Henry Bragg

Tekel or, Cora Glencoe

A Novel

Henry Bragg

Tekel or, Cora Glencoe
A Novel

ISBN/EAN: 9783337001339

Printed in Europe, USA, Canada, Australia, Japan

Cover: Foto ©Andreas Hilbeck / pixelio.de

More available books at **www.hansebooks.com**

OR

CORA GLENCOE.

A NOVEL.

" MENE, MENE, TEKEL, UPHARSIN.
This is the interpretation of the thing."—DANIEL.

BY

BRAGANZA.

PHILADELPHIA:
J. B. LIPPINCOTT & CO.
1870.

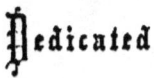

Dedicated

TO

MY COUNTRYWOMEN.

PROLOGUE.

EL PRINCIPE DE LAS TINIEBLAS

Y

LA LUNA.

AT once there came a rush of gorgeous fire
Out from the far and secret heights of heaven,
And lo! a thing of Shadow swept beneath,
And the Realms quaked and shuddered.
       Thus it was.
Luna—unblemished Virgin of the Skies,
Celestial Watcher with the Silver Brow—
Serenely smiled down on the Sons of Men,
Wooing with matchless purity of light
Their wayward souls upon the way to Heaven.
The Angel of the Bottomless Abyss
Frowned at the "Bauble" which did draw men's eyes.
"For they do stare at It—and dream of HIM,
And Hell thus loses prey. I'll go me forth
And blot out from the view of mortal sight
This comely magnet of the souls of men."
More silent than a vapor, forth he went;
Deadly and viewless crept he up the skies;
And there he balanced on a sable wing,
Within the noiseless tremor of whose plumes
Were garnered up the ashes of Corruption:
His talon hands were reeking with Pollution,
And on his breath were blasts of utter Blemish.

" With ashes will I mar this radiant rim;
I'll dash with slime of Night this zone of pearl;
With fiery blasts of Blemish will I parch
This face which men are prone to wonder at,
Then sigh—and dream—and die, and go Beyond,
Where I, with all my magic, ne'er can reach:
I'll *blacken* it—that there shall be no sign."
He hovered, putting forth his hand, when, lo!—
Ithuriel's gorgeous spear! Swift as the bolt
Which scintillates from East to West afar,
The baffled Spoiler flashed and cleft the Skies,
And down into the Bottomless Abyss
He sped him deep away—away—away!
Cowering beneath the Eye which never sleeps.

EL ESTUPRADOR

Y

LA VICTIMA.

Our Virgins are as Luna fair,
And with our stainless Women are
Chief cause of what is good in Men.
The Jungle Demon haunts the glen,
And springs upon his helpless prey,
And rends her purity away.
But, ah! it is a shame to tell,
There is no swift Ithuriel,
Equipp'd with Law and armed with lance,
Before whose ever-watchful glance
The demons of *Intent* shall fly—
And demons of the *Deed* shall *die*.

TEKEL,

CORA GLENCOE.

CHAPTER I.

THOUGH our scenes are confined almost exclusively to New York and Maryland, this brief opening chapter necessarily carries the reader, for a few moments only, to a portion of the distant Southwest where the savage, that painted scourge of the frontier, once held dominion.

Words and music, sentiment and harmony, have touchingly expressed the ever-present experience of the human breast that Home is the dearest spot on earth. Savages are no more strangers to this experience than we who read and write and build cities; and the implacable red Indian who drinks the blood of his enemies and tomahawks the children of the pale faces, droops his feathered head when, from far and biting exile, he pictures in his practical and poetical mind the graves of his ancestors, and the woods and waters of his childhood, from which he has been hurled away by the thundering car of Civilization. It is this redeeming trait, this very softening of his barbaric heart, which, upon its revulsion, sends his dread slogan on the wind and urges him to deeds of ruthless and reeking atrocity.

Those warlike savages, who had inhabited from unknown time the country embracing the upper tributaries of the Brazos River, were, years ago, driven from their domain by the ceaseless and deadly warfare of the once formidable Texas Rangers, and compelled to seek refuge among the wastes and sparse waters toward the district of El Paso.

(7)

But at intervals they girded themselves for vengeance and rapine, and, coming down like swift and noiseless foxes, would suddenly burst upon the unaware settlements, scourging the land, and chilling the hearts of the Lone Star people with their matchless deeds of blood.

Upon the fountains of the Brazos, toward the Llanos Estacados, they would pitch their lodges and divide into bands. Each band would seek a tributary of that river, and ravage it to its confluence, until both river and savages were gathered into a single stream of paramount strength and volume. With their booty and scalp-lock trophies—and among the latter might often have been found the long hair of woman, and the short, soft down of the suckling—they would retreat as they had come, dividing with the tributaries and baffling pursuit.

It was just after an extraordinarily daring and destructive inroad of this character, during which the whizzing arrows stuck within the outskirts of Waco Village, that the citizens of a wide scope of country adjacent to the Brazos hastily organized and sternly determined to follow the trail of their foes as long as there was a moccasin upon it. Like the savages, they also would divide into bands, and oppose courage to numbers and energy to craft.

With one of these citizen bands, during its quick campaign, we propose to go as a spectator. The company counted some thirty mounted men, bristling with weapons, and led by Ross of Waco Village,—probably the most effective. Indian exterminator in the Brazos country. Riding immediately in the rear of Ross was his son, a daring boy, who had already won the spurs of a Ranger, which, at that day, was no degenerate honor. By the side of the elder Ross went a gentleman whose face was of exceeding comeliness and intelligent resoluteness, and whose general appearance was aristocratic and distinguished. This was Colonel Guy Rapid, a wealthy planter and herder, and originally from Maryland. The comrade of the junior Ross was the *beau chevalier* of the cavalcade, a blithe and beautiful boy who sat his fiery horse like a young Mameluke. Almost too bonny to be a boy, he was much too manlike ever to be mistaken for a girl in male attire. His complexion was a delicate pink, and as fair as might have been his sister's. His eyes were violet, and pure as the blue ether of a summer sky. His countenance was cloudless, and his name should have been ":Joyful." In addition to the arms which he carried, a lasso hung in coils from a ring-hook of his saddle, for the boy was of the prairies. In skillful hands the lasso is a dangerous serpent; but the way now led through an impracticable forest, and he carried it from habit merely. The youth was a gentle fellow, irenic as an affectionate girl, except when on a war-path, when he was the very chief of inveterates and as swift as fire. He was mounted upon a pale, proud stallion, with black mane and black feet, and the trained choice of the prairies. Adonis, hunting the boar, was not better mounted; nor did he, when disdaining Venus, look more charmingly fresh, nor yet half so manly. The boy was the only son of Colonel Rapid, and his life had ever been as that of the bird which goeth upon the wind where it listeth. There is a distinct class of horse-killing equestrians who might well be dubbed the Whoop-and-yell Cavaliers, who, when they ride,—and when do they not? —ride all over their horses: at one moment being up to their ears in the saddle, at another down to their boots out of it. They are to be seen almost everywhere,—but in what is known as Western Texas they *abound;* and, although they may be able, at full speed, to pick a mouse from the sward, or to look back at you from between their horses' hind legs, they are scarcely more graceful or lovely in their equestrianism than would be a monkey riding a rolling barrel under compulsion and over rough ground. Young Rapid was a horseman, but not of the Whoop-and-yell class. He too could pick mice from the ground, and accomplish the feat while rushing upon a full-sized horse instead of a little mouse of a pony; for, notwithstanding that half his years had been spent at college in the East and South, he was the champion athlete, *lazador*, and sportsman in all the wide range about his Texas home. His superiority was due to a form of the finest mould, an unerring eye, and a steady nerve, as well as to his love of Western and manly sports. Young as he was, and scarcely grown, he had earned from an exacting Eastern institution of learning his diploma as a general graduate ; for, in regard to his mental culture, his father had made no petted darling of him. Out upon the prairies Colonel Rapid had permitted his boy to become an untiring physical athlete ; in college he had stimulated him to become a mental athlete ; in morals the boy had before him the example of his father ; in religion the father did not attempt to warp his son's mind this way or that, but handed him the Bible with the exhortation, "My son, this is the way; walk you in it."

Briskly the Rangers made their way up the Brazos, until, on the third day, they were brought to bay by suddenly finding themselves in the midst of an ambush, from which the feathered arrows came in troops like passing birds. Ross at once knew that he was outnumbered, and by desperate odds, divining that the band upon whose trail he had been following had been joined by other bands of the tribe. The savages, yelling and screeching like devils, rushed in from every side. The Rangers delivered their rifle-balls with mortal efficacy, and succeeded in gaining time to dismount and concert hasty measures of defense. Close quarters seemed to be their only and forlorn hope, and into close quarters they accordingly rushed. Colonel Rapid was almost immediately pierced through by a barbed arrow, and over his fallen body and coveted scalp the battle was made. Young Rapid stood over his father, emptying from either hand the contents of his deadly pistols. Ross, a tall and powerful man, with giant strength beat down the thickening savages, and young Ross, standing back to back with his father, dropped an Indian at every shot. The Rangers fought with a stern and silent energy which eloquently spoke their consciousness that the contest promised to go utterly against them. The savages were gradually closing in and preparing for a sweeping butchery. Already their eyes were glancing toward the horses of the pale faces, and here and there a warrior was being spared to secure the valuable booty. Every pistol was empty and every gun. The knife and the clubbed rifle now became the sole reliance. The Rangers looked desperately into each other's faces, as if to ask, "What shall we do?"

"*Alamo!*" shouted young Rapid in a voice as tameless as the challenge-cry of a war-eagle.

The crafty Indians drew back and began to manipulate their bows, and in a few moments every bow-thong was taut and ready to launch its feathered herald. At this crisis a young savage, fleet as the antelope, and with a prolonged cry as shrill as the shriek of panic, fled past the scene, and the red warriors melted away like a dissolving view.

"Tree!" shouted Ross to his men—"our friends are coming."

The Indian arrows began to cut from ambush through the air. The Rangers "treed," and reloaded their fire-arms; after which a stillness supervened like that which might have reigned in the depths of an untrodden wold. During this portentous calm the dusky savages, like noiseless serpents, glided here and there, collecting themselves in a more compact body. Presently, from beyond the savages, the sound of battle came. First a rifle volley,—then pistolade after pistolade, until the forest rang with mingled shouts, and shrieks, and clangor of furious onset. Ross sprang forward with his men, and the Indian braves, now themselves hemmed in by a contracting girdle of fire, bit the dust and died,—but few escaping.

Among the slain whites was Colonel Rapid. Probably no other man there could have been spared so ill as he; and as Ross looked down upon the waxen face of this dead gentleman, who had rallied from many a safe league to defend the border, between his gritting teeth he cursed every Indian upon the soil of America. Those who have spent their lives in the Atlantic and interior States have no conception of the inveterate, sleepless animosity which the frontiersman cherishes for the unmanageable, treacherous, and bloody Indian. Periodically the pioneer is called to look upon the savage's surpassing work,—to shudder or weep over the gory ruins of some one dearer than another; until he learns to lust and *yearn* for the power of hosts, that by one merciless and universal stroke he might hurl them one and all, a howling, hell-gotten heap, into the bottom of the Pacific Ocean, or grind them to impalpable atoms.

The results of the fight being ascertained, and as well as possible provided for, the sanguinary ardor provoked by this grappling, scalping, feudal combat, began to cool. Ross turned to young Rapid and said,—

"Cassel, your father's body I will take to Waco, where a coffin can be provided."

"Then," said the youth, "I will go home by the nearest route, and meet you at Waco with a vehicle to carry him to Ranche Rapid."

"Very good. Our other dead we will bury here, and mark their graves, that their friends may recover them."

Young Rapid mounted his horse and disappeared in the thick forest. He had many leagues to ride before he should rest. He headed his horse for the prairies, regardless of trail or by-path, rode all night, and at dawn of the next day emerged from the forest. Before him was a wide wilderness of waving plain, bounded only by the horizon. Over the grassy expanse, through herds of half-wild cattle, startling here and there a deer, a coyoté, or a jack-rabbit, the young Ranger took his way, trusting to his own sense of locality and direction, and to the instinct of his horse, for guidance home. At length he came upon familiar ground, where his father's branded herds were grazing, and where, far away in the unbroken, smoky distance, he could see the clump of trees in which his home was nestled. After a free gallop, during which the wind whistled through his hair, he approached the front gate of his dwelling. The trumpet neigh of the pale stallion rallied a number of negro servants to the young master's service. One of the negroes silently took charge of the horse and led him away. Those who met their young master had no customary welcome for him, but looked as though they were under sentence of death. The youth immediately observed that there was a strange and desperate gloom upon their faces. He knew that they could not have heard of Colonel Rapid's death, for the first possible messenger from the scene in the forest was himself. What, then, could be the cause of their hushed and dejected looks?

"Aunt Flora," he asked of an old family servant, "what is the matter here?"

She only shook her head and pointed to the house as one pointing to a field of horrors and of doom; and simultaneously a cry broke out from the gathered negroes which struck terror to the soul of young Rapid, for he knew that something terrible beyond the terrible had happened at Ranche Rapid. Few of our Northern readers have ever heard the wild heart-harrowing wail—the almost unearthly requiem—of a Southern black clan of slaves over the doom of some worshiped pale face—some magnanimous one whom they loved or venerated—upon whose life depended, perhaps, the future integrity of their clan and families—and whose death might scatter them ruthlessly abroad. Young Rapid hastened to the house and entered it with dread at his heart. He traversed one room and opened the door of another. Great God! What was it that overrushed and pillaged through him like a mingled icy and fiery flame, as he looked upon the contents of that room? Imagine that alone you are entering a place where rests the dead body of your dearest loved. That when you come to look upon the corpse, you see, sitting thereon, the *spirit* of the dead, in well-known form and feature. With the courage of Hamlet you nerve yourself to approach. What is that boundless consciousness which overcomes you, multiplying your fear, and grief, and agony, and horror, should you, by daring, find that the very spirit which sits upon the corpse is *dead?*

If, from the time of the Narragansetts to that of Red Cloud, the gore of every victim of Indian butchery had flowed in a crimson flood at the feet of young Rapid, bearing upon its tragic billows the upturned, appealing faces of the murdered, he could have *smiled* upon it all in comparison with what he now encountered. But over this surpassing spectacle we must suffer a temporary veil to hang; a pall, as black as impenetrable midnight. Vain would be the effort to tell what that dauntless, true, and tender-hearted brother felt, as his breast was plowed up and riven by the fell testimony before his eyes. Go up into the mountain and pluck an untrammeled pen from the wild plumage of the eagle, and dive down into the bottom of your heart for thoughts and images, and you will never reach from height or depth wherewith adequately to tell

2

of that too terrible and plaintive thing which rested in this
Western home. There it lay—a *ruin*—a WRONG, unfathom-
able in its depths, boundless in its degree, more bleak and
blighting than Arctic winter, and foul as the strategy of
hissing hell. Upon this ruin,—this inestimable *wrong*,
our narrative is founded, with the humble and sincere
hope that it may prove an *outcry*, reaching, by reason of
its simple, plaintive truth, into the secret chambers of the
soul of every *manly* reader, and echoing thence throughout
the dominions of men,—for there are laws more brittle to
be broken than icicles.

CHAPTER II.

A LETTER, dated at Ranche Rapid, directed to Rev. St.
John Hope, Creswood Post-office, Maryland, and signed
" Cassel Pontiac Rapid," left Waco Village by mail about
two weeks after the events of our opening chapter.
Young Rapid had signed his full name, not that he considered it either grand or imposing, but that there might
be no question as to the identity of the writer; for the
letter was an important one, and was intended to lead to
important and specific results. The Rev. St. John Hope,
who was an old friend of the youth's father, was requested
to direct his reply to the City of New Orleans.

In advance of this letter we must now go to Creswood,
and, with the wand of the historian, call back from the
past a few essential years.

Gale Island, which, by the fury of storms, has been
reduced to an insignificant pile of rocks, was, at the date
which we now recall, a fractional though detached portion
of the Atlantic shore of Maryland. In area it measured
about ten acres. It was not set in the sea as an island
proper, but was on a line with the low beach, which, at
either hand, was called respectively " Larboard" and.
" Starboard" Strand, the island being the central and
determining point, and intervening so that larboard and

starboard were denied a mutual view. In respect to the strand, the island, though by no means an ugly object, seemed as much out of place as would seem a house towering in the center of a pleasant street. To the rear of the island, that is, on its continental side, was a small deep bay, where a coasting-vessel might ride in safety though the sea should be in its wrath. Seaward was deep water, which led up to the front base of the island, and around it on either hand, by a moat or canal, into the little bay at the rear. The strands to the right and left were backed by abrupt and wooded bluffs, against which the waters never rose unless urged by irresistible winds.

Captain Gale of Gale Island, and sole proprietor, was a stalwart man, of middle stature; honest and rugged in his aspect. He was about forty years of age, and already it seemed that the sea, with which he had buffeted from his boyhood, had lodged some of its spray in his hair and beard. A wife, a son of six years, and an infant daughter comprised his family, to whom he was devoted, and for whom he worked hard. Captain Gale was an intelligent, self-reliant, courageous, pacific man, and a little quaint withal. When he came into possession of the island he gave it his own name, saying, with the pride of an honest pedigree, that there was not a better name on land or sea.

A neat stone cottage now crowned the ocean front of the isle, and a stout paling-fence, which inclosed the cottage, kept the little son from wandering off to dangerous places, and prevented the family cow from poking her head in at the cottage windows. A noble-looking water-dog was free to frisk or bathe, or lazily sleep in the sunny spots. The cottage was vine-clad, and a few native trees and some exotic shrubbery and phoenix-like flowers graced and garlanded the premises. It was a pleasant place, with a charming outlook, except in ugly weather.

Captain Gale was much away from "port," as he called his home, trading along the coast, sometimes as far up as New York and as far down as Norfolk.

Nautically he was only a skipper, but, as all modern titles are magnified by social or official brevet, Skipper

Gale, out of like cheap compliment, was Captain Gale, without abatement, wherever he set his foot or unfurled his sail.

He had owned several small vessels, one after another, and each had borne the name of Whitecap; and it was his scheme of life, should he ever own another, and yet another, that each should succeed to that untarnished and suggestive title.

The Whitecap had long been a welcome and expected visitor in the estuaries and inlets not accessible to sea-going merchantmen, and cut off by bad roads, or no roads at all, from the inland marts; and Captain Gale made an honest and comfortable living by his traffic with the dwellers at those rustic-marine ports.

It was late in the afternoon of a faultless October day that Mrs. Gale, for the twentieth time, went out upon the cottage portico which looked upon the ocean, and glanced southward. She was expecting her husband. Her face brightened as she saw the Whitecap riding the gently-heaving billows, and slowly making for the home-harbor. She waved her white apron, as was her custom; and Captain Gale, as was his custom, doubtless observed to his crew, with a quaint pride, that there flew the flag under which he loved to sail.

Another custom of the island, in which both Captain and Mrs. Gale took delight, was not yet obsolete. As the boat crept under the shore, little Johnny Gale, standing by his mother, hailed,—

"Sip ahoy?"

The answer came up bold and hearty,—

"Whitecap, Gale master."

"Whar 'ou fum?"

"Oyster Shallows."

"Whar 'ou boun'?"

"Port."

"'ou can pass."

"Ha! ha! h-a!" laughed Captain Gale, while the mother patted her young pride on the cheek, and told him if he continued to be a good boy he should one day have a ship of his own.

The vessel was soon moored, and the crew, being of

Creswood, were dismissed for short family visits. Captain Gale, in his sea-jacket, approached his cottage. His wife and baby, boy and dog, met him and encompassed him for caresses. He bestowed them heartily, and the family entered the cottage.

"John," asked Mrs. Gale of her husband, "are you hungry?"

"Is a shark hungry?" replied the captain.

Mrs. Gale immediately went about providing supper, while the father dandled and toyed with his children. The baby was named Catharine, brevet Caddy.

"Come to supper, John," brightly said Mrs. Gale; and the husband, whose appetite had been sharpened by the ocean air, and enhanced by the idea of eating on shore, went in to a comforting meal.

The shadow of the bluffs stole slowly out to sea, darkening the waterscape as the dusk came down, and the strand grew hazy with the gathering gloom of night.

The air was quite cool, foreboding heavy frost, and Captain Gale withdrew from the cottage portico, where, after his soothing supper, he had been quietly smoking a soothing pipe, to a cheerful fire within the cottage. He felt as comfortable, cheerful, and snug, before the bright fire, as the cricket chirping from the crevice of his hearthstone. His little housewife was brisk and busy; the children were asleep, with faces peeping from the cover; and he himself was resting from his vessel's helm, and girdled by the comforts and affection of the home where his heart was.

When Mrs. Gale had put away her cups and dishes, she came in to her husband, sat down by him, looked up in his face, and smiled. There was something so affectionate, gratified, and entrapping in the little woman's smile, that the husband suspiciously, but good-humoredly, observed,—

"Now, Sallie, you are getting under my lee. What is it,—a new bonnet, or what?"

Mrs. Gale only smiled the more pleasantly, replying,—

"John, I want nothing."

"What, then, means that insinuating sunrise on your face?"

"I am only glad that you are come."

"Oh, that's it, is it?" replied the stout captain, while he experienced a pleasant undertow of domestic emotion, and thought of the lines in which that tomb-vexed prodigy, Byron, told how deeply dear it was to hear the watch-dog's honest bark, bay deep-mouthed welcome as we draw near home, and to have some waiting bright one look the brighter when we come. "Now that I am here, Sallie," continued the captain, "suppose you give me the news."

The vicinity of Gale Island was ordinarily as quiet as an English dell, rarely enlivened except by the arrivals and departures of the Whitecap. The neighborhood wealth was monopolized by a few families, between whom sociability appeared to have reached the stage of stagnation or petrifaction. For this state of affairs various causes might be assigned, which we will not now investigate. The less pretentious of the community, however, circulated freely among themselves, seeking and extending a cheerful hospitality. Notwithstanding an almost uninterrupted calm in this uneventful region, Mrs. Gale was rarely without news of some sort for her husband when he came home. And her delight or sympathetic interest in detailing it, was only equaled by the satisfaction or neighborly concern with which he gave ear to it and made his comments.

"The most important and most melancholy news I have to tell you is that Mrs. Rapid is dead."

"What!" exclaimed Captain Gale. "Mrs. Guy Rapid?"

"Yes."

"There was not another such woman in all Creswood."

Creswood was the name of the forest region adjacent to Gale Island. It was originally Crescent Wold, but indolent tongues had contracted and moulded it into a word of easier articulation. Captain Gale continued,—

"You always liked her, Sallie?"

"I *loved* her," said Mrs. Gale. "I think she was the loveliest woman I ever saw. With all her wealth she was not too vain to visit plain people. And she was kind to the needy. In her last hours she was an angel. I was with her,—and her little children, God help them, they knew not what they were losing." Mrs. Gale, somewhat affected, wiped her eyes, and continued, "I am wrong. I forget about little Cassel,—Pony, as he is often called. I cannot tell you how that child acted; not like a frantic thing, but with a quiet, wretched, sweet, and untiring watchfulness, that made my heart *ache*."

" When did she die ?"

" Just two weeks ago. The whole country flocked to her funeral."

" That is of no consequence," said Captain Gale. "If the devil himself were to die, and die rich, there would be no lack of mourners. But how about Mr. Rapid ? Does he still talk of going to Texas ?"

" He is preparing to start this fall."

" Has he sold ?"

"Everything but the negroes and some fine stock, which he will take with him."

" He has long held that Creswood would never be much more or less than it is at present, and I am rather of his opinion."

" But Western Texas is so uncivilized," observed Mrs. Gale.

" He is just the kind of man to civilize it, or help do so."

" And make savages of his children meanwhile," returned the wife. " His little boy is but eight years old, and his daughter is almost an infant."

" He is able to educate them wherever he likes. You can rest satisfied that there'll be no lack of polish on Guy Rapid's children when they are grown. Creswood is almost as far out of the world as Texas. But who bought his place ?"

" He divided the land into small farms, which were mostly taken by the neighbors. I think his wife's death has hastened his departure, and he has doubtless sold at a sacrifice."

" Who took the mansion-house ?"

" He gave it away."

" What ! Gave it away ?"

" Yes ; to our minister, Mr. Hope."

" A good and timely deed," said Captain Gale.

" And not only that," said Mrs. Gale, " but he connected

with the gift about thirty acres adjoining the house, every article of furniture except some heirlooms, two good cows, a pair of serviceable horses, and the family carriage and harness. And he has had the ground marked off, inclosed, and put in the best of order."

" I knew there was no humbug or half way about Guy Rapid, but this is one of the few times that I have ever cast anchor alongside of the like. Such volunteers, Sallie, are scarce. And then Mr. Rapid is not a member of Mr. Hope's church, or of any other. He is, moreover, a Loco-foco and a Marylander, while Mr. Hope is a native of Connecticut and a Webster Whig. But the two men always liked each other, and whenever Rapid gave a dinner-party Mr. Hope was there to ask a blessing."

" But Mrs. Rapid was a member of Mr. Hope's church, and that, in a measure, may account for her husband's generosity," said Mrs. Gale.

" They will all go to hear the preacher," said Captain Gale, " now that his sermons will be composed in an elegant study, and drawn to church in a carriage. Respectability is the thing, Sallie. Make religion *respectable*, so that a man won't have to compromise his dignity, or a woman her vanity, in order to get to heaven. Don't you see ?"

" I hope *you'll* go to hear him then, husband, and join the church also. I don't like this separation, John,—I in the church and you barred out from me,—any more than I do your being so much away from home."

" I do go to hear him," said Captain Gale, " when I'm in port on Sundays. But as for being barred out, as you call it, I could brace sails and skip the bar if I thought it the only port of entry. But I'm not so certain that my way is not as free of rocks and breakers as yours, after all."

" What is your way, husband ?"

" I read my Bible, say my prayers, uphold the laws of my country, help poorer men than myself, and pilot the Whitecap."

" Quite an enumeration of saving clauses," said the wife ; " but I very much doubt if you ever even look at your Bible, or offer a prayer, unless you see a tremendous storm coming up," and Mrs. Gale smiled with affectionate reproach.

"Yes, I do, honey," replied the half-guilty husband, who, by way of changing the subject, inquired, "but you haven't given me all the news yet, Sallie? Let's have the whole of it, for I'm off to sea, you know, with the change of the moon."

"Oh, well, there's plenty of time; it doesn't take a woman more than ten minutes—so say the men—to tell all she knows," said Mrs. Gale with playful sarcasm.

"Women," replied the retaliatory captain, "are like shoal water,—bottom always within sight or sounding. Men are profound like the deep water: you may not be able to fathom it, but you know that the bottom is down there."

"Which knowledge does a vast amount of good," said the little woman. "But let us return to Creswood. Things are not bright at Cliff Hall."

"What's the matter there *now?*" asked the captain, emphasizing the last word as if it were usage for something to be awry at Cliff Hall, and the present occasion an aggravated succession of the oft-recurring ills which visited that unfortunate hold.

"Well, to begin," said the wife, "the Necromancer——"

"Stop, Sallie," said Captain Gale interrupting. "No Necromancer about it. Oswald Huron, you mean to say."

"Yes. And since you are so exact, I shall endeavor to be equally so in what I have to tell," said Mrs. Gale with a jaunty poise of her person where she sat in her rocking-chair. "Now you listen, and don't interrupt me. There are two brothers. Neville Huron, the elder, lives in Philadelphia; Oswald Huron, the younger, lives at Cliff Hall. You can see Cliff Hall, if you will only wait until morning, from our front portico. It is on a bluff about a mile and a fraction up the Larboard Strand."

"Sallie, don't be provoking; you know I've seen it at least a thousand times."

"Belay your tongue," laughed Mrs. Gale, "and listen. Oswald Huron, who has been away from home, returned to Cliff Hall about three weeks ago. His wife, you know, is dead. His infant daughter is, and has been, in the care of Maria Guthrie, an old but somewhat tricky family servant. Very well. Mr. Neville Huron, wife, and infant daughter have been down from Philadelphia on a visit to Cliff Hall, bringing with them a Chestnut Street nurse. Soon came a letter to Mrs. Neville Huron, informing her that her mother was at the point of death, and urging that she return immediately to Philadelphia. She went in haste, accompanied by her husband, leaving her child and the nurse at Cliff Hall as an expedient. Neville Huron's infant and the Necromancer's infant, both girls, are about the same age, and so much alike that none but the nurses can distinguish one from the other. Even the Necromancer——"

"Necromancer the dev——"

"Hush, John," cried Mrs. Gale, clapping her hand over her husband's mouth, "and let me go on. As if to enhance their resemblance, the infants have of late been dressed exactly alike, Mrs. Neville Huron having duplicated the apparel of her own child and presented the duplicates to the child of her brother-in-law. When she left Cliff Hall for Philadelphia, then the trouble commenced. The nurse which she had brought down with her became dissatisfied and cut out. There was Oswald Huron with two young babies on his hands, not knowing t'other from which, and not the mildest-mannered man in the world, as you well know," and Mrs. Gale laughed, "and with but one nurse to attend to them. He actually sent down to *me* for advice or assistance; and, after much persuasion, I induced Amy Turnbolt, your niece, who has a superstitious dread of Cliff Hall, and especially of the Necromancer, to go up there and take charge of Mrs. Neville Huron's infant. So the babies now have a nurse each, and are nourished entirely from milk-bottles and sugar-tits. Did I do right?"

"Yes, honey, you did right, as you always try to do; though we don't owe Oswald Huron any special good will. He accused me of smuggling once; that is, he called me a smuggler to my face. I asked him if he had ever made that assertion elsewhere. He replied that he had not. I then told him that he had simply uttered a falsehood of which I could afford to take no notice. He drew a pistol on me. I took it away from him, and threw it into the sea. He measured me with his eye, and though a tall and powerful man himself, he evidently concluded that I was pretty rugged, and contented himself with threatening to put an honest trading-boat in my waters. You recollect that the Whitecap for awhile had a rival. That rival was launched against the Whitecap by Oswald Huron. However, as the enterprise failed," continued Captain Gale complacently, "I don't harbor any particular malice; but I am not indebted to him for any favors. His brother, Neville, is much the better man, and as long as it is *his* child that Amy cares for, I've no objection to make. But I am surprised that Oswald Huron should have applied to you. His disposition is by no means relenting, and don't you know, Sallie, that though I can forgive him for his attempt to injure me, he can never forgive *me?* It is so with the world."

"What became of the rival boat?" asked Mrs Gale.

"As I said before, it was a failure. He sold it, and I've not heard of it since."

"John, you never told me one word of this."

"What was the use? I do not carry your troubles to sea with me, and I won't bring mine ashore to perplex you."

"That Oswald Huron is a strange man," said Mrs. Gale reflectively. "Do you believe, husband, that he is anything of a necromancer?"

"Fiddle-dee, Sallie; there are no such things,—at least on land."

"They are all at sea, are they, John?" laughed the wife.

"Sallie, what's the use reviving that old question between us?"

"Because I think you sailors are so ridiculous. Now, I want you to tell me for good and all, do you, or do you not, believe those strange and horrible legends of the sea?"

"They are like many other things, Sallie, which we are called upon to put faith in. I can't say that I actually *believe* them, but some of them have a hold upon me that I neither can or care to shake off. It is a kind of religion, and has made me shift my helm, and then laugh at myself, more than once. But there is *one* superstition which, whether I believe in it or not, I would not dare to transgress or disregard."

"What is that, John?" asked Mrs. Gale, interested beyond the ordinary.

"The sailor's Black Oath," said Captain Gale impressively.

"What sort of a black thing is it?" asked Mrs. Gale with a lurking smile.

"It's an oath which is sooner or later followed by retribution at sea, if the swearer ever violates it or perjures himself in the taking of it."

"But what does he swear by?" asked the little woman.

"Pshaw! Sallie; you will never have to take it."

"But I want to know what it is," urged the wife.

"Well," consented the husband, "the sailor pledges *'By the salt at the bottom of Neptune's grog,'*" and Captain Gale's countenance indicated that he considered the pledge no mere holiday password.

The effect upon Mrs. Gale was irresistible; and much to the surprise and somewhat to the discomfiture of the earnest captain, she greeted his grave announcement with a carol of heartfelt merry laughter.

"Tut, Sallie," finally remonstrated Captain Gale, "you outcackle a pullet over her first egg."

"But, John, it does sound so much like 'Tales of the Ocean,' which I used to read when you were a sailor lad, and I was your lassie."

The captain softened at this timely and affectionate reference. He observed,—

"During that time, Sallie, I took the Black Oath myself."

"*You* took the Black Oath!"

"Yes."

"What in the world for?"

"To satisfy your father."

"My father? Why did he require it?"

"On your account, honey. Sailors, you know, are prone to be Mormons, having a wife at every port. But you need not laugh at the sailor's oath, for punishment follows its violation as sure as fruit follows bloom; at least I have not known it otherwise. I will mention one case,—Joe Aiken; do you recollect him?"

"Yes. Was he a sailor?"

" He was a salt-water man," said Captain Gale. " Well, he took the Black Oath, and violated it when he betrayed that simple-hearted Ennis girl. He was always afraid of salt water after that, and kept away from it for years. At last, when he was a little drunker than usual, he stepped into a skiff and shoved off. The tide was flowing out. He had no oars. He was carried to sea ; and that was the last of him. The skiff was washed ashore, bottom upwards, about a week after."

" He was no loss to the neighborhood," observed Mrs. Gale ; "and speaking of him, reminds me that his son Jonas, and several other young men about here, are going to Texas with Mr. Rapid."

" What does Guy Rapid want with such a fellow as Jonas Aiken ? Of the few bad characters about Creswood he is decidedly the worst, and a mere boy at that."

" Some of them go as herders, some to seek their fortunes in the West."

" Guy Rapid is doing Creswood a service by taking Jonas out of it ; but I can't say that he manifests a due regard for the community to which he shall introduce him," said Captain Gale, laughing.

" Jonas will not be much the better of wild cattle and Indians," responded Mrs. Gale.

After a continued rambling and conjugal conversation, Captain Gale went out to make his boat snug for the night, while Mrs. Gale turned down the bedcover and beat up the pillows, with the wifely ambition of making her husband's berth with her snugger than his bunk on board the Whitecap.

As Captain Gale was stepping aboard of his craft, he heard a stifled shriek, followed instantly by a heavy splash in the water on the opposite side of his little bay. He sprang into a skiff which was always kept on duty at the island, and with vigorous strokes shot across to the point whence came the unusual sounds. Nearing the opposite shore, he saw, in the twilight of the brilliant stars, a human head, with long hair straying on the surface of the water. He grasped the hair, and attempted to drag into the skiff what proved to be a woman.

3

CHAPTER III.

"LET go my hair, Uncle John; you are pulling it *out!*" cried a feminine voice from the water.

"Thunder and lightning, Amy Turnbolt! What the devil are you doing in here?"

"Let go my *hair*, I tell you, or darned if I don't capsize your skiff;—you know I can swim;—pull me in by the arms," cried the girl in ready words but distracted tone.

"A pretty swim you'd make of it with all your clothes on," said Captain Gale as he drew his niece into the skiff. He then rowed back to the Whitecap without another word. He knew that Amy Turnbolt was either crazed or most terribly frightened. He took her into the little cabin of his vessel and lighted a lamp. He threw a blanket about the wet girl and seated her. She was pale and wild, and shivering from cold and terror. Captain Gale uncorked a bottle, poured out half a pint of still wine, and gave it to her. The wine in a measure braced and restored her.

"Now, Amy, tell me what has happened," said Captain Gale a little sternly, for he knew that there was something behind the involuntary bath from which he had just rescued her.

"Oh, uncle, it is *dreadful!*" she almost whispered.

"Tell me what it is, Amy," calmly urged the uncle.

"Oh, Uncle John, let me rest a little and recollect what it was,—it is so like a dream to me."

"Captain Gale waited. Finally he observed,—

"You have been up at Cliff Hall nursing, Sallie tells me."

"Oh, I didn't want to go there at *all* where that Necromancer was, and that was the beginning of this terrible thing."

At length the girl was induced to tell her story. It seemed that she and Maria Guthrie, the other nurse at Cliff Hall, with the two infant daughters of Neville and

Oswald Huron, had been rambling in the woods during the day. They seated themselves upon the verge of a precipice. At their feet was a deep chasm. Their seat was on a shelving rock, which, when they attempted to rise for the purpose of returning to the Hall, tilted over the bluff with them. The other nurse threw her disengaged arm about a sapling, and regained her footing; but Amy, in order to save herself, was compelled to let go her charge, and the infant was torn and dashed to pieces by a fall of more than a hundred feet. Amy fled in dismay, and hid in the woods until after dark, when she started for the island. Her terror grew with every step, and hearing noises behind her, she sped through the forest, satisfied that the Necromancer was almost upon her with an unearthly vengeance. In her haste to reach the island she fell into the bay.

Amy's story was not coherent in every respect, but the foregoing was, succinctly, about all that her uncle could make of it; and although he credited the story in the main, he thought it probable that the nurses were more careless and to blame than Amy's account admitted.

Captain Gale was proud of the unsullied though humble fame of his family. He was also, upon well-grounded and intelligent principle, strictly a law-abiding and law sustaining citizen. Therefore when Amy entreated him to take her out of the country and away from the wrath of the Necromancer, he answered,—

"Amy, if you have told me the truth; that is, if you have not had the actual facts frightened out of your mind by your natural and unnatural terror, there will be no occasion for you to leave the country; and furthermore, under no circumstances would such a course be the proper one. This unfortunate accident will undergo a legal investigation, for Oswald Huron is a confirmed litigant, and of course must have it into court. Now don't become yet more alarmed. Will Maria Guthrie corroborate what you have told me?"

"Yes, sir, every word of it," answered Amy with a possibly suspicious alacrity. Captain Gale continued,—

"Very well, then, you will have nothing to fear. I will employ Lawyer May to act as your counsel, and when the

matter is disposed of in the regular way, it will be forever
buried.   But you go running off or hiding, and you'll get
yourself into shoal water, and flounder the balance of your
life.   If you run away, it is equivalent to pleading guilty,
and might lead to severe punishment."

Amy, who was rather a headstrong girl, had sense
to appreciate her uncle's counsel. She also placed great
confidence in Lawyer May, who, in addition to his legal
and social force, had few reasons to befriend Oswald Huron, and many not to befriend him. She determined to
face an investigation.

"Uncle, I'm cold," she at length said.

"Come into the house then,—to the fire."

Captain Gale had remained so long out of the cottage,
that Mrs. Gale, by no means timorous, began to grow uneasy.   Her uneasiness was changed to amazement and
horror when Amy was brought in and her story twice told,
with this addition, that the mangled remains of the infant
had been abandoned by the nurses, who had found it impossible to reach the spot where the child lay dead.

Oswald Huron, of Cliff Hall, a tall, dark man of towering
passions, was roused to fury when told of the calamity,
and the Hall resounded with his voice and tread. He asserted rapidly and again that the nurses had murdered the
child, or trifled its life away ; and that they should feel the
weight of the criminal law, and otherwise know what it
was to come under his wrath.   Had it been reported to him
that his own child was dead, and reported by the nurse
who was responsible for its life and comfort, he, rather than
not, would have butchered the messenger before the words
were cool. As it was, he dismissed Maria Guthrie summarily, and sent the surviving infant over to Mrs. Hope,
the minister's wife, requesting her to take charge of it for
a few days. Summoning assistance, he provided himself
with ropes, and proceeded to recover the little corpse which
lay so ghastly and alone out in the gloomy chasm to which
it would long give a tragic and elegiac repute. It was piti-
lessly torn by the rude rocks against which it had raked
and rasped in its fall, and nothing but the golden locket suspended from its wrenched neck could have identified it.
In this locket was incased a daguerreotype miniature of

Neville Huron. About the neck of the surviving infant hung a similar locket with similar contents, each being presents from Neville Huron, one to his own child, the other, to the child of his brother.

The mangled body was gathered up, and clothed and coffined for the tomb, with the locket about its neck, and on the second succeeding day Oswald Huron started to Philadelphia with a clod of precious clay,—all that he could return of the priceless, warm little life and motion which had been so unfortunately left in his care. But before leaving Creswood he had not failed to place Maria Guthrie and Amy Turnbolt under bonds to appear at the next sitting of the court of criminal jurisdiction.

It is one of the most difficult things in the world for two or more persons to concert a lie, and, apart from each other, so tell it as to deceive an acute lawyer; especially when that lawyer, acting as their counsel, is entitled to a measure of their confidence, and enjoys the privilege of probing their bosoms. Not that there is any peculiar ingenuity or talent required for the simple asseveration of a direct and complete falsehood, but the trouble is to make the lie fit the truth which surrounds it, and accommodate all the tributary circumstances which flow in upon it.

Lawyer May, as counsel for Amy Turnbolt and Maria Guthrie, was perfectly well satisfied, after he had examined them, that there was a concealment, a secret between them, which, though it should be divulged, might not attach guilt to them in respect to the infant's death, but would, notwithstanding, put a different color upon that unfortunate event. What it was that they were withholding, he could neither imagine nor extract from them, but that it was something he was morally certain.

Precedent after precedent (if the phrase is allowable), and some of them illustrious in their character, has long established, among the members of the litigious bar, that it is the duty of a lawyer, in the capacity of counsel and advocate, to assert and maintain the innocence of his client, however guilty the lawyer himself may, by deduction or private confession, know that client to be.

Lawyer May, of Creswood, an honorable man, and a gentleman withal, did not sway from the established profes-

3*

sional rule when he defended Amy Turnbolt and Maria Guthrie from the exceptional and vigorous legal assaults of Oswald Huron, and brought them off innocent in the eye of the law as two young lambs.

Captain Gale honestly sustained his niece, and, indirectly, Maria Guthrie, with whose fortunes those of his niece were linked in this particular interest.

In general, Oswald Huron was an inimical. In detail, he was a foe, none the less bitter or inveterate from his consciousness of being in the wrong. Creswood, and all therein, he held in utter contempt, with the exception, possibly, of Mr. St. John Hope, whose walk in life was irreproachable, and whose years were beginning to make him venerable; neither of which facts or conditions interfered with the whims and what-nots of Mr. Oswald Huron.. Though rarely leaving his premises, he, by his wealth and vindictive mental activity, was enabled to annoy almost every one upon whom he took a fancy to fix his displeasure; and frequently his displeasure fell without premonition or provocation. Where it would fall next was as uncertain as the spot upon which the next thunderbolt would descend. Socially he was an iota, a jot. His heart was fiery and impracticable, and his disposition would have essayed discord in the presence of the great Irenarch himself. He did not care a hoot for anybody's opinions but his own, and in his action was as inconsistent as the absolute temperance reformer, who, in exhausting his subject, prematurely exhausts himself, and thereupon calls for an invigorator, a rum-punch for instance, with a green brier in it.

After the legal investigation of the causes which cut short the career of the infant Huron had resulted in the unconditional discharge of the two nurses, unusually rough words, provoked by Oswald Huron, passed between himself and Lawyer May, which, with the unfortunate and crooked temper of Mr. Huron, complicated the future history of the Huron brothers, and led to deplorable results.

Oswald Huron also set upon Captain Gale for innocently and energetically sustaining his niece, and although the dauntless mariner, out of compassion for Mr. Huron's *natural* distress, bore and forbore a deal more than was palatable, a serious personal encounter had been imminent, and was only averted by the pacific coolness of the stout captain.

Over the hills and through the forest, at a distance of some three or four miles from Gale Island, a country-store, surrounded by a few straggling houses, the nucleus of a possible village, was kept by Mr. Ichabod Nutt, who dealt in the customary articles of neighborhood barter.

Captain Gale accommodated Mr. Nutt with imported goods, in part return for which the merchant passed over to the captain the available produce of the country. Periodically a balancing of accounts current transpired between them, and it was odd if the cash balance was not in favor of the Whitecap.

In pure business transactions Captain Gale was as prompt to collect as he was prompt to pay, and for the purpose of arranging an important balance, he stepped into Mr. Nutt's place of business one fine morning in the latter part of the autumn which introduced the reader to Creswood. Having settled with the merchant and spent some time with him in neighborly gossip, he was about to return to the island, when Oswald Huron, a seldom visitor, entered the store, encountering Captain Gale almost at the threshold. Mr. Huron raised his cane as if to strike. It was a custom, nay, almost a pastime, of his, to put out his cane, tap a man on the shoulder, and accompany the action with words of sarcasm or direct insult, as the subject, to him, would seem to justify. Captain Gale caught the cane and wrenched it from his grasp. The aggressor, disarmed, used his tongue. Captain Gale turned to Mr. Nutt and made some droll remark about Mr. Huron being crazy. Oswald Huron glared at him, but the captain walked serenely away, taking opportunity, however, to turn to his foe and observe, while he held up the wrested cane,—

" You had better prefer charges against me for highway robbery."

As it often falls out, or in, soon after Captain Gale bore off the cane, Lawyer May entered the store to make some purchases. Oswald Huron, with so little hesitation that it appeared ridiculous, confronted him and said,—

" You are a scoundrel, sir."

"Your epithet is actionable," said Lawyer May, who was a tall, slender, elegant-looking man.

"Act upon it, then," replied Oswald Huron, with a haughty, ferocious look.

"Mr. Huron," observed the lawyer, calmly, "you will do me a pleasure, and (if that is no consideration) yourself a service possibly, by never addressing me again."

"Do you presume to *threaten* me, sir?" was the fierce demand, accompanied by a vehement gesture and a step forward.

Mr. May turned upon his heel, walked back to the rear of the store, took a drink of water, sat down under the clock, drew out a memorandum-book, and cast his eyes over the list of articles which he desired to purchase. Oswald Huron strode out and went home, after having left an order for some family comforts.

CHAPTER IV.

SITTING upon the portico of the cottage at Gale Island and looking with a spy-glass toward the north, that is to say, up the Larboard Strand, an observer might have seen, very distinctly, Amy Turnbolt and Maria Guthrie perched upon what was called the Tarpeian Rock. This rock was a large detachment of an overhanging crag. It had fallen upon the strand from above, and formed a kind of objective rendezvous for the eyes and steps of idlers and pleasure-walkers.

From numerous tosses of the head, mingled with other peculiarly feminine gesticulations, a lively dialogue appeared to be in progress between these whilom nurses.

As the dialogue continued, the gestures all at once subsided, and the two women evidently began to talk in earnest. It may not be amiss to intrude upon them, and learn if possible what it can be that is magical enough to reduce the rattle-tattle of two gossiping females to a sober, earnest conversation.

"But you intend to leave here, and of course you don't care," continued Amy with some bitterness.

"I'm going to leave here? Yes, I *am*, because I've got no livelihood here, and I must go where I can make my livelihood. But do you think I'd go off and let it be as it is, and leave that hateful Oswald Huron to father the child, and get gratification from it, and it not his, and Mr. Neville Huron such a gentleman, and his wife such a lady, what little I saw of them? If I had no other conscience about me I'd at least fix up to bring out the fact-justice of it, just to spite and bite Oswald Huron. I wasn't *his* help, but his wife's, which he worreted to her death, and I wouldn't a' staid with him a minute after she died only for the sakes of the baby and its dead mother."

With a look of mingled apprehension and reproach, Amy asked,—

"And who's to stay and meet him with his Satan temper and his wizzard doings? I am innocent, and have helped you out of this, and I won't let you put it off on to me," and Amy burst out crying.

"Wizzard *scratch!*" emphatically and contemptuously replied Mrs. Guthrie. "He's no more of a neckermancer than your granny. If he is a wizzard and neckermancer, why couldn't he tell his own child from his brother's? and why can't he tell what's wrong now?"

This seemed to impress Amy and encourage some hope within her. Mrs. Guthrie continued,—

"But I don't intend to leave you in his claws. Anybody that sticks to me as you did through frightenings and writs and lawyers and courts, will find that Marie Guthrie, poor slaving woman as she is, is not going to run off and leave her friend in desertion. I'm going to Lawyer May, who is a gentleman, whatever other lawyers be, and tell him the truth,—the *truth*, mind you, Amy,—and get him to put it into some writ form of suppeeny or affidavit or whatever it is, and leave it with him, and so condition him that nobody is to hear a breath of it till I get out of reach. That will throw the blame on to me, where it belongs, and my going off will confirm it on to me. When I am gone, you go to your uncle Gale and get him to make a writ form from your word o' mouth, and tell him to see Lawyer May, and fix it up amongst them the best way they can. That will pacify everything with you entirely; and Captain Gale is man enough for Oswald Huron any day, and he don't owe Oswald Huron money or favor, nor Lawyer May don't owe him money or favor, and Maria Guthrie don't owe him money or favor, and when I get away from Cres-wood to my friends down in Maryland, amongst the old Irish stock, I can give my defiance to neckermancer Huron and the devil's den of him. When I first con-trapped this thing, on the very spot where I took and held you, I didn't mean it to stand any longer than I could leave here. Supposen I had gone and told that toma-hawker that it was *his* child that was dead; he'd have blowed my brains out or cut me down to the teeth with a hatchet. Supposen I'd run off entirely, and you had run off, as you *was* a doing; what sort of a fix would we have been in, with Oswald Huron and the law officers after us for murder, and nobody left even to take the live child home? Maria Guthrie's no fool, and what she tells you, Amy Turnbolt, you go and do likewise."

Amy yielded, being almost convinced and wholly con-strained.

A few days after the above conversation, Maria Guthrie presented herself to Lawyer May, and abruptly entered upon the business which brought her into the lawyer's office.

"Lawyer May," said she, "I come to tell you something, but before I do it, I want you to swear to me on your Bible that you won't give breath to it before this day a month ahead."

"Can't you trust my discretion?" asked the lawyer.

"No discretion about it," replied Maria Guthrie; "and if there is, it's my own discretion entirely to tell you or not."

"Very well," said Mr. May, appreciating that it would be more satisfactory to know the secret and keep it than to be compelled to keep it by reason of not knowing it.

Mrs. Guthrie proceeded to administer to Mr. May an oath as binding, mixed, and particular as the so-called iron-clad oath of the present day, during which performance the lawyer could with difficulty preserve his gravity.

"I wish you to put what I've got to say into a writ

form," said Mrs. Guthrie, satisfied that the oath—for the special clinching of which she had brought along an old Bible—would most undoubtedly stick.

"You wish to make an affidavit or a deposition?" suggested Mr. May.

"Yes, sir."

"It will be necessary then to go before some magistrate, or officer with a seal."

"No officer, or magistrate, or seal shall have the first word of it under Bible oath. I want you to make it up yourself."

"I am not competent," said the lawyer.

"Not competent? I thought you was the smartest and bookiest man in Creswood."

"I mean that I am not authorized."

"Well; if lawyers aint authorized, who are?"

"Tell me what you wish to make known, and what you desire to accomplish. I can then determine upon the proper method."

"No, sir. If there are so many quirks and turns about it, I'll be a little cranky myself. I'll ask some explanations."

"I am willing to explain, but am not in a very eligible position to do so, and—it's your affair, not mine."

"I know it's my affair, and I want to keep it my affair for a month to come; but I want to put it down in witness now, with nobody any the wiser but yourself."

"I appreciate your confidence," said Lawyer May with a slight bow. "What you are qualified, under the circumstances, to do, is to make an affidavit. A deposition requires due notice to opposite parties, if there are any, and is usually attended, at least sometimes, by a cross-examination of the deponent at the time the deposition is taken."

"Can't I tell you," categorically asked Mrs. Guthrie, "and get you to write down facts and figures of dates, which will be witness at law in a case of suit?"

To this ingenious and staccato question the lawyer replied,—

"I can put into an affidavit anything which you may wish to state, you can sign it, and swear to it before a magistrate,—not before me,—and the magistrate need not know what the affidavit contains; but as to its being, as you say, witness at law in case of suit, it will only be *ex-parte* testimony."

Mrs. Guthrie was flattered by the fact that lawyer May had quoted her own words, which she doubted not were the best that could be used in that particular connection, and was encouraged to venture yet more daringly.

"But will the x-party testimony to be good in the premises of litigation?"

"It has a certain standing," replied the lawyer, compelled to smile, "and if other testimony, from a witness present, or witnesses present, in court, corroborating, that is, agreeing with it, is at hand, then the affidavit is that much the better. But alone it is not of much force."

Mrs. Guthrie reflected that Amy Turnbolt could supply the personal word o' mouth testimony, and consequently determined, after this brilliant and eminently satisfactory skirmishing, to tell what she knew.

The reader is almost aware of that which Mrs. Guthrie desired to have put into a "writ form."

"I come, Mr. May," said she, "to tell you, under my oath, that the baby which fell over the crag and was killed, was Oswald Huron's baby, and the baby alive and at Cliff Hall now, is Mr. Neville Huron's own child."

We will not stop to describe the surprise of Lawyer May. Although he was convinced that a secret of some sort was between the nurses, and connected, moreover, with the deceased infant, he was not prepared for so important a revelation as that just made to him. He requested Mrs. Guthrie to proceed.

"There is little more to tell you that you don't already know," said she. "Amy and me walked out with the children in our arms, and took a seat on a big flat rock which I used to sit on by myself with the baby I nursed before Amy come to Cliff Hall, which is the same baby as is now dead, and when we went to get up, the rock tilted over with both our weights. Amy caught by a bush and saved herself and the baby she was nursing."

"It was she, then, instead of you, as you once told me?"

"Yes; but now I am telling you the *truth*. Amy saved herself and Mr. Neville Huron's baby, which she was nursing, and it was *me* that was falling down that dreadful place, and had to let go Mr. *Oswald* Huron's baby to save my own life, and it fell and was killed, and we couldn't bring it away because we couldn't get down there to it. But at first Amy started to run with her baby, and I caught her and took and held her, and begged and worked and frighted her into doing what I contrapted for us to do about the babies; which we could easy do, because Oswald Huron didn't know his own child from his brother's, and he had driv off his old servants, or more belike they had left him, and he had bought him some niggers which were afraid to come in the house, and nobody knowed the babies apart but the nurses, and you wouldn't have knowed them apart yourself, because they was so resembling, and such young babies, which many folks can't tell one from another nohow when they are so young, and dressed just alike, as these were, and their names were identical alike in the bargain, and they had lockets around their necks, and the lockets was one and the same."

"Could you and the other nurse absolutely and always distinguish them yourselves?"

"I could distinguish them, because Mrs. Oswald Huron was my mistress, and the child was born almost into my hands, and my poor mistress died of it, and I raised the baby, and knowed it as I would my own, except that I never had one, for Mr. Guthrie died the very night we was married, poor man."

"That was sudden indeed," said Lawyer May, who, as business was not pressing, felt willing to gratify Mrs. Guthrie's spirit of loquacity. "What could possibly have put an end to his life at so happy a moment?"

"He died of a broken back," said Mrs. Guthrie, with an expression of countenance well calculated to excite sympathy.

"A broken back! And on the very night of his wedding? How did that happen?"

"The lads had sprung a Christmas-tree, for it was a Christmas-night, and they sprung it out in the yard, and, after the maiden name had been taken from me by the solemnity of the ceremony, we went into the yard, and the tree fell down, and Mr. Guthrie was under it, and his back was broke."

4

"That was very sad indeed," said Mr. May, who, by-the-way, was a widower with one little boy; "but we must now return to the business in hand. Could Amy Turnbolt distinguish the children with certainty?"

"Not till she had been nursing for two or three days. But she soon learned her baby, for it was the sweetest and the least of trouble."

"What were the distinguishing marks,—the difference, between them."

"They was not marked at all; but Neville Huron's baby had the superiority somewhat over the other one, and its eyes were a little darker, and its hair was the least bit given to curl, and it was the brightest and the lovingest, and we called it Coy, and we called the other one Glenny."

"What were the names of the infants? If I ever knew I've forgotten."

"The living and the dead was both named Cora Glencoe."

"Cora Glencoe Huron," said the lawyer, taking down the name on a slip of paper. "What was your purpose in deceiving the Hurons?"

"It wasn't that I wanted to deceive them, specially Mr. Neville Huron, but *he* was away, and Mr. Oswald Huron was the one I had to meet, and he'd a' cut my throat if I had gone and told him that Glenny, his own child, had met its death by me, which he came near to doing anyhow when I took and told him that it was his brother's baby as was dead. But I didn't never mean for it to stand this way no longer than I could make interest with my people in the off districts of this State where I am going to make my livelihood, and I come to you to set it all to rights before I go; and if Oswald Huron or his officers or his hounds comes after me, my folks are not the particularest in the world, and they will send *him* and *his* back to Creswood with the splinters of shillaly in the jowls of them. And I've told Amy Turnbolt to make the affidavit of the same before her uncle, Captain Gale, and you and him can legalize the child's pedigree and 'heritance of its father and mother. And this is the truth, under oath, so help me God, and on the cross."

"Mrs. Guthrie," said the lawyer, when that prolix deponent had finished what she mainly had to say, "can I not prevail upon you to make this affidavit within the knowledge of some other person chosen by you ?"

"No, sir."

"But you don't see the difficulty. Oswald Huron is my enemy. He imagines that I would do anything within my power to injure or annoy him. Others may imagine the same. I defended you in connection with these infants. I must now undertake to *undo*, in part, what I have heretofore *done*. I must contradict myself, and notwithstanding I am willing to submit to the chagrin in order to correct this vital wrong, it will put the case, in my hands, at a very great disadvantage. Oswald Huron will take the ground that I am his enemy, and that you are his enemy, and that for vindictive purposes we have concocted a scheme to rob him of his child. The ground will be plausible both before the people and the court to which he will appeal, for Heaven knows he has given us both cause for enmity. Could you not go before Mr. Hope, the minister, and a most excellent man ?"

"No, sir. I am a Catholic, and he would not believe me for a word."

"I am satisfied you are mistaken," said Mr. May.

"There is but one other man alive that I will give testimony to."

"Who is he ?"

"Captain Gale, who is a man of his word and bond."

"That is very unfortunate," observed Lawyer May. "Captain Gale's disabilities in this particular are similar to my own."

"And *my* disabilities are much more similar," said Mrs. Guthrie; "for if Oswald Huron had his choice, of all the heads in Creswood he would break mine first. So I must look out for myself as well as right the wrong, for who is to look for me ? I give you my affidavit, and it's not likely I'd swear myself into this if the truth was not in it, and my conscience not in it. Then I go away for good reasons as witnessed in the affidavit. Then there's Amy Turnbolt. She can stanchify the witnessing of my affidavit, and of her own, and give her own word o' mouth witnessing, herself, if the fact-justice is ever brought into the appeal of a court, which it will be, because that hyena of a Oswald Huron would claim even a skunk kitten as his own, and battle with the old skunk for it, if he took a notion to,—*durn* him !"

The last two words of Mrs. Guthrie were spoken in a low, emphatic tone, and to herself.

The lawyer drew up an affidavit, not qualified by the clause, "to the best of my knowledge and belief," but direct and positive. He appended the customary certificate of an officiating magistrate, and, with Mrs. Guthrie, proceeded to 'Squire Shaw's, the nearest authority. On their way, Mrs. Guthrie somewhat cattishly said,—

"If 'Squire Shaw goes to reading of it, I'll jerk it away from him and tear it up."

"In all probability he will not care to read it, and in any event I shall see that he does not. He has nothing to do but administer the oath, see you sign, and sign himself."

Mrs. Guthrie, having succeeded to her satisfaction in getting her secret into a "writ form," left Creswood and went among her friends and relatives in a settlement many miles distant from her late home.

When the Whitecap again rode in the little bay at the rear of Gale Island, Amy Turnbolt did pretty much as Mrs. Guthrie had done, and Captain Gale followed pretty well the example of Lawyer May. In everything which appertained to the law and its administration Captain Gale was methodical and exact, and the document which he drew up from Amy Turnbolt's word o' mouth, setting forth the "fact-justice" of the Huron family complications, was in all respects the compeer of that which was in possession of Lawyer May.

Although these affidavits were not first-class testimony, they were better than nothing in the event of an accident, such as the death or disappearance of one or both of the affiants. In those days, communication was by no means advanced to its present activity and universality, and a person might easily step aside and never be heard of more.

"Amy," said Captain Gale, "I am surprised that you have been able to keep this matter so absolutely to yourself. You did wrong to practice deception in the first place, but, having done so, you were wise not to gad it about.

Now that Maria Guthrie has gone, you will never rest until you make a confidant of some other woman. Therefore you had better tell Sallie all about it, and whenever you feel like talking it over, you can do so with her to your heart's content. But if, by your indiscretion, this secret gets wind before the proper time, it will be the worse for you, I can assure you."

Captain Gale proved himself a good *womanier*, by at once providing Amy with a confidant, and adding fear to discretion as a more potent motive for secrecy.

Although Lawyer May and Captain Gale were devoted to that justice, order, and legitimacy which are so comely in the sight of good men, they were constrained to hold their peace for the present, notwithstanding it involved a vital and accomplished fraud upon the Huron parents and the infant Cora Glencoe. Oswald Huron himself, by his inveteracy and malignancy, put it out of their power to correct the false state of his family relations. He had declared war, and waged it, and was yet waging it, upon the lawyer, the mariner, and upon each of the nurses severally; and when his animosity was fixed it was more savage and tenacious than the teeth of a bull-dog. Of what avail, then, would it be for them, or either of them, to attempt to convince him that the infant now in his possession was the offspring of his brother? He would deride the evidence, and spit in the faces of his enemies. He would declare it a vindictive conspiracy to rob him of his child. He would prosecute them one and all, wherever he could reach them, with more than his accustomed vehemence. Also, it would create a most lamentable condition of uncertainty in the family of Neville Huron; it would lead to a wretched wrangling between the Huron brothers; and, in the popular eye, disinherit the child for life of an indisputable and absolute lineage.

Lawyer May and Captain Gale appreciated the difficulties and perplexities which would accompany an effort to do the duty which had been delegated to them, or, more properly, thrust upon them. They consulted each other, as men and women *will* do, knowing in advance that an interchange of views would amount to no more than an exchange of words. Lawyer May said to Captain Gale,—

4*

"At the present time, an attempt would be futile. Before this community we have stood in behalf of these nurses, and brought them successfully out of a disagreeable and bitterly-conducted investigation, the inside merits of which we were unquestionably presumed to be fully advised of. Popularly, this matter is considered judicially and thoroughly sifted, and done with for all time. We so considered it ourselves. And now, of all men in the world, for you and myself to disentomb this calamity and cause it to resurrect* with a different face and habiliments,—for you and myself to attempt to prove by the very nurses themselves an apparently new-hatched state of 'fact-justice,'—to quote from Mrs. Guthrie, and, by-the-way, it's not a bad expression," said the lawyer, smiling,—"would be no whit short of absolutely ridiculous, as well as, *prima facie*, a crime, a concocted crime. I should be set down for a knave, and you for a fool, or *vice versa*, and we should meet with no greater success than the hootings of an indignant or jocose community might signify."

Lawyer May closed his last sentence with a smile as jocose as might have been the community under the circumstances referred to. Captain Gale observed,—

"An attempt now would make reasonable any charges which Oswald Huron might shrewdly bring against us."

"Any which he would *undoubtedly* bring," interrupted the lawyer, not, as is the professional custom, refraining from a positive and unqualified assertion which is based upon opinion merely.

"And," continued Captain Gale, "however stubbornly we might hurl the truth into people's ears, just so stubbornly would they spew it out of their mouths."

"I readily recognized the exceptional difficulties, not only surrounding this case, but imbedded in it, and the more I reflect upon it, the more I am disposed to think that ingenuity itself could not have contrived a more unfortunate and unhandy situation. Perhaps you can suggest something feasible? I myself have nothing to propose just now except to watch and wait."

"It's a dark watch, let the outlook be from bow or stern,"

---

* Not to be found in Webster.

said Captain Gale, renewing his quid of tobacco. "One thing is evident: we are becalmed, and there's no help for it but to bring on a storm, which can only result in a furious collision fore and aft, weather and lee, and probable shipwreck to the future of the infant."

"I'm told it's a very sweet little thing," said Lawyer May; "and if it should so happen that Oswald Huron shall be it's lifelong father, it will be one of those inscrutable Providences which make men reject the idea of divine supervision. If it were Oswald Huron's child which had got mismatched with his brother Neville, I believe I could conscientiously and forever hold my peace."

"I can hardly use such strong language as *that*," said the law-and-order captain; "though the child's future prospects would certainly forbid an interposition if the case was reversed. It's a pity you could not prevail upon Mrs. Guthrie to go to Mr. Hope. Amy might go to him, or to anybody, and make an open question of it, but it would rebound upon *me* in the end, as the instigator, and do the cause no good; whereas Mrs. Guthrie was not, and is not, supposed to be at the command or instance of any particular person."

"And the trouble is, there are no visible prospects for a change. This matter, I'm afraid, will vex us for a long time, like an impatient and knotty problem on our files of unfinished business;" and the lawyer took a pinch of snuff.

"Unless some person, less patient with Oswald Huron than you or I, should blow out his brains," suggested the captain.

"He does not fail to afford opportunities for such a sequel, and he little knows how near to doom he has ventured at more times than one;" and the lawyer's face grew stern with the memory of repeated insults. "But, Gale," he smilingly continued, "you are a strong man in this community. I *was*, until the public insults of Oswald Huron, and my quiet submission to them, robbed me of my character as a person of backbone. I may, however, take occasion to resume my *lumbar vertebræ*, and if we only keep ourselves on strict watch, we may find an opportunity yet of breaking the force of circumstances."

"The man's own colossal unpopularity would aid us," said Captain Gale; "but the deil of it is that everybody seems to fear him as well as hate him."

From several observations, similar to the one just made, Lawyer May felt faintly that Captain Gale connected *him* with those who feared Oswald Huron, and was delicately hinting that it was time for him to assert his manhood. Although nothing was further from Captain Gale's thoughts, it nevertheless had its effect upon the lawyer.

After conversing awhile upon wind and weather, politics and policy, the two gentlemen shook hands cordially, and Captain Gale went his way.

CHAPTER V.

MOST *able* lawyers are men of courage and fortitude. They are also, by the nature of their profession, educated to great self-control. Much reciprocal tongue-lashing superinduces in their behalf thick skins and short memories. They are not apt at taking offense for slight causes, but, with keen repartee, launch from the mouth instead of the shoulder or the pistol tube. They have too many quarrels to make, and battles to fight, for others, and for which espousals they are well paid, to allow of either inclination or leisure for getting into non-paying quarrels of their own. Physical arbitrament they regard as unintellectual, and broken heads and lodged bullets as not the proper mode. *But*, as we once heard of a very worthy parson, who, in the midst of a discourse suggested by the words of the Divine Herald, "Peace on earth and good will to men,"— left his pulpit, went down into his congregation, and trounced a disturbing element there: *so* we occasionally hear of a lawyer and counselor who abandons his neighbor's feud to settle one of his own; postponing, perhaps, the prosecution of a manslayer to go out and slay a man himself, or—get slain.

Lawyer May was an able lawyer. He was also a man of courage and great self-restraint. Oswald Huron, implacable, and growing more aggressive as he grew older, had recently insulted Lawyer May frequently; in fact, about as often as he met him. Mr. May had no family except a little son six years of age. Once a wealthy man, he had just emerged from innumerable financial difficulties, the result of faults not his own, with little else save his honor. Had it not been for the wish to retrieve his fortunes, chiefly for the sake of his little boy, a child of promising intelligence and future, he would have risked a personal and extreme issue with Oswald Huron before the insults of the latter had been so many times repeated. He knew that the community did not appreciate the influence which caused him to avoid a difficulty with this intemperate man, and one which, should it occur, would be a deadly one ; and he was acutely sensible of a diminution of respect for himself among his neighbors, who were well aware that Oswald Huron almost spat in his face whenever it was convenient. The question would often force itself upon his attention, whether it was better to take the risk of leaving his boy unprotected and unprovided for, or to forego the risk and continue to live in disgrace with his neighbors, with himself, and probably with his own child, who was a spirited little fellow. He had not been able to decide until events decided for him. One pleasant afternoon he was walking on the Larboard Strand, accompanied by his boy, whose name was Carroll. Turning an angle of the Tarpeian Rock he suddenly encountered Oswald Huron. The latter halted and stood in the immediate pathway of Lawyer May. Oswald Huron was a tall, muscular, dark-eyed, olive-faced man, slightly stoop-shouldered, and with long black hair which swept his shoulders. His beard was flowing and black, and concealed his white shirt-bosom. His countenance was highly intellectual, and, when at rest, was not unhandsome, but the least activity of his strange volcanic soul perverted it from its normal fine stamp and expression.

He sneered at Lawyer May, who stood and regarded him calmly, though with feelings akin to those which one might feel on meeting some uncertain beast or more uncertain lunatic. He then addressed some offensive language to the lawyer. The latter, still calm, replied,—

"Mr. Huron, your conduct toward me has been, and is, very strange and entirely unprovoked, and I fail to conceive in what respect it can gratify you. Let me *again* beseech you never to address me."

Oswald Huron, who had provided himself with another cane in the stead of that which Captain Gale had taken away from him at the store of Mr. Nutt, raised his stick, leant forward, and struck Lawyer May a light blow upon the shoulder. Then, still leaning forward, his countenance, working between a grin and a frown, expressed a devilish challenge, as to say,—

" *Resent it if you dare.*"

Little Carroll May, for the first time and with indignant wonder, saw his father insulted. He picked up a pebble, and, throwing it, struck Oswald Huron in the eye. The missile, though small and light, caused for the moment a distracting pain, which gave Lawyer May an opportunity of taking his son by the hand and walking away.

"Father," asked the child, still wondering, "why didn't you whip him?"

"Hush, Carroll," said the father, whose soul writhed beneath the wondering eyes of his boy as it had never done before the slights of his neighbors or the insults of his foe. He must banish that look of wonder, lest it should change to one of contempt, or he must die upon the effort.

Lawyer May, with livid cheek, walked slowly down toward Gale Island. Said he to himself, "Dueling is a practice which, heretofore, I have neither condemned nor justified; or, in other words, which I *have* condemned or justified, according to the features of each particular of that practice. As a common resort it is heartless, lamentable, or farcical, and should be discouraged by public sentiment, as it is by legislative penalty. And yet law-giving nations themselves resort to it. On a point of honor Troy fell, and Greece depleted her strength. Hector slew thousands, Achilles slew Hector, and Paris slew Achilles. Romulus killed Remus for dishonoring his walls, and Cicero preached '*delenda est Carthago*' continually, for the honor of Rome. Christians wage war to uphold the Prince of Peace, and the Saracen carves 'Mohammed' upon the shaft of his lance. Nations are insulted, exchange notes, become irreconcilable, rouse their sluggish, ponderous hearts, and rush to battle. International obligations are sent upon the wind,

ditches receive the slain, brooks and rivers bear off the
blood, the fate of brave thousands is settled, but the point
of honor is still a festering thorn. In the face of such
mighty examples, can an individual disdain to feel when
an acute point pricks him? Can an individual man, more
full of heart and heat proportionably than is a nation, refrain from breaking the laws of law-breaking legislators?
Can a Gentile be better than a Jew, or a Pagan more humble than a Christian? Can he who acknowledges weakness be more stanch than he who professes strength?
Can men fail to revolt when nations plunge headlong into
revolution? Laws are not presumed to be for glory or for
farce, but for protection and redress. But there are some
peculiar instances of wrong for which the laws are as the
lame, the halt, and the blind. The philosophy of motion
would probably be as easy to practice as to theorize but
for the resistance of the atmosphere and the impediment of
friction. So is it with statutes, which operate in a dense
atmosphere of human passions, and encounter a gumlike
friction of ignorance or corruption. The sly or vindictive
encroachments of a respectable villain upon the purity of a
woman's name or the standing of a man's character, are
among that class of subtle wrongs with which the law is
too clumsy to grapple; and the injured will be injured still,
unless the individual arm is bared for redress. Oswald
Huron does not wound my body; for if he did, I could
shoot him within the law. But he *does* lacerate my spirit,
which is as much more sensitive than the body, as it is
more ethereal. And yet I can neither bind him to desist,
nor redress myself, unless I break the laws of lumberheaded
legislators. I might sue him; he would pay the insignificant fine out of his large means, and taunt me even while
paying it. If he should knock me down, or cut or shoot
my flesh, I alone would feel the pain. But he puts a *leprosy* upon me, the leprosy of disgrace and dishonor, which
does not confine itself to me alone, but spreads through all
the ramifications of kinship, and descends to my boy, carrying its venom. He has even now brought me into wonder
and disrepute with my own child. I am not physically
able to break his head, or cane him into the proprieties of
life. But there is a leveler that I know of which, at

twenty paces or less, overcomes the inequalities of physical strength and malignancy of spirit, and as often as not gives the battle to the weak."

Thus continued Lawyer May to think, not with his wonted consecutiveness, for he felt outraged and stern, and barely succeeded in smothering his agitation before he hailed for the ferry-skiff at Gale Island.

Captain Gale sculled over the water and returned to the Whitecap with his visitors. The mariner was fixing about his rigging and preparing to sail the ensuing night, for the wind was in the right quarter to send him out to sea, and the moon promised to be fair and the skies serene. He was about to lead his visitors to the cottage, when Lawyer May observed,—

"Captain Gale, I have but a few moments to remain here, and would prefer seeing you on board," and the lawyer made a gesture toward the Whitecap.

"You are welcome to cabin or cottage," said Captain Gale, who conducted his visitors to the vessel, and offered bunks for seats.

"You appear to be getting ready for a cruise," observed the lawyer.

"I go out to-night," was the response.

"I am sorry for that. I wanted you to come up to my house for an hour or so."

Captain Gale was sagacious enough not to take or pretend to take this as a social invitation.

"If there is anything of importance," he replied, "or if I can be of any service to *you*, I will spare the time, Mr. May, and not miss it."

"It *is* a thing of importance, and I shall feel deeply obliged to you. To economize your time, I propose we go now, take tea at my house, and proceed without delay to the matter in hand."

"I'll first advise my wife," said the thoughtful captain; "but won't you come into the cottage and sit a moment?"

"No, captain, I thank you. I will await you here."

The lawyer's residence was about a mile distant from the island, up the Larboard Strand, situated on a bluff, in view of the ocean, and not very far from Cliff Hall.

Within a reasonable length of time, and after tea, Lawyer May was busily writing in his office, with a very grave though placid face, and Captain Gale was quietly waiting. Having folded several newly written documents, and directed them, the lawyer turned to Captain Gale and said,—

"Captain Gale, you are one of the few men of my acquaintance whom I consider thoroughly honest and thoroughly reliable."

The captain, taken unexpectedly between wind and water, bowed, not without grace, and replied,—

"Mr. May, I am gratified to be able conscientiously to return a compliment which I hope is as near the truth as I believe it to be sincere. No man is reliable unless he is honest, and many a man may be honest and yet not be reliable," added the ethical captain.

"I agree with you," said the lawyer, "and, without more ado, come to the pith. You are probably aware that Oswald Huron makes a pastime of insulting me. To-day he repeated his insults, without provocation and in a manner so gross that even my little boy, almost a suckling, attacked him in my defense. Longer to suffer this would be to lose my self-respect, as I have already, in a measure, lost the respect of my neighbors. The *quick* has been reached, Captain Gale, and without making use of plainer language, you may, and doubtless do, divine what my intentions are. I will only say that my resolution is fixed, and that it will be useless for you to consume the few moments which you have to spare in endeavoring to alter or modify it. I refer to this, not to involve you, but as an introduction to the request which our past friendship encourages me to make of you. My little boy may be left without protection. If so, may I have your promise that you will send him to the person and place which you see indorsed on this package, and send the package with him? I have left no will. It is not necessary to make a will, for my estate, as you know, is in its second infancy. Here is another package. It contains the affidavit of Maria Guthrie relative to that unfortunate exchange of infants. With it I have inclosed a statement of my own. At some more fitting time you may be able to restore the child, Cora Glencoe, to the true parents. These packages I will give

5

to you now, if you have decided to favor me by taking charge of them."

"It is a small favor you have asked of me, Mr. May. It shall be willingly done if necessary, which I hope will not be the case. I only regret that the favor, if it may be so termed, is not greater."

"Captain Gale, I thank you heartily. I will not longer detain you from your vessel, for I know in what manner prudent sailors rate fair weather and fortunate wind. Good-by, and may you never feel what I, for my child's sake, feel at this moment."

Within two hours of the time at which Captain Gale took his departure from the lawyer's office, Oswald Huron received from Lawyer May an unconditional challenge to mortal combat. It was accepted, and by daylight in the morning the parties, with their seconds, were on their way to the selected ground, which was one among the secluded spots in the depths of Creswood.

When Captain Gale returned from his interview with the lawyer, to the island, instead of going into his cottage he went aboard of the Whitecap, lighted a lamp, kindled a fire in the little cabin stove, picked up a pipe, sat down, and deliberated while he smoked. Creswood, thought he, once so quiet and uneventful, was getting into notoriety; and before many hours, he imagined, the neighborhood would be astir and aghast at the terrible news of *tragedy*, for he was satisfied that deadly issue was near at hand in which an implacable and domineering foe was to be met by a roused and dauntless gentleman, who, against his conscience perhaps, was impelled to risk life in order to make life tolerable.

Captain Gale well enough understood, first the forbearance, next the irresistible promptings of Mr. May. He sympathized with the gentlemanly and gracious lawyer, regarding him as a man of strict integrity, commendable pride, and strong feeling, who had been unmercifully and wantonly harassed by a neighborhood tyrant. He also sympathized with him as one who had, by fortitude and unrelaxing effort, emerged, penniless it is true, but hopeful, untarnished, and respected, from many and weighty difficulties, only to be pressed and driven into a yet more serious and exceptional position hedged by danger and irretrievable disaster.

Voluntarily to transgress the law and nullify it, or voluntarily to permit it to be transgressed and nullified, was, in the estimation of Captain Gale, as portentous of ultimate evil to the public weal, as the violation of the sailor's Black Oath was prophetic of doom to the perjured. There are many crimes which, like the far-speaking thunder peal, or the music of the thrilling wind-harp, can neither be written or defined, and in view of which there is, consequently, no statutory provision. No one condemned such crimes more heartily than Captain Gale; and yet, in a commonwealth point of view, he considered the commission of these unnamable and indefinable transgressions, one and all, as less hurtful than the lightest breach of political standard law. The former was but the plucking of a single fruit bloom; the latter was a vital hacking at the roots of the tree. The one might puncture an individual; but the other wrenched a bolt from the gates of the public ramparts.

Captain Gale put away his pipe, took down a tin bugle, stepped out on deck, and blew a blast which rioted among the hills of Creswood in ten thousand echoes. Fifteen minutes passed, when four men, his crew, hailed him from across the bay. With a skiff he brought them over to the Whitecap.

"Boys, be lively now! stow these packages, and get ready to work her out."

He then went into the cottage, where, between himself and Mrs. Gale, a consultation ensued. Emerging from his cottage, he walked if possible with a manlier step than usual, saying to himself,—

"There is, after all, no better helm for a man than a stanch Christian wife, and no better lighthouse than the Book. I felt that I was right before I went in yonder," motioning his head toward the cottage, "and now, *by the salt at the bottom of Neptune's Grog, I know* I am right."

Captain Gale's conviction must have been absolute, or he would never have dared salt water again after taking that oath, which, by-the-way, was his sole superstition.

"Run her out, boys," commanded the captain, as he

sprang aboard with an agility which surprised his crew,
who, however, were destined quickly to meet with a much
greater surprise; for no sooner had the Whitecap reached
open water than Captain Gale shifted his helm, and
ordered the vessel in a direction the opposite of the wind
and the undoubting anticipations of the crew. The sails
swung about, and refilled, and the Whitecap as gracefully
and coquettishly wheeled to the piping wind, as a sweet
gay girl, under the eye of her lover, wheels to voluptuous
music.

Captain Gale steered for Kaffir-Land. Having run
about six knots, he shifted his course, and in a couple of
hours from the time he left the island, he anchored against
the Maryland bluffs some eight miles south of his home.
Taking a small lifeboat, he went ashore, and was lost in
the gloom of the rough and wooded coast. He was absent
for the space of an hour. When he returned, he trimmed
his vessel to run with the wind, and was soon plowing
northward upon his original course, from which his first
two hours' sail had been a diversion.

Captain Gale had never found it necessary to resort to
violence in order to maintain the respectability of his name.
He avoided giving provocation, which was his chiefest
shield. If any one sought a quarrel with him, he was so
reasonable, and so firm, and so bold withal, that if the dis-
putant was not disarmed by reason, he was generally halted
by the Captain's lion-like aspect and cool gray eye. Oswald
Huron nearer than any other man had succeeded in rousing
him to the alternative of violence, but the sturdy captain
had warded off a climax so at variance with his tastes and
practices, and brought himself peaceably away without one
whit of his reputation for pluck abated.

But Captain Gale was a manner of man of which the
specimens are rare; and, as the world goes, the great mass
of men could not, if they would, follow his wake. As it is
very true that no girl ever reached the age of maturity
without having received a most provoking offer of marriage
from some quarter, it is equally true that no boy ever at-
tained his majority without one or more favorable opportunities for a personal difficulty other than that of matrimony.
Nerve and coolness, in which men generally are so deficient,

are probably more in requisition to prevent a battle than to conduct one. But with nerves of steel and the coolness of ice, it is sometimes literally impossible for a person to avoid a difficulty. He cannot even *run away* from it. In very nearly such a condition Lawyer May found himself when he sent his challenge to Oswald Huron. Captain Gale had given Oswald Huron equal cause with Lawyer May for hostility and aggression. But it did not occur to the captain that himself was a much more formidable looking antagonist than was Mr. May, and that Oswald Huron enjoyed more opportunities of insulting the slender lawyer, than he did the stalwart and itinerant captain of the Whitecap. He did not know that Oswald Huron had contemplated following him up, through the convenient medium of the United States mail, with insults deliberately and exquisitely written, and deposited in every post-office along the coast where the captain would be likely to call; and that he only abandoned the enterprise for the reasons that he could not by that means gore the captain deep enough to draw blood, and that his missives might furnish extenuating evidence in the captain's behalf, should he, by possibility, become exasperated and belabor the writer.

Although Captain Gale entertained a sincere regard, yea, an affection for Lawyer May, and took pride in him as an honorable, able, and prominent man, and sympathized with him as being one of whom care and perplexity had made a veteran, and although he and Lawyer May were in most things well agreed, the time had come, involving the life of two fellow-creatures, the destiny of children, the peace of families, and the dignity of law, in which Captain Gale was urged by his principles and conscience to oppose the practice of his friend, and endeavor to avert a calamity which would sprinkle bitter tears over infant couches, and defy the bond and order of government, and beat with reckless and impious blows upon the gates of Heaven. And yet the fact that Lawyer May had appealed to a lawless code, instead of reducing, rather augmented for him the esteem of the law-sustaining captain of the Whitecap. Is it not possible, after all, that the pacific captain was unconsciously more or less actuated by a suspicion, a dread, a well-grounded

5*

fear that his friend would meet with foul play? Who can divine even his own heart to know it?

It is proper here briefly to assist the imagination of the reader. The two hours' sail of the Whitecap against the wind, was to reach the nearest point on the coast accessible to the county sheriff's dwelling. To the sheriff Captain Gale anxiously went, and disclosed to him the contemplated hostile May-Huron meeting, to prevent which he urged the officer to spare no pains or activity. Having done all that he could possibly do, except to accompany the officer, which was not deemed necessary, he again committed himself to wind and wave, trusting that the ready and sagacious officer would forestall the mischief which was in train.

When Captain Gale turned in for the night, his last thoughts were, "Blessed are the peace-makers; for they shall be called the children of God." In these words, his wife, back at the cottage, when he had consulted her, had urged him to prevent bloodshed. Hanging about his neck, with tearful eyes and trembling earnestness, she had given him the heartfelt speedwell and good-by of "Blessed are the peace-makers; for they shall be called the children of God."

Captain Gale slept sweetly out upon the deep, where the billows rocked him gently, and the south wind bore him onward in a prosperous voyage.

CHAPTER VI.

WE have already attempted to divine the motives which prompted Lawyer May to go out into some deadly dell of Creswood, while the light of a fair December day was yet breaking through the gloomy forest.

What Oswald Huron's motives were our pen cannot conceive, unless they were founded in pure perversity. He had a risk to run as well as his antagonist. He had an eye to match as clear and vigilant as his own; and a hand as steady as his own. And yet he had not hesitated to accept an issue from which could spring no advantage whatever to himself, let it go yea or nay with him.

As Lawyer May calmly stood hard by where the seconds were measuring the ground and tossing for positions, a professional, in scanning the lawyer's fine and elegant figure, would probably have been ruffled by no more serious reflection than, if the day should go against him, that he would at the very least make a handsome corpse. Although his face was as placid as the sheltered pool, and his pulses strong and deliberate, in his soul he was living out many years during the few short moments of preparation. Oswald Huron stood apart, seemingly impatient that the action should begin, or that it were well over. The spot which had been chosen was buried in the forest's depths, and secure from probability of intrusion. The antagonists were placed by their agents in their respective select positions, and the weapons, being charged with death, were passed to them. The word to fire, followed by the customary count, was given. Two ringing shots succeeded. Oswald Huron took one step backward, but was, in other respects, apparently untouched. Lawyer May fell to his knees; then drooping to one side, he lay along the ground mortally wounded. The bullet had lodged within his lungs, hopeless of extraction, and making a rent which let in the blood upon his breath and almost suffocated him upon the spot. Oswald Huron had worn a secret breastplate. He was an amateur chemist and astronomer, at times observing the heavens through a small telescope which he had, and at times and for no visible purpose, working in metals. Hence, together with his singular personal appearance, his reputation among the ignorant of being a necromancer. A sheet of copper from his laboratory had been readily improvised for use as a hidden shield. When he reached Cliff Hall a manslayer, he found the plate of copper deeply indented where it had covered his heart. He laughed in savage triumph.

Lawyer May was taken to his home, sensible of his condition, but speechless. When his little boy came in, the child's look of horror and cry of wild dismay, and the quenching emotion pictured in his face, smote upon the father's heart infinitely sharper, and deeper, and sorer than all the insults which had urged him to this fatal *dernier ressort*. How bitter it was to the father *now* to reflect upon the results of his hazard, and how sweet it would have been to have recalled that hazard, and forever to have eschewed its like; and to have lived and gone out from the haunts of his enemy, and found a new home, in which he could have reared his son, and taught him the wisdom, unselfishness, and beauty of humility and forbearance. The film of death upon the eye gives clearer vision to the soul, thought the expiring father. It is a question, however, whether he would not have considered his life expended in a well-directed effort, had he been able to have left his son well provided with funds and friends. For this mortal problem of the duello is not altogether like the moon, a one-sided affair. It has several sides, like a triangle. But, as a rule, the bitter follows the sweet of it, as quinine taken in honey; and as an exception, the sweet succeeds the bitter, as when chewing the root of the *dulcamara*, a deadly nightshade, by-the-way. Had Lawyer May killed Oswald Huron and escaped unhurt himself, he would not have lived contented with so perfect a result. His mind would ever have lacked that serenity so pleasing and fair, and so meet for happiness and contentment. Probably the only condition upon which he could have left the contest with satisfaction, would have been the wounding of his adversary, as a painful lesson to him, and with the assurance that he would never have to repeat the lesson. A bloodless battle would have been regarded by him as an abortion. And a reconciliation, could it have been possible, would only have soothed without satisfying his wrongs; for no man can utterly forgive as Christ forgives.

Mrs. Gale, as soon as she was advised of the issue, went up to Lawyer May's residence, and ministered to him. Taking little Carroll in her arms, she wept over him passionately. She told Mr. May of the effort which her husband had made to avert this solemn sequel. A smile of gratitude was his reply. Promising to call again in the morning and see to his comfort, she returned home. But in the morning he would have no need of earthly comfort.

Lawyer May, surrounded by his neighbors, among whom

were those who had mistreated by misjudging him, died at
nightfall, of suffocation by internal hemorrhage. From the
time that he fell, until his death, he had been speechless,
as the least exertion to speak flooded his lungs. He had
managed to scrawl a note to Captain Gale, requesting him
to record, for the future information of his son, wherefore
he had met his death by violence.

In the face of this tragedy Creswood turned pale. The
sheriff had been active to perform his duty, but an Indian
jungle is not more pathless and perplexing than were the
untrodden holds and morning twilight of the dense forest.
The law, both before and after the breach, was foiled of its
capture. Lawyer May died without making any communication about the manner and cause of his overthrow,
other than the simple note which he left for Captain Gale.
Oswald Huron was silent. No one knew, or appeared to
know, who were the seconds. In a strictly legal sense,
there was total ignorance upon the subject; but the *moral
certainty* was coequal with the lack of licit evidence. No
one doubted that Oswald Huron killed Lawyer May, but
there were many who claimed it to be, not the work of the
man, but of the *necromancer*. Consequently the Necromancer's notoriety widened and deepened among the simpletons of Creswood, and not a few old women prophesied.

The Whitecap again rode at anchor in the little harbor
back of the island. The vessel was drawing fewer inches
than it had ever claimed since it was launched. Not an article of traffic was aboard, except a package or two for Mr.
Nutt, the country merchant. Captain Gale had completely
vended his stock to coast merchants and families who were
laying in their winter supplies. He dealt almost exclusively
in staple goods and groceries. "Jeems River," that is to
say, James River tobacco, was his pet. It left no remnants,
came solid, stowed solid, sold for solid cash, and always
made good ballast; for Captain Gale permitted no bilge-
water in his boat to injure his goods. He would say to his
crew, "Boys, bilge-water is hefty, and bilge-water is odo-
riferous, but it's neither ballast nor balsam." Although he
had missed his Johnny's "sip ahoy!" when he sailed under
the cottage shore, and although the weather was cold and
blustering, he walked with a comfortable and dignified bear-

ing as he approached the door of his island home, for under
his arm he carried that storm-baffling life-ballast—a well-
filled money chest,—and in his heart was the buoy of prosperity.   Entering his cottage, he found a cheerful fire and
all well.   He was shocked at the sight of little Carroll May,
sitting upon the floor patting the head of Johnny's dog,
which immediately sprang up to welcome him.   Carroll
followed the dog's example, and responded with a mixture
of gravity and cheerful childlike frankness to Captain Gale's
fatherly greeting.

"No need to ask how it terminated," said Captain Gale
to his wife.

"The very worst has befallen," answered Mrs. Gale,
who, in an undertone, related to her husband all that was
generally known or surmised in connection with the death
of Lawyer May.   Captain Gale gravely shook his head,
and sat for some time without speaking.   Carroll and
Johnny, with the dog, sported on the floor.

Lawyer May's estate at the time of his death was barely
solvent.   The house in which he had lived, and the land
belonging to it, were pledged, and would pass into other
hands.   As has been stated, he was once wealthy.   He
had lost largely by the failure of a deposit bank, and yet
more largely as security for insolvent relatives.   A few
hundred dollars would be all that his son would inherit.
This amount was in bank notes, and was inclosed in one
of the open packages which he had intrusted to Captain
Gale.   Creswood was astonished to learn that Lawyer
May had been almost penniless, for he had not failed scru-
pulously to pay his debts whenever due.

It now became the duty of Captain Gale to comply with
the request of Lawyer May respecting the child.   The
honest mariner was a just man to the world at large, and
a kind-hearted man to those who stood in need either of
assistance or protection.   A tempest in the bosom of a little
child would move his heart of oak more sensibly than the
tempests of the deep.   He was ignorant whether or not the
little boy knew what disposition his father had made of
him.

"Carroll," he asked, "do you know where you are to
live?"

With touching simplicity and confidence the little fellow replied, while he swung upon Captain Gale's knee,—

"I am going to live with you; because father said that you are such a good, brave man."

Captain Gale looked up at the ceiling. A tear slowly gathered in his eye. He was ashamed of a visitor so strange to his cheek, for he had long felt that the time of life had passed in which he should ever again be called upon to wipe away the casual tear-drop. The roughest usage of the rough world to himself would not have moistened his clear gray eye. But the little boy had artlessly touched his stout heart in a very tender spot, and the rising tear found vent through a passage which was sealed to waters of grief, unless that grief was mingled with sympathy and tenderness. He pulled out his pocket-handkerchief and blew his nose. Glancing towards his wife, he saw that her trembling lids were about to overflow.

"Let it be so, husband," said Mrs. Gale.

"I must follow instructions," replied the captain.

"But maybe you can so arrange it?"

"Not likely. 'Tis his grandparents that he must go to."

"His mother's parents?"

"Carroll," said Captain Gale, to the boy, "you and Johnny run into the kitchen and sit by the fire until I call you back." When the boys had gone, he continued : "His maternal grandfather, and his step-grandmother."

"Ah, then," said Mrs Gale, "the difficulty is reduced fully two-thirds at one stroke, if it is only a step-grandmother."

"And necessity may reduce the other third," said the captain. "But, Sallie, before any more is said, are you *certain* that you want him?"

"I am. He's a fine boy, and I can't help but love him. Then Johnny needs a companion, and he could not be better suited. They are attached already, and they play and fight and play again, with as much harmony and as little harm as any two brothers."

"His grandparents are very old, and very poor, and really not able to take care of him," said Captain Gale. "All they have in the world is owing to the former wealth and liberality of Mr. May. I am satisfied that Mr. May would have chosen me for his son's guardian, had the estate been sufficient for the support of the little one. But he did not like to put his unprovided son upon the bounty of anybody, without some claim of kin justified it."

"It will be better so, John. If we take the child of our own pleasure and accord, we are more apt to continue satisfied than if we take him, however willingly, by request."

"How do you make that out, Sallie?"

"Vanity and perversity of human nature, I suppose," replied Mrs. Gale, laughing pleasantly.

"But could you do Carroll affectionate justice in view of our own children?"

"Why not?"

"Because every cook thinks her own cake the best."

"Try me, John. I engage not to fail either in duty or affection."

"It will not cost us a great deal," said Captain Gale, "and though we are not rich, we can easily afford it. What he eats would not be missed from the table. For the next ten years, thirty dollars per annum will clothe him. His money, which is in my possession, will bring in about that amount at interest. Mr. Hope intends to open a school in which he will educate free of cost, except for books, all who are needy. That is the mercenary, financial summing up of the business, which, though important, is by no means so important as that he should have a home and a *mother*. It shall be done, Sallie, if these old people will consent. The proposition would have originated with me probably, but as I am so much away, and as the added care will fall chiefly upon you, I do not know that I should have spoken without some encouragement."

"You are a dear old lion," said Mrs. Gale, with playful affection.

"And you,—let me see, now, what *you* are;—you're a sweet little pussy," retorted the quaint captain, who tapped his wife's cheek, got up, shook himself, took down a pipe, and soon began to puff tobacco-smoke serene.

Captain Gale wrote to Carroll's grandfather Preston, who lived near the village Fortesque, some eighty odd miles away. In respect to Carroll, the mariner made offers which, whether accepted or not, could not be considered otherwise than very kind and favorable. In due course of mail a reply was received. "Old Mr. Preston was, had been, and probably would continue to be, bed-ridden. He was not able to take care of himself, and old Mrs. Preston had to care for him, and the neighbors had to care for her. She was willing to take little Carroll, but how he would get along or thrive there she didn't know. She knew of Captain Gale from the letters of the dead, and from his own good letter, that he was an upright and good brave man, and it would be for Carroll's sake that she and Mr. Preston would accept the generous proposals, and she hoped that God would stretch out His arm, not only over the little orphan, but over his timely and generous friend; and that Mrs. Gale would be a mother to the little one, and that Carroll when he came to be of stature would repay them for their deeds of care and gifts of affection."

The old lady had dictated a very proper and feeling letter, and though her amanuensis had misspelt and mispunctuated, and made of it an epistle ludicrously misdight, the sense of it was very clear; and Carroll was forthwith numbered among the inhabitants of Gale Island. He soon learned to say "Uncle Gale," and "ma," when addressing or speaking of Captain and Mrs. Gale, and glided into the family and became one of it almost as naturally and effectually as if he had traveled into it from a bed of travail. Little Johnny Gale, when he appreciated that Carroll was to be his brother, and stay with him and play with him always, thought himself hand-over-fist in luck. Notwithstanding that the boys were devoted to each other, hardly a day passed without a fight or quarrel between them; and upon occasion Mrs. Gale spanked them both soundly. Carroll was quick to anger and quick to relent. Johnny was good-nature itself, and of an equable temper, but when he did take issue and set his meg, he was about as stubborn as a mule. Whenever Carroll saw Johnny begin to look in the face like a young bull, he knew that it was time to propose something else, as a diversion. Johnny was perfectly willing to be led, but he would not be driven an inch.

The Reverend St. John Hope, minister at Creswood, proved himself worthy of Mr. Guy Rapid's gracious and graceful gift. Although he was no longer under the eye of

6

his benefactor who had moved to Texas, and now that he
was comfortable, he did not sit at ease in his study and cut
out Sunday work merely, but, exerting himself to merit in
the sight of God and man the good fortune which had so
seasonably dropped upon him, strove to share its advantages with his neighbors by making the additional influence
and opportunities which it gave him, fruitful of good. He
opened a day-school in his dwelling. The children of the
poor he instructed free of cost, and faithfully. What it was
to be poor and struggling he himself had well known, until
the munificence of Mr. Rapid had lifted him out of his poverty, and secured to him a life of temporal comfort and competency. For, strange as it may appear, as Mr. Hope's
domestic prosperity increased, the liberality of his neighbors
and church members increased likewise. There was some
distinction, it seemed, in giving to a well-dressed, well-to-
do, elegant-looking minister of the gospel; whereas the
pitiable dollar subscribed in pure charity to the threadbare
laborer in the vineyard, lost its luster altogether by reason
of the recipient's insignificance. Another reason for increased liberality on the part of his neighbors was *shame.*
Guy Rapid, who was capable, both at heart and in purse,
of the noblest acts, and Captain Gale, much more willing at
heart than his purse was able, together with a few others,
all non-professors, had habitually contributed, independ-
ently of their wives' good gifts, the greater portion of the
means which went to maintain the church and its minister.
Mr. Rapid, at the death-bed of his wife, had heard Mr.
Hope at prayer. "Surely *this* is a man of God," thought
he, "whose words rise from the depths of his soul, reaching
to the Throne;" and with one stroke of his pen he set the
minister free from the niggardly purses of his pastorate,
and put them all to shame.

Besides being a most excellent man and effective preacher,
Mr. Hope, from being a regular graduate, became a regular
student, and his somewhat advanced age found him
thoroughly educated and scholarly in the American sense
of the terms. He had not married until rather late in life,
which was the most reprehensible example, probably, that
he had ever given to the world—of young bachelors. His
family now consisted of a wife, son, and two daughters.

His wife was much younger than himself. His son Garland was eleven years of age. His daughters, Bell and Hattie, were respectively seven and five. And altogether they were a happy family. His school flourished, and became a source of convenient though well-earned revenue, which, with the product of his perfect little farm, and a moderate salary from the pulpit, enabled him to live in that respectable and unexceptionable style so appropriate to the devout, earnest, and genuine minister of the gospel.

As time sped, among his scholars were numbered Carroll May, Johnny and Caddy Gale, and Cora Glencoe Huron, the little girl who was yet astray from her rightful parents. Cora was a marked figure both in and out of school, partly because she possessed a pure and enchanting beauty of person and way, and a face of surpassing sweetness, and partly for the reason that she was supposed to be the daughter of the Necromancer. Her own loveliness, and her connection with a superhuman, invested her with the triple charm of wonder, speculation, and awe. The little boys regarded her as matchless, but unapproachable.

A short time after Captain Gale's children became pupils of the Creswood school, the captain went up to the residence of the minister, which was just beyond Cliff Hall and overlooking the sea, to ascertain how the new pupils took to their books.

"They commence very well," said the minister, "very well indeed, and they behave well also. Johnny sometimes boils over with fun, but he has progressed so far as to be able to restrain to a moderate giggle what, in the beginning, was as outright laughter as ever was heard at a monkey-show. By-the-way, captain, all my elder scholars, and myself also, had a good hearty peal at your expense on the day when your children first entered school. It was what I consider a pretty good joke on the captain of the Whitecap."

"I am sure," said Captain Gale, "that you would never laugh at a bad joke; so let's have it."

"It involves an excellent moral, moreover, showing how little we imagine and appreciate the effect which our casual or careless expressions may have upon the minds and understandings of the youthful. But here," said the minister, with a broad smile of amusement. "It is a custom of my school-room to exercise the memories of the younger pupils by quoting a snatch of something from the primary books over which they have gone, and asking them whence it comes; from what book cometh it. It was Carroll's first day, and he happened to be at the head of the class. I quoted the first two lines of 'Mary had a little lamb, its fleece was white as snow,' and where, now, do you imagine that Carroll said it could be found?"

"On board the Whitecap?" laughingly asked the captain.

"No, captain; he said that it was from the Bible.

"'Error,' said I. 'Try again.'

"'It's from Shakspeare,' said he, on second trial.

"'Error,' again said I, and was about to pass the question to the next pupil, when he spoke up quickly and decisively, saying,—

"'Then it's from the Constitution of the United States, for I heard Uncle Gale say that what wasn't in the Bible was in Shakspeare, and what wasn't in Shakspeare was in the Constitution, and *he* knows, because he's a sailor, and has been all over the world.'" And the minister laughed heartily at the droll-looking captain.

"It's a poor sailor that can't shift a joke," said Captain Gale. "If you will look in Matthew, Mark, Luke, or John, you'll find where Mary *did* have a little lamb, and as white as snow."

"Ay; the Lamb of God," reverentially spoke the minister. "I believe you are right after all, captain. Ay, *whiter* than snow."

"I appreciate the moral and accept it; but, my dear sir," said Captain Gale, smiling, "before you get off another joke upon a sailor, first see whether or not there's a turn to it."

"I'm aware that you are a shifty crew," said the minister. "I only wish that you would shift your helm so as to run into the fold of which this Lamb is the great Shepherd."

"I am not altogether a stray sheep, Mr. Hope. I believe that I belong to the common fold, though not to your flock."

" It is the safest to choose a distinct flock, and not be common to all and an alien to each."

" I'm trespassing on your time, my dear sir," said Captain Gale, who escaped from a discussion for which he did not feel himself prepared just then, and also from a " predicament" which most men dislike and few ministers have the knack of making easy or agreeable. Mr. Hope, however, was one of those few. He was, par excellence, a chivalrous, reasonable, and dulcet exhortator in pulpit and in private. He did not excite the distaste or provoke the ridicule of his company or companion with the stereotyped whang and whine of the time-serving petty theologian, but like a veteran and knightly soldier of the Cross, roused the celestial ardor and aspirations of the young, and, upon the elder sinner, urged, with no narrow views of the pulpit-politician, but with the attractive and comprehensive ability of the heavenly statesman, the timely adoption of those life-measures which would set the soul in harmony with its Creator, and array it under the Banner of the Prince of Peace. He did not, as is so often done, pencil away his cause by drawing a far-distant, microscopic Eternity, which, compared with the life-sized foreground portrait of Time with all its hurtful and innocuous charms displayed, was as the frail and uncertain butterfly to the unerring and booty-getting eagle. But out of the heights and depths of his own appreciation of the Kingdom, his divine and perpetual images overshadowed all fleeting temporalities as the firmament overcometh the earth, rendering them trivial and vapid to the soul, and as idle to the eye as the aimless wind dallying with dead leaves over the graves of the forgotten.

In the process of time, Carroll May and Cora Glencoe became, in proportion to their years, the boy-brilliant and girl-brilliant of the Creswood school; and though the minister did not permit himself to exhibit partiality, he took especial pride and interest in the orphan boy and the ill-fathered little girl. But there was a thing in connection with Cora which annoyed and distressed Mr. Hope greatly. She never spoke to Carroll, Johnny, or Caddy, or gave them an opportunity of speaking to her, though they rubbed together almost every day. The two boys soon learned to let her severely alone, though they found it impossible not to gaze at her whenever, unobserved, they could do so. Caddy Gale did not lack for playmates ; and the fact that Cora never recognized her was one to which, after her first astonishment, she soon got accustomed, losing no sleep about it, and finally regarding it as an unimportant matter-of-course. But the two boys, who had reached the age when romance usurps the place of reason and demolishes the method of the mind, *did* lose sleep about it, for they were both in love with Coy, as they called her, and talked of her by day and by night, each making a confidant of the other, and sympathizing with each other in their hopeless-ness. It would seem natural that they should have dis-liked her, but there was nothing in the manner of Coy, beyond her coyness and silence, to create dislike; nothing supercilious, disdainful, or rude. Her conduct simply and pensively said, "I do not know you; therefore I cannot speak." Or else, and more likely, "I *cannot* know you; therefore I *do* not speak." So, from talking continually of Coy, they began to dream of her; and there is nothing so creative of love-sickness, or so fertilizing to the malady, in tender youth, as those strange and ravishing interviews vouchsafed to the vivid dreamer.

It has been stated that Mr. Hope was both annoyed and distressed on account of Cora's action in ignoring altogether the existence and presence of Carroll May and the young Gales.

He was *annoyed*, because this silent feud interfered with the arrangement of his classes. Cora Glencoe was able to cope with Carroll May in all studies involving ethics, and he would have delighted in putting them in class and com-petition with each other. But he had no third pupil to put between them in the class, except his son Garland, who was much older and much too far advanced. In botany, Cora far excelled Carroll, as he did her in geometry. Mr. Hope cultivated, as an adjunct of the school-room, a small botanic garden, in which Cora was often seen, as busy as a bee among the flowers, culling knowledge whence the bee culled honey.

The minister was *distressed*, because he witnessed, nearly every day, a precocious restraint and stoicism manifested by these children, which, at times, was absolutely painful to him. But he was impotent to ameliorate or remedy what he regarded as lamentable.

He knew that Oswald Huron had made an unusual concession in permitting Cora even to attend the same school with the son of Lawyer May and the children of Captain Gale, and that this was the utmost which he could hope from him. He doubted not that the implacable master of Cliff Hall had strictly and despotically charged his little daughter on the subject of her associates; and although the minister had ever been independent of Oswald Huron and his influence, and mentally protested against this precocious feud between innocent children, he did not dare to interfere. But it was on Cora's account, solely, that he held his peace. He looked upon her as a sweet and tender flower, sporadically springing up and blooming in a place of shadow, which, should he not give it sunlight and shelter, would wither beneath the nipping frosts, or have its fragrant blonde petals rifted and scattered by the winds.

On the other hand, Oswald Huron, who was a man of mental culture, though conceding no great respect either to Mr. Hope or his ministerial robe, recognized in the minister a man with whom he could safely trust his daughter, and whose school discipline suited his fancy. The almost faultless order of Cora's progress confirmed him in favor of the school, and amply able as he was to have sent her to some more fashionable institution, he was agreed that he could not find a preferable-one, or, in all respects, as convenient and good a one as the school of Creswood. He even permitted himself to go so far as to *like* Mr. Hope, when, after repeated strict questionings of Cora, he became satisfied that the minister did not presume to dictate to her in regard to her associates.

Oswald Huron, notwithstanding he has appeared in such a bad light to the reader, possessed the elements of an excellent and eminent man. But these elements seemed to have been dislocated, and, acting abnormally upon each other, to have made him what he was, "out of tune and harsh." Some said that he was possessed of a devil; others, that he was partially deranged; and still others, that he had deliberately, though bitterly and viciously, chosen to be an Ishmael, delighting in nothing so much as to be at loggerheads with all the world.

Neville Huron, who lived in Philadelphia, differed widely from his brother Oswald. He was an equable, confiding, gentlemanly man and neighbor, almost too confiding in fact, as the sequel may show. But he was forced to regard his brother unfavorably, and there was but little intercourse between them. Neville Huron was a man of wealth and family. His son Graham, who was about five years the senior of Cora Glencoe, was his first born. Augusta was next to Cora, and Gertrude was the youngest. Mrs. Neville Huron was a well-bred Philadelphia lady, and the family, as a whole, were highly respectable and elegant in all their appointments.

CHAPTER VII.

ONE evening after tea, while Captain Gale was sitting on his cottage portico quietly smoking his pipe, and looking upon the billows which lazily rolled in the moonlight, Carroll and Johnny maneuvered about him as if meditating some sort of an attack. Carroll was the bolder scout of the two, or else Johnny had put him forward, for he finally skirmished up to the captain's chair, and said,—

"Uncle Gale."

"What, Carroll?"

"Johnny and I want to take a trip."

"Well, you can take a trip."

"When, father?" interposed Johnny, encouraged by this favorable opening.

"When the Whitecap sails again."

"But we want a *land* trip this time," said the boys.

"Where do you wish to go?" asked Captain Gale.

"To Texas," answered the boys in chorus.

"Ph-e-w!" and Captain Gale blew a column of smoke almost up to the ceiling of the portico. The boys laughed, but were nevertheless in earnest and anxious.

"What put Texas in your heads?" asked Captain Gale.

"Pony Rapid," they replied.

"Cassel Rapid, do you mean?"

"Yes, sir."

"Is he at Creswood?"

"No, sir; but we wrote to him, and got a letter from him."

"What does he say?"

"He says he wants us to come out there, and make him a visit, and if we have no money, that his father will pay the expenses, and that he will give Johnny and me" (it was Carroll who was now speaking) "a mustang pony. He can ride like a Ranger, and throw the lasso, and shoot, and almost turn himself wrong-side-outwards! He says he will come back with us. He's been going to school in New York, and is going again. He says he'll take us to San Antonio, and show us the A'lamo, where Davy Crocket was killed, and the old Cathedral in the plaza, which is nearly two hundred years old, and was built by the Spaniards. He can talk Mexican, and says that *star wano* (*esta bueno*) means *bully.* He's a *star wano* fellow, and Johnny and I want to go out and see him and Texas."

"When Johnny was a small bad boy," said Captain Gale, taking the pipe from his mouth, "he once took a notion to set up an interminable howl for the moon. His mother very properly gave him a spanking and put him to bed. Cassel Rapid is a generous little fellow, and you should both thank him by letter; but if I hear any more of Texas from either of you, I'll spank you to bed myself;" and the captain wound up his threat with a three-decker laugh, in which he was joined by the boys, notwithstanding they saw their panorama of Western travel fade away as the colors of a summer evening sky.

Four years have passed away, without memorable event in Creswood, since Johnny Gale and Carroll May had projected a trip to Texas. The two boys were nearly grown, and had arrived at that plump and happy age which immediately precedes the time when the mind begins to prey upon the flesh: the time at which thought makes a preliminary survey of the face, and registers

where it will dig its furrows in the future. Carroll's hair
was brown, his eyes dark gray, and altogether he was a
handsome and intelligent young fellow. His greatest
fault was that of his readiness to take offense at imaginary
slights, but this may be partly excused on account of his
condition,—that of a child of charity. He was destined
for the Law, in anticipation of which Captain Gale had
preserved for him the library of lawyer May, which was
comprehensive, unique, and invaluable. Carroll was not
so tall as his father had been, but bid fair to be as tall in
his profession, for he was an assiduous searcher. He
never passed a word in any sort of reading if he was not
satisfied of its signification. He would, when in doubt or
ignorance, consult Walker, Webster, and even as quaint
an authority as old Bailey.

Johnny Gale had grown to be a young Hercules.
Though not over eighteen years of age, he was taller than
his father. He was the picture of rustic health, with his
blue-black hair, dark eyes like his mother's, ruddy cheeks,
and face as pleasant as good tidings. Having, at the
Creswood school, excelled in mathematics, he had been
destined to become a civil engineer ; the result of a conference between Captain Gale and Mr. Hope.

Caddy Gale had grown up almost a tomboy, but she
was an agreeable self-acting little maid, with a charming
little love-trap of a dimple in her right cheek.

Of Cora Glencoe we must speak hereafter.

About this time, there were rumors flying around Creswood that something very unusual and alarming had
happened to the Rapid family out in Texas ; that Mr.
Rapid was killed, and his home otherwise terribly visited.
Indian raids, Mexicans, freebooters, neighborhood feuds,
and other causes, were conjectured and ascribed, and a
state of uncertainty enhanced the interest of Mr. Rapid's
old friends and acquaintances, until Mr. Hope announced
from the pulpit that he had been killed by marauding
Indians. Mr. Hope and Mr. Rapid had corresponded
regularly up to the time of Mr. Rapid's death, which
event was not altogether an idle tale to the community of
Creswood, for outside of the families of Mr. Hope and
Captain Gale was many an old woman who shook her

head with terrific solemnity and import, while muttering
something about "them Injuns."

This brings us up to the reception, by Mr. Hope, of the
letter from young Cassel Rapid, referred to in the beginning of our second chapter.

It is possible, right here, that the author may be accused
of following the example of the foolish hen, which laid her
eggs first, and built her nest afterwards. If so, we can
only ask a suspension of condemnation until the sequel
proves whether or not the eggs have turned out live
chickens.

Garland Hope, who was now a grown man, and a
worthy successor of his father, would be ready in the
course of a few months to take the old minister's place in
the pulpit. He had already, with the assistance of his
elder sister, superseded Mr. Hope in the school-room, and
had given universal satisfaction. He would doubtless
give equal satisfaction in the pulpit. As Mr. Hope was
now an old man, his sermons were growing a little stale
with age and the inevitable monotony begotten of twenty-
five years' service in the same field; and there were many
who were not loth for the young minister to make his
debut. Garland was an exemplary young man; not one
of the sinless and super-saintly kind, but a youth who
knew his way and walked gracefully therein. There was
too much genuine humility in his soul for him ever to have
professed sanctification, if his creed would have allowed
any such sacrilege. Mr. Hope, the father, having good
material to begin with, had built up his son's character
from infancy with tender, utmost care, and he had the
gratification, when retiring from the field himself, of giving
to the world another worker, who had the nerve to dare
what was right, and the grace to spurn what was wrong.
Such, briefly, was Garland Hope, with this addition, that
he was a plain-looking young man, whose manners and
comely conduct alone made him handsome.

Time, that untiring and indomitable fugitive, who is
ever going—ever coming—and ever at hand, like the belt
which communicates motion to machinery and keeps it
whirling and clicking monotonously, had added two more
years of routine and monotony to Creswood, during which

Carroll May came to be regarded as a young lawyer
worthy of small fees, and Johnny Gale as an embryo engineer, who was preparing to wake up the surrounding
forests and crags with the snort of a locomotive.

It was on a pleasant day in the spring-time when Johnny
was out among the Creswood hills with his instruments,
running experimental courses. Carroll May, for exercise,
had gone out with him, flagging for him, and otherwise
assisting him. Captain Gale was at the cottage, idle. He
had contracted for a new Whitecap, his old one having become both too old and too small for his expanding projects.
He was waiting with his customary serenity to learn, by
message from the contractors, that his new boat was ready
to launch. The time for launching was overdue, for Captain Gale had bargained with himself to be ready for the
opening of the spring traffic. But he was now well to do,
and the loss of a trip or so did not disturb his equanimity,
or increase his allowance of grog. As usual, he was sitting upon his portico; for he loved to look at the ocean.
He considered himself a wind-and-water-made man, and
felt grateful to every sweep of wind, and every billow of
brine. While he watched the dimpling sea, which here
and there white-capped a culminating wave, he heard a
clear, manly voice, at the rear of the island, sing out,—

"Gale Island, ahoy there!"

Going to the customary crossing place, he saw upon the
opposite shore a well-dressed, prepossessing, youthful figure, whose voice shouted across the water,—

"Good-morning, Captain Gale. I am glad to see you
well, sir."

"Who are you?" demanded the captain.

"A chieftain to the island bound; come ferry me over
the water," was the response.

Captain Gale crossed over, and the young gentleman,
without ceremony, stepped into the skiff and offered his
hand.

"Excuse me, Captain Gale," said the stranger, with a
very pleasant, youthful frankness, "but you do look so
natural and familiar; just as when you used to bring me
shells and oranges. Do you recall me?"

"I do not," replied the captain, scrutinizing the face of the stranger.

"Take a *good* look."

"Wait until we land," said Captain Gale.

Upon the island shore, the captain scanned from head to foot the young stranger, whose fair, heroic countenance, with a pleasant smile, invited the perplexed captain to take thorough observations.

"I'm at fault," finally and reluctantly admitted Captain Gale. "I do not know you. But I know this, that I never saw as fine a lad. I thought my own boys about the best specimens afloat, but if you are what you look to be, you can come the top-gallant over either of them. Who are you?"

Captain Gale had spoken the truth: he had never seen so fine a "lad." The stranger was apparently about twenty-one or two, and might have stood for a statue of Apollo. His countenance, compared with ordinary faces, reminded one of the difference between cut and moulded glass, or chiseled marble and plaster cast. His hair was a bronze, which the sunbeam burnished to deep gold. His face was manly, beautiful, and brave; and his violet eyes, which were pure as azure and as bright as a star, should have belonged to some high-spirited and lovely girl. About him was the grace of a trained, though unaffected, youthful athlete, and as he stood before the captain, with his hat off and dressed in a gentleman's suit of light woolen gray,—spring attire,—the old mariner thought him the very image of blonde beauty and manliness. In answer to Captain Gale's question of "Who are you?" he said,—

"Now, captain, if Mrs. Gale is at home, I'll bet you a thimbleful of gallinippers that she knows me."

"I believe there's no statute against such a wager," said the captain, laughing, "and I'll take it. Come in."

"I'll beat you, captain," said the youth, pleasantly. "Don't you know that the feminine instinct, memory, and eye are each more acute than the masculine?"

"Yes, in matters of dress, colors, gossip, and the like, but not in questions of fact and import."

Captain Gale introduced the visitor to his cottage, and

7

into the room where Mrs. Gale was sitting at work with her needle. She raised her head and looked at the stranger. Her countenance, in turn, expressed investigation, apprehension, and conviction, and simultaneously with conviction she hastily left her chair, and, almost embracing the young man, cried,—

"*Gracious me!* if this isn't Pony Rapid!"

"What! Cassel!" shouted Captain Gale. "It's a *fact.* Why couldn't I see it at first?" and taking both of Cassel's hands, he shook them heartily. "Bless me, Cassel, what a fine lad you've grown."

"Let's hear from you, Mrs. Gale," said Cassel, with a free young laugh.

"I shall not repeat what many a silly girl has doubtless told you," replied Mrs. Gale, merrily.

"I see you are not in the habit of proving what you say by your wife," said Cassel, turning blithely to Captain Gale. Then addressing Mrs. Gale, he asked, "How did you recognize me so readily?"

"I do not know. It was like a flash. I doubt if I could do it again if my life depended on it."

"Captain," said Cassel humorously, "you had better spread your nets for that thimbleful of gallinippers," and he apprised Mrs. Gale of the wager. "But where are the boys and Caddy? They must be nearly grown."

"Johnny and Carroll are out in the woods surveying. Caddy is over to see Rebecca Ruthven, an old schoolmate."

"I should like so much to have seen them," said Cassel, "because I leave Creswood immediately after dinner. I am stopping with Mr. Hope, and have been here several days; but I arrived in the night, and have not been about any, from the fact that I did not wish my visit to be known, because I have not time now to see my old friends, and they might think that I had forgotten them as clearly as some of them have forgotten me," and Cassel glanced slyly at Captain Gale. "But I anticipate calling again, and making a general tour of Creswood. By-the-way, are you all as quiet here as ever?"

"Fully as quiet," answered Captain Gale. "What surprises me is that your arrival is not within the knowledge of every one, for *here* it is an *event* for a stranger to be seen."

"Are there no other strangers in the neighborhood?"

"Not at present. A short time ago there was a man here, who, by-the-by, is no stranger to you, for he went out to Texas with you; but he is not here now."

"Who is he?" asked young Rapid.

"Jonas Aiken."

Cassel averted his face; a terrible frown passed over it, and his eyes glittered like burnished steel.

"Does he make his home here?" he finally asked, turning to Captain Gale with recovered countenance.

"He was with the men who occupy the huts down on the Starboard Strand, several miles below this. It is hard to tell where any of them make their home, for they are here to-day and gone to-morrow."

The use of the word "home" reminds us that Mr. Hope had christened his place "Gift Home," apropos of the rare title by which he held it.

For the present we must follow Cassel Rapid. He went from Creswood to the city of New York, where, in a short time, he received a letter from Mr. Hope. Half an hour after the receipt of this letter, he stepped into a Jew banking-house, Sarazzin & Sarazzin, father and son. Jepthah Sarazzin, the son, a young man about Cassel's age, met him cordially. Cassel had once saved Jepthah's life by an intrepid action, and Jepthah, by one of the most brilliant strokes of finance on record, had subsequently saved the greater portion of Cassel's fortune,—out in the wilds of Texas. Each felt under obligations to the other. How this double rescue fell out we promise to relate, should we have space.

"Jepthah," said Cassel, taking out a memorandum-book and pencil, "what is the name of that detective of whom you were telling me the other day?"

"His name is Hector O'Dare."

"Is he well named?" asked Cassel.

"Yes; he will dare anything, or hector anything, in his line."

"Is he keen?"

"Keen as a cambric needle. Give him a bag of feathers,

and give him time, and he will produce the geese from which the feathers were plucked."

"Or the persons that roasted them. But is he reliable?"

"Perfectly. Mind you, he is a *private* detective, not an officer, or policeman. But he has the best nose that ever smelt for missing money or a missing man. Say that this bank should be robbed to-night of a hundred thousand. I would check on O'Dare for ninety-five thousand, tell him to find the hundred and keep the odd five, and proceed to business by bank hours in the morning, with the latter small amount in deficit only."

"Hyperbole," said Cassel, smiling.

"The weapon of my race, in dealing with Gentiles," returned Jepthah, laughing.

"Where is Hector O'Dare?"

"He's now in Boston."

"Can you give me his address?"

"No; but any of the police can tell you where to find him."

"The police here, or in Boston?"

"I mean in Boston."

"When will he return to New York?"

"Can't say."

"Do you know him well, personally?"

"Yes. Do you wish a letter of commendation?"

"I do; and would like for you to assure him of the respectability of my bank balance."

In a few minutes Jepthah presented Cassel with a document which he said would sufficiently establish him in O'Dare's confidence.

Cassel Rapid started for Boston on the first train. A few hours before reaching that city an incident occurred, examples of which were, at that time, almost exclusively confined to the East, but which are now growing common throughout America. An old lady, with a little child in her arms, probably a grandchild, got aboard at a way-station, and came into the car in which Cassel was seated, and of which every seat was occupied. Standing at the entrance, she gazed about through her glasses, in search of a resting-place. No gentleman offered her a seat, though it was evident that she actually needed one.

Cassel Rapid, who had not got accustomed to going through life on pure business principles, observed to the gentleman who sat at his left and immediately beside him,—

"I'm going to exchange places with that old lady."

"Pshaw!" said the gentleman. "Let the conductor find her a seat; it's his business."

Cassel, however, smilingly got up, and walking down the car-way, said to the grandmother,—

"Madam, allow me to offer you what you stand in need of,—a seat."

The old lady regarded him with benevolent surprise, but thanked him kindly, and permitted him to lead her along the aisle. Following this incident came a sequel not anticipated by Cassel or any one else. While Cassel was gallanting grandmother to her resting-place, a side-whiskered, urban-looking native, who, in appearance, was as "peart" as a fly-catcher, and who had been standing, slipped into the vacant seat, and turned his back toward the aisle, as a kind of strategic position. But Cassel tapped him and observed,—

"Sir, you have my seat."

"Your seat!" replied the urban, turning about with an immense amount of manufactured amazement.

"You will be kind enough to let this lady have it in my stead," said Cassel, paying no attention to his exclamatory amazement.

"I don't recognize your title, sir," said the urban. "I found this seat vacant."

"And you shall leave it as you found it," said Cassel, taking Mr. Urbs by the arm, and forcibly withdrawing him. The much-injured gentleman strained himself up to his utmost inch, and, with a most terrific expression of countenance, seemed about to—*say* something. Cassel smiled in his face with provoking placidity. Urbs wheeled about and rushed out of the car, intimating by vehement gestures that he would, as soon as he came back, make his power felt in some extraordinary manner, and with tremendous force; which he doubtless would have done if he had come back.

"Sir," said a feminine voice immediately on the right hand of where Cassel was patiently standing. Cassel

turned about. "You can have a seat with me if you will
hold my little son time about."

Cassel accepted the offer, and while he was conducting
a conversation with the child, he overheard another conversation behind him not intended for his ear. It was between two ladies.

"But it is *not* strictly a lack of gallantry," said one
voice. "It is a sort of business or commercial custom which
has been gaining ground here since the days of the Revolution, but which is never carried into society. And now
that the women, some of them at least, talk of setting up
for themselves, the custom that one man is as good as one
woman, and, if he happens to be ahead of her, is that much
better, will become a universal practice."

"Who talks about setting up for themselves ?"

"They are just beginning to talk about it."

"What do they wish to do ?"

"Vote, hold office, go to Congress, and play. old Nick
generally, as the men do."

"My stars ! Who ever *heard* of such a thing !"

"Who ever heard of the telegraph before its time ? When
I read the newspapers and see how the men carry on, I
sometimes think that the women could do better ; and then
I think again that they would turn the country heels over
head, for I never saw two women agree who were compelled to occupy the same house. And then what we call
our prerogatives would vanish, for you may be sure that
no man will ever recognize a petticoat in a pair of panta-
loons."

"But for a woman to come out in public, and attempt
to do public business, or make a speech ; why, I should
think she would faint away and never come to again. I
know I should."

"But there are those who would not. For example,
there is one just ahead of you ; that one with the short
hair and Byron collar, who speaks in Boston to-night."

"Oh, horrid ! What can possibly be the name of such
a creature ?"

"She is one of our celebrities,—Miss Delilah Hotseat.
She can tell all she knows a half a dozen times in as many
minutes, and tell it with greater emphasis every time.

She's a regular jimplecute, shearing the locks from the men and making their seats too hot to hold them."

" What does she talk about ?"

" Women's Rights, and women's Wrongs."

" But why don't each woman get her husband to favor what she wants, and then there would be no need of this ?"

" Each woman get some other woman's husband, you'd better say," was the merry reply. " No ; if they get what they want, or pretend to want, they will have to do it by public clamor and private bribery. Suppose, for instance, that a married woman should approach her husband on the subject. Old Cross-sticks would look over his spectacles and say, ' Why, damn it, Mary, you wear the breeches *now !* What the devil more do you want?'—Or he would palaver, ' My dearest dear, if all the women were like *you*, it would be the *thing :* but except my dearest ducky of a wifey, I would not be willing to trust *one* of them, the deceitful things !' and so it goes, don't you see ? Again, unless the men themselves advocate women's rights, you might just as well try to bail a raft as try to change the ' status' as they call it. And no man is going to advocate these rights for his wife's sake, for each lord is somewhat of the opinion that his lady enjoys all the rights she's entitled to. Therefore, when a man *does* break ground on the weak side of this new issue, you can set it down that he has found an overweakness in it somewhere ; that somebody's wife or somebody's old maid has something to do with it; in fact, that there's something rotten in the state of Denmark, and he'd better not have a jealous wife at home, I can tell you. I'm not overly inclined to be jealous, but let me catch *my* old rooster of a husband cuch-a-cawing around these stray hens, and if I don't give him a sprinkling of woman's rights, he'll have nothing to thank but his shroud." Two merry voices mingled in laughter, and the subject was discontinued, much to the regret of Cassel Rapid, who had been an amused listener. Cassel formed the double resolution that, primarily, he would endeavor not to get him a jealous wife, and, secondarily, should he get him a wife at all, never to be moved into espousing the dangerous cause by any woman's convincing argument but that of his own *esposa*.

CHAPTER VIII.

It was dusk when Cassel Rapid reached Boston. The
following day was the Sabbath. He strolled out into the
city, which was exceedingly quiet, and, in comparison
with other large cities upon the seventh day, appeared
almost deserted. Cassel, who was constitutionally a
devotee, rather liked this stately calm, so meet for meditation, so suggestive of the holy sanctuary of the week, and
so appropriate to it.

Standing upon a corner, he gazed indolently up and
down the streets, while a feeling of pensiveness and loneliness stole into his heart; for he *was* alone in the wide,
wide world. With absent, dreamy thoughts, he drew out
a cigar-case, opened it, made a selection, returned the case
to his pocket, bit off the end of his cigar, spat it out,
fingered for a match in his vest pocket, found one, and
was about to strike it, when he was interrupted by a tap
on the shoulder, and a voice which said,—

"Can't smoke here, sir."

Without turning about to see by whom or what he was
interrupted, Cassel observed,—

"I reckon I can try."

"Guess you can't try," was the response.

"*No se fuma?*" said Cassel.

"I don't understand you," said the policeman.

"Neither do I understand *you*," replied Cassel, casting
about and taking an observation of a person whom he
considered an intruder.

"Do you know where you are?"

"I went to bed last night in Boston: I presume I waked
up this morning in the same place."

"You are a stranger here, are you?"

"Ah, I understand you," said Cassel, provokingly.
"You come to tender me the hospitalities of the city.
About what time does the mayor dine?"

" *No*, sir.   I come to tell you that you cannot smoke in Boston."

"You are jesting," said Cassel, with a smile.

The policeman scowled at him.

"Are you positively in earnest?   And is this a freak of your own merely, or a prank of your municipality?"

The policeman continued to scowl.

"Will you then permit me," asked Cassel, "to burn my tobacco on a chip and smell of the smoke?"

The policeman scowled yet more sternly.

"I'll get out of *your* beat, polly, if I have to travel all day;" and Cassel threw his cigar in the gutter.   Two sharp-set urchins immediately pounced upon the prohibited luxury, and struggled for possession.

Cassel sauntered away.   He was followed by the two urchins, one of whom, overtaking him, accosted him with, "Want to buy a Testament?" at the same time slyly half disclosing a lewd illustration of an obscene book.

"Clear out, you young imp, or I'll spank the iniquity out of you!" said Cassel, disgusted at this juvenile depravity.

Having walked several squares, Cassel halted on another corner.   With the view of making a toothpick, he opened a penknife and began to shave one end of the match with which he had contemplated lighting his cigar, and which he still retained between his fingers.   Pretty soon another policeman accosted him.

"Stranger here, sir?"

"Partly."

"Thought so.   You musn't make this litter on the pavement."

"Litter!   I'm only making a toothpick."

"Can't help it: regulations, you know."

"Do you mean to say that I am violating a city ordinance?"

"Yes, sir."

"Then I am mistaken.   I stopped off at the wrong place.   I thought I was in Boston."

"You *are* in Boston."

"Is it possible, then, that a man can't make a toothpick in the paradise of a whole *nation* of whittlers?"

"Let me see the size of that weapon," said the police-man.

"Weapon! You are blind: 'tis but a penknife."

"Be careful,—you might get nabbed for carrying con-cealed arms."

"It is not concealed."

"You had better close it and carry it openly."

"You've made a pun of it, but I'd see you in——"

"Hold!" cried the policeman, "or you will compel me to arrest you."

"Arrest me! For what?"

"For using profane language."

"You've broken the camel's back, by thunder!" said Cassel, laughing. "This is the most solemn occasion of my existence. Can't you enliven it a little by singing for me that good old song of 'Come tickle my tail with a barley straw,' or am I permitted to laugh? Could I, if I should happen upon something irresistibly funny, stick my head in a sewer, or under a goods box, and have a good free guffaw all to myself, without risk of fine or imprisonment for high misdemeanor? Or is the very atmosphere apportioned here, share and share alike, so that no man can take a long breath, or expend an ounce by laughing out of time, without trespassing on the muni-cipal rights and privileges of his neighbors? By-the-way, how much air is set apart here by your city council for the necessities and refreshment of the stranger? I wish to get the figures, for I might overbreathe myself, and be put to the trouble and expense of importing a score or two of cubic feet to fill up the vacuum."

A broad, open smile spread over the policeman's face (for he was an Irishman) as he looked at the handsome young stranger before him.

"Old fish," continued Cassel, with that current audacity which touring begets, "your individual style strikes me with admiration and awe. You'd whip out his Nether Majesty, and let him pick his own charcoal. You are a son of liberty,—a lover of freedom, endeavoring to over-throw this municipal despotism by making it odious. I tell you, polly (Cassel's short for policeman), this place is too much governed; stricter than a Scotch Sunday-school. But how did you ever get to be a Boston polly ?"

" Why not ?"

" Because you are a born Irishman."

" How know you ?"

" Not altogether from your speech ; but from the poise of your head, the set of your ears, the dip of your under jaw, and by that unmistakable *embouchure* so suggestive of a horn. Apropos, how do you manage to get your regular potteen ? I understood you were all running here on snow-water and flaxseed-tea! But that is not just now the main question, polly, for there *is* a main question, and I want you to answer it."

" What is it ?"

'· Do you know Mr. Hector O'Dare ?"

The policeman gave a quick glance of inquiry and interest at Cassel, and asked,—

'· Why do you put such a question as that ?"

" It's a very ordinary question, is it not ?"

" Yes. But why do *you* ask *me* ?"

" Not because you are so very accommodating, certainly," said Cassel, laughing. " But whom should I ask? I know nobody here. I wish to find O'Dare. You are as likely to know him, and know where he is, as the next man. Am I to hunt all over the city for a man who looks as if he knew O'Dare, before asking such a question?"

" Have you business with him ?"

" Yes."

" Is it important ?"

" Can a duck swim ? *Pshaw!* Do you know O'Dare, or do you not? I dare you to say yes or no."

" Yes."

" Where is he ?"

" In Boston."

" I already know as much ; but his address ?"

" You can address him through me. He is busy, and may not wish to—but are you a friend of his? or an acquaintance ?"

" I am·not. But I have use for him. I know that he is here working up a case, and may not wish to be disturbed. Here are my credentials. Examine them, and, when convenient, deliver them to O'Dare, and request him to appoint me an interview. You will put me under obligations to you, and will probably be doing a favor to O'Dare. What say you?"

"I couldn't very well say no."

"Not if you are an Irishman. Here are the credentials. When shall I cross your beat for an answer?"

"Meet me here to-morrow morning at ten o'clock."

"Will you give me your name? You have mine."

"Flynn—Michael Flynn."

Cassel made a note of it. When the policeman turned to go his rounds, the youth asked,—

"Can a man chew tobacco here?"

"If he has it, and don't spit on the pave, or throw his quids about."

"Don't you furnish spittoons? But no difference, I never chew;" and each with a laugh went his way.

Walking along, Cassel met a good-looking servant-girl. Whether he winked at her or not we are unable to say, but she cried,—

"What do ye mean, sir, by blinking at me?"

"There's something in my eye," said Cassel.

"A likely story," retorted the girl disdainfully; "what's in the eye of ye?"

"A pretty girl," said Cassel, smiling.

"Ye rogue, ye!" replied the girl, appeased, passing on, and casting a sly glance back at the comely youth.

The following morning Cassel Rapid met Michael Flynn on his beat. The latter said,—

"O'Dare will meet you on the northeast corner of Bond and Gay Streets at half-past ten o'clock precisely."

"Where is that?"

"It is the corner of this block diagonally opposite to where we now stand. Pass half way round the block and you are there."

"What is your time of day?"

"You have an hour and ten minutes to spare. Your letter from the Sarazzins was satisfactory, and O'Dare told me in his behalf to offer you my good offices."

"I'm obliged to you, and to him, and will avail myself of your kindness *now*. The weather, Mr. Flynn, is a little warm, and I would like to have a sherry cobbler, or a glass of beer, or something of the sort. I rarely ever drink; but, by thunder, your very prohibition here makes me as dry as a wooden god!"

"Oh, well," replied Flynn, with a sly smile, "you can get pretty much what you want if you'll only be a little quiet about it;" and Flynn gave Cassel directions where to go and what to do in order to succeed in refreshing himself. But just as Cassel was about to turn away, Flynn indifferently asked him where he was from.

"From most everywhere," said Cassel, "east, south, and west,—New York, Maryland, and Texas."

"What part of Texas?" asked Flynn.

"The Brazos."

"Did you know many people out there?"

"Everybody within two hundred miles of Ranche Rapid."

"Ranche Rapid?"

"Yes. Why so earnest?"

"*Jesus!* what's O'Dare thinking about, and with the letter of Sarazzin in his pocket? Come with me;" and Flynn took Cassel by the arm.

"Am I to consider myself under arrest?" asked Cassel, with some surprise.

"Arrest! No. I'm going to take you to see O'Dare without waiting. I think you can untie a knot."

Cassel went with the policeman, who took him into a building and to a secret place, and gave him a spy's view of an apartment, in which were three men playing cards.

"That is O'Dare with his face this way," said Flynn.

"Why, he's beastly drunk," said Cassel, with a feeling of deep disappointment.

"Not drunk at all. He's only foxing."

Cassel gazed a moment, with increasing interest; and then turning to Flynn, asked,—

"How do you get in there?"

"By this door; but you mustn't think of going in until I notify O'Dare."

"But I *do* think of going in. I see a man there that I want."

" Which one ?"

" The one with the sandy hair."

" Is his name Gilders ?" asked Flynn, with uncon-
cealed interest. " If it is, he is the man that O'Dare is
after."

Without replying, and before Flynn could prevent him,
Cassel opened the door and stepped into the room.

O'Dare was a man of thirty-seven or thirty-eight years of
age, about five feet ten inches in height, well and actively
built, and with a face like granite. When Cassel entered
the room the detective's hawk-like eye lit up during the
fraction of an instant from its pretended drunkenness, and
something like a frown passed over his face ; for he had
seen Flynn close the door after young Rapid, and thought
that the policeman was intruding the young man upon
him all out of time. Cassel walked up to the table and
confronted the man with the sandy hair. As each gazed
at the other, there was a world of difference between
their countenances. The man dropped his cards and
turned pale. Cassel, in a voice which thrilled even
O'Dare's veteran heart by the depth of its sadness,
said,—

" Gilders, do you know me ?"

The man dropped his gaze, and remained silent.

" Deliver to me that certificate of deposit, Gilders."

Without a word the man drew out a wallet, selected a
paper, and handed it to young Rapid.

" Gilders, I do not intend to have you arrested. You
know *why* it is that I spare you."

O'Dare looked keenly and inquiringly at Cassel, who
continued,—

" Have you any money ?"

" No," replied Gilders.

" Is there pen and ink here ?" asked Cassel, looking
around.

O'Dare, who still maintained his drunken character,
took from a pocket of his coat writing materials, observing that he was a " local," and always carried the articles.
Cassel drew a check for five hundred dollars on Sarazzin
& Sarazzin, and, handing it to Gilders, said, with an affectionate sternness,—

"Take this, and go, and sin no more"

The man's eyes gushed with tears; and, in a voice of earnestness and passion, he said,—

"Cassel, you are the noblest boy that ever drew a breath. Would to God that I had died, or had your courage when——"

"*No more,*" sternly said Cassel, while a terrible frown plowed his brow with furrows.

"I ought not to take this," said Gilders, alluding to the money check.

"Take it," said Cassel, "it is freely given, and I hope you will let your better nature predominate."

Gilders prepared to go. Hesitating, he turned to young Rapid and said,—

"Tell me good-by, Cassel, and give me your hand. I acknowledge my unworthiness, but will try to be a better man."

"On that condition," said Cassel, extending his hand, which Gilders wrung, and went his way.

O'Dare immediately doffed his drunken character, and, turning to the man who had been the third party at the card-table, said,—

"You can go."

When O'Dare's understrapper disappeared, the detective bowed to Cassel, saying,—

"Mr. Rapid, if I am not mistaken?"

"Mr. O'Dare, likewise," said Cassel, with a return bow. "Did I anticipate you?" and young Rapid held up the certificate which he had taken from Gilders.

"Just so," said O'Dare.

"Shall I keep it, or you take it?"

"Were you employed to recover it?"

"No. But I knew of it."

"Then I'll take it," said the detective.

"State your case, and show your authority."

"The case is this," said O'Dare. "John R. Lake, of Ohio, late of New Orleans, but now of New York city, general cattle-dealer, bought of Cassel Pontiac Rapid, of Ranche Rapid, Texas,—yourself, by-the-by; but I did not imagine it until I heard Gilders call your first name, for Sarazzin only mentions you as Mr. Rapid of New

York,—some four thousand head of cattle, horned cattle, and horses. Gilders, your old herder,—and I was neither certain of my man or that he still held this paper,—was in charge of a thousand head of horned cattle, as chief herder for Mr. Lake. He sold the cattle on the prairie, took the purchase money, went to New Orleans, put it upon special deposit under an alias. Lake, who was away in San Antonio, followed as soon as he learned of the robbery, but could not recover the money from bank without producing the certificate of deposit, or catching the depositor and convicting him of the robbery. The cattle had been marketed in Louisiana, and consequently were out of reach. This money remains in bank, under an injunction. This certificate will insure the surrender of it to Mr. Lake; and now that I think of it, it would probably have been better had you made Gilders transfer the certificate. That, however, is not essential. Here is my authority from Mr. Lake."

Cassel, being thoroughly satisfied, handed the certificate to O'Dare, observing,—

"Lake and I are old friends. Gilders was my chief herder. He could have served me as he did Mr. Lake, but would not, at least did not do it. That, however, is not the reason I spared him. How long have you been on this case? It's nearly six months old."

"Seven weeks. But I had to commence at New Orleans, by correspondence. And now, Mr. Rapid, I am at your service. What is the character of your business with me?"

"I expected to confer with you in a private room, Mr. O'Dare; but it seems quiet here, and there is no need of delay. Preliminary to my confiding in you, I will ask whether or not you have any conscientious scruples in regard to the death penalty?"

"In a clear case I have none whatever."

In the conference which succeeded, Cassel Rapid accomplished the object of his visit to Boston, and he and the detective went upon the street as two men who know each other well. Young Rapid had plowed up the tough breast of the detective with an inherent, imperial power, enhanced by external incentive, and had moved upon the heart of O'Dare as no other had ever moved there.

" O'Dare," said Cassel, when they were on the street, " I want you to pilot me to a glass of lager beer."

" Why, don't you know," said O'Dare, " that sweet cider is the only beverage allowed here ?"

" The only legitimate, court beverage ; but I understand that a glass of beer, a cobbler, or most anything, can be had through the back window."

" Such as it is ; for those who persist in keeping liquors can afford to keep only the most villainous and worthless stuff, for fear of seizure. Nearly all the lager beer in the city has been from cave to court and from court to cave, the mid-day sun shining on it meantime. The joke is, that the prohibitionists go and get drunk on cider, the court beverage, and then organize a special crusade against lager, overlooking, on their march, any amount of high wine and N. E. rum. But I will take you to an illustrative establishment, not far from here, where you will get the correct idea. In the room fronting the street you will find openly for sale ' Sweet Cider,' made, by-the-by, from decayed late winter apples. To the rear is another room, which you enter, if the man inside at the spy-hole is satisfied, after some little ceremony, where you find the ' ardent.' To the rear of this room is another, to be entered yet more cautiously. There you come upon the terrible destroyer, lager beer, chained and cowering in its den. The whole establishment is under one and the same proprietorship. But here we are ; come in."

" What will you have, gentlemen ?" asked the keeper.

" Sherry cobblers," said O'Dare, winking at Cassel.

" We keep no intoxicating liquors whatever," asserted the pious keeper.

" What have you wherewithal to refresh a man ?"

" Sweet cider."

" Is it full of gripes ?"

" Not so fresh and sweet as that. It has tang enough to cut the phlegm."

" Let us taste it."

The keeper produced his cider. O'Dare tasted it, and turning to Cassel, said,—

" If a man should drink three beer-mugs of this he wouldn't be sober again for a week. I should say it

8*

would cut the phlegm, and the pigeon-wing too," observed O'Dare to the keeper.

Making their way to the first rear room, O'Dare called for some whisky. A bottle and glass were handed out. Cassel smelt of the bottle, and turning to keeper No. 2, asked,—

"What do you call this?"

"Whisky. What the divil else is it?" demanded No. 2.

"I should take it," said Cassel, laughing, "to be a mixture of captured lightning, blue vitriol, and lunar caustic."

Room No. 3 clandestinely received the two experimentalists, and Cassel ordered some lager beer. It was drawn and served as of old. Cassel looked at the foamless surface of it and said,—

"Hans, this won't do at all. It is too old,—it's stale."

"Ah!" said Hans innocently, "the how older it be the so better it was."

"Have you no beer," asked O'Dare, "that has never seen a court-room, or an officer of the Prohibition?"

Hans winked, and proceeded to draw from a different keg. The lager foamed up ambitiously with an overflowing crest.

"Why, Hans, this is jolly," said O'Dare, lifting his mug. "Gayer than a young Dutchman with his coat tail afire."

"Or mit his belly full of sweet cider," replied Hans, with a sardonic grin.

Indulging in a couple of mugs each, O'Dare and Cassel withdrew, feeling much refreshed, for the day was warm and sultry. The first train carried them to New York.

The last few pages are not the less illustrative from embodying an anachronism.

CHAPTER IX.

FARMER MEDLEY and Bachelor Boyd owned adjoining farms in one of the oleaginous districts of Pennsylvania, and each awoke one morning to find himself floating in oil.

Wealth came upon them like an overflow. They had neighbored harmoniously for many years as petty farmers, and they congratulated each other most heartily, and without envy, upon the sudden good fortune which had transformed them into magnates of the land. Bachelor Boyd had, for a year or so, cast covetous glances at Malinda, eldest daughter of Farmer Medley, and taking advantage of that enthusiasm of compliance which sudden wealth begets, he cunningly and with oily tongue approached Farmer Medley, and importuned the pretty Linda, upon the subject next his heart, and which had furnished him many an hour of solitary cogitation.

Between two such well-oiled families as the Boyd and the Medley, it was only natural to anticipate that all matters, whether of import or not, would work smoothly. Therefore, with little other consideration than their mutual family respect, their common good fortune and good prospects, a Boyd-Medley alliance was formed, and Linda became Mrs. Boyd.

Bachelor Boyd, in order to do the proper, fashionable, and wealthy thing, had, prior to the nuptials, purchased an elegant residence in the city of New York,—Philadelphia not being sufficiently gay for him,—on one of the handsome streets leading into Fifth Avenue. He loved Linda, and the few gray hairs in his head made him none the less romantic and rhapsodic in view of his future arrangements. It was decided that the wedding ceremony should be succeeded by a gorgeous dinner, immediately after which a carriage should take them to the nearest railroad depot, from whence they would go on to their New York home, which was well furnished and prepared to receive them, where they would begin to concoct measures by which to people their little paradise with angels.

The minister had performed his duty, the guests had by no means neglected theirs, and the contracted couple, bearing away with them the éclat of the occasion, soon found themselves dashing forward to New York, with thoughts all for the future, when—a terrible crash and disaster spread havoc along the road.

An hour later, and Linda.was watching over a mangled husband, herself unhurt, while they were again dashing along upon an extra train which had been expressed to meet the disaster. The husband had just enough life in him to insist upon a rigid adherence to the original programme. Arriving in New York, the sight of his preparatory lovework, as he was being borne to a chamber, temporarily reanimated him. But the surgeons who were called in warned him that, if he desired to make a will, he had better be mending his pen. In the flush and fullness of his love, he willed his possessions, all and singular, to his bride, and, without more ado, slept with his fathers, instead of with his wife.

In addition to the mansion-house in the city, and its furnishings, with the oleaginous substrata back in Pennsylvania, Linda came into possession of more cash in bank than she knew how to count or what to do with, for she was but seventeen years of age, a pure rustic, and as green as grass.

Recovering from the horror occasioned by the rough and gory death of her husband, whom she esteemed, but probably did not passionately love, she determined, now that she was in the great city, and able to stay, that she *would* stay. A total stranger to the turmoil, the glitter, and the countless array which met her eye at every glance, an ambition took possession of her to comprehend, mingle with, and become a part of it. She saw fine ladies whirling here and there, dressed like peacocks, and accosting each other with theatrical gestures, and voices of peculiar modulation, and smiles of angelic sweetness. She saw gentlemen with the air of kings and heroes, spurning the pave with vigorous heel, and with a single wave of the hand, transferring, as it were, armies, navies, and bottomless exchequers. How insignificant, compared to all this splendor, and sweeping novelty, and electric life, were the greasy oil-tanks, the lowing cows, the grunting hogs, and the stale interchange, back at the Medley farm in Pennsylvania! Linda's utter ignorance of city life and the butterfly-chase of that human vortex, was the cause of her entertaining most exquisitely absurd ideas of the relations existing between one person and another in the routine and rodomontade of an urban existence and contact, and she bid fair to become an unfailing source of amusement and side-splitting laughter to her appreciative neighbors.

At the end of twelve months she threw aside her widow's weeds, of which she had become mortally weary, and came out in colors.

Upon a certain day in June she ventured upon her first airing, in a bright, new carriage, when, on returning homeward, one of the wheels, which probably lacked the original linch-pin, rolled off, and she was tossed into the street. Her hoops and dress caught upon one of the door-handles of the carriage, and she was not able immediately to extricate herself. The horses began to prance, and the carriage, so suddenly halted, caused other vehicles, both coming and going, to halt likewise, so that Linda quickly became the center of quite a little park of crowding wheels and restless animals. Her situation was getting to be alarming, for she was in danger of being trampled to death; and aside from the peril, her skirts were elevated to a degree which exposed a stitch or two too much of her chaste white stocking.

"Jupiter! what a pretty ankle!" exclaimed a young man sitting close by in a carriage whose career had been interrupted by this sudden blockade. At the same moment, and from the same carriage, a young gentleman sprang out, and rescued Linda from her peril and perplexity.

"Please take me home," said Linda beseechingly, as soon as she had gained the sidewalk.

"Will you have a carriage?" asked the young gentleman.

"Oh, no! no!" quickly answered Linda. "I live but a few squares from here, and we can soon walk it. Please do."

"Certainly I will," said the young gentleman, who saw that his charge was frightened and needed encouragement.

"Rapid, are you going to spend the day there?" cried a voice from the carriage whence came the rescuer.

"Yes," replied Cassel, for it was he. "Go on, and I will meet you at the hotel." Turning to Linda, he said, "Now I am ready to accompany you. Which way do we go?"

"I don't know," said Linda with innocent perplexity and some surprise. "I thought you would know;" and she looked up in Cassel's face."

"This is a pretty pickle!" said Cassel, with a pleasant and amused countenance. "Can't you give me your street and number?"

"Oh, yes, sir," replied Linda, brightening, and calling off the street and number of her residence. "I know it is not far from here, but whether it's this way or that way I can't tell for the sake of me."

"Come along," said Cassel, with that brotherly nonchalance which made his ways so pleasant to the girls, "and I will soon find it for you."

As they walked along the street, Cassel hardly knew how to classify Linda. Was she a resident of the city? If so, she was a very fresh one. Might she not be a very pretty servant-girl who, in the absence of her mistress, had daringly borrowed her mistress's attire, and persuaded the coachman, with a promised kiss, to take her out on a swell? But her ingenuous face precluded the supposition. Cassel looked at her dress. It was not correct, but it was expensive and rich. Her hands and feet were small, her hair soft and abundant, her cheek blooming and tender, her eyes modest, her manner neither of the country nor the city, but absurd, preposterous, and unique. But in spite of it all, she was unquestionably a pretty piece of flesh, and Cassel did not think it tiresome to take her home.

Arrived at the Boyd mansion, he was urged both by Linda and a growing curiosity to follow her into the house, the superb front and balcony of which served but to enhance his bewilderment.

Linda had recognized in Cassel a gallant, handsome, city-going person of the masculine gender; and now that she was at her own house, and being indebted to him withal, she felt under obligations to invite him in, and ambitious to entertain him in a style which would, while evincing her gratitude, establish at once her reputation as a genuine, gilt-edged, metropolitan lady, capable of all the fine arts of society. During the days of her mourning Linda had properly secluded herself, postponing all pomp, display, and profusion until the time when she should lay aside her widow's weeds. She had looked forward to that hour as to the breaking of seals; and to it she had referred so many things to be done and begun (in the imaginary midst of which things she failed not to recognize her own figure as chiefest), that the arrival of the bright period had been anticipated as a *puerto* which would let her in upon numberless essential urban responsibilities, duties, and pleasures, which, unfamiliar though they should be, she had so conned, and imagined, and rehearsed, that she was satisfied, in her own mind and unsophisticated little heart, they would become familiar on sight and self-adapting on contact. But now that she had occasion to test the practicability and scope of her theories so often pondered, her conceptions of the proper and opportune were not as clear as crystal or more ready than Glendower's spirits. She was satisfied that a great deal of gesticulative and wordy ceremony was demanded; but as to the character of it, whether it should be grave or gay, familiar or reserved, she was in a mire of doubt and ignorance; for, in all her rehearsals, she had never anticipated a carriage accident, a predicament of peril, an elegant, youthful, and noble-looking rescuer, with the self-imposed exigency of having to entertain him off-hand. Moreover, here was a double demand upon her undeveloped resources. She must not only give *style* to her hospitality, but a proper degree of significance to her gratitude. Cassel was fortunate enough to be the first object of her superlative attention and solicitude, this being the initiatory act, after her emancipation, of the brilliant play of " Life in the Great City." And however unprepared she felt herself to be, she was determined not to fail for lack of an effort. There was but one point connected with Linda, as she assiduously maneuvered about the splendid parlors, and about *him*, upon which Cassel's mind was perfectly clear. The point was this : that she undoubtedly considered the present an occasion of no ordinary consequence, and, whatever she might be herself, was strenuously essaying to do the double-distinguished bon-ton, and, by-the-way, making a most ridiculous farce of it. Out of and into the parlors she hurried, giving him no time to introduce himself, apparently apprehensive that she would lose caste if she allowed a moment to slip by unaccompanied by civilities, wine, cake, and the like, with which she crowded him, and anon observing that "she had plenty of servants to do the waiting, but they were asleep or away where she could see neither hair nor hide of them, and even if the servants were at hand, it would be more grateful in her to wait upon him herself." Cassel, out of courtesy, partook of the cake and wine, mentally observing, "she is no servant-girl, at all events ; but that does not solve the mystery,—it only aggravates it. I shall introduce myself as soon as she lets up, and capture her name." But Linda withdrew, requesting Cassel to be amused with the illustrated periodicals which covered a center-table, until she should return. He was utterly confounded by Linda, who was so entirely out of keeping with her surroundings, for he was unable to connect her with those elegant rooms in which he saw nothing to criticise but misplaced books and newspapers, and too much furniture perhaps. He waited, in anticipation of he knew not what, unless it should be the appearance of some elder member of the family on a thanking and inspecting expedition. A full half hour passed. Becoming restless, he mentally weighed whether he should expediently take unceremonious leave, or neglect his unimportant engagements in the city, and follow up this, his latest discovery. He inclined to the latter alternative, for, as the moon will, now and anon, peep through the rifts of the banked cloud, so he, by glimpses beyond the van and parade of her tomfoolery, saw that Linda was pure, perfectly sincere, and—the most outrageous little ignoramus within all the wide compass of his knowledge and acquaintance. At the expiration of thirty-five or forty minutes, a

door opened, and Linda, dressed to the very summit of
absurdity, entered and approached Cassel with an air
which, with all the screws he could put upon himself,
rather got the better of his risibles. In an effort to hide
his face, Cassel arose and made a most profound and long-
continued bow, to which Linda responded with an equally
protracted courtesy, while Cassel's sides shook with suppressed laughter. But he could not keep his head down all
day, notwithstanding that the laugh was in him and was
not going to stay there; so, after maintaining his bow until
it was getting to be worse than the alternative, he raised his
head and gave out a carol, as free and clear as the neigh of a
young wild stallion. Picking up a newspaper over which he
had been glancing, he turned to a comic picture, called Linda's attention to it, and reading the corresponding facetious
paragraph, succeeded in making her join him in his merriment, without suspicion as to its source. She even felt
gratified at his appreciation of her center-table literature,
and observed that she had laughed, and laughed, and
laughed over that very same thing that very morning.
She then seated herself with the air of one who was about
to entertain a regular and expected visitor. Cassel took
this opportunity of introducing himself by name.

"Law me!" exclaimed Linda, blushing, "I forgot all
about the introductions. My name is Mrs. Boyd. It used
to be Linda Medley."

Cassel had, in all his mental roaming, never once conjectured that this young girl was a wife.

"Is Mr. Boyd in the city?" he asked, thinking it possible that some city man of money, rusticating, had found a
wild flower to his liking, and transplanted it.

"Gracious goodness!" said Linda, "Mr. Boyd has
been dead more than a year."

Cassel remained an hour, during which time Linda told
him, artlessly in fact, superstylishly in manner, all her
history. When Cassel descended from the front vestibule
of the Boyd mansion, he said to himself,—

"She is the sweetest little fool that e'er the sun shone
on—ha! ha! h-a!"

A week passed, in which Linda returned numerous old
calls, and went a bit into society. But hardly a day went

9

down without finding her in tears. She was disappointed utterly. City people were so heartless and supercilious. She could not find congeniality, or a companion. Nothing fell out as she had anticipated. In a company of half a dozen she was of no consequence whatever. The lady at her side would be invited to some select affair, and she be overlooked, slighted. She met with a cold welcome and a warm good-by; with suspicious, sneering glances; caught here and there a whisper, or a suppressed titter; had often to repeat her name to some self-sufficient dame three or four times within the space of half an hour. She had been desolate and lonely enough in the days of her weedhood, but had been buoyed and cheered by anticipation of a happy and transforming era; but now that the era had come, it was a winter succeeding spring, nipping the fruit-buds of her coming pleasures, enjoyments, and worthy deeds of social renown and conspicuity. Her bright dreams faded even as the glory of an evening cloud, and the great city which she had contemplated with awe and wonder, and as containing an exhaustless store of happy, seemly, gorgeous, good, and unimaginable things, became at once a thing to fear, a mingling merely of mercenary millions, whose hearts, to her, were not responsive, whose stare was shameless, whose words were indifferent and unfeeling, and whose houses looked cold, mysterious, and unapproachable. Linda did not feel herself to blame, for she was not sensible of her exquisite faults; but she felt keenly that she was not appreciated, not expected, not welcomed, not wanted as a member of coteries, clans, and impromptu knots of confidential, golden gossip. And all in all, the last week of her life in the city was infinitely more painful and disheartening than her first week of mourning. She had bethought herself, aforetime, of returning to Pennsylvania, and she would have done so, had she not, in her ignorance, imagined great difficulties attendant upon an absolute removal, and had she not, in equal ignorance, looked forward to happier and less lonely days. Disappointed and desolate, she was now in a mood to give up the city and all its ungenial brilliants, and go where she knew that the sympathy for which she craved awaited her. But she was not destitute of courage, ambition, or perseverance, and she could not, without a sense of cowardice, abandon so abruptly her scheme of life. She had read of heroines who never *did* give up, but fought their way through dangers, contumely, and powerful adversaries to the very pinnacle of their ambition and desires, and dictated to those who were wont to trample on them. Linda had proud blood in her veins,—but then she was so green, and tenderhearted.

CHAPTER X.

IT was quite natural that Cassel should desire to see Linda again, and equally as reasonable that he should at once perceive and appreciate her great need of a guardian and honest mentor, and yet more natural that he should imagine himself as competent and fit to stand in relation to her as quasi guardian and actual counselor.

He therefore went to see Linda, about ten days after his first adventure with her. She was unmistakably glad to see him, for he was the one of all others whom she had met in whose countenance was genuine sunlight, and from whose heart came inspiring warmth.

Cassel led her to talk of herself, and gradually stole away from her the pomp and phantasmagoria of her creative imagination, and reproduced her as what she was, a pretty country lass, to be pitied, and probably to be loved.

As the negative takes to the positive, Linda was attracted to young Rapid, and in all her innocence and ingenuousness, unbosomed herself to him. In his presence she grew cheerful, and unconsciously a little jaunty, like a sweet young girl who knows her company. She gained his sympathy by word, and eye, and blush, and by the unselfishness of her spoken thoughts. She unreservedly discussed her own affairs, sensible that he could advise her if he would, and doubting not his willingness to do so. Among many things, she stated that she was so very lonesome; that the city people were so stiff and cranky; that

she had no pleasure, and did not know how to pass her
time. Then the servants were such a bother, and the
shopkeepers cheated and imposed on her; that a wine
merchant had sold her wine not a month old, making her
believe that the newer the better. That she did not drink
wine herself, but kept it for company. That sometimes
when she had company she drank it as a hospitable duty,
but it always put her in such a good humor that she would
nearly kill herself laughing; and then she would have the
headache afterward.

Cassel could imagine with what gusto a covey of *au
fait* city women might get around this innocent little
maid-widow, force her to drink wine through scruples of
hospitality, and then tickle her into immoderate screams
of countrified laughter.

"I hardly know what to do with myself," said Linda,
with a deep-drawn sigh, and a pensive brow.

"Don't you find society pleasant?" asked Cassel.

"They laugh at me," said Linda, with quivering lip.

Although Cassel had laughed at her himself, he felt his
heart rouse within him. Said he, tenderly,—

"Let me be your brother, and let me teach you, and
they shall never laugh at you again."

Linda was taken by surprise. She looked at him wistfully, and asked,—

"Will it be right?"

"We will *make* it right," said Cassel. "I have no
kindred, and, like you, I feel the need of sympathy and
affection."

Linda looked at Cassel and thought that one so bright
and beautiful could have no need, no want, unprovided
for. What a luxury it would be to have him for a brother,
and give him all her wakeful sympathy and affection!
How infinitely fair and assuring to be within the care of
him, with his dauntless pure eyes upon her, his manly
arm to shield her, and his refined experience to guide her!
Linda felt that a treasure had been laid at her feet, which
she should gather to her bosom and never, never spurn
away.

"Oh, if I could be your sister, and you would not be
ashamed of me!" she said with sincere pathos.

"Ashamed of you I shall never be. You have told me your history, and I recognize all your disadvantages and difficulties. They can be made to melt away as the snow before the sun. A pure heart and a sister's affection is what I want; I can form the rest. It is not a legion of acquaintances that will make you contented and joyful, but a few chosen, sympathizing, and right-hearted friends."

Cassel talked Linda into a gay and happy mood. A new vista was opened to her, down which she saw many comely and ambrosial things. Finally Cassel asked,—

"Are you living entirely alone?"

"No, sir; Uncle Jesse lives with me."

"Now tell me all about Uncle Jesse."

"Well, father sent him up here to live with me, and keep me company; but he is no company at all. He does nothing but sit in his room, and copy maps and pictures, and write notes on slips of paper. He takes thin paper and puts it over the maps, and then marks off the lines with a pencil."

"Quite an interesting occupation," said Cassel, with a smile.

"Then he's so cross," said Linda, pouting. "He sometimes actually calls me a fool. If he was not my uncle, and poor, I would almost send him away."

"It is better that he should be here," said Cassel. "He is your only protection."

"No protection at all," said Linda, laughing, not at what she had said, but at what she was about to say. "Let me tell you about him. A burglar might rummage the whole house and he would never know it. He won't even let me dust his room. He locks me and every one else out of his 'study' as he calls it. I went in there once when he was at breakfast, and began to dust the room. He came up and caught me at it. Looking about for something which he instantly seemed to miss, and not being able to find it, he frowned at me, and gritted his teeth at me. Seeing some scraps of paper in my apron, he clawed them out, and shaking one of the slips at me, said, while he gritted his teeth,—

"'How dare you take this out of my study?'

"'What account is that?' I asked.

9*

"'*Damn* it," said he, almost choking, 'it has an *idea* on it; a thing which seems never to have entered your head.'"

Linda laughed gayly, and Cassel amusedly asked,—

"What did you, then ?"

"I told him it must have been the only one *he* had or he wouldn't be so outdone about losing it, and then I came away. I didn't want to treat Uncle Jesse disrespectfully, but sometimes he is so provoking, and makes nothing of calling me an idiot, and crazy, and such like. He says that when I visit my parents again he is going to make father keep me there in Pennsylvania; that I have no business in a city, trying to be what I wasn't made for; that I ought to be milking cows instead of wearing silk dresses and aping she-monkeys of fashion; and that when he gets the benefit of about as much of my nonsense as he can stand, he's going to burn the house down and clear out and take me along with him."

Notwithstanding this terrible array against Uncle Jesse, Cassel had an idea that he would like the old gentleman.

"Is he a student?" asked Cassel. "Is he engaged in any scientific or literary pursuit?"

"I don't know what he's up to," said Linda. "I know that I have paid out three or four hundred dollars for histories and maps and old atlases, just to gratify him. He says he only looks in the history books for dates, and not for facts; that he doesn't need anybody's words, but the figures, which won't lie; and that he can fill up the balance with what he calls his regular old wild-hog sense."

Cassel was rather amused at Linda's portrait of Uncle Jesse. The old gentleman had doubtless become disgusted with his niece on account of her hard-headed efforts to act the fine lady, regarding her as a fashion-ape, and a poor one at that, and probably contented himself with keeping her from actual harm, if so much. But although Linda went to work, as you might say, wrong end foremost, her ambition was by no means the ambition of a fool. She was wealthy, and young, and she had a laudable desire to take rank in society as a useful, happy, graceful, recognized member of it, to enjoy and dispense its benefits and pleasures, and be an acknowledged equal wherever she should choose to go ; in all of which she had, at the very outset, been bitterly disappointed and coldly rebuffed, and had fallen back upon sighs and tears, a woman's last alternative. Young Rapid's present visit could not have been more happily timed for Linda ; and she, had she searched the world over, could not have found a truer or more dauntless breast upon which to cast her cares, or a gentler and more competent guide from whom to seek direction. It was fortunate for Linda that Cassel crossed her path so soon after her widow's weeds had perished with their season, for many a one would soon have been on the alert to lead her along the primrose path to hell. But he would never do it. It was not in his nature ; and *had* it been in his nature, his experience would have stormed against it, for he himself knew of something worse than death, and fit alone to stand in the very gates of hell. To develop Linda into a well-versed, charming, and fashionable young lady, and yet leave her spotless and green-hearted, there was no one who might have better taken the venture than Cassel Rapid. With leisure, and without attachments to preoccupy him, being the last of his race, and homeless, and recognizing Linda's peculiar, desolate, and dangerous condition, he could well make up his mind to fashion her according to the demands of her natural beauty, and purity, and of her fortuitous wealth. He could see no reason, and there was none, why he should not rescue this little innocent, and gird her with knowledge and experience. At all events, he determined to undertake it, and make a mission of it. Aside from any other consideration, it would be a delight and a pastime.

" Will you permit me to visit you freely ?" asked Cassel.

" I would be so glad to have you come," eagerly replied Linda. " You are so kind and homelike."

" What do you mean by homelike ?" asked Cassel.

" I mean," said she guilelessly, " that you have no style."

Cassel smiled. Linda unconsciously had paid him the highest compliment he had ever received. It was the very perfection of his manner which put her at ease and caused her ignorantly to suppose that he had no style at all. Her conception of style was a mate to that of those

stage actors who tear a passion all to tatters, and by
Hamlet condemned.

"Have you any intimate friends in the city?" asked
Cassel.

"None that I like," said Linda.

"Who manages your affairs for you?"

"I manage the house myself; Lewis & Capelle are my
business agents. They managed for Mr. Boyd before I
was married."

"What are they—bankers?"

"I don't know. I check on them for money."

"Have you their street and number?"

"I can get their card," said Linda, rising. "You can
then see what they are and where they keep."

Linda brought a card, upon which Cassel read "Lewis
& Capelle, Bankers and Real Estate Brokers," following
which was street, number, etc.

"Now I must go," said Cassel.

"When will you come again?"

"Will you be glad to see me?"

"Indeed I will," said Linda.

"I will come to-morrow," said Cassel.

"And what am I to do until then?" asked Linda, with
an expression half pensive, half mischievous.

"Behave yourself, and let Uncle Jesse's papers alone,"
answered Cassel with a pleasant laugh.

When Cassel had gone, Linda became restless. Without knowing anything about him, she had surrendered
herself to his keeping. It never entered her head to
doubt him, or imagine that it was possible he might
deceive and take advantage of her. Not that she was
totally deficient of caution or sense of virgin propriety,
but his face was the sign-manual of Honor, and in his voice
was the harmony of Truth.

On the next day Cassel returned to the Boyd mansion.
Linda was ready and double ready to receive him. With
him she forgot her mistaken airs and civilities, or abandoned them from a glimmering sense that they were
entirely superfluous. She ceased to importune him with
untimely hospitalities in the way of refreshments, discerning that he did not care for them. She learned to listen,

and that it was not necessary for her to busy herself or keep up a ceaseless tongue-clatter to make the time pass pleasantly or properly. She consequently appeared to much better advantage, with the single exception of her excessive attire.

"I have brought you something," said Cassel, handing Linda a letter.

"A letter!" cried Linda, springing for it; and without saying "by your leave," or excusing herself in any way, she broke it open and read it,—as Cassel intended she should do.

"Why, I know all this before," said Linda, looking up with a countenance upon which was questioning surprise. "What is it for?"

"*How* did you know it?" asked Cassel.

"How did I know it? Why, I just *knew* it," said Linda, laughing.

"No," said Cassel, "you knew nothing about it. I brought it to you as a testimonial upon which, in the beginning of our acquaintance, you could rely. As we learn each other better, you can then form your own opinion of me."

The letter was a commendation from Sarazzin & Sarazzin, and indorsed by Lewis & Capelle, Linda's bankers.

"And now," continued Cassel, "from this day forward I am to be your brother, and you are to be my little sister."

Linda blushed with modest pleasure. She said,—

"It seems so strange that you should be so kind to me, and want me for your sister."

"Why?" asked Cassel.

"Because I am not like you, who know everybody, and can go here and there when you please, and be happy, without a thought of me; and then nobody ever takes any interest in me, and I am so different from every one here."

"For those very reasons you need a brother; and for those reasons I offer you a brother's affection and guidance. You are a wild flower blooming alone, but none the less sweet and dear to the wayfarer, who would shield you from the nipping frost, the foul breath of the sirocco, and the ruthless tread of the rushing herd. It is not all unselfishness in me. The florist cultivates the rose, not from the love of labor or that the bush may merely thrive, but for the pure blush and fragrance which it gives him."

"I love to hear you talk," said Linda. "You do not talk like other people, and are no more like them than I am. If I am run wild, as you say, please to tame me, and teach me what it is that I must do."

"We will teach one another," said Cassel, "and begin by making a compact not to be angry or feel hurt with each other."

"I could not be angry with you," was the confiding reply.

"I will straightway test your temper," said Cassel.

"I wonder how," replied Linda.

"By introducing a very delicate subject. How many dresses have you?"

Linda had never been asked such a question by a gentleman, and she was in doubt whether it was a proper question to be asked or answered. With a little hesitation, however, she said,—

"I have but six new ones. My black dresses are all laid away. I am to have six more new ones this week."

"Where did you get those which you have?"

"From Madame De Lude."

"She is properly named," said Cassel, "and has deluded you thereby. Are your other dresses to come from the same place?"

"Yes, sir."

"You must countermand the order."

"Why?"

"You are being imposed upon—cheated. You have worn a different dress each time that I have seen you, and none of them are in vogue, and never have been."

"How is that?" asked Linda.

"Your dresses are not the fashion," said Cassel plainly.

"They must be," insisted Linda. "They are just finished, and Madame De Lude bragged on them as being almost ahead of the style."

"Ahead of the style they certainly are," said Cassel, with rather a droll smile, "and so far ahead that I'm afraid the fashion will never catch up with them. But seriously, they are mainly last season's style, altered. Probably second-hand dresses thrown off by fashionable ladies, bought up by the mantua-maker, changed a little, and for the worse, and put upon you as the mode, which they are not, either in pattern or make."

Linda was overthrown. No one except herself knew how long, and with what mental preparation she had been anticipating the exchange of her sad weeds for the unfettered magnificence of the current brilliant mode, or how she had calculated upon securing the very latest, most exquisite, graceful, and exact style of outfit, or how complacently she was contemplating *having done so.* And now, when she was conscious of having failed in all her other endeavors, and was only consoling herself with the comforting belief that at all events her *dresses* were of model tuck and stitch, to be told and convinced, by a *gentleman,* that she was wearing merely the cast-off trumpery of some gay belle of a gone season,—ah! it was indeed too much. It plunged her into the very Valley of Humiliation. Linda was miserable under Cassel's rather free criticisms; unpardonable they would have been, but that he *wished* her to feel miserable for the moment, and remember and profit by it. She hung her head, rich with golden hair, and buried her face in the cushions of the sofa on which she sat. She was very pretty and desolate where she drooped, and Cassel might have taken her in his arms and consoled her. Instead of which, he urged,—

"Now please do not be angry with me."

She raised her head. Her face was deeply blushing. With an energetic, self-disdaining air, she said,—

"I am not angry *at all.* I am *ashamed.* Uncle Jesse is right when he calls me a fool."

"Nay, do not be cast down," said Cassel, soothingly and cheerfully. "Your error is not beyond repair."

"I know you are ashamed of me," said Linda, the tears starting to her eyes.

"I am ashamed of nothing which is so innocent and fair as my little sister," said Cassel. "It is a matter of no particular importance, only you must not allow this cheat to continue. Your order for the other dresses must be countermanded, with the reason why."

"But I am *afraid* of the dressmaker, and would rather pay for them than meet her," said Linda.

"Order your carriage. I will go with you. You need not speak a word. I will manage it myself."

The carriage was ordered. Cassel and Linda got into it and were driven away. Arrived at Madame De Lude's, they entered the superfashionable establishment. Linda was most charmingly accosted by the female head, who, with a gracious nod to Cassel, said,—

"Ah, Mrs. Boyd; your last dress is just finished. I was upon the point of sending them around to you."

"Let me see them, if you please," said Cassel politely.

"We never admit gentlemen to our dressing-room," said the female head with killing prudery and concealed misgivings.

"Be kind enough, then, to bring them here," said Cassel.

After some shuffling back and forth, the dresses were produced. Cassel took one of them, and examined it with the dexterity and eye of a fashionable woman. He took his penknife and ripped a binding.

"See here," said he to Linda, pointing to the stain of perspiration at the armpits; "this dress has been worn."

"You are mistaken, sir," haughtily asserted the female head.

"Whether I am or not," said Cassel, "it is of last season."

He picked up one dress after another, and found them all cheats but one, which also would have been had not Linda taken a stubborn fancy to a certain pattern, and refused to be comforted unless she got it; refusing to be dictated to and declining advice, as she had not done in respect to the other dresses.

"Madame," said Cassel, holding up a garment, "here is a walking-dress, the features of which are twelve months old. By mistake you have inserted a width darker by a shade than the original fabric. That would not be much of an objection were it not intended for open day wear. It would probably pass a street lamp without criticism. But it is useless to discuss the dresses. You are even better aware than I am of the objections to them. We cannot accept them."

Cassel then withdrew Linda from the establishment under a furious fire from the female head. In the carriage Linda said,—

"I would not have gone through with that by myself for anything in the world. I *couldn't* have done it. How she did get mad!"

"Let her remain so," said Cassel. "If you do not claim your own, here, you will soon have nothing to claim."

Cassel took Linda to a more honest establishment, and engaged for her a complete outfit. As Linda's order was unusually comprehensive, the Madame accompanied her and Cassel from door to door, and, between the three pairs of eyes, succeeded in making very elegant and tasty selections; Linda deferring almost wholly to Cassel and the Madame, the latter of whom observed,—

"You have very good taste, sir, for a gentleman."

"You compliment me at the expense of my sex," said Cassel.

"Not at all, sir; for most of gentlemen pride themselves in not knowing a ribbon from a rolling-pin," gayly replied the Madame.

When Linda retired to be measured, the Madame, who went with her, coming out of the sanctuary in advance of her, asked of Cassel,—

"Is she your sister?"

"Yes," replied he.

"She has a splendid form," said the Frenchwoman.

"See that you fit it," enjoined Cassel.

"I'll make her look another sort," was the reply.

Linda came out, and Cassel took her home. She had been in paradise while selecting, under intelligent guidance, the rich and innumerable things which went to make up her outfit; and now that it was over, she would be in a tremor of expectancy until her wardrobe should make its appearance and be tested.

Cassel called to see Linda every day. She responded so unaffectedly to his kindness that his interest in her was daily on the increase. It gave him joy to give joy to her, and he was beginning to control her, and she to obey, as though they were blood and bone of each other. He came in one morning at his usual hour, and Linda met him in an evening-dress, with bare arms and shoulders, which were of a mould fitly to be put on exhibition.

"Are you not afraid of taking cold?" he asked.

"No, sir; it is so pleasant to-day."

"But that dress will certainly give you cold if you wear it in the *morning*," said Cassel.

Linda understood him. She arose with some confusion and was about to withdraw and change her dress, when Cassel said,—

"No. Do not go to that trouble now. It is not necessary. I came this morning on a special errand. I have not seen a servant, except the bell-maid, and her but now and then, since my first morning with you. Where are they?"

"In the basement, I suppose."

"How many do you keep?"

"Let me see; there's the cook, the washwoman, two chambermaids, coachman, marketman, and errand-boy."

"What do they do?"

"I do not know," said Linda.

"Two women and a man are all that you can possibly need. Why don't you discharge them?"

"I'm afraid of them," said Linda; "and then I was told that all nice families keep as many."

"The nicest families in the city keep no more servants than they have use for. They are like bad debts—the fewer you have the better. Show me the way to your basement. I'll go down there and see what I can do for you."

"You had better not go alone, because the marketman is as impudent as he can be."

"He is the first one whom I mean to discharge," said Cassel, "for you have no more use for him than I have for a chignon."

Linda laughed, but with some apprehension led Cassel to the head of the stairs which descended into the basement. He went down, and remained about ten minutes. When he returned, Linda anxiously asked him what he had done.

"I discharged all but the coachman, the cook, and another woman, who will do the washing, chamber-work, and answer the bell. Those three I put on call from six o'clock in the morning until nine o'clock at night. Your coachman is to act as messenger, and make himself generally useful. The marketman wouldn't be convinced until I knocked him down."

" Did you knock him down?"

" I did. He was insolent without provocation, for I treated them all with consideration. What do you suppose they were doing when I went down? Eating breakfast, and it's now eleven o'clock! And a very fine table they spread of it, indulging even in breakfast wine, at your expense, of course," and Cassel laughed at Linda, who blushed and laughed also, for she was glad that her affairs were being corrected. " I paid those whom I discharged, whether rightly or wrongly I do not know, and I'm sure *you* don't; so let it go. I will collect from you whenever convenient. Are your new dresses delivered yet?"

" No, sir, but I get some of them to-morrow."

" On to-morrow then I shall have a proposition to make."

" Make it now," said Linda; "it will tease me so to wait."

" Very well. We will take a carriage drive to one of the parks. It is to be a gala-day, and you will have an opportunity of seeing a little style."

" I know I shall enjoy it," said Linda affectionately. " I have had no one to take me anywhere."

" I know it. You would be lost at the turning of the next corner. But good-by; I am rather busy to-day. Run away now and change your dress."

Linda obeyed like a happy child.

CHAPTER XI.

WHEN Cassel called in the morning, Linda came in smiling, and blushing from consciousness.

"Why, little sister," said Cassel blithely, "you are so very lovely this morning. What has happened to you?"

"I have on one of my new dresses," she replied, with innocence and ardor. "They are all done, and so nice and sweet. I am *so* much indebted to you for your care."

Linda was really beautiful. She had a fine elastic form, and when she moved without assumed airs and paces, and without confusion, she displayed the natural and undulating grace of the silver-footed wild gazelle. Cassel felt a twinge at his heart for having ticketed her as his sister merely. But then he could overleap the brother mark, if he would, at a single bound.

"I came to tell you to be ready within half an hour for our drive. I will call for you with a carriage."

"Why not take my carriage?" asked Linda.

"Because your horses are not carriage animals. They are draft horses, and we must exchange them. I know what a horse is, and will look out for proper ones, and make you up a handsome pair, suitable for the city."

In half an hour Cassel returned with a well-appointed turn-out. Linda in the mean while had dressed herself anew; but Cassel, on sight of her, cried,—

"Oho, birdie; that dress will never do for the carriage. Run and get the one with the spots on it about the size of a mouse's ear, and bring your light shawls."

Linda tripped away as if heeding a brother's chidings, her heart overflowing with happiness, and her thoughts crowded with anticipation. She very soon reappeared with the proper dress on, and with an armful of shawls, which she spread upon a large sofa.

"Which shall it be?" she asked, with perfect confidence in Cassel's discretion.

"Exercise your taste," said Cassel.

With some hesitation and diffidence she made a selection, and said,—

"I like this best."

"You are correct; it is the best for this occasion. Now let me put it on you *à la mode*, that is, according to the present approved style," and Cassel adjusted her shawl, and pinned it where he wished it to stay.

"How do you know about all of these things?" asked Linda, who had her back toward him.

A sudden and sweeping change came over Cassel's face. He turned away with a frown so terrible and an eye so fierce, that he scarce recognized himself in the mirror at his side. Cassel once had a sister.

"Now for your hat," said he, not replying to her question, while the light of his eyes' fierce gleaming, which had momentarily banished their customary and genial holiday glow, subsided, smouldered, and died out.

"I have not a single hat; nothing but bonnets and hoods," said Linda.

"We must have a hat," said Cassel. "A sudden descent upon some fashionable milliner is now in order."

"But what shall I wear to the milliner's?"

"Nothing," said Cassel, pleasantly.

"What! Go upon the street bareheaded!"

"Why not? You will be in the carriage; and did you never go bareheaded in the country?"

"Yes, sir. But here—in the city?"

"There's not so much difference as you imagine. You are nobody's slave, to be made to do this or that. You have freedom here, as well as in the woods. Look now, out at this window. Do you see that young miss tripping along, bareheaded, swinging her hat by the ribbon, and just in time to furnish me with an illustration? It so happens that I know her family, one of the best born and wealthiest in the city. She is well bred, and knows her steps, and yet she trips with hat off. Why? Because the day is warm, she is on the shady side of the street, and it suits her mood and pleasure not to wear her hat. She is but a girl, it is true; but when she becomes a young lady, she will never depend upon Mrs. Jones for her walk, Mrs. Brown for her bow, Mrs. Tinker for her attitudes, or upon

10*

anybody's smirk for her smile. However, as you are not
a school-miss, you might wind a veil about your head
until we get to the milliner's. But I want you to notice
particularly, as we go, that nobody will take an observation as to whether you have anything on your head or
not; and should they, it would only be because your head
is so pretty, and——"

"There!" said Linda, "my hair is all down; and it
will take me a quarter of an hour to fix it."

Cassel, while adjusting Linda's shawl, had pulled out
all of her hairpins, and her hair, relaxing from its abundant coil, fell about her shoulders.

"No," said he. "I can arrange it in one moment,"
and he shook it into a showery golden fleece. Linda
looked into a mirror, and protestingly said,—

"Why, it makes me look as wild as the woods."

"And most vexatiously bewitching," said Cassel. "Come
along now, and let your hair alone ; you couldn't improve
it with a day's effort before the glass."

At the milliner's, a tasty hat, with a plume, was tied
upon the young widow's pretty head, and Cassel felt that
he would not be willing to exchange companions with any
one. To the park they smoothly rolled along, and Cassel
took occasion to lecture upon every salient point in view.
"The best-bred people," said he, "are the most moderate
people in the world. They never overdo. (Driver, go
to the right, and drive slowly.) Look you now, my little
sylvan, at that handsome carriage, with the gray horses,
standing there. The occupants are Mr. Withe, his wife,
and his daughter. Everything about them is rich and
elegant, but not glaring, or in gaudy colors. Miss Withe
is trimmed pretty much as you are. You will notice that
they talk as easily and quietly to the gentleman on horseback as though they had met him on a country road, and
no one but themselves were present; whereas there are
fifty pairs of eyes now leveled at them. The gentleman,
you will see, sits a little sidewise on his horse, as a man
might sit who had met a neighbor on the highway, and
was exchanging gossip or bargaining for corn. The attitude of the two ladies is most comfortable and natural,
and as unconcerned as though they were at home in the

family room. You might imagine that they have no style; and yet they are counted of the very best style in the city. Were I to present you to them, you would feel at ease in a moment; whereas, should I put you in among the *apes*, you would be very uncomfortable indeed. They would kill you off with their overcoming nonsense and sweeping importance. But turn this way. There goes a carriage full of what are called high-flyers. They are rich, only,—and thereby vain. See them bowing themselves into double-bow-knots, laughing immoderately at their own wit, dispensing honey-dripping smiles, or supercilious stares; attracting merely the attention of the idle, exciting the disgust of well-bred people, and the admiration of fools. Helter-skelter! look there, following them; and burlesquing them to perfection, male and female; a stable groom exercising livery horses, and airing his Dulcinea. See how the fellow noses the air, as a running pointer would snuff an atmospheric scent. An El Paso Indian would take them for prince and princess; but look at that newsboy, with his finger to his nose, and one foot raised in derisive 'all hail.' The stable groom glories in the wake which he follows, and is enjoying himself at the expense of the high-flyers, whom he can readily distinguish from the thoroughbreds. Here is another picture. See that glittering turn-out, and the nonchalant pair exquisitely languishing and lolling. Notice the extraordinary display of jewelry, the woman's gaudy fan, the man's indolent cigar, and look of sleepy disdain. The man is a professional gambler, and conducts what is called a 'hell.' The woman, whose cheeks owe their color to paint, may be his wife, and as likely may not be. They are beyond the pale of good society. See yonder; a sward cotillon party; youth enjoying itself, like kids upon the lawn, and as unconstrainedly as your father's lambkins out in Pennsylvania. I might show you pictures until the sun went down; but you shall have other opportunities to look and learn. These things are all new to you; metropolitan society is new to you; and it is natural that you should lack confidence coequally with your inexperience, and not know what to expect, or what is expected of you, when thrown with these veterans of social turmoil. Not to excite your vanity, but to sow the seeds of confidence in you, I will assure you, that during our drive, so far, I have not seen a lovelier or more stylish-looking girl, or one more tastefully dressed, or who has behaved in better manner, than my own little golden-haired sister by my side. And do you know the reason? It is this. You have laid aside your assumed mannerism, which you have dreadfully and mistakenly learned, and appeared simply as Linda. Always be Linda, pure and simple, and never enter upon anything which you do not in part comprehend; I mean, never attempt to repeat a lesson until you have learned it. You saw that handsome young fellow stoop from his horse and whisper to me while we were driving slowly? What do you suppose he said? He asked me what beautiful little bud this was in the carriage with me. And what think you I told him? That you were my little sister, from the country. 'You selfish fellow,' said he, 'she is city bred.' Now think of Claude Melnotte, as his acquaintances call him, one of the most fastidious and discriminating young gentlemen of New York, asserting that you are a genuine city bud. From this, you can judge how well and correct you appear, when you do not *try* to appear well. That fact should not make you vain and sufficient, but encourage you not to lay aside your natural loveliness for the unlovely *style* of *anybody*. Do you know what you are, right now? You are a delightful little country girl, recently come to the city to learn what cannot be learned in the country. There are thousands just such, but you are the only one I ever saw without guide or protector; without some one to lead you intelligently, and assist you here and there to discover and comprehend. You have much to learn, and you cannot learn it all at once. You must take it gradually; for you are young, and have plenty of time. Although you live in a great city, which appears to go, day in and day out, by compass and rule, it is by no means a social martinet, whose rigid and minute behests you are to obey with utmost precision, but the indulgent mother of innumerable children, who can run and play in their own fashion, preserving only a degree of congruity, and neither expected nor desired to be all alike, or imitators of badly-

conceived and self-appointed models. There is an individuality about *every* person which renders it impossible
for Linda ever to become Lucinda or Clorinda, though she
should spend a lifetime in perverting herself to that end:
and furthermore, it is easier and far more distinguished to
be a good original than to be a copy, whether good or bad.
You are fortunate in two respects: first, in having so little
to unlearn; second, in possessing a native capacity for
pure, well-toned, and unaffected society. With a guide, a
few hints, a little restraint here, and a little urging there,
you will, almost before you know it, be at home in the
city, and as free and happy as when gathering nuts, or
climbing cherry-trees, away in Pennsylvania. But you
must accustom yourself to do your own thinking, notwithstanding your guide; and endeavor to look not only upon
the surface, but into the deep of everything around you.
When you are perplexed, or need advice, or assistance of
any kind, always come to 'brother,' and he will take pride
and pleasure in aiding you. But let there be a limit to
your confidence even in *me*, your brother; for I cannot
stand to you as a mother or a father, and it is better,
always better, especially for a girl like you, to hold a
certain reserve of trust; which, like the bullion held by the
banks, is the basis of security, and reputation."

"I feel that I could trust you without the reserve which
you recommend," said Linda.

"*Don't do it*," said Cassel; "for the heart of man is deceitful above all things and *desperately* wicked. That is
a passage of Scripture the truth of which is universally
admitted by Christian and alike by Pagan. But I have lec-
tured enough for one day. I am coming now to a scheme
which I have in my mind, and which, if carried out, will be
a better school for you than all the teachings of which I am
capable. Listen, and I will state it in full and particular.
You say that you are lonesome; and I am not surprised at
it. I could introduce you into city society to-day, or to-
morrow, but you would be doing yourself an injustice, without some preparatory training, to adventure it. Here is
my scheme. You have a great deal more house than you
need. You have room for at least ten persons additional
to your present family, and without inconvenience. We

will say that you take, as guests, self-supporting of course, a few ladies and a few gentlemen, of unexceptionable merit and connection, and who themselves visit and receive freely. They could be readily obtained, and made to comprehend your object, which would be to collect about you a goodly company, a little colony of refined and cultivated people, who would intermingle pleasantly, and make you their queen and darling. Your house would then be lighted from cellar to garret, and your home be full of life and cheerfulness. In a single month you would become more capable of the outer world than in a lifetime spent as now."

Linda was fascinated. She wondered why she had not thought of it before. She adopted the scheme at once and eagerly.

"Do not be in any haste," said Cassel, "or you will get company which you may repent of. I expect to aid you, and to come live with you myself."

"You are to come, of course," said Linda, "or I should be dreadfully amiss in everything." ·

"Leave the matter, then, entirely to my arrangement, and I will make your house so cheerful that you will almost wish to move out of it," said Cassel gayly. "I will get companions for you, such as you need. I have several in my mind at this moment, who will be glad to come, and whom you cannot fail to like. But the sun is almost set, and we had best go home."

Arrived at the Boyd mansion, Linda timidly asked,—

"Would it be proper for me to invite you to tea with Uncle Jesse and myself?"

"Nothing more proper in you, or more agreeable to me," said Cassel, who felt like chucking her under the chin, for she looked so absolutely free from guile and self-assertion. "And now that we are here, I am going to get you to show me over your house."

"Do you wish to see it?" said Linda brightly. "You can then tell me if I need anything. Come."

As they went over the mansion, Cassel made his observations.

"Your parlors and first floor are just a little overcrowded with furniture. You can have some of the

articles moved up-stairs. I'll tell you which. Here, on
your second floor, you have two connecting rooms. I
already know a family to occupy them,—a gentleman, his
wife, and two young daughters. Ah," said Cassel, peeping
into a large apartment which looked upon the street,
"here is *my* room. Please remember, for it is exactly
what I want."

"You shall have your choice," said Linda. Where she
stood, mainly on one foot, while tapping the floor with
her other little boot, she was so very pretty, and fresh,
and fair, and uninvaded, that Cassel was almost tempted
to take every room in the house at one grab, with Linda
in the choicest of them, and probably would have done so,
but for a secret fire within his heart which brooked no
other flame.

"These rooms here," he continued, "are suitable for
young ladies. On our third floor we will put our single
gentlemen, should we have any."

"Are you not single? asked Linda."

"Yes. But I am to help you manage, and must be
convenient to all parts of the house. You must not call
me Mr. Rapid any more, but *brother*, and then we will
feel so easy and at home together."

"What will you call me?" asked Linda.

"Sister, and Linda, and little Sylvan, until I make you
to become a little urban, about which time I expect you
will be taking some other name, and I will have to exchange them all for that one."

Linda blushed. She had no thought of marrying, for
she did not know what it was to be a lover. Cassel could
have taught her in the three magic words "I love thee,"
but as he had never spoken except as a brother, the little
volcano of her heart was asleep, and she felt that it would
be the complement of happiness to have him for a brother,
now and always.

"I want no name but Linda," she said. "You can
always call me Linda, and sister, if you will always be
my brother; but I dream at night that you have gone
away, and I wake myself with my own sobbing."

"You find me on hand in the morning," said Cassel.

"Yes; but then I fear at night that my dreams are true.

No one cares for me but you. In the day my heart *aches* with joy, as if it were too full. At night it aches with fear, and is bleak and empty."

"Linda, do you ever say your prayers?"

"Yes, sir."

"Then; in the night, when it is so silent that you can hear your watch ticking off the time, do not think of *me*, or let your peace hang upon a thing so slight and evanescent as I, or my existence. You overprize me. I do not wish to weigh so heavily against your individuality and life mission. I shall not leave you, you little dove; but do not suffer me to become the corner-stone of your tranquillity, for to-morrow I might die, or, as all humanity is prone, do that which might shatter your hopes where they cling. Do you ever go to church?"

"I have no one to take me, and I should be lost there."

"To-morrow is Sunday. I will call, and we will go together."

Tea was announced, and Linda invited Cassel to the supper-room, where she presided with charming abashment. Uncle Jesse, a caustic, fool-hating, have-my-own-way looking old bachelor, whom Cassel had never before met, walked into the supper-room with an air which said as plainly as the nose on his face, "*I stand no nonsense.*"

Linda accomplished the introductions, and Cassel made some pleasant remark, to which Uncle Jesse replied with a "Humph."

During tea, Linda told Uncle Jesse of her happy day's drive, and of her projected scheme of gathering a select company of permanent guests at the Boyd mansion. Her prattle lasted until Uncle Jesse had swallowed his tea. His only reply, as he arose and started for his den, was "Twad," by which he meant "twaddle," and immediately he disappeared, gritting his teeth.

"Now don't you see what he is?" protested Linda, with a pensive humor in her face.

"I like him," said Cassel, laughing freely. "He's a gem. Just the kind of uncle for you. Leave me to bring him around."

"Maybe, after all, I am accountable for his strange ways, disgusting him with my simpleton's doings," said

Linda, and she and Cassel laughed merrily at the too probable truth of her remark.

In the morning, which was the Sabbath, Cassel called to take Linda to church.

"What shall I wear?" was Linda's first inquiry.

"Your blue silk; and over it your lace shawl. I will adjust the shawl for you."

"Please do not pull my hair down again."

"No; it does very well as it is."

"Where are you going?" asked Linda, as Cassel stepped to the hall and started up-stairs.

"To see Uncle Jesse," said Cassel, smiling.

"Goodness gracious! you had better not stir *him up now*," cried Linda, with eyes wide open; but Cassel laughed pleasantly, and proceeded to knock at Uncle Jesse's door. The old gentleman opened his door, and looked at Cassel with harsh surprise.

"Good-morning, Uncle Jesse."

"Who told you to uncle *me*, sir?"

"I do so out of respect, I assure you."

"What do you want?"

"Permission to accompany your niece to church."

Uncle Jesse looked at Cassel almost askance, while over his harsh features came a faint expression of abated severity.

"Go 'long," and he shut his door.

At church, the sweep of the grand organ, and the rich and soaring of voices the choir, overwhelmed Linda, and thrilled her through and through. She trembled with excitement, and in her wakefulness to all that was about her, looked as wild as a young chamois.

"How did you like it?" asked Cassel on their way home.

"It almost killed me with—with—I don't know what."

"Would you like to attend regularly?"

"Yes, sir. I did not know there was such a—such a— grand place in the world."

"There are churches of much more imposing grandeur than this one; but you must remember that they are all humble gateways to the world beyond. The pew which we occupied *was* mine, but I have transferred it to you.

11

A pew at church is considered by many to be essential to respectability, if not to salvation, especially among your sex."

"You are so good," said Linda.

"No, I am not. But I wish you to be."

"I will be, if you will teach me how."

"I will point you the way, but mine is not the unerring judgment which you must obey, or the invincible arm on which you must lean."

"When we came out of church, the streets looked so strange, and worldly, and heedless."

"Yes. You saw people hurrying to dinner as if their salvation depended upon hot soup."

"Is a theater anything like these city churches?"

"No. But you shall see and judge for yourself. Tomorrow night I will take you to see a most excellent play, well rendered."

"Is it a proper place for me to go? But I need not ask, for you would not go yourself if it were an improper place."

Cassel smiled at Linda's guilelessness, but it was a smile of increasing affection, not one of ridicule. He said,—

"You have determined to lead a metropolitan life; therefore you must know what it is that you are inhabiting. There are *some gems* among the innumerable baubles upon the stage, and where we shall go to-morrow night you will find the pomp and array of wealth, a chaste and thrilling entertainment, and an opportunity of enlarging your stock of ideas. Generally, theater-going is not good; selectedly, it is profitable and instructive. I intend to take Uncle Jesse along with us," humorously concluded Cassel.

"Uncle *Jesse!*" exclaimed Linda. "*Impossible!* But what shall I wear?" asked the girl-widow, abruptly changing the subject. Cassel laughed heartily.

"Oh, that ever-recurring and vexatious question," said he. "But lose no sleep, Linda; you are provided. For a dress, your white foulard with the black fringe and velvet bows. I will send around a hair-dresser to curl your hair. For a head-dress, all you need is a pair of sugar-tongs with a humming-bird's feather just a little drooping. I intend to make more than one person envy me, and ask what little golden head it is by my side."

Cassel's object was not to flatter Linda, but to make her feel intrinsically at par with all the world, for he intended soon to take her into *Society.* She was now as wax in his hands. She regarded him as the monarch of circumstances—everything seemed so facile and right with him. When under his pure eye, and hearing his rich, soft voice, she teemed with delight and contentment. He could flood her heart with joy as easily as the Mexican irrigates his little *pedazo de tierra.*

The next morning, Cassel, who had got an inkling of what Uncle Jesse was "up to," appeared at the old gentleman's door with an armful of the quaintest, as well as of the newest, *maps* which he could find in the city. In less than ten minutes he and Uncle Jesse were closeted together, and the ensuing evening found the old gentleman ensconced, with Linda and Cassel, in a box at the theater. The fact was, Uncle Jesse was about as near lost in the city as was Linda, and only needed such a cicerone as Cassel to make him as adventurous as a night-cat and as gay as a badger.

At the theater, Linda's cheeks glowed, her budded bosom heaved, and her bright eyes gleamed with the passion of the play, and Uncle Jesse cut his tobacco with the rapidity of a sheep chewing up sweet daisies in the spring. During the play, an old gentleman, crusty as frozen and double-frozen snow, appeared on the stage, and, with a single harsh word, testily and with amusing eccentricity "cut" every one who dared to approach him. Linda, referring to the caustic actor before the scenes, turned to her uncle and said,—

"Uncle Jesse, that's *you.*"

The delighted old gentleman roared with laughter, and the benches taking their cue from the boxes, the whole house indulged in a crashing storm of mirth.

"See what a fuss you've kicked up," said Cassel mischievously to Uncle Jesse, who subsided at once.

"Who did you say this young fellow is who brought us here?" asked Uncle Jesse in a whisper.

"It is Mr. Cassel Rapid, of the city," replied Linda.

"Well, I can say this much for you," continued Uncle Jesse: "he's the only person you ever took up with in New York that's got any sense."

Linda thought that her uncle was saying a good deal for Cassel but not much for her. But she didn't care; she was happy.

"Brother," said Linda, blushing at the affectionate word even in the twilight of the carriage while on their way home from the theater, "what are you going to do for me next?"

"Uncle Jesse," said Cassel, replying indirectly to Linda's question, "I am going to teach her how to dance."

"She used to dance with the best of them," responded the now tractable Uncle Jesse.

"Nothing but cotillons," said Linda.

"That is enough," said Cassel; "for beyond the Cotillon, innocence and propriety are said not to remain intact."

"I always *thought* there was something wrong about these hug-dances," said Uncle Jesse, "and we agree. I was just telling Linda here that you were the only person she ever took up with that had any sense."

Cassel couldn't resist the impulse to pinch Linda's arm, and the two youths laughed merrily at Uncle Jesse's discretion.

CHAPTER XII.

ONE morning a jeweler called at the Boyd mansion, and succeeded in selling Linda a set of what he stated to be "genuine Indian Ocean Luna Lustre Pearls," for which she gave her check on Lewis & Capelle for four hundred dollars.

The jeweler left, and in a few moments Linda was standing before a parlor mirror, adjusting and admiring her pearls, when Cassel Rapid came suddenly in upon her.

"Vanity of vanities!" he exclaimed. "Whoever invented the mirror should be canonized by the ladies. But what have you there?"

"A set of new pearls; the genuine Indian Ocean Luna Lustres," said Linda, with enthusiasm. "And the jeweler let me have them at cost price in Europe. He is going back to France for a new stock, and these were all he had unsold, and he did not wish to take them back with him."

"Let me look at them."

Linda passed the pearls, which were in fact nothing but wax, over to Cassel. A little darkey down South once observed, that "alligators chaw a feller all up." Cassel looked at Linda as if he would as willingly as not imitate the manner of the alligator, and chaw *her* up.

"Why, you little goosey of a *goose!*" said he, taking the Luna Lustres and crushing them in his palm as he might have done so many humming-bird eggs.

Linda was terrified. She saw at once that she had been swindled, and she was very unhappy to think that Cassel would condemn her as an incorrigible fool.

"Come here," said he, and he led her into an anteroom, where he put on a disguise which he had borrowed from the office of Hector O'Dare, and, to Linda's amazement, the jeweler stood before her.

"Little sister, this is caution number one. Until you grow wiser, let your motto be, 'never trust a stranger.' I hope I shall not have to repeat my lessons."

"Brother," said Linda, despondently, "you will never be able to make any more out of me than a monkey."

"Then I'll make a very nice little monkey of you," laughed Cassel. "But now to business. To-morrow I will bring you a cook,—a man cook." Linda opened her eyes. She had never heard of such a thing. "He is to control your basement. I shall also bring you a housekeeper, a respectable woman, who will take charge of the house above the basement. You will then be prepared to receive your guests, and have leisure for improving yourself. On the day after to-morrow I shall introduce, as guests, Mr. Lake, his wife, and their two daughters, one fourteen and the other about five years of age. The

11*

family are unexceptionable, and have had the advantages
of travel. With Mrs. Lake you will be at home almost as
with your mother. She is both competent and willing to
teach and advise you. They will occupy the double
rooms on the second floor."

"When are *you* coming?" asked Linda.

"On the same day. I see you have plenty of stable
room for my two horses. I will keep them here. Your
carriage horses were too heavy; I have traded them off.
You now have a matched pair of elegant equine antelopes,
as vain, and prancing, and high-headed, though not so
hard-hearted, as young belles."

"You think of *everything*," said Linda, pouting with
self-disdain. "I am no account at all." Then brightening a little, Linda added, "But, brother, I had a visitor
yesterday."

"Who was it?"

"Mrs. Colver. Is she of the *ton?*"

"What do you know about *ton?*"

"But she was so easy to entertain."

"And consequently you thought she was nobody.
There is just where you mistake it altogether. It is the
genuine dollar, and not the *counterfeit*, which brings its
own welcome and makes its stay untiring. But I will
show you what Mrs. Colver is to-night. She gives a
large party this evening. I have an invitation from her
for you. You are to go, and I am to go with you, if you
will. I promise that you will see sights."

"Then her call was a made-up thing between you?"
suggested Linda, with some penetration.

In the evening Cassel was with his young protégée,
assisting her to perfect her toilet before one of the parlor
mirrors of the Boyd mansion.

At Mrs. Colver's, Linda was dazzled; but Cassel kept
her upon his arm until he had explored the novelty with
her, and given her a clear, synoptic idea of what she saw.
The music was excellent, and Cassel, who danced well,
but had not indulged himself for a couple of years, took
Linda out upon the floor and put her most ravishingly
through a set of cotillons. Linda thrilled with pleasure
from top to toe, and with the buoyancy of opening, charm-

ing life, felt as if floating and swimming upon some ambrosial tide. Several young gentlemen sought introductions to her, and soon discerning how guileless and sweet she was, took especial delight in keeping her under a shower of joy.

Late in the evening, Linda was sitting with a young lady upon a sociable, in distinct view, there being no other persons near. Cassel was perambulating with a haughty belle, who, by-the-way, was somewhat affected toward him, and secretly jealous of his interest in Linda. She knew as well as any one who Linda was, but in her imperious, depreciating way, she asked of Cassel, while she glanced toward the sociable,—

"What silly thing is that sitting over there?"

Cassel divined with what this shaft was tipped, and he determined instantly to turn it back upon its haughty launcher.

"Why, that is your sister," said he innocently.

"Oh, *no!* I mean the girl beside her."

"I beg your pardon," said Cassel. "I mistook your reference,—the girls are so close together, and I didn't observe anything peculiar about the other one, who is *my* sister."

Cassel's companion bit her lip, and almost stamped upon the floor, at what was to her an intolerable thrust. She soon requested to be seated. Cassel resigned her, saying to himself, "She forced me to be rude. Linda is worth more than she in every particular. She has nothing to uphold her but wealth, which is more often inherited by the fool than by the sage, and far more often acquired by the knave than the honest person.' Let her keep her silly sister away from Linda, and her silly remarks away from me."

"Linda," asked Cassel, on their way home, "which do you enjoy the most,—the church, the theater, or the party?"

"I believe I like the party best of all," said Linda honestly.

"Don't run wild now about parties," said Cassel. "You will soon get used to them, and they will become as ordinary as beefsteak for breakfast."

Linda would have gone with Cassel anywhere, and listened to him always. She was fully awake from her tiresome and dreary dream, to a real existence, full and overflowing with charming particulars. She felt that she was a different person from the late solitary, apprehensive, heavy-hearted, and circumscribed Linda. Her outlook was inviting now, and becoming familiar. The stately buildings swallowing up their throngs, and heretofore wearing a shroud of mystery through which her imagination and conjecture vainly attempted to make their way, were being turned inside out to her. She felt more at home in her own house, as though she had a right there, and not as if every one who entered its halls held prior sway, and might order her to begone.

We may now consider Linda, the guileless, in a pathway 'on either hand of which is happiness. Out of his nobility of soul, a wealthy and enchanting young stranger, who could, with much less outlay of pains and patience, have put her perhaps upon the road to despair, chose joy, and not shame, for her.

Cassel, Pontiac, Rapid:—rather a singular name, indeed; and in some respects having a singular owner. Two years ago, as we have before said, that name might well have been "Joyful." *Now*, it might better be "Indomitable." Linda, to whom he had been so generously gentle and true, and who repaid him with such unalloyed trust and affection, was no more essential to his inner life than the butterfly which fans the flower is essential to the breeze that rocks the forest. Although he prized Linda, and would doubtless have laid down his life in her defence, yet, had it been his fate to have done so, it would have been for him a fate like that of one, who, organizing a chief battle, falls prematurely in some insignificant skirmish. In the play of young Rapid's countenance there was a feature, or the absence of a feature, which was, in all probability, unique. His face, regular, pure, and chiseled in manly beauty, never wore an expression of absolute gravity. When it was at rest, the beholder was reminded of a finely-cut countenance upon which the sculptor's genius had kindled the light of a coming smile. The ordinary perplexities and mishaps which make men swear and contract their brows, were pondered by him with this pleasant and unruffled light ever upon his face. If his reflections became lighter, or droll, or blithe, he either smiled with frankness or laughed outright. But if they took an opposite and peculiar turn, his expression leaped over the point of gravity altogether, and a frown as implacable as *War* gathered to his brow. And when he was alone, this frown often came upon his face, and with the quickness of light transformed its placid beauty to the grim and relentless aspect of an avenger. The observer would be compelled to the conclusion that at such times a merciless pang was shooting through his brain, or that there was some one thing in this world which he utterly hated with most ravening desire, the bare thought of which was sufficient to rouse a raging lion or a Lost Angel within his breast. Accustomed calmly and with iron nerve to stand in the vortex of peril, his hand trembled at his own frown, whose terrible gathering seemed but the outward signs of an emotion within him which was as volcanic as Truth, and resistless as the waft of storms. It would be false to say that Cassel Rapid was now habitually or consecutively unhappy. It would be true to say that at times, and often, memory swept through his soul, scorching its way like a flame of exquisite ills.

CHAPTER XIII.

WHILE Cassel Rapid was training and cultivating the fair exotic, which, in its state of neglect, had excited his sympathy and enlisted his care, there were several persons ranging about Creswood who were not regarded as legitimate denizens of that fastness of tranquillity. One of these strangers, who appeared to go alone, or to *desire* to go alone, was an erect, active, good-looking person, with an acute, intelligent countenance, and a keen, vigilant eye, notwithstanding the superfluous glasses which he wore upon his nose. He was dressed in substantial, well-cut clothes, and seemed to be ever intent upon picking up shells from the beach, examining pebbles, and pricking into clefts of the. rocky bluffs with a steel instrument after the fashion of a stiletto. Strapped to his shoulder he carried a small satchel, into which he sometimes dropped a specimen from the ocean, a chip from the rocks, or a sample of the soil. The latter he packed in jar-shaped vials, which he corked and sealed with wax. He could be seen almost every day, walking about and discovering the geological characteristics of Creswood. He would loosen a stone, hold it off at arm's length, and glare at it through his spectacles, then draw it close up to his eyes and examine it as minutely as if searching for fossilized animalculæ. He gave out that he was a geologist, employed in the interests of science, and would remain in that neighborhood for an indefinite period, as he found it an exceedingly interesting spot, abounding in fossils and traces of hoary antiquity. He seemed particularly attracted by the Larboard Strand, and the line of bluffs which rose abruptly against it; and, by a shrewd observer, might have been detected in topographical as well as geological investigation. However, as it is not our intention to excite the curiosity of the reader, it may be as well to state at once that the geologist was none other than Hector O'Dare, the person with whom young Rapid held an interview in the correct city of Boston, and one of the most cunning fellows in the United States. Cunning though he was, he was destined to be put to his wits in a very few days after he made his appearance at Creswood. With the exception of a very few persons, the dwellers of Creswood knew as little of geology as Towser knows of taxation, and in less than a week the geologist became the wonder of the neighborhood, and was pestered beyond all ordinary patience by the curiosity of the people, especially the younger ones, who would follow him about for half a day at a time, in a vain endeavor to discover or comprehend what in the mischief he could possibly be after. Some said he was hunting for gold, or silver, or precious stones, or coal, or buried treasure. Others asserted that he was crazy. And others, that he was a necromancer, and was in league with Oswald Huron in

some Devil's doings. But what he had most to fence
against was the interest which Garland Hope manifested
for the progress and results of his researches. Garland
was himself a student of geology, and now that a scientific and practical geologist had come into his neighborhood, it was a chance too rare to be lost, and nothing but
the very coolest civility on the part of O'Dare restrained
him from opening up the boundless subject for discussion
and information. He would go out into O'Dare's chosen
range, and fish up some specimen which he himself could
neither name nor locate, and about which O'Dare knew
absolutely nothing. The detective could have canvassed
Theology with the young minister with infinitely greater
scope and understanding. He was a proper feeling man,
and did not wish to treat any deserving person uncivilly,
but with all his hedging, and deafness, and foxing, he
could not, in this instance, avoid doing so, without great
risk of an open exposure. He glided out of answering a
number of direct interrogatories in a manner which Garland regarded as very singular indeed, and was finally compelled to inform the young minister that *"he never discussed
Geology with amateurs ;"* at the same time facetiously adding to himself, *"or with anybody else."* With the rustic
bumpkins who stared at him and anon ventured an inquiry, he resorted to the tactics of the negro phrenologist
who, being interrogated, replied, "that amativeness and
costiveness meant exactly the same thing,"—O'Dare telling
the bumpkins that geology and genealogy were synony-
mous, and meant *Pedigree.* They all knew the meaning
of pedigree ; for during the last season some one had kept
an ass in the neighborhood, and not to know the pedigree
of that ass was to be considered a greater ass than the ass
itself.

But curiosity, like young birds, will, unless it is continually fed, pine away and die ; and as O'Dare discreetly
reduced his movements to the monotony of an empty
craw, the curiosity of the rustics died of famine. So, after
having run the gantlet of the entire neighborhood, he
was left alone to pursue his researches. After numerous
walks up and down the Larboard Strand, and repeated
investigations of the wall of rock which backed it up, he

one day took from his satchel and unfolded a sheet of canvas about a yard square. With a pencil he traced the strand and the wall of bluff, Gale Island at the lower or southern end, and Cliff Hall in view at the upper or northern end of the strand; the island and Hall being about a mile and a half apart. Upon that part of his tracery representing the beach and bluff some two hundred yards north of Gale Island, he made a distinct mark; and upon the corresponding actual locality he marked the rock wall with a cross of red chalk. Between the red cross and Gale Island, and about fifty yards from the cross, a bridle path led up to the hills and into the forest. Between the red cross and Cliff Hall, to the north, there was, for at least a mile, no access to the hills; no way to escape from the beach except by way of the ocean. We are particular in describing Larboard Strand, because it is to be the theater of a tragedy, swift and mysterious.

Several miles south of Gale Island, on the *Starboard* Strand, was a ragged string of huts, the property of no one in particular, and occupied at will by itinerant nondescripts. In one of a group of these huts, at the present date, were three persons: Amy Turnbolt, the niece of Captain Gale; Jonas Aiken, the young villain whom Guy Rapid had taken to Texas with him, and now a grown man; and Gilders, also originally of Creswood, the man whom Cassel Rapid had compelled to deliver up a certain valuable paper at a card-table in Boston.

Amy was in a bad humor from some cause, and went out of the hut. Jonas Aiken wheeled his chair, turned his back to Gilders, and stuck his feet out of a window. Gilders got up softly, drew a revolver, pressed the trigger, and cocked it without clicking it, and leveled the pistol at Jonas Aiken's back. In this position he stood for ten seconds. His countenance changed, and lowering his weapon, he said to himself,—

"Something urges me to make sure of him; but he is not my game, and I will not rob the owner. If ever I had a prayer, it is that the hand of that gallant, noble boy may not fail him when he comes upon this hellion."

Gilders sat down as softly as he had risen, and Jonas Aiken never knew how near he then was to the pit of death.

Amy Turnbolt reappeared, and sat down.

"How much do I owe you for board?" asked Gilders.

"Eleven dollars," replied Amy.

"Here is your money, and here is my good-by," said he, extending his hand.

"Where are you going?" asked Jonas Aiken.

"To California, maybe."

"I wish you'd let me have about twenty-five before you start. I'm strapped."

"You are already in my debt, of old; and I have no money to spare."

"Suppose I should *make* you spare it?" said Aiken, with a fierce, contemptuous look.

Gilders did not answer, but with his hand upon his pistol and his eye upon Aiken, he backed out of the hut, and was seen no more in Creswood.

Very soon after Gilders' departure there was a distinct knock at the door of the hut. Aiken actively withdrew, for his crimes made him apprehensive, and Amy, answering the knock, found herself face to face with O'Dare. She had seen the geologist and had heard a great deal about him: she consequently invited him in with some curiosity. O'Dare, greatly to his surprise, had met with Gilders a few days before, and had gained information from him. Gilders had recognized O'Dare as a person whom he had met in another and very different character, but the detective had secured the silence of the cattle herder by mentioning the name of John R. Lake, and, in a very friendly manner, hinting him off to California.

O'Dare saw that the room into which he was invited contained three chairs only; and he managed to discover, before taking a seat, that two of the chairs were warm from recent occupation. He was satisfied that at least one person had left the room at his approach.

"Are you the mistress here?" he asked of Amy.

"Yes."

"You do not live alone?"

"No. I keep a few boarders, but they are now away."

"Laborers, are they?"

"Well, yes; that is, I believe they are."

"When will they return?"

12

"That is more than I can tell."

At this moment O'Dare's quick eye detected a man spying into the room between the chinks of the hut. A few seconds passed when a door opened and the man walked in with a proprietary air.

"Good-morning, sir," said O'Dare, at the same time observing to himself, "You are my man and no mistake."

Jonas Aiken was a muscular, dark man, rather tall, and with hooded eyes, out of which looked evil, cunning, suspicion, and alertness. With investigating eyes he said to O'Dare,—

"I don't think I ever saw you before."

"Nor I you," answered the detective, who noticed that Aiken kept his revolver handy.

"Where are you from?"

"I am the gentleman from Geology," said O'Dare, adjusting his spectacles in a very eccentric manner, "traveling about in search of the vestiges of the Silurian, Devonian, Carboniferous, Reptilian, Mammalian, and Golden ages."

"And otherwise a damn'd book-fool," said Aiken to himself. "Well," continued he, addressing O'Dare, "what do you want here?"

"A man to do some work with a pick."

The interview between O'Dare and Aiken resulted in a bargain, this being Saturday, that on Monday morning Aiken should go to work picking the drift from a crevasse where O'Dare had marked, with a red cross, the rock wall of the Larboard Strand, and to continue to excavate until O'Dare, by stopping his pay, should notify him to quit.

When O'Dare left the hut, Aiken turned to Amy, and with a selfish, unpleasant laugh, said,—

"Any damn'd fool ought to know there's no gold in these bluffs. This fellow is crazy. I've heard of him, roving about here pecking into rocks, bottling dirt, and bagging shells, for the last week or two. But I'm strapped, and if I don't work any gold out of the bluffs for him, I'll work some out of his pocket for me, and keep it up as long as he dares to, unless I get wind of the Devil on horseback."

"Who is this 'Devil on horseback,' and what makes you so afraid of him?" asked Amy.

"I tell you again, Amy Turnbolt, he's a handsome devil that rides a pale horse with black mane and black feet. He's been here once, but went away, I hope, for good. I don't want to meet him; so, if you hear of him, it will stand you in hand to let me know of it. I owe him, and he's determined to collect."

"And I tell *you* again, Jonas Aiken, that you must hunt some other place to board. I do not like this skirmishing about every time that any person knocks at the door; and I won't prevaricate for you any longer. And furthermore, I am going back to Uncle Gale's. I was a fool for ever leaving him."

"Very well," said Aiken; "when you go, I'll run the shebang myself. These huts are as much mine as yours, anyhow."

"Not until I get out of them, sir," said Amy resolutely. "When it comes to that, I'll see who has the most friends in Creswood between us."

On the morrow, which was Sunday, Jonas Aiken went upon the Larboard Strand to have a look at his field, or rather his spot, of labor.

"Not so hard after all," said he to himself, as he looked at the red cross chalked upon the rock; "and if I don't tinker the work for as many days as that fool can be coaxed to pay, then let some sensible man kick me into the sea."

Strolling up the Strand, he came upon Cora Glencoe, who was seated on the Tarpeian Rock. She was reading, and must have been exceedingly interested, for she did not observe Aiken's approach, and was only apprised that he had stopped in front of her by the deep growl of a powerful dog which lay at her feet. She raised her head, and Aiken saw that she had been weeping.

"What is it that distresses one so beautiful?" asked Aiken, who did not lack for words or blandishments.

Cora answered him nothing, but kept her firm dark eyes fixed upon him as though he had been some dangerous animal from the overhanging forest.

"Why do you weep?" persisted the man.

Cora gazed at him resolutely and silently. She felt that the man was one to beware of. But she did not know that she looked *Hell* in the face, as her sweet, unquailing eyes rested upon him.

Aiken glanced up the strand: there was no one in sight. He glanced southward, and seeing Johnny Gale with his mother and sister pleasure-walking, he turned away and continued his stroll.

Cora Glencoe had never spoken to any member of the Gale family. Notwithstanding this fact, the Gales bore her no malice, for all their charges were laid at the threshold of Oswald Huron, with whom, they were satisfied, Cora led a most wretched and withering life. They had often pitied her in their fireside conversations, for they knew from Mr. Hope that she was a pure-hearted, lovely, dauntless little girl, fighting daily and hourly with the fate which bound her to an almost intolerable existence. Out of human sympathy, then, when they were about to pass her, they looked over toward the Tarpeian Rock on which she sat. What was their surprise to see her acknowledge their regard with an inclination of her head, which had more of apology than condescension in it. Very kindly and politely they responded, and passed on.

Thinking of the man upon whose evil countenance she had just looked, and fearing that he might return and find her alone, Cora descended from her seat upon the rock, and, in the rear of the Gales, proceeded slowly toward Cliff Hall.

Carroll May, who apparently had been delayed at the island, and was endeavoring to overtake the Gales in their promenade, came briskly along, and was about to pass Cora, when, hearing his steps behind her, she turned suddenly and looked him full in the face. With a politeness, possibly indiscreet, but certainly irrepressible, he bowed to her, not expecting her to regard him in the least. But he, even more than the Gales, was astonished, when, with a manner exquisitely sad, she bid him good-day, and courageously requested him to halt. Before his happy wonder had time to expend itself she handed him the book which she had been reading, and said,—

"Mr. May, here is something which belongs to you. I picked it from the strand but an hour ago. I have read it twice. Ignorance of its contents, and finding it open and astray, caused me to look into it. A glance made it impossible for me to close it. I know that I have trespassed upon what to you is sacred. But consider that to me it instantly became as essential as it is sacred to you, and you will forgive me. May the good God bless you, and forever prosper you!" and Cora turned and walked away.

Carroll felt as if he had been shocked by a sensation battery which had agitated every chord within his breast. Never had Cora looked into his eyes or vouchsafed him a word before. He knew that it was madness to love her, but who is ever mad from choice? or who that *is* mad can help being mad? He knew that the very tie which now existed between himself and Cora was a bloody one, which effectually severed them forever, and yet the fated command to *forget* her caused him the more intensely to remember.

The book which Cora had restored to its owner dispelled a life-long illusion. It had been originally a blank-book, in size about five by six inches. It was filled with manuscript, plain, regular, and neat as print. It contained over fifty pages, devoted exclusively to Carroll's family history, from which he learned of his father's character, and particularly of the motives which impelled him to seek an alternative which resulted in his death. The name of Oswald Huron frequently occurred on its pages, and furnished the irresistible attraction which caused Cora to begin what, when once begun, could not be relinquished until it was read and re-read. It was a faithful record, but totally devoid of bitterness. It was a vindication of the motives of the slain; not an arraignment of the slayer. It was discernible that the heart of a good man had influenced and guided the head which had arranged, and compacted, and tempered the facts recorded. Instead of inciting to revenge, they breathed a sigh, pensive with regret, and exhaled a perfume which quieted the spirit with an exquisite sadness, like that which is borne through the senses to the soul by the scent of flowers blossoming over the tomb. In this record, Captain Gale had more than complied with the request of the dead that he should acquaint the son wherefore the father died by violence. Next to the sarcoph-

agus which held his father's ashes, that little book was
sacred to the boy. He had unaccountably dropped it on
the strand; but that Cora had found it and wept over it,
and hallowed him with a blessing fresh and spontaneous
from her pure heart, gave joy to its loss and rapture to its
recovery. But in his heart there came and sat a wretched
pang when he thought of the rivulet of blood which jetted
from his father's breast and sang of death as it ran between himself and Cora; that rivulet, like an impassable
flood, over which no earthly sail could bear him to her
side.

CHAPTER XIV.

IT was Monday, the day succeeding the events recorded
toward the end of the last chapter. A summer evening's
rosy pomp clothed the sea-waters with a coat of color, and
gave to each ambitious wave a jeweled crest. As myriad
kings have risen in the earth, received their crowns, and
fallen back to dust, so these aspiring waves, towering,
were only jewel-capped in time to sink again into the
eternity of waters.

Cora Glencoe sat upon the Tarpeian Rock, her brave
dog at her feet, while the sea lapped the beach as though
its sands held everlasting and uncloying sweetness. In
a voice of touching melancholy she was singing "Beautiful Venice, the Bride of the Sea," and looking far away
to where the rim of waters joined the horizon. Where she
sat the celestial glow gave luster to the rich auburn of her
head. Her eyes were very dark, and thrilled with an
intense longing, as if she would fain go where she gazed
afar. Tears dew-dropped her lashes, and hung upon cheeks
as pure and fair as tinted porcelain. Her mouth was as
tender as the "there, then" of a young mother to her
first born. Lovely as imagination, she was equally sad
and bleak, in these the days of her early youth. Oswald
Huron—her strange father—filled her mind with dread,
and her bosom with almost every feeling but that of respect

or affection. Not that he abused her person; but his
mind was dark, his soul tempestuous, and his character
blemished and awry. She could not love him, and she
had no one else to love. She was famishing for life's
fragrance, and often, when alone, her heart would gush
with agony and pent affection, and she would give her
very dog those tender, fiery, and priceless bosom-caresses
which otherwise must waste upon the air. Cora had long
learned to think for herself, and in every glance of her
eyes there seemed to be a reckoning. She was writing
out, and adopting, a code to govern her through life. It
was founded in the religion taught by her venerable pastor,
Mr. Hope, and embodied her own ideas of right and
wrong. When it should be finished, she determined to
cling to it, let the world stray as it might. She was now
adding a new chapter; a chapter prompted and dictated
by the contents of the little book which she had picked
from the strand, and which revealed to her, or reminded
her of a phase not yet considered. If, before, she had
regarded her father with feelings akin to horror and
mingled with fear, she now saw him robed in the gloom
of the murderer, the man-slayer; and although she could
not doubt the truth of the indelible story which she had
read, at times she revolted against it with the very pathos
of protest, and endeavored to flee from a fact which she
could only contemplate with utter dismay and despair.
She even canvassed in her mind whether it was not her
Christian and ethical duty to cleave her existence forever
from that of her father, and go out into the world and
buffet for a new life. But she was restrained and bound
by a lingering hope that at some good hour and day he
would scourge himself, and cast out his evil nature. She
herself might conduce to that end. Cora's sorrow and
lamentation was vital, and would have consumed her had
it been mute; but she gave it voice, sobbing in her
chamber, crying to Heaven, or singing mournfully to the
heedless waves.

Looking down the strand, which lay between the bluffs
and the sea-line like a sanded street backed by the rude
walls of nature and fronting on a boundless waterscape,
she could see, some hundreds of yards away, the Geologist

and his hired man—O'Dare and Aiken—at work against the face of the rocks. She saw O'Dare quit the spot and start up the beach, leaving Aiken to continue his labor alone. He would soon pass her, and she had a curiosity and a desire to have a good look at him. The science of which he professed to be a practical student had often carried her mind down into the catacombs of the buried Ages. Her life was distressingly lonely, and, when not employed in domestic duties, she almost dreamed the hours away, by the shore, watching the water as it bolted the sands at her feet. As the sprig of mountain-sorrel, or the Alpine rose, carries the imagination to dizzy heights and snów-capped shafts, so the simplest shell washed up by the waves, plunged her thoughts away into the vast beds of the ocean, where they reveled in submarine scenery, with its couched grottoes, its hill places, and its plains, until Imagination snapped upon its stretch, and rose to the surface, impotent as the air-bubble.

As O'Dare was about to pass Cora, he, as if upon second thought, halted in front of her and addressed her thus,—

"Permit me, young miss, with the greatest respect, to greet you 'good-evening.'"

Cora looked at him mildly. His voice was kind, his appearance respectable, and his air reassuring. She answered,—

"I could not refuse so simple a request, accompanied as it is."

O'Dare bowed, and continued,—

"Do you not fear to go alone so much?"

In reply, Cora patted her dog on the head. He growled at the stranger.

"A faithful guard," said O'Dare, looking at the dog, "but not always a sufficient one."

"What have I to fear?" asked the young girl.

"Why, *me*," said O'Dare smiling, "in the absence of something more frightful."

"Why should I fear you?"

"You do not then take me to be crazy?"

"I regard Geology as a Science, not as a Lunacy, if you refer to your repute among us rustics."

"Neither do you take me to be dangerous?"

"Not from your appearance."

O'Dare drew from his breast a small, ivory-handled revolving pistol. It was a gem weapon.

"Do you see this?" asked he, holding it up.

"I do," said Cora, turning a shade paler than her wonted color. Then, with an expression of features which O'Dare could not interpret, she added with vehemence,—

"It is a *demon!*"

"True," said O'Dare, "and demons use it! therefore men are compelled to pit demon against demon."

"Rarely," was Cora's reply.

"You say you have nothing to fear, here and alone. What prevents me from killing you?"

"You are eccentric in your questions," said Cora. "But if there were no other restraint, absence of motive would prevent you."

"You answer well. Can you imagine anything worse than to be killed?"

"Yes."

"What is it?"

"To kill."

"Anything worse than that?"

"No."

"Your innocence puts you at fault."

"Is there a worse thing than the murderer?"

"Yes."

"What is it?"

"The *Spoiler*," said O'Dare, with deep emphasis.

"I do not discover your meaning," said Cora, after a moment's reflection.

"Have you read Shakspeare's works?"

"Yes."

"The whole of them?"

"Yes."

"Do you remember Tarquin?"

A sudden light was thrown upon O'Dare's meaning. The young girl said,—

"Please discontinue your catechism."

O'Dare tossed the pistol into Cora's lap. The dog sprang up to defend his mistress. The detective quickly took off his spectacles and fixed a brilliant, piercing eye upon him. With a deep growl the faithful animal crouched at Cora's side.

"I have disarmed myself," said O'Dare. "You now have both dog and demon. Permit me to speak to you as a man who especially knows the world. I have already done you a service by recalling to your mind the name of Tarquin. Let me tell you, Cora Glencoe, that every age has its Tarquins, and the present is prolific of them. You go too much alone; but if you *will* go alone, accept that demon which I have tossed into your lap, and carry it, for it may ward off a yet greater demon; such a one as Tarquin. Look what it will do;" saying which, he drew another pistol, a mate to the first, and directing Cora's eye to a small white blossom against the bluff, he raised his arm and fired. The bullet cut the stem of the flower and the bloom fell below. O'Dare went and picked it up, and stuck it in his button-hole. "I drop you some bullets here upon the sand. I would put them in your lap but for your mastiff. Keep your pistol dry, oil it now and then, and you will have no need to reload more than once a year. Do not, in your innocence, throw it away as the gift of a fool. Neither must you consider this the freak of an eccentric man, for I am in no sense eccentric, and have a matter-of-fact, steady, guiding reason for all my deliberate acts. At another time I may inform you why I took the liberty of accosting you, why I give you that pistol, and, as a sequence, why I urge and counsel you to acquaint yourself, without delay, with its use, and fail not to carry it, if you must needs go alone."

O'Dare bowed and walked away, leaving Cora to wonder at him. "Granted that he is mad," thought the young girl,—"he is at least methodical, and points his words with rationality." From looking at the pistol Cora began to handle it. She condemned its uses, but possessed no prejudices against either its material or its mechanism. As a concrete Ingenuity she regarded it as of almost matchless power, able, in the twinkling of an eye, to drive out the spirit from the body, and send it into the presence of God himself. She had never shot a pistol, but she knew how it was loaded, and how it was discharged. O'Dare's

words were not without effect upon her, and in recalling
the fate of Lucrece, she thought of the man—Jonas
Aiken—who but yesterday had stopped before her with
his evil face and repulsive address. But the more she
.became reconciled to the dangerous gem, the more was
she at a loss to conjecture the inquisitive interest of the
geologist in herself, and his singular mode of manifesting
it. The fact of its singularity, however, determined her
to carry the pistol in her dress-pocket when she went
alone. She already began to feel an accession of power
with the weapon in her hand, and at all events it would
serve to frighten if not to kill.

Had Cora's intimate friends (supposing that she had
such) urged her to carry a pistol, she would either have
considered them crazed, or disregarded them as jesting;
and a moment before O'Dare had tossed the pistol into her
lap she would have thought of carrying a cannon as soon.

Cora was now sixteen years of age, and had acquired
a complete common-school education. She had studied
well, having had nothing to consume her time or distract
her attention except the heartache, from which she fled
to her books, and to the shore, which was a ceaseless study
to her, as untiring as the waves themselves.

Oswald Huron, who was satisfied with his daughter's
progress, determined to take Cora from the Creswood
school, have her devote one year to history, and then send
her to some finishing institution, where she would be
enabled to see a little more of the world, and the kind of
people it contained, than would ever be seen at Creswood.
This determination was formed upon the suggestions of
Mr. Hope, who was probably the only person living to
whose advice Oswald Huron would so much as listen, or
to whom he would concede a single grain of disinterested
wisdom.

Cora was naturally elegant and lady-like. Her "style"
was pure and unaffected, and therefore correct and beautiful. What she needed was something beyond home
views, and home experience, and it was now essential to
her expansion that she should, for awhile, be cut loose
from the withes which bound her. She was preparing
herself to enter creditably whatever institution she might

be assigned to, and looked forward with some relief to the time when she should escape, for a season, the gloom of Cliff Hall. But there was no brightness in her future. To her the future seemed as a long vista, hedged and overhung with evergreen weepers, through which peered· the sad faces of the desolate, and each face bearing a mournful resemblance to her own.

Captain Gale had steadily watched for an opportunity of restoring Cora to her true parents. But he had never found the time at which he was satisfied that the evidence he possessed would be accepted as conclusive, or that it would not be combated by Oswald Huron with all the vigor of animosity and hate. He had altogether lost the polarity of Maria Guthrie, the most important witness, and did not know if she were alive or dead. Her affidavit, mere *ex-parte* testimony, would, in the handwriting of Lawyer May, breed suspicion. Amy Turnbolt's word, written or spoken, considering the relations existing between Captain Gale and Oswald Huron, would be subject to attack before any court of justice or equity. Toward Captain Gale, Oswald Huron had never relaxed a muscle or relented a thought, and the mariner wished, above all things, to guard against raising the question of Cora's parentage, and leaving it in a state of painful and maddening non-solution. Better let her remain as she was yet a little while longer than submit her to be torn to pieces by a controversy which he was satisfied would be as bitter as gall on the one hand, and, on the other, as wakeful as want,—the want of the true parents for the child of their blood. And so Captain Gale had put off the day of restoration from month to month, and from year to year. What was to strengthen his arm and equip him with greater power, he was unable to see, either near at hand or in the distance; but confiding in the justice of Heaven, and the inscrutable ways of Providence, he bowed submission to the fiat of circumstances, and compelled himself to be partly contented with endeavoring in his prayers to hasten up Providence a little, and precipitate the sequel of its unaccountable and mysterious ways.

It is time that the reader should be informed that Garland Hope, the young minister, was in love. The object of his fondest thoughts was a mild, celestial-looking girl, a young blonde of Creswood. Her name was Rebecca Ruthven. She was tender-eyed and affectionate, and returned the young minister's fondness with a discreet and gentle love which thoroughly satisfied him, for the present. Her father was dead. She lived with her mother and her grandfather, and attended the school of which Garland was the head. He took especial pains in educating her, and she repaid his prospective care by assiduous study, modest ambition, and anon a tender glance. She was an amiable, lovely, and precious girl, and Garland contemplated her expanding beauty and intelligence with a deep and happy calm, for he felt secure in her love, and there was neither rival nor bugbear to fright him in his dreams. His father commended his choice, except that he would rather have seen Garland and Cora Glencoe together, but did not interfere to make it so; and Rebecca's mother and grandfather regarded him as a well-girt Christian knight, under whose shield their daughter could safely shelter when they were laid in the grave. But Rebecca was quite young, and would not be ready for a year or more to submit herself to the manipulations of Matrimony. Garland, however, was content to wait, having no fear, and desiring firmly to establish himself, and count his temporal success as a stone already hewn and set, and not as one to be searched for in the quarry.

The Hope family had exercised a very salutary influence upon the community of Creswood. By their teaching and example they had given direction to the random thoughts and aspirations of the dwellers, and had bound many of them as a sheaf, ripe and fitted for the garner.

But there were a few strongholds which resisted all their Christian lances. Cliff Hall was one of them. Oswald Huron was regarded both by Garland and his father as beyond the influence of anything short of the death-bed, and, as likely as not, proof and stiff-necked even there would he be found.

Then there was Gale Island, which was but half redeemed. It had long been the heavenly ambition of old

Mr. Hope, who had delegated its consummation to his son, to bring Captain Gale into the church as an avowed and communing member. There was no reason to complain of Captain Gale's pecuniary fellowship, for he gave freely, and, in addition, volunteered sensible and timely suggestions in regard to the temporalities of the church ; but he neither broke bread nor drank wine at the table of the devout, and the reverend father and son, and many members of the church, felt an uncommon interest in the sure and prescribed salvation of a soul so worthy the strivings of the people of God.

But the resolute captain had peculiar notions of his own ; and so long as it was required of him to conform his views to the general, specific, and promulgated views of the church, he could not in conscience take the vows.

For instance, he did not believe that the human race is the issue of one man Adam and one woman Eve, and he stoutly maintained that Genesis does not teach any such doctrine.

Again, he did not believe in the universality of a world-submerging flood ; or, granted that it was all-submerging, there must have been a subsequent creation, he contended.

"Before the mast," said he, "when I was a youth, I sailed the world over. I have seen too much and many, to believe that all things now existing came out of Noah's Ark in embryo. In the Sandwich Islands I saw creation. In the South Pacific I saw creation. In other oceans I saw creation. How did it get there ? With a good ship, compass, and crew, and knowing that these islands existed, it was no summer day's sail to reach them. Human beings, the savages in occupancy, don't know how they got there themselves. It is possible that their ancestors *might* have made the voyage in some way now obsolete, and, in fact, absolutely unknown. But did they carry with them animals, beasts, birds, reptiles, insects, worms, and fresh-water fish ? If not, it is not an unreasonable question to ask 'how—did—these—things—get there ?' The simplest answer in my mind is, 'they were created on the spot.' Just as easy to create in one place as another. Some say that continental and marine convulsions scattered the land and water every way. If these islands were separated from continents and sent to sea, when did the convulsion occur? According to the universal, all-submerging theory, they could not have been sent to sea *before* the Deluge, or they too would have been deluged. Neither is it likely that they could have been convulsed away *since* the Deluge, for such a period would have been more memorable than the Deluge itself, and would have been the theme of Tradition down to the age of letters and statistics. Moreover, every continent from which an island was torn must have been restocked from Noah's Ark, or the fragments would have gone to sea destitute of creation; and such a convulsion, even at *this* teeming and prolific day, might tear many an island from many an uninhabited coast. I divide this question into three.

"One.—The Deluge was not universal.

"Two.—If it was, there was a subsequent creation.

"Three.—Is it not feasible that Deluge was accompanied by Convulsion, or Convulsion by Deluge, one causing the other, and scattering the hills and the waves abroad, and leaving the face of the earth about as it now is, with here and there its *nuclei* of life, each probably, like the man who ran away from the battle, reporting itself the sole survivor?

"But I leave the solution (as one not essential to salvation) to the time when Eternity shall enlighten us all. To the magnificent old Prophets I strike my flag, always. Coming still further down, the Sermon on the Mount is ample to save the world; and on an endeavor to imbibe its spirit I trust to get to heaven, church dogmas to the contrary notwithstanding. If," said Captain Gale to Mr. Hope, "you will cut your Temple from the solid Rock, I will sit with you therein. Let God be the Creator, Man the Sinner, Jesus Christ the Mediator, and His plain teachings the Guide, and I am with you. Put down all that is not plain, as distorted light, coming to us through a defective medium, the medium of human scribes and linguists."

The stanch captain continued to rest so calmly and meekly upon his simple faith, that the Hopes deemed it safer to leave him where he was, than, by attempting to force him forward, drive him backward.

Hector O'Dare, having got his man regularly to work, left Creswood. Jonas Aiken pecked away at the packed drift in the crevasse, day after day, and to all questions replied that he was digging for gold.

"Have you found any?"

"Yes."

"How much?"

"Two dollars a day and tools furnished."

Finally he was left alone to his hired endeavor to crack open the cliffs of the Larboard Strand.

We next find O'Dare in Cassel Rapid's room at the Boyd mansion. On a table he had spread a sheet of canvas, over which he and Cassel were bending.

"Do you recognize it?" asked O'Dare.

"Yes. Here is Gale Island; here is the path leading down to the beach; here lies the strand against the rock walls; and here is Cliff Hall. Where is your excavation?"

"Here," said O'Dare, putting his finger upon a cross in red ink. "It is about fifty yards from where the path comes down to the beach."

"Just as I would have it," said Cassel.

"You will find him armed to the teeth," said O'Dare.

"Just as I would have it again. And now, Mr. O'Dare, I have to thank you for a favor. The fact that I pay you for it takes nothing from it in my esteem."

"Mr. Rapid," said O'Dare, professionally, "I have simply obeyed instructions without asking questions. It is not for me legally to know your purposes. But, judging you by myself, and by every other *man*, I can anticipate what probably will soon be a startling sequence in that quiet neighborhood. If you come out of it alive, or whatever may transpire, I am, you will remember, not to be mixed up with it in any shape."

"You are, and shall be, free from all contagion which this matter may breed. But how much do I owe you?"

O'Dare named the sum.

"Permit me to double it?" suggested young Rapid. "I thought it would be at least five times as much."

"I never alter my figures," replied O'Dare. "I am

charging you only for my *time*, not for my conscience. The one can always be bought, the other is not for sale. But what I will not sell I sometimes give away. I have done so in your case. My conscience, speed, and wishes go with you, free of cost. As I said, he is armed to the teeth. He cannot fail to see your approach, and have ample time to surrender or fight. You never asked me to arrange for an assassination, nor would I have done it. Everything is calculated for a compulsory but open battle, as you desired. That is and was as much as Hector O'Dare could undertake. But I do not hesitate to empha- • size what you already know, that he deserves *no such consideration* as time, or opportunity, from *you*."

"Here is a check for the sum I owe you," said Cassel, not replying to O'Dare's unmistakable and friendly mean- ing, but observing, "I don't intend to commit you by say- ing a word."

"You are doing worse," said the detective, smiling. "You are checking me down in black and white. Never mind the check, but pay me in notes or coin when con- venient. I want no banker's books to record me for future reference."

When the detective took leave, he held out his hand to Cassel, saying,—

"Young man, I like you. When you return, come see me. Good-by; which, being interpreted, means 'God be with you.'"

Cassel shook hands with O'Dare, and the latter went his way.

Taking from a trunk a fine, solid, steel dagger, young Rapid went to the banking-house of Sarazzin & Sarazzin. Calling for Jepthah, the junior partner, he retired with him into a consultation-room. In ten minutes he came out, and returned to the Boyd mansion. Going through the house and the garden, he entered the stable, which was at the rear, and fronted on an alley. He went into a stall and met the salutation of his favorite horse with an affectionate patting on the neck and head. Manipulating the noble animal himself, he equipped him for a ride. In a few moments he was on the street, "a handsome Devil riding a pale horse with black mane and black feet"

In a couple of hours he returned to the stable, and
having groomed his steed, was going to the house through
the garden when Linda met him, and with enthusiasm
said,—

"Oh, brother, my flowers are so beautiful, and such
willing bloomers. Please come and look at them."

They went to the borders, and Cassel saw that his
selections had proven good, and that the plants had responded gratefully to the care which they had received.

Touching a delicate pink rose, a monthly, which was
• just opening, pure and fresh, he said,—

"Little sister, this is the color of your cheeks."

Linda blushed with modesty and pleasure.

"Oho," laughed Cassel, "now it is *this* one," and he
touched another rose of crimson hue. Then, turning to
her affectionately, he continued,—"There is but one thing
more beautiful and tempting than the rose's blush, and
that is, the rosy spray upon the modest cheek. But look
you here : see this one, half opened. Down in its heart is
a crimson glow. But down there also is the *worm*. It is
thus I treat all such," and with that terrible frown upon
his face he plucked out the worm and set his heel upon it.
"Let no spoiler get down into your heart, or it may
wither as that flower would have withered, and I shall
have to set my heel upon him as upon that canker-worm."

Cassel proceeded to give Linda a complete and affectionate lecture. At its close he asked,—

"Now, can you tell me why I am lecturing you?"

"Because you know I need it," said Linda.

"That is not the immediate and prime reason. It is
because I am going away."

Linda turned pale with instant agony and dismay.

"Now you are a Lily," said Cassel. "You have lost
all your color."

She burst into tears, and springing to his breast, clung
to him with the tenacity of want and affection.

"Ah," said she, while her young form shivered, "I shall
die. Please do not leave me, oh, my brother! Please do
not go away and leave me to perish of desolation! If you
need money, I have it. If you need a home, it is here.
If there is any one you love, bring her here and she shall

be my sister. But do not leave me, oh, my *brother*, please, *please* do not leave me !"

Putting his hands on each side of her wet face and lifting it up, Cassel said,—

"Your entreaty would melt a harder heart than mine. Charmed with it, I did not attempt to stop it. But do not waste another tear. I hope to be away only for a few days. There is now no place on earth so welcome to me as your pleasant lodge, hallowed as it is by my little sister's love. But you must learn to be more self-dependent. Do not look upon your brother as so essential. I have often told you that something might occur which would separate us forever. What then ?—You were kind and tender, but possibly not discreet, in offering to frank me through the world with your money and your home. You must know that I could not accept even *your* bounty. But I do not need money, for I have more of it than you have. But I do need a home, and it shall be with my little sister, until a stronger man comes and turns me out."

Linda looked into his face, with tear-drops on her cheeks and lashes, saying,—

"Oh, how dearly you rejoice me. You have led me out of the night into the day, and if you should leave me it would be night again. You have taught me, and I begin to see what a social heathen I have been. You have cared for me, and thought for me, and spent your time and patience on me, when so often I have been a shame to you in my ignorance, and you so competent for all the world. Why *is* it," asked Linda, realizing yet more fully the aptness of her question, "that you are so good to me ?"

"If I am good to you, it is because your innocence and rarity delight me, and your tender gratitude repays me." Over young Rapid's face now came an expression which Linda had never before seen there. Said he, "I am far more alone in the world than my little sister. I have no kin above the sod. No father to guide and restrain me. No mother to say my prayers for me, and kiss my brow. No brother to jostle my head upon the pillow. No— no——"

He stopped. With all his nerves of iron and dauntless

firm heart, young Rapid broke down. He turned away, and with his handkerchief dried the water which came from the depth of his heart to his eyes. Again turning to Linda, he said,—

"I do not go until to-morrow, and then you shall kiss me good-by."

He left her, and going to his room, locked himself in. Opening a trunk, he took out a pistol. It was empty. He loaded it carefully and returned it to its place. Next he withdrew a long lasso, and balanced it in his hand.

"I had better take this also," said he. "It may prevent an escape."

Opening his door, he stepped into the hall with the lasso in his hand, and whistled. Presently a dog came up the stairs at the far end of the hall and frisked up to him. With a stern chiding he stamped upon the floor, and the dog scampered away. Cassel wielded the lasso and sent it like a flying serpent along the hall. Just as the dog reached the head of the descending stairs the looped coil of the lasso dropped upon his neck, and brought him to a frightened halt. Cassel coaxed him into renewed confidence, released him, and returned to his room, saying,—

"It is surer than either powder or steel."

On the next day Cassel called again upon Jepthah Sarazzin. The young Jew took him again into a consultation-room, and handed him a package. Cassel unrolled the package and took out the dagger which he had given to Jepthah the day before. A slip of paper, which had been wrapped about the dagger, he handed to Jepthah, and requested him to read from it. As Jepthah read, Cassel compared the manuscript with the engraving on the blade of the weapon.

"It is correct," said Cassel. "I hope you have encountered no risk?"

"None," said Jepthah, smiling. "I defy even O'Dare to trace it to me."

Within an hour Cassel Rapid had kissed Linda goodby and was on board of a vessel bound for the Chesapeake. Among the animals aboard was a pale stallion with black mane and black feet.

CHAPTER XV.

CAPTAIN GALE'S new boat had been successfully launched, and the bridal trip had been satisfactory ; and as the captain brought her for the first time under the shore of the island, his greeting, as he shouted to his wife who stood above, was,—

"*I—tell* you, Sallie, she's a spanker !"

It was very early in the morning when the new White-cap rode into the little harbor, and gracefully balanced upon the calm bosom of the miniature bay. The great quality of this little bay was, that, at the point where Captain Gale always moored his boat, the waters were self-adjusting. A storm from the sea might rush the mad waves against the island, and against the beach on either hand, but as they crowded into the mouths of the canals which formed the island they passed around the two sides of an immense horseshoe, and, their force well-nigh expended, met and mingled at the toe ; the effect of which was a regular, gentle heaving of the water which supported the vessel at anchor. Hence the real security of an apparently unsafe basin of water not over two hundred and fifty yards from an almost open sea.

Captain Gale came up to the cottage and gave his wife a kiss which smacked of vigor and enthusiasm.

"Sallie," asked he, "have you had breakfast?"

"No. I was just preparing it when one of the boys told me that you were in sight."

"Very good. And now, honey, if it will not be too much trouble, we will take breakfast on board the White-cap. The stomachs of my crew are as empty as a charity box. Here, Johnny, you and Carroll and Caddy come and help your mother. Look lively now, for after break-fast the island takes a pleasure cruise. I intend to carry everything to sea for half a day at least, even down to the dog. How is the cow, Sallie? I think I'll take her along too," added the quaint captain.

"John, you are just like a boy. You shall not disturb my cow, for her calf is but two days old."

Captain Gale laughed, cut the pigeon-wing a time or two, and went lightly down to the Whitecap.

"He hasn't been so frisky in ten years," said Mrs. Gale to herself. "But he always did delight in a nice boat, and I think he now has what he never had before,— just the kind of vessel to suit him."

After a hearty and merry breakfast, Gale Island, except the cow with her young calf, went to sea, and did not return to its moorings until mid-day.

Early in the afternoon, when the shade of the cliffs began to encroach upon the beach and make it a pleasant promenade, Captain Gale went, for a walk, upon the Larboard Strand. Coming to where Jonas Aiken was at work, he said,—

"Well, Aiken, I'm glad to see you so industrious."

"Getting good pay," was the answer, accompanied by an unpleasant laugh.

Captain Gale continued his promenade until he came upon Cora Glencoe, sitting in her accustomed seat upon the Tarpeian Rock. Cora saw him coming, and knowing him to be the author of the little book she had read and restored to its owner, and recognizing in its authorship the spirit of a just, good, charitable, and generous-hearted man, she got down from her seat and went out to meet him.

"Captain Gale," said she, "will you not give me your hand?" at the same time offering hers.

"Certainly, my little dear, and my heart also," answered he, while into his bold face came a look of compassion and gentleness.

"Can we not be friends?" she asked very sweetly, and almost beseechingly.

"I have always been your friend, you little lamb, and ever expect to be."

Cora looked up into his face with an intense longing. How desolate must she have been to be seeking friends upon the highway! But here was a man whose sturdy strength and integrity was a bulwark to himself and to his family; a man of stout virtues, whom she had continually passed by, without deigning to look at him. Duty, repentance, and appreciation, the fruits of a recent revelation, now taught her, in defiance of her father's expressed will, to seek both his forgiveness and affection. Cora was careful not to cross the will of her father, unless that will degenerated into a whim which crossed her own fixed conceptions of right and duty; but, although Oswald Huron boasted that he ruled the land, upon occasion, when he roused the unconquerable spirit of the queen eagle in the breast of Cora Glencoe, she stood before his fury as dauntless as death and inflexible as marble, denying his right, and with her calm, dark, desperate eyes, defying his power and usurpations. As Captain Gale looked down into Cora's face, unsullied except by care and sadness, he was almost tempted to take her in his arms, carry her to the island, and fortify it against the thunderbolts of Cliff Hall. Instead of this extreme measure, however, he adopted the milder measures of his compassion, which urged him to partly anticipate that which he hoped and trusted would be the young girl's eventual history.

"Cora," asked he, "do you believe me to be a truthful man?"

"I do, thoroughly," she answered.

"Should I assure you of something, which, to your mind and inexperience, would appear vague, almost impossible, and beyond comprehension, would you believe it?"

"If reason could accept it, or conjecture account for it, I should believe it. Otherwise, I might think you mistaken; nothing more."

"A very discreet reply," said Captain Gale. "What I am going to tell you is in the nature of a prophecy. What you require to believe and trust in it is, faith in my word, and faith in the beneficence of Providence. I know that you are not happy as other children are happy; and I know the reason why. Now listen to me, and remember what I tell you. Just as well as I know that you are not happy, I also know that it will not be forever,—before you are fully grown, perhaps, until you *will* be happy, as other children are; and I also know the reason why. This

is strange language to you, and I hardly hope that you
will establish your undoubting faith upon it. But I tell
you of this as a thing to come, that your heart may be
encouraged; that you may cherish a hope through the
long days, and dream of it when you have said your
prayers, and pillowed your head for the night. I can give
you no glimpse of an explanation now, except that there
are some things which the old do not tell to the young
until the young grow older. My prophecy is not absolutely *certain* of fulfillment, but I can assure you that it is
as certain as that a young tree will grow if you plant it,
or that human affairs in the future will be a copy of human
affairs in the past. I am not volunteering an attempt to
cheer you for an hour, and disappoint you forever, but I
tell you a truth, not yet accomplished, but seeking and
nearing fulfillment, and bearing directly upon your destiny
and happiness. You cannot conjecture what will work,
or what will be, this change, but you can think of it, and
dream about it, and hope for it, and expect it; and let your
heart be lighter and your spirit less cast down. Let it be
your half-secret, as it now is my whole secret. Trust that
there are sunbeams across your pathway ahead of you,
and that you will yet overtake them. Trust in God,
and—the laws of your country," added the captain, not
altogether ineptly, or from force of habit. "That this
may be the last and freshest thing in your memory, I will
leave you to think of what I have said. Do not read any
more to-day, but think of all the wildest events in history
or fiction, of all which you may be able to collect from
your own brief experience, and if you choose, number this
strange but coming thing of which I tell you as among the
wildest, and, God willing, the happiest."

As Captain Gale returned home, he repeated to himself,
referring to Cora,—

"I think I have lodged some hope there."

For more than an hour Cora sat upon the Tarpeian
Rock, wondering and wildering. She had seen but little
of the world, and did not profess to know of it beyond her
native woods, except through elementary books. Reflecting, she began to imagine that she had altogether misconceived the world and the ways of it, and also the character

of that wisdom and insight which are the prerogative of age
and the fruit of experience. She had just been informed
by Captain Gale that there were some things which the
old did not tell to the young until the young grew older.
She had often seen old women shake their heads mysteriously and hint to younger persons that the time would
come when they "would know." Even Mr. Hope had put
her off at times by saying, " This is something which I
could not explain to you now. When you grow older, and
see more of the world, then you will comprehend it."
What could these inexplicable things be? Were they
secrets forbidden to be told by mortal tongues, but to be
whispered into her soul at some mystic moment and by
some mystic agency? Again, was the great world, away
from Creswood, so different actually from what she had
conceived it to be? There were reasons for her to think
so. The three most traveled persons of whom she knew,
to wit, Oswald Huron, who was a tourist,—the Geologist,
(O'Dare), who was an explorer,—and Captain Gale, who
was a mariner, were each in some sense incomprehensible;
while, in contrast, the common people of Creswood were
as fathomable as the primer-book of her childhood. Was
her father so strange in his ways because that he saw and
knew so far beyond her own limited scope? Was this the
reason why the Geologist appeared so eccentric and peculiar? Could she account in this way for Captain Gale's
extraordinary language? Was it the common property
of those who knew the great world, to comprehend and
daily deal with matters which to her were enigmas?
Where, then, was that fountain of which she could drink
and become as one who had been abroad in the earth? or
must she too go abroad? What was that thing of which
Captain Gale so earnestly spoke, which was to come to
her as a happy visitation, and be her own? Must she
indeed expect it and hope for it? Although her mind
caught at hope, it was occupied by a vague dread. She
began to feel that she was the focus of some concentering
event, which, notwithstanding it might bring Happiness,
would be forerun by Terror; the terror perhaps of a super-
natural Revelation. The reader will remember that Cora
was a little forest-bound girl, trained only by her old

14

pastor, and by him to perfect purity and simplicity of reasoning upon all the eventualities of life. But her imagination had carried her beyond her training-ground, and she was lost.

Wildering thus, she was just in that mental condition to see what she soon did see, in its most frightful aspect. She was startled from her meditative mazes by a savage cry which came up the strand from the direction of Gale Island. A pistol-shot accompanied the cry. Looking down the strand she was transfixed. She saw Jonas Aiken, fleet-footed as the hind, running up the beach toward her. Behind him, a rider upon a pale horse came like a rushing bolt. Three times she saw Jonas Aiken fire his pistol as he ran, then dash it to the sands and stretch away with all the speed of Panic. Onward came the pale horse, whose rider poised in the air that deadly serpent of the Southwestern Llanos, the terrible lasso; more deadly than the flying arrow or the hissing ball, and surer than the cheetah's spring or the silent drop of the treacherous boa. Cora knew not what it meant. She knew not what dread fate lay in the unerring hand, the cast, the looped coil, the wheeling of the steed, the dragging to earth, and the ruthless rasping of the flesh from the bones, at the whirlwind feet of the frantic speeding horse. But Jonas Aiken knew what it meant, and he knew the steel-blue eye that was upon him, and despairing of all other escape he ran into the sea and plunged beneath the waves. The rider dropped his lasso on the beach, and drawing a dagger whose sheen flashed into the eyes of Cora Glencoe, he rushed his horse into the shallow sea and caught the diving fugitive by the throat. Three times did Cora see that shining dagger lifted and driven to the hilt in the heart of Jonas Aiken, whose vile body was then spurned to the fishes. As the rider came out of the waves, without dismounting he plucked his lasso from the ground. As he recovered himself, Cora saw in his corrugated brow and glance of fire the very frenzy of retribution. Looking upon her for the first time where she sat upon the rock, in tones as stern as war he commanded,—

"Go *home*, you *sparrow!* the falcons of *Hell* are abroad!"

He then turned his steed away. Cora fainted, and lay as one dead upon the rock. Down the beach rode the horseman in an easy walk; up the path the pale horse clambered, and with a wild neigh plunged into the forest, and was seen no more.

Alternately her dog licked the face of his fainted mistress and howled desolation on the air, until he revived her. She came out of her swoon as from a dream of dismay. She saw her book resting where she had placed it upon a projecting ledge of the Tarpeian Rock. The strand was quiet and deserted: so quiet, it seemed impossible that but a few moments ago a swift and terrible action could have swept it. Was it indeed reality which she had looked upon? Or was it but the powerful supervening of Imagination, with its vivid, rioting, and lifelike images? She went home, not certain that she had seen anything actual, and barely satisfied that she had seen Captain Gale, and listened to his prophecy.

Captain Gale, after his conversation with Cora, had gone back to the island and seated himself upon the cottage portico, where he loved so well to sit. The cottage was too close, he would say, and the portico gave him plenty of breathing room in front.

Caddy Gale's morning voyage had made her sea-sick. She was in bed, and her mother was ministering to her and laughing at her for a landlubber. Sea-sickness rarely excites sympathy. Ridicule and banter appear to be the specific compound with which to overcome it or cast it out.

Carroll May was copying matter for a neighborhood attorney, who, if talent and legal acquisition were taken into account, should have been copying matter for Carroll.

Johnny Gale was making himself familiar with a new and full case of instruments, a concomitant to his adopted profession of civil engineering.

Captain Gale, upon the portico, at intervals looked up the Larboard Strand to where Cora continued to sit after he had left her. He would then let his eyes rest for a moment upon Jonas Aiken where he was at work. Then out to sea he would turn his gaze. Then down upon the

Starboard Strand, which was solitary and uninteresting. Thus he continued to employ himself for more than an hour. But it was getting almost time for him to have another look at the Whitecap, away from which he found it as uneasy to stay as a youth from his love. Rising, and taking a last glance up the beach, he saw Cora still upon the rock, and Jonas Aiken apparently hard at work. He then went down to the Whitecap, and taking a skiff, rowed twice around her, went on board, looked about, and in a dozen minutes was back in his accustomed seat upon the cottage portico. The neigh, as of a wild horse, came down the wind, which was blowing steadily and gently from north-by-west, and recalled the captain's attention to the beach. Jonas Aiken had disappeared. The howling of Cora's dog now caught the captain's ear, as it came faintly down the wind. Cora was not in sight, but he could see the suggestive motions of the dog, as he howled and then turned to lick the face of his prostrate mistress. Captain Gale was about to get his spy-glass and have a nearer view, but at this moment he saw Cora rise up, sit awhile, descend from her rock, and with her dog, walk slowly homeward. How he pitied her. Jonas Aiken was not yet in view, and the captain again turned his eyes seaward. The surface water was slowly moving southward from the action of the wind. The captain lighted his pipe. Tobacco was the beginning and the end of his dissipation; and he could see no harm in what ended in smoke. For half an hour or more he continued his leisurely puffs, when his attention was attracted by a couple of sharks, playing or contending about an object floating in the deep water in front of the island. Unmooring a skiff, he rowed out to investigate the floating object. Approaching it, he discovered that it was a human body. Coming upon it, he recognized the upturned, death-sealed countenance of Jonas Aiken. His nerves tingled with horror and amazement. The sharks, fearing to be deprived of their prey, became active. Captain Gale struck at them with an oar. They drew the body under, but it rose again within reach of Captain Gale's hand. He reached out for it. His hand met the handle of the dagger which yet remained in the breast of the dead man. He grasped it. One of the sharks struck the skiff with its tail, almost upsetting it. The heart of the dead relaxed its hold upon the dagger, and it drew out in the hand of Captain Gale, as, with urgent activity, he restored the equilibrium of his skiff. He threw the dagger in the bottom of the skiff, and renewed his attack upon the sharks. They, becoming savage, furiously assaulted the dead, bore the body away, struck it with bristling jaws, tore it to pieces, cutting and whizzing through the water with ravenous commotion, and finally disappearing in the depths, their prey devoured, or carried to their still home. A moment after the body had been carried below, Captain Gale saw something leap into the air, and, falling back again, rest upon the surface of the water. Securing it, he found it to be a large flask. It contained a few drops of whisky.

"This," said Captain Gale, "is what floated him so well. Is it possible that he has committed suicide? If so, how did he get to sea? But, no; such men as he never turn their daggers against themselves."

Captain Gale went upon the beach where Aiken had been at work. He saw nothing there but the tools of the laborer, his dinner-bucket, and the belt and holster of his pistol. Walking up the strand, he discovered the pistol where the fugitive had dashed it. Upon its handle he saw, roughly carved, "J. Aiken." It was empty, and four of the tubes bore marks of having been recently discharged. The two remaining tubes were probably discharged several days before. Captain Gale saw no tracks of any kind indicative of an encounter. Both pursuer and pursued had taken the edge of the water where the footing was firm and smooth, and the faint traces of their speed were soon bolted out by the busy waves. There were a few horse tracks where the horseman came upon and left the strand, but they were no uncommon signs there.

Captain Gale now possessed all the evidences and vestiges which had been left of the tragedy. Except Cora Glencoe, no one in Creswood had seen the pale horse come or go.

Captain Gale went back to the island, with dagger, pistol, belt and holster, dinner-bucket, flask, and tools, and
14*

startled the family by his consequent announcement. He gave an account of his contest with the sharks, their victory, his going upon the strand, what he found there, and ended by making a display of the articles which he had brought with him.

Caddy Gale forgot her sea-sickness entirely, and sprang out of bed fully restored and with eyes wide open.

The articles which Captain Gale had brought to the cottage were scrutinized, and turned over, and scrutinized again, until Carroll May discovered that the blade of the dagger was covered in an unusual manner with engraving. But before he could satisfy his curiosity, Captain Gale ordered,—

"Here, boys, give me those articles. They must be deposited with an officer of the law. You'll get them scattered about, and some of them lost, in all probability. I must put them away and let your curiosity have time to cool. Here, Carroll, give me that dagger; to-morrow you may decipher the engraving."

The boys reluctantly handed over the articles, and Captain Gale locked them up.

"Caddy," said Carroll, "I thought you were sick!"

"I was," answered Caddy, "but father gave me such a big dose of fright that I got well before I knew it."

CHAPTER XVI.

CARROLL MAY had seen just enough of the engraving upon the dagger which Captain Gale had withdrawn from the breast of Jonas Aiken to awaken an interest and foster a curiosity to examine it more completely.

Captain Gale, to all appearances, was going to be very leisurely, and very deliberate, in the ceremony of again exposing the articles which he had found to a further and more minute inspection.

On the following day, Carroll, who had been put off several times, and who was growing impatient, in a tone partly in earnest and partly in playful appeal, said to Mrs. Gale,—

"Ma, make Uncle Gale show me that dagger."

"Let him see the dagger, husband; he's not going to eat it," said Mrs. Gale, quietly.

"Now, Sallie," said Captain Gale, half in remonstrance, "if *you've* set sail in that quarter, I may as well shift my helm at once."

The lawlike captain regarded the articles as important for developing the mystery of Jonas Aiken's untimely end, and he wished to preserve them just as they were found, especially the dagger, for of the tragedy it was the central piece. Around its steel handle must have grasped the fingers of the person who had urged it on its deadly mission. In order to dispose of the issue, however, and possibly with the view of getting off a little of his quaint humor, he handed Carroll a key, saying,—

"Carroll, unlock that drawer; take out the dagger; set it up and look at it; look at it far; then look at it near; then reverse it, and look at it far and near; measure its length; measure its breadth; measure its diameter; measure its circumference; weigh it; copy the engraving; then give it back to me for evermore."

When Captain Gale got through enumerating, he was compelled to laugh heartily along with the others. He had always treated Carroll as his own son, reproving him, petting him, or scolding him, with the manner and emotions of a parent.

Carroll took the key of the drawer, inserted it in the lock, and slowly turned it, while he looked at Captain Gale with a roguish expression which reminded one of a headstrong, mischief-loving child, whose especial delight it was to half tease its parents and get a good-humored spanking.

He opened the drawer and picked up the dagger. With pen and ink he proceeded to copy the engraving, it being the object of particular interest with him. When he had finished transcribing, he replaced the dagger, locked the drawer, and returned the key to Captain Gale.

Carroll read over the words which he had written down with an intense interest which seemed to fascinate him.

"What is it?" asked Captain Gale, observing the countenance of the spell-bound youth.

"I hardly know," replied Carroll; "but it is a most extraordinary inscription."

"Read it," said Captain Gale.

Below, we give a fac-simile of the engraving on the dagger:

To the Lawgiver.
See Chapter 118, Section
17, Revised Statutes
of Maryland. See kin-
dred Sections in the
Penal Codes of other
States of the Union;
and ask of your
mother, wife, or
sister, *why*, a-
gainst these
Statutes, this
Dagger
dares to
write

T
e
k
e
l
.

"What can it mean?" asked Captain Gale, reaching for the copy. "Let's have a look at it, Carroll."

"Ma, shall I let him have it,—or make him wait until to-morrow morning?" laughed the youth.

"Give it to him, Carroll," said Mrs. Gale, smiling. "You know he relented just now in your favor."

"Relented!" exclaimed the husband. "I unconditionally backed out—as soon as you enlisted against me."

"And now you are as anxious to see what it is as Carroll was," retorted Mrs. Gale, merrily.

"Then it's the *first* time that my curiosity ever got ahead of yours—aha! ha! ha! h-a! h-a!" and Captain Gale roared as he had not done for six months, his wife and children bearing him good company.

While Captain Gale read over the copy, Carroll went to his own little room and brought out the Revised Statutes of Maryland.

"Uncle," said he, "please call off the chapter and section mentioned in the engraving; there must be some special design in the reference."

"Chapter one hundred and eighteen, section seventeen," responded Captain Gale.

Carroll turned to the chapter and section, and read rapidly to himself. A light broke upon his mind and gave direction to his conjectures. In a tone of some excitement, he said,—

"It does mean something, uncle. Here, read this."

Captain Gale took the law book and read the section referred to. He looked up into Corroll's face and exclaimed,—

"Aha! Here is matter for speculation. Carroll, in my blue chest, in the cabin of the Whitecap, I have the laws of Virginia, Maryland, Delaware, New Jersey, and New York. I always keep the laws of whatever coast I trade with. Bring them here. Here is the key. The chest is on the left—but never mind—that will not throw any additional light on this particular case, and I can compare the books at another time."

"What's all this lawing and fuss about?" asked Mrs. Gale, who had been quietly looking on.

"Belay your impatience, Sallie," said the old mariner, with wicked humor. "I don't intend that you shall get a rope's turn of this until it becomes dead stale. There's law for you—*lex talionis*," and the captain savagely shook his mane at his wife.

"This tragedy appears to me to be a farce," said Mrs. Gale. "I begin to suspect that it's all a hoax."

"No hoax to Jonas Aiken, I can tell you," replied the captain, "or to the man who killed him."

"Might it not have been a woman?" suggested Mrs. Gale, who sometimes, out of mischief, asserted the new-born rights and capabilities of her own sex.

"Since you mention it, Sallie, it might well have been a woman; better, probably, than a man."

"John, is the man really dead? or is this but a ghastly marine joke which you are attempting?"

"Dead without a doubt, and eaten up by the sharks under my own eye."

"Did the Black Oath have anything to do with it? You remember his father?" asked Mrs. Gale insinuatingly.

"Sallie, don't talk of things which you never went to sea and saw," said the captain, a little vexed.

"And couldn't see, if I should go to sea," replied Mrs. Gale, following up the mariner's style of expressing himself. "The fact is, then, that the dagger killed him,—is that it?"

"It came out of his breast," said Captain Gale. "I had no time to act as coroner, but I judge that the dagger, in the hands of some person unknown, caused his death. But what is this last word, Carroll, in your copy? You have blotted it almost out."

Carroll took the paper and looked at it.

"Uncle, it is so blotted I shall have to refer to the dagger."

Again taking out the weapon, Carroll looked at the blade, and, from the point of it, read,—

"*Tekel.*"

"Tekel?" echoed Captain Gale, somewhat at fault.

"Tekel?" said Johnny, reflectively.

"Tekel?" followed Caddy, at a loss.

"Tekel?" repeated Carroll. "I have both heard and seen the word—often."

"So have I," said Captain Gale.

"So have I," echoed Johnny.

"So have I," followed Caddy.

Mrs. Gale, who had held her peace, conscious that they were puzzled, said,—

"Well, I reckon it's *my* time to sail in, seeing that you are all aground;" and notwithstanding the subject was a grave one, she could not but laugh at their blank faces until the tears ran down her cheeks.

"What is it, Sallie?" asked Captain Gale.

"Now you belay *your* impatience," said Mrs. Gale, retorting upon the captain.

"Pshaw, Sallie! I know what it means, if I could only think of it."

"Yes,—but that's the trouble,—you can't think of it. I thought you told me you read your Bible."

"Come, honey," said the husband, with beseeching impatience, "if you know the meaning of it, let's have it. It is doubtless the key to the whole matter."

"Of course it is," replied Mrs. Gale, who was mistress of the predicament; "but before I furnish you the key, I must know what it is that you wish to unlock."

"Well, that's a fair compromise," admitted the captain, and he pointed her to the section of law which he and Carroll had been reading.

"Is this referred to on the dagger ?" she asked.

"Yes; and the kin law of all the other States. This is Maryland law."

"The meaning, then, is as plain as daylight. This man Aiken has been a *demon*," said Mrs. Gale.

"Ay, no doubt of it; but what does the word Tekel refer to ?"

Pointing to a wall of the room, Mrs. Gale, as if reading from the plaster, said,—

" Mene—Mene—Tekel—Upharsin."

It was now almost as familiar to the auditory as the Lord's Prayer.

"But why the single word, *Tekel?*" asked Captain Gale.

"Refer to the feast of Belshazzar and you will learn," answered Mrs. Gale.

"Caddy," said the captain, "bring me the Bible. Wife, where will I find Belshazzar ?"

"Look in Matthew," answered Mrs. Gale, with secret mischief.

"Sallie, don't make me out more of a heathen than Belshazzar himself. I know it's not in the New Testament."

"Look, then, in Daniel," said Mrs. Gale, laughing merrily at being foiled in the perpetration of so glaring a joke.

Captain Gale turned to Daniel, and finally to Chapter V.

" Belshazzar's Impious Feast." ❥

Verse 1. "Belshazzar the king made a great feast to a thousand of his lords, and drank wine before the thousand."

Verse 5. "In the same hour came forth fingers of a man's hand, and wrote over against the candlestick upon the plaster of the wall of the king's palace: and the king saw the part of the hand that wrote."

Verse 8. "Then came in all the king's wise men: but they could not read the writing, nor make known to the king the interpretation thereof."

Verse 13. "Then was Daniel brought in before the king." * * * * * * *

Verse 17. "Then Daniel answered and said before the king," * * * * * * *

Verse 25. "And this is the writing that was written, MENE, MENE, TEKEL, UPHARSIN."

Verse 26. "This is the interpretation of the thing: MENE; God hath numbered thy kingdom and finished it."

Verse 27. "TEKEL; *Thou art weighed in the balances, and art found wanting.*"

"Now you see what points the dagger," said Mrs. Gale.

"Carroll," said the captain, laying aside the Bible, "go down to the Whitecap and bring me those law books I mentioned. This is a subject to which I have heretofore given very little attention."

When Carroll brought the books, Captain Gale notified the young people that their presence just then was not needed. Turning to particular sections of law in each State code, he glanced through them and pointed them out to his wife, observing,—

"These are the kindred laws referred to by the engraving on the dagger."

Mrs. Gale read.

"And most pusillanimous, *unmanly* laws they are," said she, her soft brown, motherly eyes flashing. "This is the interpretation of the thing, John Gale. The dagger *challenges* the sufficiency of these laws—and so do *I.* Jonas Aiken has polluted some helpless, innocent girl, you may depend. He has suffered death for it; and I, for one, say, may the hand *live* that drove the dagger."

"Wife! wife!" remonstrated Captain Gale.

"I *say* it," cried Mrs. Gale with fiery vim; "and I'll say it on my dying bed,—may the hand *live* that drove the dagger. Now, Captain Gale, granted that we interpret this engraving correctly, and suppose that it had been Caddy,—what would *you* have done?"

"Wife, do not ask me such a question."

"I *know* what you would have done, you lion. And I say shame upon *any* man who, for the honor and purity of his house, would not drive daggers and give the Spoiler to the fowls of the air and the fishes of the sea."

"But why be so excited, Sallie?"

"Excited! Hasn't this villain been within reach of Caddy and Cora Glencoe, ever since the day he set his foot in Creswood? That very blade may have saved us from infinite shame and heart-rending,—and you from doing you know not what, unless what has been done."

"But how know you," asked Captain Gale, "that the inscription on the dagger has any reference to Jonas Aiken?"

"It proves itself," answered the shrewd and consecutive little woman. "What murderer leaves his knife behind to track him up and bring him to the gallows? No. That dagger was driven by some gallant arm, and left as a testimonial that at least *one* dauntless soul dared to retribute the purity of his house, and deal death for deathless pollution. What if it *is* against the laws? What are such laws as these to the ruined girl, the parents, the kindred, the friends? They are but a farce,—and an *invitation* instead of a terror to such men as Jonas Aiken."

Captain Gale subsided. To rid himself of all responsibility, he would hand over to the proper authorities the articles he had collected, tell what he knew, and there let the matter rest.

The death of Jonas Aiken created no sorrow in any breast. It was regarded as a neighborhood wonder, but not as a neighborhood calamity. Cora Glencoe was the only witness of the deed which hurled his soul to judgment; and for many months she did not tell to any one what she had seen. Her father was a man-slayer. Him she could not approach upon a subject of blood; for his present was overclouded and fitful enough without rousing him to memories of the past. For a long time Cora did not go upon the strand, but remained at home, and saw no one but Oswald Huron and the servants. Before she again appeared where she might communicate with the little world about her, the event of Aiken's death had become stale. Imagining, if at so late a day she should come forward with an account of the tragedy, that she would not be credited, and that it would do no good, she held her peace. She had been so dismayed at the time, that she could at best have given but an imperfect idea of what had occurred. She could not have described either the horse or horseman, though each was a marked figure; and could only have testified that she had seen one man kill another. She shrank from being dragged before a goggle-eyed public, simply to tell (what everybody knew) that a man had been killed, and that somebody had killed him.

Such were the views of artless Cora Glencoe. An inquest, or a prosecuting attorney, might have held differently.

CHAPTER XVII.

PROBABLY every coast is more or less infected with salt-water notions and superstitions. The reader may have discovered that Creswood was not in this respect an exception.

It is not astonishing, then,—when it became generally known that Captain Gale, a man of undoubted veracity, had seen Jonas Aiken alive and at work, and, half an hour after, had seen him unaccountably dead and at sea, with a strange dagger in his breast,—that a cloud of superstition swept through Creswood, and rested here and there in many minds.

The elders remembered Jonas Aiken's father, and how, when the land would not punish him for his wickedness, the sea drew him out upon its bosom, took his life, and heaved his corpse upon the shore.

The wonder-weavers, therefore, found it easy to connect the fate of the son with that of the father,—doubting not that the son had inherited, with its curse, the mantle of the father,—doubting not that he had himself been guilty of distinct crimes,—and doubting not that the mysterious genius of the ocean, exasperated at the tardiness of the shore, had caught the doomed man from the very beach, struck him, and left, in the life-seat of the wretch, the unmistakable arraignment of the laws of *Terra Firma,* " Thou art weighed in the balances, and art found wanting."

The wonder-weavers, in their own social sphere, were masters of the mystery, and would probably continue so to be,—until the mystery should be dissolved.

Amy Turnbolt presented herself before Captain Gale, who was sitting in his accustomed seat upon the cottage portico. The captain was impatient to get to sea, but was detained as a witness in a legal investigation of the singular fate of Jonas Aiken, which investigation was appointed to commence on the following day, before a primary tribunal of the neighborhood. There had been no inquest, and, as events were so rare in Creswood, it was determined by those who hungered and thirsted after *sensations*, to have a public powwow in honor of this doubly interesting incident of death and mystery. And it was determined that the powwow should be a *legal* powwow, so that all possible elements should be enlisted to make the occasion one to be remembered after it had been enjoyed. The investigation done with, and knots of wise heads having unknotted the knotty question, the snowy sails of the spanking Whitecap would court the breeze without more delay.

"Uncle John," said Amy, as she appeared before Captain Gale, " I've got in a good humor."

Amy, in the past, had married a man by the name of Bowden, against the remonstrances of her uncle. Bowden, who proved to be a harmless, good-for-nothing sort of a fellow, had died of cholera. Amy had again been received and cared for at the island; but as she was subject to fits of cattishness, she had occasionally gone off in ill humor, vowing never to return to the island again. Her uncle had habitually told her that when she got in a good humor she could come back. Her experience down among the huts, as landlady, had pretty well cured her of her resolutions to paddle her own canoe; and she had returned to the island in a more humble and accommodating state of mind than on any previous occasion. Captain Gale welcomed her, and merely observed,—

"I am glad of it, Amy. Go in and tell Sallie, so that she can assign you a room as of old."

"But, uncle, I have something to say to you first."

"Very well. Let's hear it."

"It's about the Jonas Aiken matter. You know he's been boarding with me, until I turned him off. Several other men have been boarding with me also, and they are down at the huts now. Last night I heard two of them in conversation. I listened, and found out that they were talking about you and Jonas Aiken. They agreed to get up a report that I had turned Jonas Aiken out, and he had threatened to drive me out of the huts, and that you had on that account killed him. They are to take some rascal of a lawyer in with them, throw suspicion on you, and force you to give them hush-money, or force you, in order to clear your own skirts, to direct suspicion somewhere or anywhere that will give them a chance of squeezing out hush-money,—they professing to act as Aiken's friends. They said that most any man would pay a hundred dollars or so, if suspected, to have the matter dropped; and that one such payment would give them a hold to which they would hang, as long as it could be made to pay. I am not certain which of the men it was, or what lawyer they were going to take in co-hoot with them; but you can look out for something of the sort."

Captain Gale smiled with a disdainful confidence. He, who for more than a quarter of a century had been the umpire of order and legitimacy, and the appeal of his neighbors,—to be blackmailed by some villainous attorney and a couple of unsubstantial conspirators! He merely observed,—

"You are right, Amy, to tell me of this, but don't you be uneasy on my account. You need not say anything about it to Sallie until this judicial inquiry is over, which will be by to-morrow evening, for she might conjure up a bugaboo. I do not know of any lawyer in this neighborhood who would undertake to conduct such an enterprise, unless it should be that lank pettifogger who rides the lank nag known throughout the county as 'Famine.' But if he can make something out of nothing, he has improved amazingly since I last heard of him."

Captain Gale, in his secret thoughts, gave Oswald Huron credit for conceiving the plan, and organizing the meditated attack upon him. Whether the captain was right or wrong we are unable to say, but we do know that he felt firm, and even saucy, in his integrity.

On the following day Captain Gale was prompt to respond to the summons of Justice. Carroll May went with him, and before the investigation was fairly begun, the affair assumed somewhat the courtly aspect of plaintiff and defendant; the rogues of whom Amy Turnbolt had spoken being plaintiffs,—and Captain Gale being defendant, and at the same time, witness.

The captain told what he knew,—neither more, neither less. A number of questions were then asked and clearly answered, during which the rider of the nag "Famine" was conspicuous as an interested party. He appeared in behalf of the dead and the friends of the dead, and succeeded in creating an impression that there was something to be developed, and that he was the person capable and engaged to develop it. With much ado about preliminaries and precedents, he instituted a cross-examination, in which it was his intention to get Captain Gale upon his hook, and in which, as the reader will discover from a few of his questions and the replies elicited, he displayed extraordinary research, tact, and shrewdness.

It is not on account of any intrinsic merit in the following little comedy, however, that we are induced to include it; but for the purpose of introducing, without recommendation, the rider of "Famine,"—otherwise Mr. Attorney,—who will appear again before this history is written to the end.

Assuming that impressive and penetrating air which a certain school of lack-brain attorneys habitually affect with the view of befooling fools and imposing upon wiser men than themselves, Mr. Attorney very pointedly asked of Captain Gale,—

"You say you drew that dagger from Jonas Aiken's breast?"

"Yes."

15*

"Maybe you can inform the court who stuck it there ?"
"No."

"You say he was floating on the sea, half an hour after
the murder ?"

"I said nothing about murder."

"Do you deny that it was a murder ?"

"No."

"Very well. Now what made him float so soon after
being killed ?"

"You can answer your own question. I have already
given my theory about the loss of blood, the large empty
flask, etc."

"You say he had his coat on ?"

"Yes."

"Now is it customary, in the heat of summer, for men
at hard work to wear their coats ?"   .

"It is a prudent habit with laborers, while resting, to
throw on their coats if they are perspiring freely and the
wind is blowing."

It was evident that Mr. Attorney's object was to entrap
Captain Gale into an inconsistency, and throw doubt and
suspicion upon his testimony, and upon himself.

"You say there were a few horse tracks upon the
beach ?"

"Yes."

"Are horse tracks common, or are they singular, to the
Larboard Strand ?"

"They are a common mark there when wind or water
does not wear or wash them out."

"Is the strand a thoroughfare, a drive, a resort for
animals, or what ?"

"It is a watering-place."

"Aha ! Animals drink salt water, do they ?" demanded
the attorney, brightening.

"Not unless backed by an attorney."

The court was compelled to cry "order, order."   .

"How then is it a watering-place, hey ?" persisted Mr.
Attorney, who was not willing to let go what he conceived to be a "holt."

"It is not uncommon," said Captain Gale, "for well-
kept horses to be brought there and washed in the sea.

Hence, for your sole comprehension, the tracks. A little salt wash, and a little rubbing of the hair backwards, would doubtless help that nag Famine of yours, Mr. Attorney."

A roar of laughter again elicited the cry of "order, order," and Mr. Attorney, thus reinforced, with a very piercing and mysterious eye, asked,—

"Captain Gale, are you the sole witness in this affair?"

"So far as I know."

"Aha! Have you any suspicions of the guilty party?"

"None."

"You suspect *no one?*"

"No one, or no dozen."

"No person or persons whatever?" persisted the attorney

"No man, woman, or child; no men, women, or children."

"Have you *heard* any suspicions expressed?"

"No."

"Have you heard or do you know of anything which might *lead* to a suspicion?"

Captain Gale was well aware that he was answering unauthorized questions, but he nevertheless replied,—

"I never attempt to hunt for a needle in a hay-stack, unless I first know that the needle is *in* the hay-stack. But as you urge me to express an opinion, and direct suspicion to some quarter, I am free to say that I know of no one more likely to have done the deed than yourself."

Mr. Attorney bristled up.

"I submit to the court that the witness, in his reply, makes a clean shift."

"And I," said Captain Gale, "with due respect to the court, submit that the attorney needs a clean shirt."

Another roar of laughter was pronounced out of order.

"I challenge the action of witness in evading questions," said the attorney in great wrath.

"I challenge the right of attorney to ask such questions," replied Captain Gale, smiling at the court.

"I demand the right of a licensed attorney!"

"I demand an exhibition of Mr. Attorney's license," was the reply.

Mr. Attorney could not produce his license.

"And I adjourn court," said the justice, who was satisfied that the time for adjournment had arrived.

In the character of witness, Captain Gale may have
appeared flippant to the reader; but by those who knew
the rider of Famine, and who were present during the judicial proceedings, the captain, in both word and manner,
was considered appropriate, rosy, and quaintly gay.

The captain himself came out of the court-room laughing heartily, the court arming him and laughing also.

"Hoo-ray for Captain Gale!" cried a number of appreciative urchins who had gathered about him.

"Hush,—you little spankers!" good-humoredly remonstrated the captain.

As they walked along, the mariner said to the justice,—

"Squire, I risked the clemency of the court in order to
give that rascally attorney his deserts; for he is a rascal,
be assured. I could not forbear touching him on his nag
Famine. She is known the county over, and is a standing, or rather a staggering, accusation against him. Then
his shirt," continued the captain merrily, "was an insult
to the purity of the bench."

"I own," said the justice, "that I was somewhat
surprised at you, for in all matters pertaining to law, you
have the reputation of being as sedate and methodical as
law itself. In fact, Gale," continued the justice jocosely,
"I have been told that your very dreams are lawful. I
would have restricted Mr. Attorney to legitimate grounds,
but seeing that you were getting the best of it, and the
bench being amused withal, I gave unusual latitude to
the proceedings. But I want a little advice. You are
the only person who knows, originally, anything about
this matter. What would you counsel me to do?"

"What *can* you do? The man has been killed, and
the sharks have held an inquest. Beyond this there is
not a spark of light. The dagger, in my opinion, ex-
plains *why* the killing was done. But you are not called
upon to do this or that, or to say yea or nay. The case
dismisses itself for lack of evidence; leaving no ground
for the commitment or indictment of anybody."

Nothing more was attempted by the authorities to clear
up the mystery of Jonas Aiken's death, or to discover

who slew him. The intelligent portion of the community doubted not that the dagger told a true tale; a tale which we hear almost every day,—that of some defenseless girl shrieking in the polluting grasp of the Spoiler, and of an outraged kinsman, friend, or commune, dealing out merited and thrice merited death. The insufficient law which commissions justice to use the sword's flat, merely, where its double edge should cut and cleave, is met daily from some quarter of this land by the stern *Tekel* of the single-handed Retributor, or by the righteous fury of a mob, and few there be who are so mean and spiritless as not to say amen.

It would seem, with some exceptions, when men become legislators, that eagles are turned vultures. That the manly and chivalrous sentiments of the free and knightly citizen are suspended in the legislator. That roaring like lions when stalking for votes, means acting like jackals when assembled around the public carcass. What man could, without shame and confusion, look his wife, or his daughter, or his love, in the face and say, "I have voted for a law which sets a price upon your purity and chastity? I have made the robbery of your purity equivalent to the theft of a horse, and the violation of your chastity equivalent to the violation of a senseless revenue stamp !"

Captain Gale again wound his bugle, and waked up the hills of Creswood with echoing melody.

The blast was promptly followed by the appearance of his crew, and the Whitecap was soon at sea..

CHAPTER XVIII.

GRAHAM HURON, son of Neville Huron, and brother of Cora Glencoe, came down from Philadelphia, on a visit to Cliff Hall. He had never seen his Uncle Oswald since the time when a little corpse was brought up from Creswood and lodged in the family vaults at Philadelphia; and he had not seen his sister Cora since she was an infant.

Neville Huron, who did not wish to permit a strict and
permanent alienation to become established between his
own and his brother's family, had suggested to Graham
that he might spend a few days or weeks very pleasantly
at Creswood with his cousin Cora, who was now almost
a grown young lady. The youth, who was by no means
unappreciative of the girls, and who would as soon toy
with a pretty cousin as a pretty anybody, was pleased
with the suggestion of his father, and without more delay
than is necessary to outfit a young gentleman of the city
and of the "period," was on his way to Creswood.

Graham was a fine-looking fellow, rather tall, with a
rich head, olive cheek, dark eyes, pleasant manners, and
finished collegiate education. He had no idea of the country cousin whom he was going to visit, and when he arrived at the Hall he was delightfully surprised by the lovely
girl who warmly received him and welcomed him to Creswood.

Cora was very glad to see Graham, and would have
been glad to see any one of his promise, male or female,
who stood in the relation of cousin.

The sepulchral atmosphere of Cliff Hall needed some
such visitation to change it into one of breathing, open,
sunny air, and give the place an appearance of life.

Oswald Huron was perfectly satisfied with the aspect,
tone, and manner of his nephew, and, from the beginning,
left Cora free to entertain him as she liked.

It required but a short time for an attachment to spring
up between Graham and Cora, and they were together
almost continually.

Oswald Huron regarded the fondness of the young people with complacency and growing interest, and finally
bethought him that his daughter could not do better than
to secure, in her wealthy and handsome cousin, a future
husband. He encouraged their ripening intimacy, and
even hinted to Cora the eligibility and aptitude of such
an arrangement. She answered him with a blush, and a
quiet look, which he interpreted as willingness and appro-
bation.

The young couple were out every day upon the strand,
in the forest, on the cliffs, and occasionally on a visit,

until the gossipers of Creswood openly connected their names as those of affianced lovers.

Gossipers are not always at fault, and in this instance they were certainly half correct if not wholly so; for Graham Huron soon learned to love Cora Glencoe as he would not have done had he known her to be his sister.

But with all his tact, and his experience with wary, fencing, and alluring belles, it was impossible for him to determine whether or not his affection was met by Cora's secret heart as he would have desired. Infinitely tender and attentive as his cousin, she seemed hedged by an impenetrable thicket whenever he would advance upon her as a lover on his lassie. She did not discourage him as one who was unwilling to cope with him, but as one who was altogether innocent of his designs, and ignorant of the battle which he vainly maneuvered to precipitate. If impetuously he assaulted her, with a sisterly air she artlessly disarmed him, appearing as unconscious the while as if he had invited her to take a glass of water. Graham was both piqued and headlong in love.

"If she does not love me," he would say to himself, "why is she so very, very tender, and so charmingly shy? If she does, why can I not surprise her into some betrayal of herself? What would the young fellows say if they knew that I had fallen in love with my country cousin, and wasn't able, with every opportunity, to read her mind? I could only tell them that if they would like to be bewitched, to come down to Cliff Hall. It is not Uncle Oswald who is the necromancer, but it is Cora who is the little witch. I am afraid to tell her plumply that I love her, for she would either be greatly shocked, or, what is worse, she would laugh at me."

There are very few girls—probably not any—situated and surrounded as Cora Glencoe had always been; cut off from the most of those things which attract the youthful mind, and develop the young heart; and too ready to lavish their soul's wealth upon the first object which promises at all;—there are very few, we say, who could or would withstand the manly onsets and loverly assiduities of a sensible, handsome, and elegant young person such as Graham Huron. Cora was in a very dangerous

situation.   Oswald Huron had already settled her destiny
in his own mind.   He saw that Graham was fascinated
by Cora, and doubted not that he was in love with·her.
He reflected that Graham had prolonged his visit much
beyond his originally set time, and that he would probably continue to prolong it until Cora had said him yea or
nay; and the father was determined that the daughter
should not say nay.   If necessary, he would make use of
all those wearing and despotic influences which the old
and crafty so well know how to bear upon the young and
guileless, and he did not even question his success.

Cora was just ready to form attachments.   She was
aged and conditioned to hail with eager joy anything
which would mark the beginning of a new and happier
era in her life.   What then was ·she likely to do,—what
could she do,—against the wishes of a willful father and
the entreaties of a fine young lover, combined?   Is it
strange if she gave her promise true, and surrendered the
castle of her heart?   Is it strange if she was captivated
with the vision of a new life, full of romance, variety, and
love, and cast in some beautiful spot, away from the gloomy
chambers of Cliff Hall?   Away from her father whom she
could not love, and away with her lover whom she could?

It was a beautiful summer evening in the latter part of
August, when Oswald Huron, with a small telescope, was
sitting at an east window of Cliff Hall, watching for the
moon to show itself above the crest of a hill which lay
between Cliff Hall and that part of the sea immediately
toward the east.   The sun had set, and dusk was gathering when the full moon rose slowly up from behind the
hill, and became visible at the window where Oswald
Huron waited.   From the time that the upper rim of the
orb appeared in view, until its lower rim rested for an instant on the hill-top as if the moon were balanced there,
he kept his glass upon it.   Though Oswald Huron, in his
temperament, was the very opposite of celestial, he was
fond of looking upon celestial phenomena; and though he
had, during a long series of observations, seen many remarkable things in the heavens,—as meteors, storms,
auroras, hazes, and eclipses,—he had never yet observed
upon the face of the moon so singular a phenomenon as

met his eye upon the evening in question, at the moment the moon was clearing the hill-top. In it, he saw distinctly a man and a woman,—standing, and facing each other; and so close together that their persons almost touched. They appeared to be gazing into each other's faces,—and conversing, as a slight gesture of the hand or movement of the person would indicate. They then to all appearances joined hands, and embraced; the head of the woman resting evidently upon the breast of the man; in which position they slowly sank into the depths out of which the moon was rising.

Forty yards to the right or left of Oswald Huron's position, an observer would have seen nothing but the ordinary, mild, and unobstructed visage of sweet Luna as she rose up to queen the Night.

Did Oswald Huron note this strange phenomenon, with the view of advising with some astronomical coterie? He did nothing of the kind. He smiled a smile of possible triumph, and rang for a servant. When the servant appeared, he asked,—

"Are Mr. Graham Huron and Miss Cora Glencoe in the house?"

"No, sir."

"How do you know they are not?"

"Tea has been waiting for them, sir; and I have been twice to their rooms, and to the parlor, to call them, and they are not there, sir."

"Where are they,—do you know?"

"They walked out upon the cliffs late this afternoon. I have not seen them since."

"You can go," said Oswald Huron, who stalked back and forth in his laboratory, saying to himself, "I will make even Cora and Graham believe that I am a necromancer, by telling them of what I saw in the moon." Then, after a little reflection, he continued, "No: I'll say nothing to them about it. It will be better to let them carry out my wishes of their own accord, and imagine that they are having the fun all to themselves. Lovers are said to be very fond of looking at the moon, ha, ha!— I wonder how these two would feel if they knew that I had caught them embracing in it!" and Oswald Huron

16

laughed as if the world were wagging to suit him. "Quite a romantic astronomical incident," said he; "and if I did not know Cora to be so stanch a little soul, it might be well for me to look after her."

When Graham and Cora returned to the Hall, their minds seemed preoccupied, and, while they took tea in the presence of a dining-room servant, very little passed between them.

On the next morning Graham was to return to Philadelphia. He would visit Creswood again in the autumn.

That night Cora and Graham went pensively to their pillows. Cora said to herself,—

"I wonder if Captain Gale meant *this*, when he assured me that happiness and content would come to me?"

CHAPTER XIX.

CAPTAIN GALE made a longer stay at sea than usual, when, for the first time, he put the new Whitecap into trading waters. As a preliminary he had to steer for a wholesale port and lay in an entire stock of fresh goods. Next, his vessel being larger and of greater capacity for the sea than any former Whitecap, he spent some time in enlarging the boundaries of his traffic.

Mrs. Gale had often urged her husband to quit the sea, as he was getting a little old and weatherbeaten, and was able to retire upon a competency. But the captain had striven for a boat which would fill the measure of his ambition; and having got it, he would now strive for a fortune which would put himself and his family above the ordinary wants which harass the human race. He would be independent in fortune as he had ever been in principle; and that he might be the more comfortably independent in principle, he aimed that his fortune should be large enough to bear, without serious detriment, those oft-recurring sacrifices which a strict adherence to principle fails not to demand. This was a worthy ambition in Captain Gale, and he had good reason to hope that in a very few years he would be able to compass it.

When he returned from his protracted cruise, his wife, who always became anxious when the Whitecap was tardy to return, asked,—

"Husband, where in the world have you been so long?"

"It would take half a day to tell you, Sallie," answered Captain Gale in the best of spirits; "but the boat does so well that I had a good mind to run her to Liverpool. She catches a breeze quicker than I could kiss a pretty woman," with which the buoyant captain took his wife in his arms and smacked his lips over her.

The next morning, as the thriving mariner sat upon his cottage portico, smoking his breakfast pipe, and calculating the profits of his next trip, Amy Turnbolt came to him and said,—

"Uncle Gale, I am so much relieved to have you back at the island again."

"Why, Amy, there's nothing wrong, is there?" asked the captain, who imagined that his niece had probably, during his absence, got into one of her tantrums.

"Nothing wrong here at the island,—but up at Cliff Hall I'm afraid there is, or will be."

"At Cliff Hall? What's the matter there?"

"Uncle, I have been very near to letting out the secret which I have kept so long. I've been almost crazy to tell it, and would have done so, but Aunt Sallie made me see that it was better to wait until you got back."

"But what is the matter?" asked Captain Gale, anxiously, and fearing that Oswald Huron had been guilty of some intemperate and outrageous act which had roused Amy's quick and willing ire; for Amy had always loved Cora from the time that she had been an infant, smiling like a little hooded cherub into nurse's face from nurse's lap. Amy felt as if she had almost as good a claim to Cora as anybody. In reply to her uncle's last question, she answered,—

"Uncle John,"—Amy sometimes said Uncle John, and at other times Uncle Gale,—"it is this. Cora Glencoe's brother, a very handsome young man, has been down to

Cliff Hall on a visit, and all Creswood says that they are in love with each other, and engaged to be married."

"May the great God prevent!" exclaimed Captain Gale, starting up. "Who would have anticipated such a fatal entanglement as this? But are you certain there is foundation for these rumors?"

"There undoubtedly is," answered Amy. "I have seen them together myself,—often,—among the cliffs, and on the strand, down by the Tarpeian Rock. This young Huron, her brother, is a splendid-looking fellow, and no girl that I know of in Creswood would turn her back to him."

"And Cora," said Captain Gale, "is too lovely to be passed by; and what is more against the purpose, she is tender-hearted, lonely, and famishing for some worthy object on which to lavish herself, and from which to claim a lavish return. Amy, the time *has come*," said Captain Gale; "whether these rumors are true or false, the time *has come:* for the longer this thing is delayed, the worse it gets. I have always regretted that I did not fight it out at the start."

"What are you going to do?" asked Amy.

"Have you the courage," asked Captain Gale, "to be firm and consistent in the fierce battle that will rage over Cora as soon as I throw up the first signal light?"

"If you will stand by me, uncle, I will have the courage to do anything for that little girl. I have loved her and bemoaned her almost as I would have done my own child if it had lived, for little Cora Glencoe has had a hard, hard life of it, and I am much to blame, and often feel so down-hearted when I see her darling sad eyes."

"Of course I will sustain you. And not only that, but Neville Huron, who is a different man from his brother, will sustain you. You will only have to make a confession, in court, and tell exactly the truth. You may be reprimanded, or even fined for misdemeanor, but you need not fear the reprimand, and I will pay the fine myself, in the event there should be any. The fault is mainly upon Maria Guthrie, she being a grown woman, and at that time a permanent member of the Cliff Hall household, and you but a thoughtless wild young girl, and only temporarily engaged with the family. Moreover, Maria Guthrie admits the fault as chiefly, if not entirely, her own, and has sworn to it in an affidavit which I now have ready to be produced upon occasion."

Captain Gale designed to so strengthen Amy that, notwithstanding her fear of Oswald Huron, and law benches, she might boldly proclaim the consistent truth, and fearlessly stick to it.

"I was a superstitious fool," said Amy, "and it is only within the last few years that I have got rid of my terror about Oswald Huron being a necromancer. I'm afraid of him yet,—that is, he might shoot me,—but even that would not frighten me like the old terror." And Amy laughed at her girlish dread of the Necromancer.

"Are the circumstances clear to your mind now? You will remember it has been fifteen years since," said Captain Gale.

"As clear as on the day after the accident."

"Let me hear you repeat them."

Amy did so, and Captain Gale continued:

"That is correct. And now, as a strict preliminary caution and injunction, let me impress upon you the importance of not discussing this matter with *any* person. When the news runs like escaped lighting through Creswood, a thousand tongues will be busy, and people will be running to you to know about it, and one will say that you stated *so*, and another one *thus*, until they will confront you with witnesses who will swear that you said everything that can be imagined. Do not say anything about it whatever, except to tell them that when the case is at the bar they may learn the facts from the evidence. You will have enough to do to keep your account straight when you are cross-examined, without having to encounter ten thousand things which you might be reported as having said elsewhere."

Amy promised to keep her mouth under lock and key. She then asked,—

"When will you commence, uncle?"

"For Cora's sake, I must wait until the last moment before the next session; for this matter will have to be adjusted by law, I am satisfied. It would be cruel to open the subject now, as Cora would be compelled to remain with Oswald Huron until her lineage was determined, she in the mean while not regarding him as her father."

"But how do you know that Oswald Huron will not give her up after he is told about it?"

"How do I know it? How do I know that the water buoys the boat, or that the hyena loves blood? It is his nature not to give her up. He would not yield her if he *knew* she was his brother's child, unless he should be the first to discover that fact. Out of deference to his own discovery, he might propose a restoration of the daughter to her parents, but he will abide no other person's discovery on this or on any other subject."

"Then what is she to do when the business begins?" asked Amy. "She will be in his power until some result is reached."

"I hardly know. I both feel and fear for her," said Captain Gale. "When Oswald Huron's mind becomes eclipsed by what he conceives to be a laudable spirit of personal vindication, it is bloody and strange, and halts at nothing; and I firmly believe that he would kill her, rather than be defeated and compelled to give her up."

"You will go to sea and return then before you attempt to do anything?"

"Yes. I shall probably have time to make a couple of cruises before the period for action."

"But what if her brother comes down to Creswood again while you are at sea?"

"That *is* a question to be considered," said Captain Gale, reflecting a few moments. He then continued : "If he does come, and you are not expecting me back when he arrives, go to Cora and tell her that Graham Huron is her brother. Tell it to her as coming from me, and she will the more readily believe it. At all events, bind her to keep it secret until I come."

"What if she will not believe me?"

"She will at least await my arrival. You do exactly as I tell you, and not a whit more."

Captain Gale again put to sea, steering in the path to fortune over a pathless deep.

Indian Summer, with its azure haze, its frosts and yellow leaves, was beginning to throw its dreamy spell upon tranquil Creswood, when Graham Huron made a second visit to Cliff Hall.

It was hardly time for the Whitecap to be expected at the island, and Amy Turnbolt grew very uneasy as she thought of the task which was set for her to do, in the making of her strange communication to Cora Glencoe. She put it off from day to day, fearing to go to Cliff Hall, and finding Cora attended by Graham whenever the young girl left the Hall for a walk or ramble.

A week thus passed, and Amy was getting to feel wretched, lest she should delay too long, suffer irretrievable wrong to result, and merit the stern censure of Captain Gale, and of her own conscience. She spent a great deal of her time upon the Larboard Strand, hoping to meet Cora unattended, but Graham was always in the way. Growing desperate, she determined to separate Cora from Graham the next time she should see them, and tell to Cora what she had been commissioned to say. The opportunity soon presented itself. About one o'clock one pleasant Indian Summer day, she saw Cora and Graham sitting upon the Tarpeian Rock, enjoying a picnic. Amy nerved herself and started up the strand. Ordinarily, she could have met either Cora or Graham without trepidation, but she now felt as if on an exhuming expedition, and she went forward with something like fear and trembling. She walked slowly, attempting to fix in her mind and on her tongue the exact words, and no more, with which she was charged; for the subject in hand was one of deep interest to Amy, and once fully open for discussion, would be exhaustive of nearly every word in her vocabulary. Irresolutely she approached the Tarpeian Rock, until Cora recognized and spoke to her. Graham bowed carelessly.

"We are taking a snack," said Cora to Amy. "Come and share with us."

"Thank you, Miss Cora, I am just from dinner. I came here to see *you*."

"Very well,—I am here, and at your service. What is it that you wish to see me about?"

"I have something to say to you," said Amy, glancing

at Graham in such a manner that he would have been
dull not to have understood her.

"I am *de trop*," said Graham, smiling at Cora as he
proceeded to get down from the rock and step apart.

"Now Amy,—or what must I call you?" asked the
young girl pleasantly.

"Call me Amy,—or Aunt Amy if you like, for I am old
enough to be your aunt."

"Well now, Aunt Amy, what can we do for each
other?" asked Cora very sweetly.

Amy felt like clasping Cora in her arms, and making a
clean breast of it. She glanced toward Graham to be
certain that he was out of ear-shot, for now was the
coveted time in which to make her revelation. But just
as she drew in a supply of breath upon which to begin,
she saw the Whitecap gracefully rounding the bluffs in
front of Cliff Hall and sweeping home to anchor.

"Bless me!" cried Amy, relieved and disappointed at
the same time; "there's Uncle Gale and the Whitecap."

"What a beautiful boat!" said Cora, as she watched the
Whitecap cleave the wave, "and oh, how I should like to
take a ride on it!"

Amy thought that she had never seen Cora so bright
and unfettered as at this moment. She said,—

"Uncle Gale would take you riding almost any time.
He gives us all a short trip down at the island whenever
he thinks we want it."

"I know he would take me," replied Cora, still watching the queenly Whitecap. "But what was it that you
wished to say to me?"

Amy hesitated whether to speak or wait and let her
uncle determine what should now be done. She decided
upon the latter course, and very prudently; for had she
ever opened her mouth, Cora would have won from her
everything that she knew, and perhaps more. But she
must answer Cora and account for requesting a private
interview; and not knowing better what to say, she replied,—

"It is something which Uncle Gale told me to tell to
you some time ago, but now that he has returned, it will
be best that he should tell you himself."

" That is not fair now, to make me curious and then leave me so," said Cora, coming as near to a pout as she ever did. It then flashed upon Cora's mind that this communication might have some connection with the prophecy which Captain Gale had vouchsafed her on a previous occasion, and she was impatient. " It is not fair now," she repeated. " Can't you tell me yourself?"

" I know it is not fair," said Amy, " but it is best. Uncle Gale will meet your curiosity more readily perhaps than I could, and satisfy it better." Rather hesitatingly, Amy asked a favor. " Miss Cora," said she, " will you please let me see your hand?"

Cora, who had been lunching with half fingers, pulled off a glove and extended to Amy a perfect model of a hand. Amy took it and kissed it.

" Now please let me see the other."

Cora extended her other hand, which Amy took, kissed likewise, and released.

" You are very kind," said Cora.

" I saw those little hands when they were not one-tenth so large,—and kissed them too," said Amy, losing a measure of her prudence.

" Did you, indeed?" exclaimed Cora brightly.

" Yes I did. I was your nurse once," added Amy, losing yet more of her prudence.

" Why, you dear woman," said Cora affectionately; " I did not know that. Come and let me kiss your brow."

Cora plunged headlong down into Amy's heart when she put her arms about her neck and kissed her, and smiled sweetly in her face, and kissed her impulsively and cutely again, and then pushed her playfully away, saying,—

" *There* now,—there's my love."

Amy would have died for Cora on the spot. Almost overcome with an emotion half maternal, she withdrew and went home. As soon as she could see her uncle privately, she told him what the reader already knows, adding from her secret gainings,—

" Uncle, I fear the mischief is partly accomplished. I asked to see her hands, and on one finger is a ring which looks new and bright, and for all the world to me like an engagement-ring."

"What does an engagement-ring look like?" asked Captain Gale, who did not pretend to be *au fait* in such matters.

"I don't exactly know, but this looked just like one to me," was the somewhat paradoxical reply, at which Captain Gale would have been inclined to smile, had he not been in too serious a mood. A very grave expression came upon the mariner's face, for there was a duty immediately before him, which, however painful and delicate it might be, was yet more dangerous than it was delicate or painful.

"You must tell her, uncle," said Amy.

"I intend to tell *him*," replied Captain Gale.

"Who,—Oswald Huron?"

"Yes; Oswald Huron."

Amy for a moment looked terrified; but she had so much confidence in the courage, discretion, oak-like firmness, and physical strength of her uncle, that her terror subsided into mere anxiety.

"When and how will you tell him?" she asked.

"I shall go up to Cliff Hall this afternoon, and tell him in plain English. I trust that nothing has transpired between Cora and Graham to make them regret their relationship when it shall be discovered to them."

"Cora is as pure as snow," said Amy.

"Pshaw!" said Captain Gale; "I am not speaking of her purity. I mean that it is to be hoped that the two young people have not suffered themselves to become lovers to such a degree as will make them unwilling or disappointed to be brother and sister."

"I believe they are already lovers," said Amy.

"In that event," said Captain Gale, "love's young dream must be rudely broken up. To know that they are brother and sister will serve to soften their disappointment, if not to displace it altogether."

"I hope you may come away in triumph and safety," said Amy, going into the cottage.

Captain Gale, after sitting and reflecting awhile, got up and went down to the Whitecap. Unlocking a chest, he took out a revolving pistol which he was accustomed to take to sea with him, where, upon one or two occasions,

he had found technical use for it in restoring discipline
during the panic of furious storms. But if ever a man
flinched or mutinied in time of peril, that was his last trip
on the Whitecap. Captain Gale could overlook or pardon
a little constitutional timidity, when the tempest roared,
and the air and sea were ablaze with fire, and the Ocean
Eagle went screaming and kiting through the lurid storm;
but he never forgave that dogged submission which, mingled with meanness, induced a man now and then to give
up, fold his hands in negative mutiny, and obstinately
refuse to do duty except under cover of a pistol tube.

CHAPTER XX.

It was late in the afternoon when Captain Gale walked
up the Larboard Strand on his way to Cliff Hall.

He had not been upon the premises for more than
twenty-five years, and would likely never go upon them
again.

He was better aware, probably, than any one, that he
had no ordinary man to meet, and no ordinary interview
to conduct.

He was sensible of the personal danger he was about
to encounter, but he could not delegate the interview to
any other, and would not.

As he walked up the strand, his usually resolute face
was doubly resolute with the determination to do his
duty, and to do it with such firmness and coolness as
would likely countervail the personal risk he would have
to dare, and carry convincing proof of the fact he was
about to reveal.

He found the Tarpeian Rock, which Cora so loved to
frequent, desolated of her sweet form and presence, and
he met no one in his way to Cliff Hall.

Nearing the mansion, a gloomy, ancestral looking pile,
he saw Oswald Huron standing in the main entrance,
which fronted to the south.

Oswald Huron, recognizing Captain Gale and his intention of entering the front gate, turned about, withdrew
into the building, and armed himself.

As Captain Gale approached the door, Oswald Huron
again appeared, coming along the hall, and confronting
the captain as the latter stepped upon the threshold.

The two men halted and looked at each other, as if, on
Oswald Huron's part, they were the only two men on
earth, and he did not know that the other existed until
that moment; and, on Captain Gale's part, as if he were
considering whether it was man or beast that confronted
him.

"An unsolicited honor," finally said Oswald Huron,
bowing to Captain Gale with freezing mock politeness.

"I come to offer you neither blandishments nor honors,"
calmly replied Captain Gale.

"Probably to make a *demand*," said Oswald Huron,
showing his white teeth.

"You owe me nothing, and if you did, I should hardly
trouble myself to come to you for it."

"You are here then to grant me a *favor*, possibly ?"
was the rejoinder, in which a little fierceness and a good
deal of sarcasm was mingled. He added, "I ask *none*,
sir."

"Mr. Huron," said the unmoved captain, "you might
question me for twelve months, and then conjecture for as
many more, and you would not even approach the cause
which brings me, consciously unwelcome, into your demesnes."

"Probably you will be so kind as to inform me, then,
before I invite you into my house," said Oswald Huron,
who, during the interview so far, was leaning forward towards his visitor, with one foot advanced, as if in the act
of springing or rushing upon him.

"I do not court an invitation into your house. You
can invite me in or not. If I should go in, it would be
solely on account of convenience to myself. I can perform my errand here."

"What is your errand, sir ?"

"It is one in which you are concerned ; not I. It
is one in which the interests are your own; not mine. I

am here, not from any anticipated pleasure, but from a sense of duty. Although I come not to dictate to you, you will do well to listen to me. And furthermore, to put myself upon a proper basis, I will tell you, Mr. Oswald Huron, plainly, that if *you* were the *only* person concerned I should not have come at all."

"Gale," said Oswald Huron, with a dash of humor, "I like your boldness. It entitles you to a seat at least. Therefore, if your errand involves any discussion, for the sake of convenience we will go in and be seated;" and he led the way, followed by the brave captain, into an ante-room, where each took a chair.

"Now, sir," said Oswald Huron, after they had settled themselves, "I am ready to listen to you."

"Mr. Huron," said Captian Gale, "it is hardly necessary for me to remind you that we have not for years regarded each other as friends."

"That is plain enough so far," was the reply.

"Nor is it for the purpose of courting your favor that I frankly admit and assert to you that I have as little desire to injure you as to befriend you."

"Gale, I am convinced that you are not afraid to speak the truth, and consequently I grant that you are sincere. Had I known you better sooner, we might have been better friends." This was said rather gracefully by the proprietor of Cliff Hall. "But I am waiting for your communication."

"What I am about to tell you," continued Captain Gale, "will not only surprise and amaze you, but it will stir you very deeply; and as I approach the subject, I wish to prepare you, only asking that you will endeavor to be calm, and bring your reason, not your temper, to bear upon it."

The countenance of Oswald Huron indicated that he was becoming interested. Captain Gale continued :

"When I have made to you a revelation of fact, which for years has been withheld from you, your first wonder or question might be, 'Why has it been so long withheld?' and your next, 'Why is it now revealed?' When I have told you what it is, I will then endeavor to abate your wonder and answer your questions."

17

Oswald Huron was becoming excited in spite of himself, and his efforts to maintain his calmness were commendable if not successful. The surest way to unhinge the nerves of a person is to mysteriously and portentously caution that person to keep his nerves on their hinges. This thing of preparing people for good or bad news is generally not a good, but a bad plan. It is like bleeding a patient to give the patient strength for a severer operation; like exercising a horse to the verge of fatigue preliminary to the straining race. Captain Gale, however, had properly conceived both the measure of his purpose and the mettle of his man. It was not the sensibilities of Oswald Huron about which he was solicitous, but the preservation of his reason and moderation. The captain kept his eye upon him as upon some doubtful and dangerous creature. Oswald Huron waited for the captain to proceed.

"Mr. Huron, there are some strange things in this world; and one of the very strangest, but as true as it is strange, is the fact, which I now announce to you, that Cora Glencoe is not your child, but the child of your brother Neville."

Captain Gale barely had time to deliver the words before Oswald Huron sprang up, and, with electric eye, grimly said,—

"You are a *liar !*"

Captain Gale had also risen, simultaneously with his adversary, for such he may be called.

"Oswald Huron," said the unruffled mariner, "in the performance of a duty and the expiation of a delinquency, I came prepared to ignore any insult which you might offer me. I also came prepared to defend myself against any violence you might unreasonably attempt upon me. But I wish to address your reason, not your passions. Take your seat now, and hear me. Then, if you consider me a liar, you shall be welcome to your consideration, so far as I am individually concerned."

Oswald Huron, glaring upon Captain Gale, slowly resumed his chair. There was but one circumstance which curbed him and fortified him with sufficient reason longer to listen. It was the well-remembered fact, which, at times, flitted through his mind, that he had never known the infant children one from the other ; and that, on the night he went out and gathered up the mangled remains of what he supposed to be his brother's child, a fearful doubt had swept into his soul, which was only allayed by the reflection that Maria Guthrie knew the infants, each from the other, and that she had assured him the surviving child was his own. When, therefore, he resumed his seat, it was with an undetermined mind, which suggested a mental inquiry as to the possibility of Captain Gale's truthfulness, and the scope of his information on the subject. Evidencing a reluctant willingness that Captain Gale should proceed, he listened to a minute detail of the circumstances surrounding the fact which bereft him of a daughter.

Up to this time, Captain Gale had only referred to the confessions of Amy Turnbolt. He then handed Oswald Huron the affidavit which Amy had made more than fifteen years ago, and but a short time after the calamity. Mr. Huron read the affidavit and passed it back. Captain Gale then informed him why the imposition had been practiced by the nurses, why the fraud was not sooner exposed, and why, in view of Cora's brother, he was compelled to make the revelation now. Oswald Huron, with all his fiery, sulphurous soul, was softened and partly convinced. Relenting, he asked, with evident sadness and concern,—

"Captain Gale, is this, *can* this be true?"

"Mr. Huron, I am as firmly convinced that it is true as that the sun shines to-day."

"Have you no other evidence than that of Amy Turnbolt? Aha!" he exclaimed, his eyes beginning to gleam; "what of the other nurse? What of Maria Guthrie?"

"Her evidence is to the same effect, and yet stronger, for she acknowledges the deception as one suggested and enforced by herself, Amy being constrained by her terror of you as a necromancer."

"Where is her evidence?" demanded Oswald Huron, who was becoming nervous with well-founded excitement.

"I have it here," answered Captain Gale, who drew out and delivered the affidavit of Maria Guthrie.

Oswald Huron took the paper and read it. A fierce

and sudden change came over him, and the very devil looked out from his countenance. He had recognized the handwriting of Lawyer May. He was about to tear the affidavit to pieces, when Captain Gale snatched it from his fingers. Springing up with uncontrollable fury, he shouted,—

"*Conspiracy!* It is a conspiracy from *hell!*"

He drew a formidable knife, with which he had armed himself when he first saw Captain Gale approaching his gate. Captain Gale prepared himself for a desperate encounter in the event that it could not be avoided. At this moment, Cora Glencoe, attracted by the unusual noise, and just returned from a ramble, came into the room, her hair loose flowing, and she in most lovely woodland deshabille. Oswald Huron, in his rage, seized her by the hair, and waved the glittering blade over her upturned face, with every indication of eye and hand that he would plunge it into her bosom. With the bound of a lion, Captain Gale was upon him instantly, and with a rugged strength which many years of peace had husbanded for war, he bore the madman to the floor. Cora was utterly confounded with amazement, fear, and horror. Graham Huron, attracted also by the noise, and led by a habit which he had of following up Cora wherever she went, appeared at the door while Captain Gale was struggling with Oswald Huron, and Cora standing by, pallid as wax. In his hand Graham held the gem pistol which Hector O'Dare had given to Cora, and with which he had been practicing in the forest. Not understanding the situation, and seeing a stranger pressing his uncle to the floor, and Cora standing by, mute with accumulating terror, he cocked his pistol and fired it at Captain Gale. But Cora struck the weapon up, and the ball passed into the opposite paneling.

"*Hold*, Graham,—my father is *mad!*" cried the young girl, vigorously interposing between the pistol and Captain Gale. Graham was perfectly bewildered, and suffered Cora to take possession of the pistol.

Captain Gale, with an outlay of all his strength, succeeded in mastering the bloody tiger who struggled with him. Disarming Oswald Huron of his dagger, and also

of a pistol which he had attempted to draw, Captain Gale
sternly said, addressing Graham,—

"Young man, take these weapons and put them beyond
the reach of this wild-hearted man ; and don't be so handy
with your pistol. See you this little girl ? She is your
sister ! Take her and protect her as such, until to-morrow, from this incarnate fury, who is *not* her father, and
who would murder her. · Woe to the Huron blood if you
do not heed my words."

Graham led Cora away. Captain Gale suffered Oswald
Huron to rise from the floor, standing meantime upon his
guard. Oswald Huron was merely checked, not changed.
Disarmed, he was compelled to submit to the sturdy
strength of his vanquisher, and to permit him to depart in
his own chosen way. Captain Gale left the premises
without saying a word. He knew it would be useless.
A prudential impulse caused him to stop at the gate, and
consider whether he had not better return into the house
and 'renew his cautions more distinctly and comprehen-
sively to Graham and Cora. But he had already been
forced to take more liberties with the premises and the
proprietor than was customary to be taken by one man
upon the fee-simple of another, and as it was growing
dark withal he determined to seek his home, and postpone
any further action until the morrow. It would have been
better if Captain Gale had increased his caution to the
young people, and convinced them that he was literal in
his meaning, for both Graham and Cora regarded his
words as tropic and hyperbolic, used in an extreme, and
not relating to their actual kinship, but to the exigency
which made it necessary for Graham to act as Cora's
brother in protecting her from an unnatural and murderous father. Although Captain Gale, upon reflection, was
sensible that such an interpretation might be applied to his
words, he trusted reasonably that no harm would result
before the morrow, from which time, with a relentless
activity, which, if necessary, would consign even the
Whitecap to worms and water-rot, he would prosecute
the cause of Cora Glencoe, until, for weal or woe, he could
say "it is finished." ˙ It was his intention first, to provide
in some way for Cora's safety and security from personal

danger, and then to start immediately for Philadelphia to confer with Neville Huron, whose buried paternal love, plucked from the ashes of the little sarcophagus which rested in the family vault, and resuscitated to the double glow which burns for one who was dear to the heart, and *was* dead, but liveth, would arm him with shield of brass and blade of magic, to battle with his tiger-hearted brother for the lost child of his loins.

CHAPTER XXI.

In a far room of Cliff Hall sat Cora Glencoe in the very acme of exquisite despair. She could not but regard her own father as a murderer, in act and intent. She knew that he had killed Lawyer May, years ago; and now, with her own eyes, she had seen his hand ready to strike the killing steel to her breast; and what was more terrible and sickening still, she had seen his eye gleam and glare upon her with a tragic light which was the unmistakable flash of the hell-fire that burned within him.

While she sat like a chained innocent in a wilderness of woe, Graham Huron came into the room, sat down quietly, and somewhat wearily said,—

"He is busily writing."

"Graham," said Cora, while she seemed almost to droop away from life, "I am as desolate as a lost soul."

Such words, coming from this brave little girl, who, from her infancy, had been trained to fast upon hardness and sorrow while looking upon softness and joy, and to famish with emptiness of heart while other hearts seemed full with plenty, meant that she was in the midst of the very abomination of desolation.

"Cora," said Graham, with a depth of feeling which shook his voice, "let me again tell you that you are dearer to me than all the earth. I cannot offer you all the earth, but I can give to you a world of love in some sweet spot, out and away from this gloomy cell; away where requiems shall be turned to songs of joy, and your memory soothed by the lotus leaf of love. Come with me, and cast your burdens here," and he touched his breast. "I have spoken to your father, and he has consented that you shall be mine. Of two things he is one,—a madman or a fiend. Heaven grant, what I believe, that he is mad. It is my duty to shield you from him, and your own duty to flee for a time from his murderous frenzy. In coming with me you violate no command or ultimate calm wish of his. Let us go to-night, and let my arm be your stay and shelter, and my breast your home."

Cora fainted, and fell into the arms which were ready to receive her.

On the following day there were strange words being whispered from mouth to ear in Creswood, of events transpired the evening before and during the night, and of which Cliff Hall was the mysterious and gloomy center.

Captain Gale was astounded and thrilled to hear that Graham Huron and Cora had fled the Hall, and had gone to Mr. Hope's, where, it was supposed, they were secretly married, and whence they went—no one knew whither.

Captain Gale hired a dozen men, mounted them upon horses, started them in pairs in every direction, and charged them to spare neither flesh nor foray until they had halted the couple and sent word back to him where they could be found. To each pair of horsemen he intrusted a short and hasty note for Cora. He then went to Mr. Hope's and made inquiries. Finding the minister, as he conceived, somewhat reticent and by far too tranquil, Captain Gale unfolded to him the secret which had been kept for years. Mr. Hope turned pale with interest. To a question, he answered,—

"No,—they were not married by me. They wanted my advice,—that is, Cora did. I gave it, but whether it will be followed or not, it is impossible for me to foretell. I do not even know where he has taken her."

"Mr. Hope," asked the roused and anxious captain, "do you believe in direct providential interposition?"

"I do," replied the old minister.

"How is it secured?"

"By earnest prayer."

"Then down upon your knees, you godly man," cried
Captain Gale, volcanic with emotion and concern, "and
let your soul *teem* with entreaty for this youthful pair.
Where is Garland? Let him join you, for his heart is
warm for supplication with the fire and blood of youth."

Garland was summoned, and made aware of the emergency. The two ministers knelt, and old Mr. Hope led
in prayer. Captain Gale also bent the knee, notwithstanding that on this particular ground of faith his mind was
skeptical. But in the way of duty he was determined to
take all chances, as, in a storm, a doubtful port was better
than none. As he listened to the venerable minister calling upon the great God in the very ire of earnestness, and
pleading as a child to a tender-hearted father, as if the
Father were there, manifest, and in the room, he almost
looked up to see that Face on which no man looks and
lives. When the supplication was finished, Captain Gale's
Amen came from the center of his sensibilities, and he rose
up greatly reinforced. After a few moments' silence, Mr.
Hope observed,—

"I omitted to inform you, Captain Gale, that Cora
has her maid, a middle-aged woman, with her."

"That is a good indication," said the captain, who
took his leave by depositing upon a desk a bank-bill of respectable denomination, and saying,—

"This, gentlemen, is for any purpose to which you may
see proper to apply it,—Church, Sunday-school, or Charity,—and if the good wishes of a sinner will do you no
harm, accept my earnest desire for your welfare."

When Captain Gale had gone, old Mr. Hope, turning
to his son, said,—

"Garland, I fear I shall die yet before I get that bold,
good man into position."

"His heart is right," said Garland, "but his head is a
little out of plumb. If we could once get his head right,
he would be a pillar against which the gates of hell
would never prevail."

"Garland," said the old minister, continuing a subject
upon which he had dwelt before, "if I should die before
he is garnered, never lose sight of him. He is too good
a man to be risked from heaven; and too good an ex-

ample to have outside of the church. You must get him into the church, for, independent of his own salvation, there are at least a score of adults who would follow him, and no calculating how many of young and old who would follow them. There was Guy Rapid; a man of a different type it is true; a man whom the world would regard as more polished and loftier in his aims, but intrinsically the same character of man as Captain Gale. I never could get *him* into the church. And yet we, and the church also, temporally speaking, owe him more than is due to all the citizens of Creswood put together. He was a good man," added the old minister, " and I hope that it is possible for his soul now to be in heaven."

"Father," said Garland, changing the subject, "you promised to tell me about the Rapid family, and what it was that destroyed them in Texas. What was it?"

" I will tell you, Garland, but it is under the seal of confidence. The family is not all destroyed. Cassel, as you know, is yet living. When Mr. Rapid went to Texas, he took with him a squad of rather wild young men who were better suited to that region than to this quiet place. He thought they were merely wild, without being vicious. Among them was Jonas Aiken, who, when he left here, was only a lad, but a bad one by inheritance and acquisition. Also a man by the name of Gilders went out with Mr. Rapid. Aiken and Gilders were the chief herders of the Ranche. Mr. Rapid prospered with his herds, and as his children, a son and daughter, grew up, he had them educated at Eastern and Southern institutions. Cassel, who is as beautiful as a Greek statue, you have seen. You used to know him when he was a little leopard of a boy. His sister Diana was as lovely as the dream of a Mohammedan, and as high-hearted as Shakspeare's Lucrece. She was a pure and perfect blonde, a youthful lady, and a most charming girl. I saw her once in New York. She was just that kind of girl which makes young men go mad, and sets old men like me by the ears with delight. I know of no one to compare with her unless it is Cora, whose life and experience however have obscured her natural starlike luster, and marked her brow with a pensiveness which should not be there, and which I hope

some day to see disappear, if this unfortunate elopement
does not terminate fatally.   Well, marauding Indians were
devastating the settlements along the upper Brazos, and
Mr. Rapid, with Cassel, the Rosses, and other formidable
frontiersmen, went out to punish the savages.   Diana was
left at Ranche Rapid with the negroes and the herders.
The Indians were overtaken, and, after a desperate battle,
were destroyed; but Mr. Rapid was killed by an árrow.
Cassel went immediately home to arrange for the trans-
portation of his father's remains to Ranche Rapid.   But
when he arrived at the house and entered it, the fate of
his father dwindled to insignificance compared with that
which he looked upon.   On a couch lay Diana, his sister,
dead.   In her exposed white bosom a dagger was stuck
to the hilt, pinning to her bloodless flesh a note which
told of the Plutonian horror and insufferable pollution
through which she had passed.   The note was from her
own hand and was addressed to her brother.   The dagger
was her refuge, and it seemed that she had put the note
upon her bosom and thrust the dagger slowly from point
to hilt through it and into her heart, and had then lain
down, calmly and desperately adjusting herself to die.
From the note, Cassel learned that Jonas Aiken, taking
the opportunity of the absence of both father and brother,
had violated the chastity of his sister, and there she lay
in the embrace of Death, to which she had fled from the
embrace of a *demon* worse than Death.   What he must
have felt I cannot tell you.   No tongue could tell it,
or inexperienced heart feel it; but from that moment,
mercy for the Spoiler was forever routed from his heart.
And, Garland,—this tragedy of the Larboard Strand,—
I have the key to it; for as certain as we now sit here,
the dagger which Captain Gale drew from the breast of
Jonas Aiken, is the same that Cassel drew from his sister's bosom."

   "Father," asked Garland, who was intensely interested,
"is there any punishment too great for the crime of which
Jonas Aiken was guilty?"

   "There is no earthly punishment which I can conceive
of too great, or even commensurate.   Unlike most other
crimes, which are the result of provocation, poverty, or

feud, this is a premeditated, unprovoked, blasting perpetration, by the strong upon the weak, for which, in this immoral and abundant world, there is no excuse whatever. The laws upon this subject are dastardly and unmanly; and until they are changed, noble souls *will* be guilty of slaughter. It is nature, — irrepressible, — and the laws should provide for it, and not attempt to repress it. In this State the law approaches to a just conception of this crime. But in most of the States, under the laws, as they now read, the punishment of a blameless man, who, from overwhelming and irretrievable outrage, slays the ravisher of his family honor and chastity, and thereby strikes a fiend from the paths of his countrywomen, is greater than the legal punishment of the fiend himself,— the fiend who desolates the hearts of families, and consigns a weak woman, an innocent pure-hearted girl perhaps, to a life-long tryst with shame, or to death by reason of unbearable pollution, as in the case of Diana Rapid. Meanwhile the Spoiler, if not turned loose upon a disgusting technicality, works out his crime within the walls of some prison-house, as one would work out a task, and, in a few years, is again set free upon the community to desolate more families. There should be a law as universal, as firm, and as fatal, as the law of poison, which should be a bulwark to the chastity of our homes. Every man knows that if he violates the law of poison he will surely die. To guard our countrywomen, chivalrous men should make a law, the violation of which would be deadly bane to the Spoiler. Cassel Rapid felt that the law mocked him, and he disdained to appeal to it, as he would have disdained to appeal to Satan to purge Hell of sin. He must visit the punishment with his own hand, and to the extreme; but even then, the life of a thousand such men as Jonas Aiken, such men as commit these crimes, is inadequate to atone for the destruction of a single life like that of Diana Rapid, who, to her brother, was a matchless sister, and consummate object of affection and devotion. From the day that his sister was buried, Cassel has hunted her destroyer through jungle, forest, swamp, and city, with unremitting and increasing purpose. There are many senseless heads, speaking from senseless hearts, and say-

ing that if the spoiler is killed in the *attempt*, the slayer
is excusable ; but that after the *act*, and the lapse of time,
the blood being *cool*, the slayer is inexcusable. Can the
blood of a man *ever* cool, when it circles as it were in a
furnace of ceaseless and innumerable fiery thoughts?
You may as well wait for the sun to cool. Every thought,
and every reflection, but aggravates the heat; and even
now, when I think of Diana Rapid, *my* old blood boils,
and my arm volunteers to strike. Jonas Aiken endeavored
to induce Gilders, the other herder, to be an accomplice.
Gilders refused, and would have averted this matchless
calamity, but Aiken drew a pistol, at the mouth of which
he bound Gilders, hand and foot, with a lasso, and then
went about his demon's work. Gilders did all that he
could to save Diana, and afterwards went with Cassel
upon the hunt for Jonas Aiken. At San Antonio, Cassel
started out alone. He had got upon the track, and following it, compelled it into the Llanos Estacados, where the
Comanche holds away. That determined boy went into
the very heart of the Comanche country, and into the
presence of its savage chief Espanto, whose name means
everything that is grim and fearful, and who had never
turned his knife from the scalp-lock of a pale face. Cassel,
in Spanish, told his mission. Espanto, in savage wonder
at the surpassing boldness and beauty of the youth, and
partly conceiving the royal spirit which brought him into
those terrible demesnes, called his warriors about him and
scoured his vast country for the guilty fugitive, but without success. Aiken escaped into the States. He had stolen
sufficient money from Colonel Rapid's desk at Ranche
Rapid, to enable him to change his location at will, and
take every advantage of his pursuer. He was ever upon
the alert, and being a man of cunning resource, he escaped
until his money was exhausted and he was compelled to
work and shift for a living. He came back to Creswood,
his old neighborhood. Cassel was here almost as soon as
he, and Jonas Aiken vanished as darkness vanishes from
light. Cassel left Creswood, and Jonas Aiken came back
again. Legally, I know nothing; but morally, I am certain that Cassel Rapid slew Jonas Aiken. What the
Geologist had to do with it I do not know; but I know

this, that in Cassel Rapid's breast there beats a heart as noble as any that ever beat within the breast of man,—an unregenerate man," added the old minister, "such as, in extremity, meets the commandment 'Thou shalt not kill,' with the Mosaic Law, 'an eye for an eye, and a tooth for a tooth.' It is true that I have seen but very little of Cassel since he was a child, but the diamond has only to be seen to be recognized. This thing has often moved me deeply. I never *can* forget that pure, heroic girl, so spirited, lady-like, and lovely, and so well constituted to enjoy and dispense the brightest things on earth, but destined, alas! to be ruthlessly quenched by a foul fate, which, to her, was insufferable and incurable, and beyond the reach of any soothing hand but that of Death—a fate too oft recurring, among our women and virgins, for the honor of Americans and the laws which they vote into our statute books. Cassel showed me the laws of almost every State in the Union, upon this particular subject, and I can but denominate the majority of them as legislative abortions—*shameful* abortions. Before any human can condemn Cassel, let that human put himself in Cassel's place, and answer the self-question, 'What would I have done?' When a legislator makes laws bearing so directly and vitally upon his countrywomen, then, if at no other time, there should be some manliness in his conceptions and his voice. *He should vote as though the woman whom he loved was sitting by his side and looking him in the eye.* Men make laws for themselves, and *also* for the women. Therefore every principle of manhood and chivalry *demands* that the laws should protect and defend our women, not as with an ægis of paper and a spear of wood, but as a gentleman would protect his lady, or as a strong man would defend his house. Where a woman unfortunately has no masculine arm to guard her, the laws should so read as to cherish her, and be her knight, steel-clad and gallant for her service. Lawgivers might well enliven their prosaic sections with the spirit of chevaliers, when prescribing for those who depend upon them, and who are trusting—perhaps too confidingly—to their honor."

"From the amount of gallantry they are accustomed to display among the fair visitors in the lobby, one would be reasonable in supposing that they would break a lance for them in the forum of the assembly," observed Garland, when his father, who, though an humble minister, was a gallant-hearted man, had closed his remarks.

Garland returned to the school-room, and the old minister soon became immersed in theological commentaries.

CHAPTER XXII.

THE runners whom Captain Gale had sent in search of Graham and Cora were coming in again for several days, until the last of them returned, without a particle of information having been obtained. The youthful pair had not been heard of in all the region round about Creswood.

Captain Gale had ascertained that on the night of the elopement, three horses had been taken from Oswald Huron's stables, and he reasonably presumed that Graham and Cora had left Creswood on horseback, the third horse being for Cora's maid. As to their mode of travel, Mr. Hope was deficient in accurate knowledge, having, in the surprise and disarrangement, forgotten or failed to inquire about it.

Captain Gale had not been so outdone in all the days of his life. He was as impotent as he felt himself to be responsible. An irretrievable family disaster might occur, nay, may have already occurred, and he, the only person who might have prevented it, had neglected to do so until now that he was as powerless as one stricken with the palsy.

Oswald Huron, also, was making efforts to have the fugitives arrested. By officers of the law he would have Cora arrested as a minor, and Graham as a horse-thief, and brought back to him. However willing he might have been that the two young people, regarded as cousins (and he so regarded them), should marry each other, he

could tolerate no infringement of his authority, though
that infringement should conduce to bring about the very
end at which he aimed. He was that kind of man, who,
never so hungry, would not suffer ever so good a dinner
to be *thrust* upon him.

Neither was Oswald Huron satisfied as to the character
of the elopement; whether Graham had carried off Cora
as his presumed sister, or as his bride. If she had gone
as Graham's sister, especially would he appeal to the law
for her recovery. He would have had Captain Gale
arrested, and held, for violently entering and acting upon
the premises of Cliff Hall; but a cunning prudence
prompted him to forego such a measure, and in the suit
which he intended to institute for the possession and control of Cora Glencoe, be she bride or sister, to impeach the
testimony of Captain Gale, and all testimony which he
might superinduce, upon the ground of enmity, vindictive-
ness, and conspiracy; backing up his impeachment, in
part, by what he would make to appear, and what he may
have actually considered, an unprovoked and unlawful
assault upon him in his own house,—and in other part, by
establishing proof of the long and well known unfriendly
relations existing between himself and all who were likely
to be concerned against him.

Captain Gale was in a mighty muck of indecision as to
what was best to be done, or as to what *could* be done.
At times, this tenacious, anxious, and courageous man
was almost ready to throw the whole matter overboard, as
probably past cure, or altogether beyond the power of
arrest. But there were several considerations which held
him to his original purpose, and also whispered encouragement. First, his conscience pricked him, and would not
permit him to abandon Cora. After, he had confidence
in Cora, and a strong trust possessed him that she would
do nothing precipitately. That she had left the home of
Oswald Huron was not, in the estimation of Captain
Gale, an evidence of precipitation, but of prudence rather.
Her application to Mr. Hope for advice was favorable, and
indicated that notwithstanding she might and doubtless
did have great confidence in Graham, her confidence was
limited, and subservient to her trust in her old mentor,

Mr. Hope. The minister's advice could not be other than good, and Cora, having long looked up to the now venerable man with reverence, and love, and profit, would not be likely to break away from his counsels unless under an extreme and mighty stress.

Mr. Hope was no advocate of Quixotic measures, and ordinarily would have detained the young girl by force or persuasion, and advised Oswald Huron; but when Cora told him, as far as she knew, what had occurred, he took the responsibility of charging her not to return home, not to remain in the neighborhood, and not to say where she was going; but to go, keep her maid with her, do nothing which could not be undone, and when the hue and cry was over, to let him know where she was.

"I would like to know *now* where you are going, but it may be better for me not to know, for I might be compelled by your father to divulge it in a magistrate's court, or refusing to do so, suffer for contempt."

Such had been Mr. Hope's farewell words to Cora, as she started out into the night, knowing as little as he did whither she was going.

Opposed to Captain Gale's hopes and encouragements was the fear that under the manly persuasions of Graham, Cora would yield herself up, and forever elope from the melancholy, grimness, and terror of the past, to a future whose sunshine and promise were the more bright, seductive, and summer-fair, on account of the starless night out of which she was escaping.

Captain Gale determined to go to Philadelphia and lay before Neville Huron the evidences of Cora's parentage, and inform him of the very peculiar and alarming relations which, it was supposed, existed between the brother and sister. It was possible that he might find Graham and Cora under their father's roof.

When Captain Gale arrived at Philadelphia, he sought out Neville Huron, and made him master of the details of the subject which induced his visit. The unprecedented disclosures of Captain Gale threw the Huron family into a maelstrom of hope, dismay, and indescribable feeling. At first, Neville Huron thought it best to conduct a secret search for Graham and Cora, but Captain Gale maintained that rumor was more active than lightning, and more pervading than mist, and that the sooner the world knew all about it the better, that the news might spread, and probably reach the young pair before the fleetest and most untiring searcher would ever find them. All the news-papers were consequently charged with notices, the tele-graph spoke far and near, and quick-witted men were put upon the alert and started in every direction. Among these latter was our old acquaintance, Hector O'Dare.

O'Dare went alone, with all speed, to Creswood, out-running Captain Gale. He would trace the fugitives from the doors of Cliff Hall—from the very starting-point. He soon ascertained that Creswood had learned nothing of the whereabouts of Graham and Cora. He avoided Os-wald Huron, but from a loquacious stable groom at Cliff Hall he obtained a minute description of the three horses which had disappeared simultaneously with the clope-ment. O'Dare, whose experience as geologist had given him a pretty good idea of the topography of Creswood, knew that there were not many ways of getting out of that neighborhood either by hoof or wheel. After having collected every item of any value, or which it was possi-ble for him to discover, he went upon the main road which led from Cliff Hall towards the interior. About half a mile from the Hall he stopped where the roads forked ; one fork leading westward, the other northward. With him he had a good horse, which he had been leading. He sat down on a log by the roadside, as if to whet his wits, and pick his nose for a keen scent. O'Dare was puzzled. He had no idea what his next step should or would be. Half an hour passed, during which he began to think of other things than his present enterprise. Finally, he heard the sound of hoofs. His horse pricked up his ears, arched his neck, and poising his head, neighed most lustily. The neigh was answered several times from the direction of the approaching hoofs, and in a few moments there came in sight, on the north fork of the road, a man riding one horse, leading another, and followed by two others. The man, contrary to rural custom, passed O'Dare without greeting him good-day, or evincing any desire to be him-self greeted.

18*

"That's all well enough in the city," said O'Dare mentally, and taking out a memorandum which he had just made; "but people don't do that thing in the country as a generality. I'll examine your marks. You have some reason no doubt for keeping your mouth shut. Don't want to invite tedious questions probably. Very well; I'll carry on a little dialogue between me and myself, and see what we will make of it. So:"

Question. "What animal is that which you are leading, with a side-saddle on?"

Answer. "It is Miss Cora Glencoe's dapple gelding, and no mistake about it."

Q. "Just so. What sorrel horse is that, with three white feet, shod all round, natural pacer, man's saddle, and follows so well?"

A. "It is Mr. Oswald Huron's riding-horse, which Mr. Graham Huron took from the stables at Cliff Hall, on the night of the elopement."

Q. "Just so. What bay mare is that, with a colt in her belly, black mane and tail, left fore foot white, fox trot, side-saddle, and anxious to get home?"

A. "She is the mare which Miss Huron's maid rode off the night of the elopement."

Q. "Just so. Where did these animals come from, all together, and in such good trim?"

A. "They came from the direction of the runaways, and the man who has them in charge will return in the same direction, and Hector O'Dare will go with him."

"Thank you, sir," said O'Dare, as if addressing some accommodating individual, while he laughed at his own solitary drollery, and smiled at the prospect of game ahead. "But I'll watch this man and see what he does with the horses."

Approaching Cliff Hall and ascending an eminence, O'Dare saw the man ride to within a hundred yards of the stable inclosure, and there turn the three animals loose. They started for their stalls. The man then wheeled his horse and came rapidly back upon the road, barely giving O'Dare time to get into position again where the road forked. The man was about to hurry on without noticing O'Dare, when the latter, by a maneuver of himself and horse across the road, compelled the countryman to draw up.

"Don't be in such a dreadful hurry," said the detective, "and maybe you'll get company."

"Don't want any company," was the answer.

"But I do," insisted O'Dare. "I wish to find my way. This is your road, and I think it's mine. We will go along together for a little while at all events, and talk the matter over. I may be able to learn from you whether I am on my road or not. I won't trespass on your time by detaining you here, but we can balance probabilities as we jog along, and if I find that I am out, I can ride back again, and no harm done."

"But you can't keep up with me," said the man, with an evident desire to get rid of O'Dare. "I'm going in a whoop."

"Oh, I can go in a whoop as well as not, and carry a bucket of water on my head for that matter. My horse can beat yours at any gait you may choose."

The man was riding a fine country horse. The rack being probably his best gait, the countryman seeing that O'Dare was likely to stick to him unless he could get away by superior speed, told O'Dare to mount, at the same time starting off, and shouting back,—

"Rack!"

O'Dare nimbly mounted, and overtook the man with all ease, for he was riding a trained horse of the best breed.

"Where are you going to?" asked the disappointed countryman, slacking his speed, and changing his tactics.

"That is exactly what I wish to find out," replied O'Dare, with good-humored impudence.

"But how do you expect to find out?"

"From you," said O'Dare, with cool presumption.

"How the devil do *I* know?" demanded the exasperated countryman, whose eyes began to snap with kindling ire.

"You might consider the matter for the sake of good company," said O'Dare, with no whit of his persistency abated.

"But I don't *want* any company."

"You don't?"

"No, I *don't.*"

"I *do*, though," said the detective.

"Well who's to have his way now, you or I?" demanded the countryman, who seemed to think that matters had come to a pretty pass when a man in a free country couldn't choose his company.

"I!" was O'Dare's answer.

"You are the dam'dest man I ever heard of," said the countryman, who halted his horse and indignantly looked upon the strange customer who seemed determined to stick to him like a burr.

"I'm just that very thing," assented O'Dare, who likewise halted his horse and faced his unwilling companion.

"Look here, Mister, you may find it a little dangerous riding with a man against his will, and the more so the farther you get. Do you see this?" and the countryman tapped the butt of a pistol which was belted to his waist.

"I have two of them," said O'Dare, with provoking nonchalance, "and I can beat you shooting with my left hand."

"If you don't leave me," said the man, who hardly knew what to make of his companion, "or let me leave you, the very first house I come to I'll have you arrested as a highwayman."

"*Stand* and *deliver*, then!" said O'Dare, presenting a pistol which covered the man's breast. "I'll have the benefit of your arrest at least."

"Do you want my money?" asked the countryman, who had been taken off his guard.

"Yes," said O'Dare, sternly, "and your pistol, and your horse. We'll see who is quickest at an arrest."

The countryman prepared to dispossess himself, when O'Dare, putting up his pistol, very pleasantly said,—

"Neighbor, you misjudge me entirely. I do not want your money, or your arms, or your horse; but I *do* want your company. Come now, don't be so exclusive; give me graciously what I need, and what will leave you none the poorer; be neighborly, and I think we can get along together as softly as a chunk floating down stream."

The countryman, greatly relieved at not being robbed of his valuables, rode along with doubtful confidence in his companion, while O'Dare secretly amused himself by watching the suspicion that lurked in the corners of the man's uneasy eyes.

We will leave these two agreeables to agree or disagree, while we join Captain Gale,—remarking by the way that O'Dare knew he was on the right trail, and was going to stick to it at all hazards. He was confident that the man had come from the direction of Cora and Graham. The manner in which he had returned the horses evinced a desire and purpose to come and go without being seen, suspected, or followed, or in any way connected with the fugitives. O'Dare might have told him squarely his own purposes, and why he was so fond of his company all at once, but the detective judged correctly that the man would have put no faith in him, but rather would have considered him a citizen of Creswood, in the interests of Oswald Huron, and in search of the very parties the finding of whom would be contrary to the interests or desires of the countryman. But O'Dare considered himself a match for any single man, and now that he had the countryman within his grasp, he would worry him into a spell of sickness before he would suffer himself to be outdone, or thrown from the track, which he doubted not would lead him just where he wished to go. "Ride on, my hearty," said O'Dare jocosely to himself; "I'll keep within hoof clatter of you if I have to starve for a week."

Captain Gale took advantage of his visit to Philadelphia to make some exchanges of produce for merchandise, which would render it necessary for him to put into that port with the Whitecap.

Arriving at home, he found Creswood agog. Innumerable rumors and tales were upon the wing, out of which could be extracted nothing but confusion, and the single fact that the three horses, which had been carried off by the fugitives, had returned, no one knew how or whence, and were found quietly browsing a short distance from the stables of Cliff Hall, saddled and bridled, and in good condition.

Captain Gale also learned that he himself was inextricably mixed up with the events transpired 'and transpiring at Cliff Hall, and that, on account thereof, the citizens had never been able to determine whether they were called

upon to mourn a catastrophe, or rejoice over a happy but
undiscovered or unannounced *denouement.* In answer to
a thousand and one questions, the mariner simply suggested to the curious and overcurious that it would be
just as well for them to "belay their impatience."

Captain Gale trumpeted his crew from the hills, and
having stored everything snugly, set sail up the coast,
that is to say, northward. Not being blessed with a very
jealous wife, he did not hesitate to hug the shore; and
wherever he could touch it he did so, buying produce and
stowing it away in his new and capacious Whitecap; for
he was on his way to Philadelphia to meet his engagements. His progress was slow on account of his stop-
pages, and on the second day, in the afternoon, he was not
more than thirty miles by coastline from Gale Island.
He was passing a section of abrupt shore wall against
which he had never ventured to anchor, for it was a bad
place for breakers. With his glass he was examining the
bluffs more critically than he had ever done before, with
the view of determining whether there could possibly be
an eligible spot for casting anchor and establishing a fair-
weather trading post. While scanning the shore, he spied
a man waving a flag, and, to all appearances, hailing the
Whitecap. Shifting his helm, he cautiously ran the vessel in towards the shore, and while he stood upon the
wind, a shouting conversation ensued between himself
and the man with the flag,—the flag being a large handkerchief.

"Where are you bound?"

"Philadelphia."

"Can you take a passenger and horse?"

"Yes. How's the water next to shore there?"

"Don't know; but it looks deep. Send your jolly boat
ashore and take soundings."

"Teach a tar to tie a knot, will you? But where do
you wish to go?"

"Out of this wooden country."

"Can't you swim?"

"Yes, but I'm not in a hurry; I'll sail—with you."

"Ha! ha, h-a!"

Captain Gale, instead of anchoring and going ashore in

a small boat, very carefully and very skillfully lodged the Whitecap against a natural pier, and to his surprise met—

"Mr. Geologist!"

"Just so," said O'Dare. "Interesting country this."

"Any dead horse around here—mammoth bones—or old bird-nests?" asked Captain Gale, with rather a sly look at the whilom geologist, in whose assumed character the mariner had never put much faith.

"Nothing more ancient than coon tracks and pheasant wallows," answered O'Dare, laughing.

From far up a pathway, which, like a straggling thread, led to the very top of the hills, there came a pure mountain cry, and down the pathway sped a young girl, agile as the wild chamois, and stopping not, until, with the spring of a squirrel, she was in the arms of Captain Gale, with her own tender arms clasped tightly about his sturdy neck. It was Cora. She had seen "Whitecap" in plain letters on the vessel, and to her who had never been away from home until now that she was away under such peculiar circumstances, that name was as sweet as a babbling brook would be to the traveler in some scorching desert.

Graham soon made his appearance. The landing of a vessel at that no-port was as unexpected as it was without precedent, and all the inhabitants, some half-a-dozen, came down to open their eyes upon it.

Hector O'Dare, who had stuck to his man like a motherless colt to a stray mare, or poor kin to rich relations, had succeeded in finding Graham and Cora. The countryman, who eventually was made to understand the incentive for so much pertinacity and audacity on the part of O'Dare, got to believe that the detective was a capital fine fellow and regretted to see him preparing to leave the neighborhood by sea; for by land, he would have gone half a day's journey with O'Dare, simply for the pleasure of his company, which, in the beginning, was so extremely irksome to him.

O'Dare succeeded in getting his horse aboard of the Whitecap, after which he and Captain Gale went apart for a talk; for Cora had whispered something into the captain's ear while she hung about his neck, and he felt will-

ing to anchor for twelve hours, if necessary, rather than
sail away empty-minded upon the subject which was
nearest his heart.

CHAPTER XXIII.

THE time may be remembered when Oswald Huron,
from an east window and through a telescope, saw Graham
and Cora clasping hands and embracing in the moon.
For a moment we must go back to that time.

When Graham first came to Cliff Hall, Cora very
naturally was delighted with him, and he very naturally
was enchanted with so sweet and lovely a young cousin.
There was all the difference between Cora and the girls
whom Graham had been accustomed to tryst with, as
there is between metropolitan atmosphere and pure hill
air; and before he was aware of it, Cora, to use his own
words, had bewitched him, and he, with the ardor of a
young lover, but the caution of an old one, consequently
laid siege to her heart.

If it should appear strange that Graham, accustomed
to the fascinations, dash, and spirit of fair and fashionable
city girls, should so readily have loved Cora, with her
simple dress, her woodland air, and her untrite talk,
sweet and thrilling as passion-murmurs, but weighted
and depreciated by an element of *sense*, it will appear still
more strange that Cora, to whom Graham's advent at
Cliff Hall was like some brilliant meteor lighting up a
gloomy vale, did *not* return his love, other than as an
affectionate cousin. It was in the young girl's code that
first cousins, with very little more propriety than brothers
and sisters, could either love as lovers, or marry as men
and women; though a theoretical and paper code, never
yet put to the test, *might* have been pierced and torn
to pieces by Cupid's amorous archery. But upon first
greeting, Cora had given her love to Graham unreservedly
and tenderly as a cousin, and that love had become fixed
in its character and temper, as the waxen seal is fixed

when it is stamped and cooled, or as original volcanic ore is fixed in its combinations. To change it, she must pass through fire and fusion. Through the fitful fires of Cliff Hall, built by Oswald Huron, she was passing every day, and though her susceptible and exquisite nature never could become tempered to them or acclimated, her moral nerve had been strung to the snapping-point, where fortitude, utterly discouraged, subsides into supine hopelessness: and into such hopelessness Cora inevitably sank when Oswald Huron waved the murderous dagger over her head, with a yet more murderous eye. Her own father to be her murderer! This was an extreme heat which was affecting the crystallized cluster of principles which formed her code, and made her wail out that she was as "desolate as a lost soul." Added to this was the apt and knightly urging of Graham that she should make his breast her home. But heat does not always melt,—it sometimes hardens, as with the process by which the diamond is said to be produced. Cora, with all her past life before her eyes, with the scenes through which she had just passed standing out in bold and fearful relief, felt that the hour had struck when she must choose between bitterness on the one hand and gall upon the other. An overpowering conflict in her bosom stagnated her blood. She fainted, and fell into Graham's arms,—those arms which had never yet held her statuesque sweet form, except when once upon a time, to gratify his intense longing, and in giving him a farewell, she had suffered him to clasp her hand and give her a brotherly good-by caress, all of which demonstrativeness or tenderness, against the chaste bosom of La Luna, Oswald Huron had observed from his east window, through his telescope,—and chuckled over.

When Cora recovered her consciousness, her maid was in the room with her, almost making a dead darling of her. Graham also was anxiously there.

"What shall be done?" asked the young man, as Cora got up, looking like some frightened captured bird, which would fain escape.

"It is night,—is it not?" asked the young girl.

"Yes," said Graham; "it is nine o'clock."

19

" Graham, is the world all as hard as it is here ?"

" No. There are many places as bright as this is dark, and where the vicissitudes are as soft and fair as here they are hard and gloomy,—if you will but come with me."

"Miss Cora," said the maid, "listen to the brave gentleman, and go with him. I belongs to you, and I'll go with you to the world's end. This is no place for the like of you."

"Aunt Mag," said Cora to the maid, "get yourself ready. Graham, take me to Mr. Hope's. From there we will adventure."

The maid was but too willing to get away from Cliff Hall, and was ready in a trice.

Cora, by her interview with the old minister, was strengthened and confirmed in the policy which she had conceived to be her duty to herself and to others.

By the light of stars the party of three set out, not knowing so much where they were going, as caring that they were leaving Cliff Hall behind them.

In the silent night-gloom of the forests which they traversed, Graham renewed his entreaties of love. Cora resisted him firmly, but with an affectionate consideration which only served to check him for the while, and to throttle instead of destroying his hopes.

They rode all night. Cora was chilled through, and became sick with fatigue and cold. The road had dwindled into a bridle-path, and seemed about to terminate in trackless woods, when the dawn, coming up from the east, revealed to them, just ahead, the dimpled, tumbling sea. Approching, they came upon a country-house overlooking the ocean. Dismounting, they were kindly and curiously received and entertained by the family in occupation— plain, honest, and surprised-looking people. Graham gave out that he and his party were lost,—whioh was as true as the Gospel itself, for he had not the most remote idea of his immediate whereabouts.

Resting a day and night, Graham, professing to be charmed with the surrounding scenery, but secretly enchanted with the romantic situation in which he now found himself with Cora, and not knowing or much caring what better to do, engaged to remain with the family as long as he might find the locality pleasant and novel.

It is not at all improbable that the family suspected that they were entertaining a Gretna Green party, but the fact that Graham and Cora occupied different rooms, and the rather distinguished appearance of the young couple, together with the unusual appendage of a maid, convinced the country folk that they were at all events harboring respectability.

After a number of days had passed, Graham, who became more and more unwilling to terminate his direct hourly guardianship of Cora, and who, like Cortes, was willing to burn his ships, cut off retreat, and force his fortunes to complete establishment or complete overthrow and annihilation, compounded with his landlord to deliver at Cliff Hall the three horses which had been taken from Oswald Huron's stables. In order to effect the clandestine delivery of the horses, Graham was compelled to confide, in a measure, the situation of his affairs to the landlord, and also to confide to the cautious countryman, in fee, a seductive amount of cash.

O'Dare was just in time to secure an unwilling guide to this country spot, which was so secluded and so little thought of that, in the general search for the fugitives, it had either been overlooked or ignored.

It is not necessary to give O'Dare's experience with the countryman, but many a time has he laughed over it as one of the raciest rides he ever enjoyed. He outmaneuvered his man at last, and came upon the fugitives. He took Graham apart and overwhelmed him with the revelation of his relationship to Cora.

The feelings which were stirred up and created in the breast of the young man are beyond our power to conceive or put to pen. They were doubtless a mixture of everything akin to amazement, disappointment, gladness, regret, pain, pleasure, and chagrin.

To Cora, this life-reversing fact came like a pregnant wonder out of the very heavens. A troop of revolutionary emotions swept through her bosom, succeeded by a pure and ravishing delight, gushing in and out of her heart and singing its songs of joy. *This*, then, was the glad thing that was to come to her, of which she had been admonished by Captain Gale, into whose stout arms she rushed from the hill-tops and sprang, agile with new life, and hope, and joy.

We are now brought up to the time when Captain Gale landed the Whitecap at what might be called No-port, and Cora hung upon his neck like a wreath of beauty about the lion's mane.

A few words with O'Dare and Graham apprised Captain Gale that Cora, with a veteran fortitude and rocklike firmness, had passed unharmed through the peculiar and extreme dangers and seductions by which she had been beset as by bristling bayonets, clinging, even in the very depths of her despair, to the horns of that altar on which she was accustomed to make sacrifices of all that she deemed wrong, and about which she wove perennial garlands of what she deemed goodly and right.

The conscientious and anxious mariner, who keenly felt his responsibility in respect to Cora, was never so relieved, exalted, and enthused before. He broke away after the young girl, and finding her, cried with fiery admiration and affection,—

" *Come*, you glorious, steel-built little *woman*, and let me press you again to that breast from which you have heaved the heaviest cargo that ever weighed upon it !" Catching her in his arms, he said, almost beside himself: "God bless you for a regular little lightning-rod !"

Cora disappeared into Captain Gale's capacious embrace like a bird into a wooded hill-side, or a cricket into the breast wool of a bear. What with his immense whiskers, his sailor's overcoat, and the gauntlets which he held in his hand, he could hardly find Cora when he came to release her. He put her down, and, looking at her almost wistfully, with vigorous staccato, he continued,—

"You brave, *gallant*, little craft ;—never will you want either captain or crew as long as my old head is hot. I could almost *eat you up*, you sweet dove."

Cora, in her joy, could not forbear laughing at the stormy captain, notwithstanding she appreciated him thoroughly. With genial playfulness, not unmixed with earnestness, she said to him, while she looked up in his face with her bright, brave eyes,—

"Captain Gale, somehow I feel that you and I could whip the whole world."

"And then challenge the moon," replied the captain;— "I, with my strength, and you, with your sense and sweetness."

Graham and O'Dare now approached. Cora had recognized O'Dare as the geologist of Creswood, and she was not now certain how to classify him. She did not contradict his character, however, and at this moment addressed him thus:

"Mr. Geologist, as you are about to leave us, I wish to return to you this pistol which you were kind enough to press upon me. I told you then that it was a demon, and it has proved itself; for it came near to killing my dear, firm friend, Captain Gale."

"It might have been called upon to kill as great an enemy as he is a friend," answered O'Dare, taking the pistol. In view of Cora's daily proximity to Jonas Aiken, down on the Larboard Strand, O'Dare's conscience had urged him to do what he *had* done to add to her security, and the caution of his mission had restrained him from doing or saying more.

In the midst of her joy, Cora could not but feel sad when she thought of Creswood, and of Cliff Hall, from which her destiny, as she read it, would take her away forever. It was probably best, however, that her happiness should be tempered somewhat with sadness; for she was by no means completely emancipated from her bondage, and might yet count her future as uncertain as her past had been pent and gloomy. Over her head was a thunder-cloud, as black as night, and from its bursting she was to be saved, or by it be engulfed. But Cora looked upon her future as secure, and her mind was divided between the future and the past. She had but few filial ties to sunder, it is true; and, outside of the Creswood School, and the scope of the Larboard Strand, and the bird-singing forest, few pleasant memories to woo her back into the dead years. But her mind *must* go and dwell upon Oswald Huron, her uncle,—once her father,— and picture her life and association with him from infancy almost up to the present hour. Compassion, and roused

19*

latent affection even, now mingled with the horror which
his image called up. Except upon a memorable and recent
occasion, Oswald Huron had been fitful, fierce, and terrible, not *upon* Cora, but *about* her, and within her unhappy and horrified ken: she had never felt personal fear
of him, for ever and anon she had met him upon a question of right and wrong, involving herself essentially and
directly, and he had never failed to yield to what he
denominated her "incorrigible stubbornness." Also, he
had often, when in the mood, fascinated her by his brilliant
conversations, in which, with her, as with no other person,
he gave freedom to his thoughts and fancies, frequently
discussing both sides of a question, and appearing as Paul
and Saul at one and the same time. These conversations,
or disquisitions rather, swayed Cora's mind as they progressed, but when he would finish and she have time to
reflect, it was rarely that she did not discover a meta-
physical unsoundness in his premises and deductions.
He would have no one to talk to now, thought Cora, and
with all her past experience with him she could not but
feel sad to leave him in his solitary gloom. Then there
was Creswood, and the strand, and the sea, with all their
painful, pensive, sweet associations; it would be sad indeed to leave them all forever. And there was her dog,
and her dapple gray, each of which she must leave behind.
A feeling of reproach came into her heart as she thought
of her faithful dog, which, she doubted not, was howling
desolately for her at that moment, or frantically snuffing
the wind to find out where was his lost mistress.

Graham wished to take Cora to Philadelphia on the
Whitecap with Captain Gale and O'Dare, but Captain
Gale did not think it a prudent step, for several reasons;
Cora's parental allegiance not having been established, or
determined, or defined, by law, admission, or otherwise.
Oswald Huron had already denounced the evidence of
Cora's lineage as the fruit of a conspiracy, and there were
too many circumstances to bear him out. It was not at
all improbable that the "conspiracy" view of the inevitable controversy would appear the most reasonable, natural,
and best sustained, to whatever judge, jury, or umpire it
might be submitted. Oswald Huron could prove strong

probable motive other than for the sake of justice and
legitimacy, and long, unusual delay—criminal in fact—in
all the affiants, witnesses, etc. whose testimony he would
be called upon to oppugn. He could make it appear that
Lawyer May had lived and died his enemy. He had
himself driven Maria Guthrie from Cliff Hall. Therefore,
the affidavit of the inimical Maria Guthrie, in the handwriting of the inimical Lawyer May, would be of little or
no weight. Again: he would prove that Captain Gale
was his living enemy; that Amy Turnbolt was Captain
Gale's niece; that Captain Gale had written out her affidavit, and would doubtless control her as a witness. In
conclusion: that it was a four-handed conspiracy, gotten
up by four persons, all friendly to each other, and all inimical to him; that the conspiracy was almost overthrown
years ago by the death of Lawyer May, and was only
now revived by Captain Gale's increasing enmity and vin-
dictiveness, which his late violent conduct at Cliff Hall
would go far to indicate and prove.

The master of the Whitecap was aware of the weak
links in his armor, and would do nothing more whatever,
unless it should be absolutely essential to the issue, by
which Oswald Huron would be furnished with additional
weapons. He would, if possible, avoid any and every
appearance of arbitrary and vindictive action. For these
reasons he informed Graham that he could not ship with
Cora, on the Whitecap, for Philadelphia or any other port.

"What shall be done, then?" inquired Graham of Captain Gale and O'Dare. "She cannot go back to Cliff
Hall. Nor can she stay here."

"Why can't she stay here?" asked O'Dare, as if it was
the most eligible spot on the map. Graham looked at
him in blank surprise, approaching to indignation.

"What!" said he, "remain in this wilderness, and in
such a rookery as that up on the hill!"

"I *could* take her," said O'Dare, paying very little attention to Graham's exclamation points, "to a place where
none but an angel would ever find her. But it might not
be pleasant,—at all events not so pleasant as here. This
is a spot which only a rambling fool would be at all
likely to discover—after sunrise," added O'Dare, laugh-

ing at Graham; for Graham had discovered it, but before
sunrise. "Therefore it is a place of security. When we go
to Philadelphia (Captain Gale and I—not you and your
sister), the Whitecap, on her return-trip, if the sea is in
as good a humor for landing as it is now, can bring you
everything but society and a billiard-saloon to make this
a very agreeable place — a very *charming* place," added
O'Dare, who saw that Graham didn't relish the prospect
at all. "Your father will be consulted, and whatever
may be determined upon will be acted upon. But until
you get further orders,—from head-quarters,—as the agent
of your father, I order you, Mr Graham, to remain with
your sister, here."

"And I," said Captain Gale, "as an old friend of Cora's,
and one well versed in the history of the matter in hand,
advise you to obey orders."

The reader will understand, if it has not been previously
intimated, that Cora was not present during this conference. She had gone on board of the Whitecap to investigate what, to her, was all but a novelty.

Graham scratched his head: not that he was head-
strong, but he was headed off. Had Cora remained his
sweetheart, he would have been delighted at the prospect
of continued love-making while swinging in the vines of
the deep woods, sitting on the margins of autumn brooks,
or cosily ensconced by a country fire, and talking by the
light of a tallow candle. But now that she had become his
sister, he "wanted to go home," and to take her with
him;

> "For there he had sweethearts
> And here he had none."

He made another effort for liberty, which was not entirely without result.

"When I first came to Cliff Hall," said he, "it struck
me that my Uncle Oswald was very slightly deranged in
his mind. I watched him closely, and my first impression,
instead of being eradicated, was deepened by continual association with him. It is now, and has been, my deliberate
opinion that his mind *is* deranged, and that it is becoming
more so very gradually. He is fitful, and at times as un-

reasonably domineering and dangerous as the devil. To put my sister again in his fierce charge, shall neither be done nor risked, Mr. Hector O'Dare to the contrary notwithstanding," and Graham bowed to the Expert, who returned his bow, smilingly. "To remain here, is to risk just what I wish to avoid, and what I will take steps to avoid, whenever my reason urges me to do so."

"Your views with reference to your uncle's mind are not without foundation," said Captain Gale. "They are, to review his life and acts, almost an inevitable and sequential conclusion, and would make palliating plea in behalf of his heart, governed as it may be by a disordered head. But I can suggest nothing better at present than for you to remain here with Cora. What say you, Mr. O'Dare?"

"I still adhere to my first expression—that it is best for Mr. Graham"—(Graham did not like to be so addressed or referred to, and O'Dare had been malicious enough to discover it; but he thought the young man had just a trifle too much style, and he was after dampening the starch in him a bit)—"that it is best for Mr. Graham," repeated O'Dare, a little emphatically, "to remain here with his sister, until you and I can run up to Philadelphia, see Mr. Graham's father, give him our information and views, let him decide, then act. It will take but a few days, and there is no danger of your being molested in this serene and lovely spot. But, if you *are* unearthed by your uncle, take your sister out of Maryland and *not* into Pennsylvania, but—let me see—here, to this address," and O'Dare wrote on a card, with a pencil, the address of Mrs. Linda Boyd, in the city of New York, and commended Graham to the acquaintance and friendship of Cassel Rapid, in whom, to use his own words, he had more confidence than in any other young blood that ever wore high-heeled boots. "This matter of States, and your locality, *may* make some difference in the end. I don't assert that it will, but I am like you,—taking all advantages and no risks. Therefore let the responsibility of your flight from Cliff Hall continue to rest upon you alone, or upon you and your sister. Do not mix your father up in it, for he will doubtless be a prime party to a lawsuit. Don't mix up Captain Gale in it, for he will

doubtless be a prime witness in a lawsuit. If you go
from here to your father's house in Philadelphia, on the
Whitecap with Captain Gale, you will be doing both of
these prohibited things at a single effort. Now, sir, that's
official, and though I am paid for it, it is none the less
friendly. It's good advice too, and if you have half the
sense which your young sister has, you'll take it."

"You are full candid," said Graham, laughing, "and
business-like also. I suppose I shall have to submit."

"Do not allow yourself to feel as though you had submitted, but simply as if you had adopted," said O'Dare,
blandly.

"See how he garlands the points of his bayonets!" exclaimed Graham, turning good-humoredly to Captain Gale.
"O'Dare, you would make a successful tyrant—inducing
your vassals to shout 'adoption' instead of murmuring
'submission.'"

"I'd take some of the overdone out of you," replied
O'Dare, laughing. "But make out your bill of wants, and
I will file it with your father. He can send the articles
down by the Whitecap—that is, if the weather will permit the vessel to put in here, and if it don't, you can rough
it awhile—it won't hurt you."

"I wouldn't mind roughing it if I had company," said
the young man, lugubriously.

"What better company do you want than your sister,
I'd like to know! She has not expended a breath upon
complaint, and you great strip of a fellow must needs
whine around because you have to live a few days in the
garden of Eden, as our first parents did!"

"O'Dare," said Graham, "you have no more sympathy
than an oyster. What you can do best is to open your
mouth, for you have neither heart nor conscience. But
come; we will board the Whitecap, get a sheet of paper,
and arrange the list of those possible things which this
garden of Eden sadly lacks. I do not think that I could
find even the forbidden tree hereabouts."

"If you could, you would need no tempting Eve to induce you to partake of the fruit thereof."

On board the Whitecap, Graham sat down and penciled
a column of wants which occupied an entire page of letter-

paper. O'Dare took it and looked over it, and then opened upon Graham with a laugh which no one would have imagined was in him.

"What's the matter now?" asked Graham. "Are my very wants to be the subject of your ridicule and horsehead mirth?"

"What will your sister and her maid do for clothes, I wonder, while you are smoking up these boxes of cigars, and reading these unillustrative novels?" asked the detective. "Here, take this sheet to Miss Cora Glencoe, and let her specify her wants. You have only brains for yourself."

Graham, somewhat crestfallen, went in search of Cora. When he returned, O'Dare took the sheet, on which the young girl had penciled her simple wants, and looked over it.

"Your sister Cora is worth two of you," said O'Dare, with provoking sincerity.

"That is doubtless true; but I am as good as any other *man*," replied Graham, a little nettled at the detective's persistent strictures.

"Miss L., on Chestnut Street, didn't think so, one night, when you would kiss her, and she wouldn't."

"What the devil do you know about *that?*" demanded Graham, with a look of great surprise and a conscious blush of detection.

"I know every door-step lip-sucker and rich-daddy swell between the Atlantic and the Alleghanies, but I know of only one who can kiss Miss L., and you are not that festive fellow by a mile or more," and O'Dare stared into Graham's face with all the encroaching impudence of a grown-up *gamin*.

"Captain Gale," pleaded Graham, "sail away with this man—he knows too much; and be careful to keep him in the waist of your vessel, for if you ever let him get to the one side or the other, the weight of his knowledge will capsize your craft. He carries a heavy head, I can tell you."

"Well, Cora," observed Graham, as the Whitecap disappeared around the northern coast, "what shall we do to

kill old Tempus?   I feel as if I was treed by an overflow,
or blocked by a snow-storm."

"In such an event we should have to wait for the flood
to assuage or the snow to melt; and I do not know what
better we can do now than to wait patiently, or impatiently, if you please," replied Cora, with a smile of fortitude.

It was some time before Graham could thoroughly undo
his heart of lover and set it up properly as that of an affectionate brother.   He would toy with Cora's abundant
brown hair, and kiss her, now that she suffered or welcomed it, oftener than he ever kissed his two young sisters
at home.   Several times he told Cora that he wished that
his or her name had been anything else but Huron.   He
talked to her of her parents, and assured her that she
would love them,—and of her two sisters, Augusta and
Gertrude,—Gussie and Gertie,—who were both younger
than Cora, and very pretty, but not, said Graham, "so
lovely as you." Gussie had her beaus, and wore long
dresses; but Gertie was in short dresses, was a school-
miss, and although she could get beaus, her mother would
not let her have any, which was very cruel on little Gertie,—and so Graham would talk, by the hour.

The Whitecap appeared to be in no haste to return,
and the days were becoming very tedious and anxious,
not only to Graham but to Cora also; for they had no
books to read, and nothing in the world to do; and their
"hotel," though a kind and willing one, was not comfortable, and could not be made so with the means at hand.

It was a blustery, uneven day, when the sea was chop-
ping, and the air was raw, that the Whitecap again
appeared in front of No-port, but not daring to lay along
side of the rock-built pier.   Graham and Cora, as they
looked upon the vessel where it stood, apparently still,
about three hundred yards from shore, were extremely
anxious to communicate with it, but to do so seemed to
them impossible.   As they watched it intently, they saw
a small boat lowered from the davits, and come toward
shore, like a shell tossed at will by the irregular and
dangerous waves.   They ran down to the verge of the
sea.

"Stand by there," shouted Captain Gale, "and catch the tow-line when I heave it to you."

Graham stood ready to assist the landing. As Cora looked upon the dancing, rearing, and dipping boat, her bosom panted with apprehension, and she wondered how so frail a thing could live among those domineering, treacherous, and collapsing waters. But there was an iron hand and fearless eye at the helm, and skillful arms at the oars.

"Look out for the lead," said Captain Gale; "don't let it strike you;" and, with one hand at the helm, he threw the end-loaded hawser ashore. Graham caught the rope and braced himself while the mariners actively made the boat secure, and in a few minutes discharged the cargo. Captain Gale came ashore, shook hands, delivered a package of letters, and said,—

"I have no time now to answer questions. Your friends are all well. These letters will advise you. I wouldn't have stopped here for a thousand dollars. The sea is getting ugly, and ten minutes lost time may send me and the Whitecap to Davy Jones's locker. Cora, use your own head, and don't be persuaded by your brother's impatience. Good-by!" And Captain Gale, after a perilous short passage, again reached the Whitecap, and trimmed his sails for a speedy run to the safe anchorage at Gale Island.

Graham divined, from the trunks, boxes, etc. which were put ashore, that he was doomed to stagnate yet longer in this next to nothing of a place.

In the package of letters Cora found four—one from each member of the Huron family in Philadelphia—addressed to herself; the contents of which we leave the reader to imagine.

A letter from Neville Huron to Graham informed the latter of a decision arrived at between Captain Gale, O'Dare, and the writer, that Graham should remain with Cora where he was, until the father could go down to Creswood and have an interview with his brother Oswald, with the view of making an effort to adjust the claim to Cora Glencoe in an amicable, quiet, and brotherly manner. If he failed, he would then advise Cora and Graham what

20

to do. If he succeeded, Cora would be brought immediately home to Philadelphia.

"His mission will be a failure," said Cora.

"I have no doubt of it in the world," replied Graham.

As Graham unpacked a number of boxes of cigars, a
lot of novels, and a variety of other tranquilizers, he was
encouraged to hope that he might possibly live through
it all.

Cora was stirred with new emotions and affections, as
she read the yearning letters of her parents, and the
warm-hearted words of her young sisters. She was impatient to speed to them, but from what she had gathered
of her peculiar situation, she could not but fear that there
was a high wall to be overgone before she should receive
the heritage of love and peace which awaited her on the
other side.

CHAPTER XXIV.

NEVILLE HURON arrived at Cliff Hall. His brother
Oswald met him calmly, but somewhat sternly, saying,—

"Neville, I divine what brings you, a stranger, into my
country. You may as well take your stirrup-cup, and set
out on your return-journey."

"Not until I have had a talk with you, Oswald," answered the brother, mildly.

"Very well: say your say. I will answer it all with a
single word, of two letters."

"I came down to see you about Cora."

"True enough; but what have you to do with Cora, my
own child?"

"Oswald, she is *not* your child, but mine."

"I presume you can prove what you say," replied
Oswald Huron, sarcastically.

"I have both seen and heard the proof, and I am thoroughly convinced," answered the brother.

"I have both seen and heard the proof, and I am thoroughly *not* convinced," rejoined Oswald Huron, who, upon
this occasion, maintained an extraordinary calmness. "Ne-

ville, you may strive in vain to change my purpose, which is firm and firmly rooted, and based upon the knowledge and conviction that there is, and for years has been, a systematic and vindictive conspiracy to rob me of my inestimable little girl, my only child. Do you think," said he, in a deep, thrilling voice, which told of the electric power and pent-up fury which slumbered beneath his calm exterior, "that I will submit to be *plundered* of my child?—of the only sunbeam in all the passage of my lonely life?—of the only thing I love?—of the helm which guides me?—of the stanchion which sustains me from overthrow?—of the star which woos me from *hell?* NEVER, sir, will I countenance your claim, or countenance you as a brother, so long as you make such a claim! I bid you defiance, and all your backers. I have anticipated everything, and am prepared to meet you and your conspirators. Bring this matter, if you please, into a court of judicature. I will meet you there. And all who are engaged in it I will prosecute and hunt to the uttermost, for this piracy upon me. Now, sir, abandon your wild demand and wilder convictions, or leave my premises, for I will not brook the company of bandit or brother who would rob me of my child."

Nothing which Neville Huron could urge had the least softening influence upon his brother Oswald, and the Philadelphian left Cliff Hall, conscious that Greek would be met by Greek in the coming strange and unhappy contest for a daughter.

It was evident to the elder Huron, after his interview with his brother Oswald, that should he ever recover his daughter it must necessarily be done by legal process; for there was left him but the alternative of appealing from the personal fiat of his brother to the master voice of Public Justice. And in those days Justice did actually exist, and had a voice, and was sufficiently well bred to speak when spoken to. Neville Huron lost no time in addressing himself to it.

It is not our purpose to furnish the minutes or follow the forms of a trial between *meum et tuum* in a Maryland court; for we are free to confess that we could not draw up even a *precis* of the legal proceedings involving and evolving Cora Glencoe's destiny, so accurate and technically true to the then current usage as to withstand the critical glances of the gentlemen at the bar.

The contemplated struggle for the parentage and possession of a child was probably without precedent in all Maryland, certainly so in the Creswood district; and, in those strict and lawlike times, it was with no little hesitation and consultation that the jurisdiction was agreed upon, and that the cause was determined to be tried before the district court within whose commission was included the neighborhood of Creswood. It was also determined that the head upon the bench, and not a jury, should be the umpire.

Although the whereabouts of the daughter, for the possession of whom the suit was about to be instituted, was, to one side of the controversy, and apparently to both, as uncertain as became that of the waggish ass which kicked up its heels and ran away while two claimants were disputing and fighting for its ownership, all such minor difficulties were eventually reconciled, by pliancy, emergency, and agreement, to a regular legal process; the personal presence of Cora being deemed not necessary to the integrity and symmetry of the suit.

The session of the court would be held in the county town, not many miles from Creswood.

Oswald Huron went up to Baltimore, and engaged the wisest men of the city.

Neville Huron, against the remonstrances of O'Dare, obtained his counsel from Philadelphia. "Your brother will have the advantage of you," had said O'Dare, "for the Baltimore lawyers will be fighting on their own dung-hill, and are of course more familiar with the laws, forms, usages, etc. of Maryland than are the Philadelphians; and in the country courts there is always a prejudice against imported lawyers; or if, in the beginning, there is not, the home lawyers will see to it that, in the end, there will be." Notwithstanding this shrewd advice, Neville Huron, in some things obstinate, in others weak, retained his chosen counsel without addition or subtraction.

The legal gentlemen engaged to conduct the Huron war came down to Creswood in advance of the session of the court, and almost bedeviled the people out of their wits by the pertinacity with which they elicited, fished up, and minutely gathered the history of Creswood and of every person whose residence there was of fifteen or more years' duration.

Some of the old women were looking for the millennium to succeed this avalanche of curiosity and investigation. They were confident that these black-clad investigators were searching for and gathering up data by which to separate the tares from the true seeds, and the manner in which not a few good old souls avoided committing themselves was irresistibly laughable.

The children, on the other hand, were of the opinion that Christmas was at hand before its time, which impression was due to the ready dimes which the new-comers threw among them from day to day.

There never was such a to-do in Creswood before. You could not hear an undisputed assertion about anything whatever, but you *could* hear a disputed assertion about almost everything. Old men looked at the skies and babbled of fearful things. Old women looked down into wells and droned out tales in the chimney-corners. The ghost of Jonas Aiken had been seen working by moonlight at the crevasse in the bluff. And the whole neighborhood was on the *qui vive* for Terrors. All this, because of a few black-clad, distinguished-looking personages, who were nosing about Creswood, going in and out at Cliff Hall, visiting Gale Island, interviewing the elders of the people, taking notes, citing witnesses, *et cetera*. About one-half of the adults of Creswood were summoned as witnesses, direct and indirect. Although old Mr. Grain was painfully desirous of gathering his late crops, the trial was at hand, and he must go to court. Grandmother Feathers had some fall broods of chickens which required her constant attention, but she too must go to court. Old Aunt Hives wanted to prepare her bees for the cold weather, but she also must go to court. And so it was, that Creswood issued out in the morning and swarmed in at night, with ceaseless gabble and wonderful speculation.

Meantime, Graham Huron and Cora were captured by officers of the law, and brought back to Creswood. Gra-

20*

ham was arrested as a horse-thief, and bonded to appear
before a criminal court. Cora was arrested and detained
as a stray and fugitive minor, but, much to the relief of
her friends, Oswald Huron sent her to Mr. Hope's, to remain there, subject to his demand, the minister pledging
himself to be responsible for her.

Oswald Huron's native fury seemed to have been transformed into cunning and prudence. He did nothing to prejudice his cause, and many things to strengthen it. The
ability and calmness exhibited by him excited the wonder
and admiration of numbers who had aforetime feared or
condemned him. For years he had been so little seen by
the people of Creswood that they had, in their imagina-
tions, invested him with a mystery, a habit, and an appearance not his own. Tall, dark, well dressed, dignified,
alert, and even bland on this occasion, the deep purpose
which brought him out seemed to have given a royal
power to his magical eye, symmetry to his mind, and reason, bordering upon forbearance, to his actions. As an
oak, firmly rooted in the soil, he appeared to think himself
established in his right, proof against overthrow, and monarch of the field. He appeared confidently to feel that he
could reach out his hand and crush, as with an iron grasp,
all who might dare to be inimical to the legitimate order
of his house. He seemed actuated and sustained by motives honorable, sincere, and deeper than his ordinary sea
of life. Men who had felt the weight of his cane about
their shoulders, came around him and even courted his recognition now,—licking the hand that smote them at will,
as hounds fawning at the feet of a hard but apparently
relenting master. To all who did not stand entirely aloof
from him, Oswald Huron acted most graciously and gracefully, and his action was the more charming and friend-
winning because of its being so unexpected, such an agreeable surprise, and so contradictory of all his former ways
and repute. His bearing went far to confute the many
tales which were told of his ungovernable temper, his
wrathful violence, and his haughty, ruthless enmity and vin-
dictiveness ; for what would be more apt to rouse his bitter fury and pour it out red hot than a persistent effort by
his personal enemies to pillage his house of its lovely child

and only light,—the only light whose ray seemed ever to have reached his own dark soul?

Several days were devoted to the examination of a cloud of witnesses, for and against; establishing character here, and destroying it there ;—and more neighborhood and family secrets, scandal, odds, ends, and intervals of speech, and misgathered testimony were soon upon the wing, than it was possible for the atmosphere to sustain or the ear to register.

Captain Gale came home to the island each night, looking as if some heated action had spared him for a moment, or as if the angry seas had pursued and battled with him to his very door. He felt that he, chiefly, was responsible for all this turmoil, and would be forever accountable to Cora, her friends, his own strict and sleepless conscience, and to a yet more sleepless Heaven, should the struggle in which he was now engaged result in the calamity of defeat.

"Carroll," said Captain Gale, coming home one night more anxious than ever, "you saw how things went this morning while you were there. Get, from your library, the books which are listed on this slip of paper, and bring them to court with you to-morrow. Our lawyers need them ; for every three minutes there is a controversy about what is admissible testimony and what is not. They also need some one to point them to precedents, references, and such like, and keep them clear on numberless little points in the Maryland practice, with which they are not familiar. You must go inside of the bar to-morrow, and sit with them."

"How is it going, uncle?" asked Carroll.

"Like the sea when the wind suddenly shifts against the waves and chops them to pieces ;—rough enough. Oswald Huron has impeached all the testimony, so far, and has raked up and perverted the truth of everything that has transpired in Creswood for twenty-five years, to bear him out. If that man had a good heart in his breast, I do not know of his equal anywhere. His brother is no match for him, and is greatly dispirited. I believe he even begins to doubt that Cora is his child."

"Have you been examined yet?" asked Carroll.

"No. They are reserving me, they say, for a center shot; but how I am to reach the center for them is clearer to them than it is to me, for my testimony is necessarily indirect. But I have many things to say which I trust will put a different color on the case. If I am discredited, however, I fear the struggle is hopeless, unless Maria Guthrie can be found and produced in court;—but the finding of her, in time for good, is an impossibility. Nobody knows where she is, or whether she is dead or alive. Oswald Huron has nullified her affidavit, which was but bastard testimony at best, and has turned it to his own advantage. He accepted it as a genuine document, but attacked and ridiculed it as a contrivance of your father, in whose handwriting it is, and succeeded in making a very unfavorable impression in regard to your father's memory."

Carroll sprang up. He was very fiery, even to undue haste. With a flashing eye, he said,—

"It then becomes my first duty, if Maria Guthrie is in the world, to seek her out; and whether I find her soon or late, to purge from my father's memory the venom of this Oswald Huron. If I cannot do that, I'll stop his breath by letting his blood."

"Sit down, Carroll," said Captain Gale. "This is not the time for such action. You will need both money and the assistance of a man like Hector O'Dare, if you ever prosecute a search for Maria Guthrie."

"Uncle," said Carroll, "I *have* the money. You know I've not been idle since I could work. I've done everything that a young lawyer *can* do. I've been a two-bit attorney, a ten-cent counselor, have drawn up bushels of documents for older men in the profession, kept the minor affairs of Creswood straight, and taken every job offered, though the fee amounted to no more than five cents. I wish to *redeem* myself, uncle, from a dear and affectionate bondage, and lighten the burden which you so nobly took upon yourself."

"Carroll," said Captain Gale, "you have stuff in you, and I'm glad of it." He then added, "You have been no burden to me, boy;" and turning away, he went out of the room and into where his wife was.

Carroll May was interested in the Huron war in more ways than one. If Cora Glencoe was Neville Huron's offspring, Carroll was not so hopelessly separated from her, as he had always conceived himself to be, by a red and impassable stream—his father's spilt blood.

He had, before the revelation of her parentage, mastered, not his preference, but that love and passion which school-room views and subsequent casual encounters had bred within him, and he now had his affections well in hand, to curb or give them rein as fortune might invite.

Whatever would be the after-difficulties which he should have to encounter, he would fain sweep the bloody and absolute barrier from between himself and Cora, that it might be possible for him to pass over to the other side. All this, and much more, without his having spoken to her a dozen times in his life.

On the following day, which was to be principally devoted to the examination and cross-examination of Captain Gale, Carroll appeared inside the bar with the weighty legal heads from Philadelphia, who found the young lawyer of great service in minutiæ, and by no means inferior to the importance of the case.

If the court-house had been packed full before, it was to-day packed and jammed, for it had gone abroad that Captain Gale was to take the witness-stand, and intensely interesting developments were anticipated. The curious and eager were not destined to disappointment, for before Captain Gale was told to stand aside, he gave a complete thirty years' view of Creswood.

When Oswald Huron saw Captain Gale upon the witness-stand, and Carroll May "busying himself" inside the bar, the iron bands with which he had harnessed himself down, came near to bursting. With a tremendous and persistent effort, however, he maintained his calmness, and, as before, assiduously supplied his lawyers with searching, skillful, and pertinent questions.

Over the head of Captain Gale the battle raged to the culminating degree of intensity and heat. Up to the time at which he was introduced as a witness, Oswald Huron, to all popular appearance, had decidedly the advantage of his brother. But the well-known and well-proven sturdy integrity of Captain Gale, his unimpeachable veracity, his long recognized respect for law, order, and legitimacy, and the vast amount of tributary light which he threw upon the subject of dispute, corrected the unbalanced scales of Justice, and left them suspended in the air, trembling, if at all, in favor of Neville Huron. After a most exciting day, closing with a most exquisite cross-examination of Captain Gale, court was adjourned until the next morning, when the lawyers on either side would enter upon their brain-fuddling arguments and summing-up.

But during the night which was to intervene, there was some fine work done by all hands, and the suit was virtually transferred from the court-room to a room in the village tavern, in which were gathered Oswald Huron with his counsel, and Neville Huron with his counsel, with the latter of whom also sat Captain Gale and Carroll May.

The judge before whom the trial had been progressing, and who was to decide the case, though not altogether inferior to his position, yet felt himself rather small in comparison with the trained and talented lawyers from Baltimore and Philadelphia. He therefore experienced a desire to get the benefit of other people's wisdom and opinions before he should risk his own; and for this reason he solicited a private interview with Captain Gale, whom he regarded as a clear-headed, reticent, reliable man, and as one who appeared to know more about the case in hand than was known by any other person with whom he could safely confer. The judge, furthermore, desired to do right, intrinsically as well as legally, and he thought that by a private talk with Captain Gale he might be able to enlighten himself upon points which were yet obscure, and would otherwise remain so, on account of the inadmissibility of certain mooted testimony which alone could make them clear. We will venture the assertion that very few protracted and exciting trials have ever been prosecuted to a close, without creating a *desire* in the bosom of a conscientious court to call a witness aside and ask,—

"By-the-way, Mr. Brown, what was it you were going to tell about, when, under the customary rulings, I was compelled to stop you?"

Now whether the judge did right or wrong in consulting privately with Captain Gale, we put it down in extenuation, if need be, that he undoubtedly *meant* to do right; and Captain Gale was one of the few men who, however much he might be interested in the result of a trial, would not endeavor to seduce the judge to substitute sympathy for law. But he would and did, in this case, endeavor to ascertain the probable view which the judge entertained in respect to Cora's lineage, and the probable decision which he would render; the evidence being before him *in extenso*, and having been thoroughly sifted and winnowed by cross-examinations. Although the judge was careful not to commit himself, Captain Gale was conscious of having obtained the cue for future action. The captain divined about as follows:

That the judge, as a private citizen, was not in doubt as to Cora's lineage; but that the same judge, in whose keeping was the conscience of the Law, *was* in doubt. That a continuance would be granted on the motion of either party to the suit, but preferably on the motion of Neville Huron's counsel, upon the ground that Maria Guthrie—an important, even a deciding witness—was not at hand, but might be produced at a future session of the court. That, if forced to a decision now, the testimony being incomplete, and, in many things, superficially conflicting, the court would be compelled to run in the old grooves in respect to law and evidence, and the decree would necessarily be in favor of Oswald Huron.

Captain Gale left the presence of the judge, with a scheme in his head, the salient points of which he unveiled to Carroll May, who caught at them instantly, and not without reason or forecast. The scheme of the firm and fertile captain—which led to the assemblage of the two Huron wings in the tavern-room—may better than otherwise be conceived from the following short dialogue:

"Carroll," said Captain Gale, "there are two things to be done. One of them is feasible — and the other may be."

"What are they, uncle?"

"First — the case must be continued. Next — we must, in advance of a continuance, endeavor to effect a compro-

mise by which Cora will be rescued from the immediate
control of Oswald Huron, and have an agreed guardian to
take charge of her."

"But is there a man alive," asked Carroll, "with whom,
or under whose guardianship, Oswald Huron could be
brought to trust Cora?"

"There is one—and a good one."

"Who?"

"Mr. Hope."

"True. I had not thought of him."

"And now for the terms which will recommend the
compromise which I intend shall be proposed," said Captain Gale.—"Cora, you are aware I presume, has left the
Creswood School, and is devoting a year to history,—or
was, prior to this turmoil,—and is preparing herself probably for some classic institution to which it is Oswald
Huron's intention to consign her. Her preparatory year
is almost gone. What I advise to be proposed is this:
the Huron brothers shall contract with each other that,
following a continuance of this suit, Mr. Hope shall be
chosen to take charge of Cora, act as her guardian, and
send her, say to New York, where she can pursue her
studies, and remain for a year at the least, during which
time Maria Guthrie may be found; in which latter event
I have reason to know that we shall win. If this thing
is properly managed, Oswald Huron can be brought to
terms, for the terms will in no essential sense change his
premeditated course with Cora. As likely as not he may
consider it a triumph, for he was as restless as a worm in
hot ashes under my testimony to-day, and I saw well
enough that his previous exulting confidence effectually
failed him. Moreover, such an arrangement will involve
an important admission on his part,—the admission that
his right is doubtful. But it will not do for either you
or me to make this proposition. That would steel him
against it at once. He must be led up to it by one of
Neville Huron's counsel, we in the mean time seeming
rather to object than to sanction."

"Give it in charge of that sharp-nosed attorney. He
will manage it, if it can be done at all," said Carroll.

"I agree with you," said Captain Gale.

" This has been a hard fight, uncle."

" Worse than cold pitch and a storm at sea," was Captain Gale's reply.

So it was, in pursuance of Captain Gale's interview with the judge, that the Huron brothers, each attended by his staff of lawyers, met in conference.

But the cunning scheme of the captain of the Whitecap would have proved abortive had it not been for one circumstance. His private interview with the judge of the court was already within the knowledge of the watchful lawyers engaged by Oswald Huron, who were not, as they boasted among themselves, to be tricked by either bribery or collusion, without knowing when, where, and by whom it was done. They communicated to Oswald Huron their suspicions relative to this interview, and put him on his guard, and the very fact that Captain Gale and Carroll, in the subsequent conference, objected to the compromise which Neville Huron's sharp-nosed lawyer skillfully maneuvered before the assemblage, prompted Oswald Huron to accept the proposals,—which, by-the-way, came more in the shape of suggestions than propositions,—and induced him to feel that he had hedged his enemies.

When the court resumed its session in the morning, the cause of Huron *vs.* Huron was continued, on the motion of Neville Huron, and upon the ground already indicated —the absence of an important witness, Maria Guthrie.

This disposition of the cause left the Huron affairs, legally, *in statu quo ante bellum;* for it was not within the province of the court to bind either party to good faith and performance in the equitable arrangement resulting from the Huron conference in the tavern-room.

Oswald Huron might even yet forfeit his pledged word, ignore the contract, and resume control of Cora ; for there was nothing to prevent him but his own conscience and sense of honor—no lawful, physical force or agency by which he could be restrained from such a course. Notwithstanding this, and that he was accustomed to brook no opposition, but to have his way whether or no, there was one thing on earth which this strange man loved, admired, respected, yielded to, and even feared—the stanch little girl whom he regarded as his daughter. He was not insensible of the fact that he was possessed of a devil, and, to do him justice, he strove against it, but, often, as ineffectually as he, who, night and day, was in the mountain and in the tombs, crying and cutting himself with stones, and whom no man could bind. There were times when Oswald Huron, knowingly, but from an irresistible, reckless perversity that was in him, had aggressed upon Cora in ethical matters which she held dear to her integrity, and she had stood out against him like a steel shaft against a pelting and pitiless storm. At such times he had been *compelled* to yield or kill her where she stood. When she was brought back to Cliff Hall from her elopement, she read him the law of right and wrong, and promised him firmly that unless he abided by it, nothing but iron chains would ever keep her with him. He saw from the desperation in her eyes that another time had come in which he must yield, or she would wrest her fate and fortunes from his keeping, and leave him forever. For Cora, whom he loved with a fathomless though insane affection, to turn her back upon him and seek some other refuge, would, he thoroughly felt, pluck the last glimmering light from his soul, and crown his dark life with a wreath of midnight blackest flowers. He knew that the hunted girl was awake to her new-born situation, and that if he did not abide by her roused dictation, and by the agreement which had just been made between himself and her champions, that she would hardly abide with him. Under these influences he was coerced—and forewarned to act in good faith.

Cora, the child of compromise, consequently remained with Mr. Hope until, for certain considerations which will appear, he determined to send her to the city of New York, where she might prosecute her studies.

When Captain Gale unveiled to Carroll May his scheme in regard to Cora, among the several features of it the incidental suggestion of the captain that Cora might be sent to New York, was the one which to Carroll was the most attractive; for Carroll himself was going to that city to remain probably for a year, possibly for always. His contemplated change of base would be in pursuance of Captain Gale's paternal advice. The captain, to whom

Creswood was a sweet spot but by no means the kuown world, once upon a time said to his young protégé,—

"Carroll, Creswood is a happy, tranquil place for those who are established, and for others who have no ambition; but it is not a place for a man to make his way. You may successfully vegetate here, but that will hardly satisfy you. If you wish to escape the slow growth of a shaded sapling, you must go out into the world and foster yourself. This is but the outer edge of the universe. Go to the center, son, and you may do something. You' will either succeed or fail, and it is better to succeed, and, as well to fail, at the center, as anywhere else."

"What do you call the center, uncle?"

"Some large town or city, where there is business to be done by those who are willing to do it."

"New York is the largest, and busiest," said Carroll. "I will strike boldly, and go there."

"Very well. And if you are starved out, why, then, you can come back to Creswood. I will send Johnny with you, that he may learn something besides 'ma' and 'pa,' and complete his theoretical study of civil engineering. How do you like the prospect?"

Carroll was delighted, and lost no time in seeking out Johnny and concocting with him a world of schemes.

And now that Cora was destined to the same city as themselves, they numbered the fortunate fact as chief among the attractions which loomed so gayly up in the pathway of their future. Johnny did not care so much about Cora, for he was grown to be a large, lubberly lad, who would almost as soon fondle with a dog as with the daughter of a duke. But Carroll, although he might never see Cora in the great city, would feel a foolish sort of satisfaction in knowing that she was *there*—in the same metes and bounds with himself.

Graham Huron, laughable to relate, was actually tried for horse-stealing. His uncle prosecuted relentlessly, and would have added to the grave charge that of abduction, but for fear of Cora, and for the fact that she was not now under his care. Graham got off, as it were, by the skin of his teeth, for technically he *had* stolen the horses, and law goes by technicalities. But as he proved the emergency

under which they were taken, that they were seasonably
returned, unharmed, and by his orders, and also established
a good character, the jury jocularly agreed to return him
"not guilty." It was a source of great amusement to
Graham's acquaintances in Philadelphia,—his arrest and
trial as a horse-thief,—and he was likely never to hear the
last of it. He was advised by no means ever to run for an
office, if he did not wish to be known all over the continent
as a horse-thief and a man of desperate character.

This assault upon Graham did Oswald Huron no good,
but detriment rather, as it necessarily brought before the
public the scene at Cliff Hall which had induced the young
man to take Cora and flee. Oswald Huron thereby lost
the prestige which he had gained by his calm brilliancy
during the trial for the possession of Cora Glencoe.

Had it not been for an overruling Providence, Cora's
future would probably have been like that of a tender
lamb, sent out into a world of brambles, to be torn and
robbed of its fleece continually. But with Mr. Hope she
was harbored safely, and under his guidance and instructions might safely adventure upon an expedition into the
world.

CHAPTER XXV.

WHEN the smoke of battle cleared from about our young
heroine, there were but few people in Creswood, or in the
adjacent country, who had decided opinions about the case,
or distinct ideas of its merits or demerits. It was evident
to all, that Captain Gale had been the bulwark of Neville
Huron, against which Oswald Huron had charged, as
waves against rock. But the testimony of Captain Gale
was neither direct nor conclusive, and, in the nature of his
knowledge, could not be. The intelligent few of his acquaintance, and of those who had heard his honest voice,
and seen him with unshaken firmness and uninterrupted
consistency withstand a cross-examination which elicited
everything bearing upon the case of which he had known

or dreamed for the last twenty years, believed as he believed, with the exception of Oswald Huron, and possibly,
Oswald Huron's lawyers. The simpletons of Captain
Gale's acquaintance were with him in opinion and sympathy, simply because he was with himself. But there
were many goggle-eyed lookers-on, who knew none of the
parties to the controversy, whose fuddled condition was
downright amusing. One old countryman went away
saying, "that he'd be-dog-gone-his-cats if them lawyers
hadn't twisted his noddle, and beat up his brains so, that
he would have to put in a double *crap* the next spring to
git himself straightened out again. He wouldn't git done
thinkin' and dreamin' 'bout it fur a year."

Now that Cora was disinherited of one father and not
given another, she began to regard herself as almost an
alien in the house of the Hurons.

Neville Huron visited Cora before he left for Philadelphia. Their meeting was too affecting and too difficult of
description for the prosy pen. He was all that she would
ask as a father, and she filled his bosom as a daughter.

In the matter of visiting Cora, wherever she might be,
it was deemed prudent by Mr. Hope, inasmuch as Oswald
Huron was not likely to seek her often, and inasmuch as
it was not desirable that he should do so, that Neville
Huron and his family should be restricted to periodical
and not too frequent visits. Oswald Huron being similarly restricted, there would be no reason for complaint on
either hand. Neville agreed with Mr. Hope, and promised not to stir up his brother Oswald by permitting his
family or himself too frequently to see Cora. He would
give his brother no excuse to depart from the agreement
between them.

Our heroine, in some respects, was better situated than
young girls generally are. She had two fathers,—at all
events there were two wealthy men claiming her as their
daughter, who were each willing and anxious to supply
all her personal wants, furnish her with plenty of money,
and see that she was assiduously cared for, while in this
state of suspension. In addition, she was in the possession of a kind, indulgent, venerable guardian, who would
give her all the freedom she craved, and encourage her

21*

not to despond, but to look aloft, and remember the everlasting covenants of her Maker.

Oswald Huron, during his manly, keen, and superb
struggle for Cora Glencoe, had earned a reputation for
defensive and offensive ability for which no person had
ever given him credit. But after the excitement was well
over, his mind collapsed; and losing the calm power of
his lucid interval, he became as savage as a punched tiger,
and as haggard as famine.

He worried himself continually, talked wildly by day
and by night, and frequently woke up the servants at un-
seasonable hours, for trivial and unreasonable services.

When, years ago, he first came to Cliff Hall and made
it his home, he brought white servants with him from
Philadelphia. They remained with him a few months,—
until the death of his wife,—after which, as by accord,
they all left him, with the exception of Maria Guthrie,
who, being attached to Mrs. Huron, had promised her on
her death-bed to nurse and nourish her child. Bereft of
his wife, and bereft of servants, Oswald Huron bought
slaves. They were compelled to remain with him, like or
dislike, and, with their issue, were with him now. Ordinarily, he was not severe upon them, but when the spirit
moved him, and they happened to be in the way, he made
them *walk.* They soon learned pretty well to dodge him,
however, and taking it all in all they had an easy, lazy
time of it.

Not long after the Huron war had been suspended by
an armistice, Jim, the "body-servant" of Oswald Huron,
was waked from his slumbers about midnight, by a bell
which communicated with his master's chamber, and
which was so arranged that it would tinkle right into
Jim's ear whenever the master saw proper to pull it after
the servant had retired and composed himself to rest.
Jim sprang from his couch, went up-stairs, and with fear
and trembling, tapped at his master's door—and was
ordered in. Oswald Huron was walking the floor, like a
caged tiger. The negro stood, half asleep, notwithstanding the tremor of his soul, waiting for his master's orders.
Oswald Huron wanted a fish,—a fresh, live fish,—and he
commanded Jim to get him one immediately. The negro

looked at him almost speechless with amazement. This was the most unreasonable and untimely demand which had ever been made upon him.

"Master," said he, with anxious humility, "dey aint no fish in dees woods."

"I want a *fish!*" sternly and despotically said the master, with a frown which made the negro quake, and with a wave of the hand which notified him to leave and go get it.

The negro went down, waked up the cook, and counseled with her,—telling her meanwhile that he thought "master had done gone clean crazy."

There was no place in all Creswood where a live fish could be had at this witching time of night, and Jim, as the next best thing he could think of, concluded to try and fool his master with a mackerel.

When he tremblingly went back to his master's room, with a doctored mackerel on a string, as if he had just hooked it from a trout pool, he found Oswald Huron seated, and asleep, with his head resting upon a table. A pen lounged in his nerveless hand, and before him was paper and an ink-bottle. Jim quietly and joyfully withdrew.

On the initial page of a letter sheet was written,—

"CLIFF HALL.

"MY DARLING DAUGHTER CORA:

"Night and darkness are in the house when you are away from me. My heart yearns for——"

The above is all that was penned, before sleep, fatigue, or some other influence overcame him, and cut short his lament.

In the morning, Oswald Huron was unusually calm, and, to the infinite relief of his servant, did not allude to fresh fish or any other untimely matter. He merely asked if the windows had been closed, remarking that he had caught cold overnight.

During the day, Mr. Hope, who was one among the few visitors who ever appeared at Cliff Hall, was announced. Oswald Huron received him with due consideration and civility. After a short and quiet conversation upon extraneous and indifferent subjects the old minister observed,—

"Mr. Huron, I thought that you might like to see Cora before she leaves Creswood."

"Where do you contemplate sending her?"

"I have concluded to place her for awhile in New York."

"In the city of New York?" asked Oswald Huron, not without a slight elevation of the eyebrows, indicating surprise.

"Yes—in the city."

"I have never heard that New York city was distinguished for its educational facilities."

"Nor I," answered the minister. "But I am advised of a place in the city, which will, I think, be more advantageous to Cora than if I should send her to some strict seminary. I was thinking that it would be more agreeable to her and her relatives, should I place her in a private family, where she will get the benefit of select society, and, with other pupils, be instructed in her studies at the family mansion. This is the arrangement which I have in view, but I have refrained from making it positive and final until I shall have conferred with you upon the subject."

"Mr. Hope, if you will exercise your own judgment with respect to my daughter, and not suffer yourself to be influenced by my enemies, I am willing that you should have absolute control of her for the time. I have every confidence in Cora. Wherever you may place her, she will be as stanch as those cedars of Lebanon which you preachers so greatly glorify."

"Will you see Cora before she goes?"

"I would like to see her, but I am submitting to the compromise."

"We must all abide by the agreement," rejoined Mr. Hope; "but it will not be best for her to see *none* of her relatives during this suspension. I have thought it both prudent and tender toward her that she should see you on the one part, and your brother's family on the other, about once in every three months, if you or they should find it convenient to visit her that often. What do you think of it?"

"You are the arbiter, Mr. Hope. I confide in you, and will make no objections—at present."

"What shall I say to Cora,—that you will be over to see her, or not?"

"Tell her that I will come. Probably,—yes, I feel better to-day, and I may as well walk over with you when you return."

After some further conversation Oswald Huron accompanied the minister to his residence.

When Cora saw Oswald Huron she went to his bosom. She could not hold back. From her infancy she had lived with him and regarded him as her father. And now, in his haggard calm, and the new relations which had arisen between them, with thoughts of his loneliness, and the firm, bold battle he had made to keep her, she was melted to compassionate affection. He pressed her to his heart. His breast was convulsed, and heaved with the power of suppressed emotion. He knew not how much he loved Cora until this moment, and she knew not until now, that with all his fiery faults and gloomy terrors, he was very dear to her heart. Their interview was not long, and was principally devoted to exchanging endearments. Oswald Huron experienced a softening of his heart, which he had never felt before. Under the influence of roused affection, he asked her to forgive him for having overshadowed her young life as a deadly nightshade, and to strive if she could love him in future, when he would be gentle with her. He poured out a purer than his wonted spirit upon her, and blessed her fervently in the name of Heaven and its great God.

"Ah!" said he, "my little one, if you knew of the Apollyon against whom I have to contend, the Apollyon who haunts my pillow and my steps, and comes upon me with his infernal power, and sits in my heart, and sways my faculties, you would pity as well as dread the unfortunate man who claims you as his child."

This was the first time that Oswald Huron had ever alluded to himself in this manner. In his deep rich voice there was a thrilling sadness, the echo, almost, of despair.

Cora's tender heart was rent by these writhing words, and she clung frantically about his neck while her eyes flashed fire and alternately issued tears.

The young girl had never had an intimation, other than from her own observation, that a disordered mind dictated the actions and dominated the heart of Oswald Huron, rendering him, oftener than not, perverse, bitter, and uncontrollable. Her bosom now ached with compassion and teemed with palliation for him.

Oswald Huron took leave of Cora, after having exhorted her to abide with those principles which he knew to be her guide and stay. He seemed never to have realized as he now did — his mind being perfectly clear — what a firm, heroic, invincible spirit this woodland child must possess, to have lived alone with *him* from the cradle almost to womanhood, and performed her duty faithfully, without murmuring, but hopelessly. He could not remember the time when he had had just occasion to reprove her; nor could he remember the time, if ever, that he had taken her to his heart as he had done to-day. He could look back and see her as of yore she stepped about him, with serious, sad eyes, — or wandered out with her dog to seek companionship among the birds of the forest, from the voices of the winds, or the splashing of the waves.

He went home, cleft to the very soul. The ensuing night, he was taken from the floor of his chamber, in fearful convulsions. A dangerous illness succeeded, from which he slowly recovered, and during which Cora willfully postponed her departure from Creswood, left her guardian, and watched over her uncle until his malady abated and health returned.

Prior to Mr. Hope's special visit to Oswald Huron, and the return-visit of the latter, the old minister had received the following letter in answer to one which he had written immediately upon the commencement of his authority and responsibility as Cora's chosen guardian:

"Rev. St. John Hope.

"My Ever-esteemed Friend,—Your letter of the 10th inst. is just at hand. I am glad to be able to answer it satisfactorily, I trust, and without delay. Don't mention *trouble* to me, my dear sir, in anything which concerns or will accommodate you. I have what you inquire for, ready made, here in New York, without going any farther. If you should search the country, you could not find an accessible temporary home, so well suited to the young lady you describe, as she will find in the mansion of Mrs. Boyd, where I have the honor and pleasure of being domiciled. The mistress is a wealthy young widow, who, for the sake of society, admits to her house, as permanent guests, a few well-chosen persons, mostly of her own sex. She is honest, gentle, correct, and delightful. She keeps about her an unexceptionable circle, such as any young girl may safely enter and abide with, and certainly find agreeable. There are pupils resident in the mansion, which is visited daily by professional masters and mistresses of arts and sciences. A superb piano, also, which Miss Huron can use almost at will. To enumerate, we have, in the way of company, or colony :

"First—Mrs. Linda Boyd, the Queen Bee of the hive.

"Second—Uncle Jesse Medley, Mrs. Boyd's uncle, an old bachelor, and, if you will pardon me, a trump. He stands no nonsense. He and I are great friends.

"Third—Mr. Lake, a gentleman ; Mrs. Lake, a lady ;. Miss Lake, fifteen years old ; Missie Lake, five years old ; an interesting, cultivated, proper, traveled family.

"Fourth—Miss Lightner, a morning teacher in one of our first-class schools. Her afternoons are devoted to the pupils in the Boyd mansion. She is a young lady whose presence is invariably profitable.

"Fifth—Two young misses from the country, under Miss Lightner's control and instruction.

"Sixth—There are two vacancies, one of which will be reserved, until I hear from you, for Miss Huron.

"If Miss Huron were my sister, and I were going to Europe or anywhere, I would leave her here, or with you.

"I will take pleasure in meeting the young lady at the cars, and conducting her to Mrs. Boyd's, if you should decide to consign her to this place. Or, if it would commode you, I will come down to Creswood for her. I have nothing of moment to occupy my time at present, and would be glad of an occasion to visit Creswood, and see some of my old friends there, chief among whom are yourself, Garland, and the Gales.

"With veneration and respect,
"I remain sincerely your friend,
"CASSEL P. RAPID.

"P. S.—Miss Cora Huron need not contemplate bringing a maid with her if she comes here. The maid would be useless.—C. P. R."

"Cora," said Mr. Hope, after his conference with Oswald Huron, which was in pursuance of the letter just published, "your destination is fixed."

"Where am I to go?" asked the young girl.

"Here—read this letter. It will tell you better than I could tell you myself."

Cora read Cassel Rapid's letter, and turning to Mr. Hope, inquired,—

"Who is Cassel P. Rapid?"

"He is the son of Guy Rapid, of whom you have often heard me speak."

"He is very kind," said Cora.

"He *is* kind, and that is not his only virtue," said the old minister. "Also, he has relieved me of much anxiety. What that letter says, we can both rely upon. You will have a pleasant place at Mrs. Boyd's, without any doubt."

"He writes like a *young* man," said Cora. "Where have you known him?"

"I knew him when he was a playful little cub of a boy. I have seen him within the last six months, and on my word he is genuine. I intend to put you somewhat under his care and guidance, for when you get so far away from home, you will need a referee; and I know of no person with whom I would trust you so confidently as with him. He inherits numberless good qualities from his most excellent and worthy dead parents."

"How will I go?" asked Cora.

"Garland and his sister Bell will go with you."

Cora was relieved. She did not fancy Cassel Rapid as a lone escort.

"When will you be ready to leave ?" asked Mr. Hope.

"I am ready now, or at any time which may suit your convenience. You must forgive me for refusing to get ready while there was sickness at Cliff Hall."

"You were a little headstrong, my dear, but I do not know but that you were right, after all. I will lay no blame against you there."

Cora kissed the brow of the aged minister, and withdrew to her own chamber to contemplate the future which was about to come actively upon her. Life, to her, had been thus far like a passive existence, in which she was called upon chiefly to resist. Now she was about to enter upon activity and unfettered endeavor—unfettered except by her inexperience.

But she was fitted for contact, and would more naturally absorb and gather, than lose and dissipate.

CHAPTER XXVI.

SIMPLE, unsophisticated Creswood was getting to be *blasé.*

After the eventful, heated term through which it had passed, numbering among its items and incidents, bloodshed, elopement, strangers, ghosts, lawsuits, and a general ganging and mixing up of the people,—and all crowded into a single summer and autumn,—nothing less rousing than an earthquake or a wedding would elicit remark or capture a glance ;—and as neither earthquake nor wedding was at hand, the greeting of the people fell into "dull times" as they met and separated on their way. There was no newspaper in the neighborhood to startle the populace by wonderful editorial asseverations one week, and still more wonderful contradictions and innuendoes the next. Consequently Creswood became itself again, and so continued for a season.

But as long as Cora Glencoe remained in Creswood, the gossips would gabble concerning her and her family rela-

tions.   But Cora was about to leave, and very unkindly
bear away with her the last breath of the gossips.

As Mr. Hope had promised, Garland and his sister Bell·
accompanied Cora on her journey to New York.   When
they arrived at the Boyd mansion, Cassel Rapid was out
of town, boating on the Hudson, it being a pleasant, breezy
day.   Linda, also, was out in the city ; but Mrs. Lake received Cora, told Garland that she had been expected and
provided for, that Mrs. Boyd would soon be at home, and
every needful attention be bestowed upon the young lady.

Garland, who was perfectly satisfied with appearances,
took leave, and, with his sister Bell, went on to Connecticut to visit some relatives.

Cora felt at ease with Mrs. Lake, who was an inviting,
lady-like matron, and perfectly at ease herself.   Mrs. Lake
was not slow to recognize in the new guest a superior
quality of girl, and a most acceptable acquisition to the
Boyd colony.

Linda had so improved under the tutorship of Cassel
Rapid, and by daily contact with those whom he had
secured for her companions, that she was now competent
to pass muster almost anywhere.   Ignorance and diffidence
were supplanted by increasing comprehension and modest
confidence, and, her heart remaining pure and domestic,
she had already become an agreeable, well-behaved girl,
charming and sweet at the fireside, in the parlor, or on
the boulevard.

So soon as Linda had got an elementary understanding
of city life, and of her true position, she emerged from
the fog which had enveloped her, as the moon bursts
through banked and rifted clouds.   She seemed to comprehend everything all at once, and speedily learned to
blush at her former ignorance and simplicity.

Mr. Hope, in his correspondence with Cassel Rapid, had
given the young man a sketch of Cora's life and experience, and had fully disclosed to him her present peculiar
situation, that Cassel might the more knowingly judge
what would be the tenderest and most balmy treatment
for her.   ·He also delegated to Cassel the eye and arm of
a guardian, requesting him to take an interest in the
young stranger, look after her, and see that she avoided

all harm. Nothing but the almost boundless confidence which the old minister had in both Cassel and Cora, could ever have reconciled his conscience to the course he was pursuing with his young protégée, or ever have prompted such a course. Ordinarily, he was furnishing the young gentleman with undue opportunities, and subjecting the young lady to some of those insidious perils which wait upon the pathway of innocent and unsuspecting youth. But the old minister had brought himself firmly to believe that in Cassel's soul was neither snare nor ambush, and that Cora was not a girl to be taken either at will or by surprise.

Accepting the trust which Mr. Hope had gently urged upon him, Cassel, with the design of preparing the way for a proper performance of his assumed duty, acquainted Linda with Cora's character as described by the minister, and cautioned not only her but all the inmates of the Boyd mansion upon the recent prominent points of Cora's history. He was interested in the coming pupil, in advance of her coming, and closed his instructions to Linda by saying,—

"Now, my little Urban, you must not imagine, because Miss Huron has been raised in the woods, that she is necessarily as green as you were when I first found you," and Cassel and Linda laughed merrily. "Therefore, do not attempt to patronize her, but receive her as you would your present other self,—just as you would like to be received should you go down to Creswood. To begin with, remember that Miss Huron is from Creswood, and that Creswood is Cassel Rapid's birthplace."

"Creswood should feel very much indebted to Cassel Rapid for condescending to be born there," replied Linda, with playful sarcasm. She then added, "Brother, don't get vain, for if you do, I shall follow your example."

"Follow my *advice*, and you will do better than to copy from my example," said Cassel. "I am your mentor, remember,—not your exemplar."

"You are my brother," said Linda, affectionately, "and for your sake, if not for hers, I will endeavor to win Miss Huron's heart on sight."

As before said, Linda and Cassel were both absent when

Cora arrived at the Boyd mansion, a total stranger in the midst of a myriad. When Linda returned to her house Cora was alone in a sitting-room, Mrs. Lake having left her for a few moments. Linda, learning that Cora was in the house, went to meet and welcome her. As she came in at the door, Cora looked around and saw a half-hesitating girl, scarcely older than herself, with a tender, pretty face, stylish form, and an air of modest investigation and curiosity. She had no idea that this was the Widow Boyd, the mistress of the mansion. Linda was enchanted with her first sight of Cora, and her heart went out to the young stranger on the instant. She stepped forward; Cora left her chair, and facing the new-comer, each stood looking at the other with a half smile.

"Shall I introduce myself?" asked Cora.

"No. I know you,—but I had no conception that you would be so sweet and lovely. Do you know me?"

"I do not."

"Guess who I am."

"I cannot."

"Would you like to know?"

Here the girls both laughed.

"Yes, if your name is half as pretty as you are," said Cora, returning Linda's compliment.

Linda announced herself. Cora was rejoiced and amazed. This young rose-lipped girl to be a widow, and the mistress of the mansion! She could hardly realize it.

Linda, approaching nearer, held out her arms, and said,—

"Come—let me welcome you."

Cora met her embrace, and two tender bosoms throbbed against each other.

"I am so glad you have come," said Linda. "I know that I shall love you, because you are so sweet and fresh from the country."

"Do you love the country?" asked Cora, whose preconceived idea of the Widow Boyd was of a different person altogether from the one now before her.

"I do indeed—and everything from it. I am but a rustic myself, transplanted from the backwoods. But let me show you your realm, and get your baggage together." And Linda took Cora to the room set apart for her. "Has your baggage arrived?" asked Linda, glancing about.

At this moment the alert housekeeper looked in, and pointing to a small trunk, observed,—

"That is all the baggage which came."

"It is all I have," said Cora. "I will be outfitted here in the city."

"You are right," said Linda, "because our country dresses generally look odd in the city."

The housekeeper went off, better satisfied than she had been with the pomp and circumstance of one small trunk; for when she had noted the insignificant amount of baggage, and had taken a glance at Cora, she had said to herself,—

"Very nice, but very poor."

Underlings are apt to judge by outlying circumstances. A cart-load of baggage has made many a porter polite, and a diamond ring on the finger of a fop has rendered many a dining-room servant obsequious,— whereas, the person without so much baggage, or so much ring, might be by far the better of the two.

It required but a moment's observation—such as females rarely fail to bestow—for Cora to discover that there was a difference between her dresses and those of Mrs. Lake and Linda; for although her dresses were complete, they did not have the appearance, in her memory, of being as *finished* as those of the city ladies. This, however, was not a matter greatly to trouble a girl of Cora's good sense and financial readiness, and to tell the truth, there was but one person in the whole city whom she felt a backwardness about meeting, attired in whatever dress she might be. This person was Cassel Rapid, whom she reflected upon as a critical and fastidious city gentleman, who was to exercise over her some control, along with which would probably go the right or privilege of scrutinizing her attire. In most things Cassel *was* both critical and fastidious; but in the matter of a country girl, or any other girl, he would always be enlisted on the side of purity and intelligence. Let him once see Cora's face, and he would be her knight, regardless of the pattern from which her last

22*

dresses were cut. If there was a man in the world who forgave trifles, it was Cassel Rapid. If there was a man in the world who was considerate and tender toward the tender and inexperienced, it was Cassel Rapid. And if there was a man in the wide world who was the relentless foe of despotic evil, it was Cassel Rapid.

Although Cora had anticipated a friendly welcome, she was not prepared for the sweet and loving one which Linda gave her. She was destined to yet another surprise. In Cassel Rapid, the chosen one of Mr. Hope, she expected to see a black-dressed, professional, and somewhat caustic-looking young gentleman, whose outward appearance would be faultless, whose city politeness would be killing, and whose manners would be regulated by square and compass, and by no means amiss so much as a hair's-breadth. Why she had so conceived him she could not even tell herself, but she was constantly conscious of an effort at mental preparation to put herself, when she should meet him, between the veritable P and Q.

As Cora, with Linda, came out of her room into the hall, she heard. a pleasant, manly, laughing voice, and running footsteps, coming up the stairway, and in a moment Cassel Rapid appeared at the head of the stairs, shaking his finger in saucy triumph at some one below. He was dressed in sailor's habit, and was just off the water, where he had been boating. As he came along the hall, Cora, not in the least suspecting that this was the formidable personage who was to hold a sort of dominion over her, did not hesitate to let her eyes rest upon him. Cassel was barely twenty-two years of age, very youthful in appearance when he was happy, and, when on a frolic, looked no other than a boy. He was just now from below-stairs, and from kissing little five-year-old Lily Lake, who had chased him up the steps in an effort at reprisal. As he came along the hall, his face lighted with sportive animation, his step unstudied, and his sailor's dress suggesting the freedom of the wind and billow, Cora thought that she had never seen so bright and manly a youth.

"Oh, here is my brother—Mr. Rapid," eagerly said Linda, half to Cora and half to Cassel, as he approached.

Cora was far more surprised than when she learned that

the girlish Linda was the Widow Boyd and the mistress of Boyd mansion. Was it possible that this school-boy was Mr. Cassel P. Rapid, her *quasi* guardian? and was he Linda's brother?

When Cassel, with a smiling look of inquiry, halted before Linda, she, glancing at Cora, said,—

"Mr. Rapid, Miss Huron has arrived,—permit me to present you."

Cassel, in defiance of cold etiquette, held out his hand. Cora looked into his face, and after an instant's hesitation, daintily placed her hand in his.

"I always seek the grasp," said Cassel, pleasantly, "of any coming from Creswood under the blessing of Mr. Hope. Have you just arrived?"

"Yes, sir,—but half an hour ago."

"Sister," asked Cassel, turning to Linda, "is everything comfortable?"

"If it is not, it's your fault," replied Linda, "for you have been away on the water altogether out of season."

"This," said Cassel to Cora—and smiling at Linda, "is the Queen Bee of our hive. I perceive," he added, glancing into Cora's room, "that she has given you a sunny cell. Do not let her spoil you with favoritism."

"I am in danger, I assure you," said Cora, with a lovely blush of pleasure. "I feel so very much at home already."

"You *are* at home," replied Cassel with that smile and pleasant eye of his which never failed to win. "But would you not like to write back to Creswood announcing your arrival?"

"I would indeed," replied Cora.

"I will bring you writing material," said Cassel, going to his own room.

"Is he your brother?" asked Cora of Linda.

"Oh, no,—we are no kin. But I call him brother, because he has been so kind and noble with me. I have no brother of my own, but I never want a better one than brother Cassel. He made me call him brother when I first knew him, and now I've got so accustomed to it that I would hardly know how else to address him. Don't you think he is handsome?"

"I do," answered Cora.

"Oh, he is *beautiful!*" said Linda, with enthusiasm. "And then he is so very, very thoughtful and kind; so gentle, to be a man. You are bound to love him,— you can't help it."

"Is he a sailor?" innocently asked Cora.

"No," replied Linda, laughing at the question. "Did you ever see a sailor with so white a hand and neck? He has just returned from a water frolic."

Cassel now reappeared with writing material, and handing it to Linda, said,—

"Little Urban, do the dainty duties of your house by depositing these in Miss Huron's room."

Once upon a time, Cassel told Linda that when she ceased to be a country girl, and got to be a city lady, he would cease to call her little Sylvan, and get to calling her little Urban, when he did not use the privilege of addressing her as "sister." The time had already come when he felt justified in using the appellative of "little Urban." Turning to Cora, he observed, smilingly,—

"Miss Huron, in Spanish they do not say that a distinguished person 'has arrived,'—but 'has finished to arrive.' You have simply arrived. When you have written to Creswood, announcing that welcome fact, and conveying to Mr. Hope my reverence and love, then you will have finished your arrival. You see that little box—there by the window-side, at the head of the stairs? That is our mail-box. Place your letters in it, and they will go out upon the first train."

Cassel was about to withdraw, when Lily Lake appeared at the head of the steps, and seemed waiting for an encouragement to come forward.

"Come here, Lily," said Cassel. "Here is our new friend."

Lily, a dulcet, open-eyed little creature, skipped up to Cora. Cassel duly presented her. Cora took her and kissed her. Lily said,—

"Mamma told me to come up and give you welcome. He is a rogue," said she, abruptly, pouting and turning her eyes upon Cassel. "He steals kisses from me every day; and if you don't mind he will steal 'em from *you.*"

Cora blushed, and Cassel, bowing to her in gay humor,

and as if he would as soon steal a kiss as not, withdrew and went down-stairs, but soon passed back again to change his clothes. Cora invited Lily into her room.

"No," said Lily,—"mamma said for me not to bother you, but to give you welcome and come away, and when you got rested, that I might come to see you some days. May I?"

"Yes, you little sweet!" and Cora released Lily, after kissing her pretty mouth over and over. Lily ran down-stairs, elated with the success of her welcome.

Cora withdrew to her room, where Linda, with her own hands, was making it as comfortable and tidy as possible.

"What shall I call you?" asked Linda.

"Call me Cora."

"If I knew that you would like me," said the girl-widow, "I would ask you to call me Linda."

"I already like you," answered Cora, whose soft eyes thrilled with that appreciation which she felt but had not spoken.

"I shall *love* you," said the artless, open-hearted Linda.

"I am certain to return your affection," responded Cora, who felt a world of need for something to love. The two girls would probably have gone into each other's arms, but each feared that the other might think such a demonstration somewhat foolish or overdone. They did not reflect that it was the fashion among girls to be foolish and to overdo in such matters.

Linda left Cora, feeling that she would like to court the pure-eyed, statuesque, self-dependent girl, with whose lovely face and sweet manners she was delighted and charmed. In doing her duty, she had done herself a pleasure. In the beginning, she was essaying to satisfy her brother Cassel. In the progression and conclusion, she lost sight of her brother's injunctions, and acted from self-impulse.

Cora was fully alive to her exceeding and unlooked-for welcome, and realized speedily and happily that she would be among companions in the Boyd mansion. She wrote to Mr. Hope, telling him that the sun had risen clear,—giving promise of a cloudless day.

After tea, Linda introduced Cora to the parlors, where

was gathered the Boyd colony,—except Cassel, who was either in his room or away in the city, and except Uncle Jesse, who stood no nonsense. Mr. Lake was first presented to Cora. He was a middle-aged, substantial, good-looking gentleman, who engaged Cora in a pleasant conversation, into which Mrs Lake soon glided,—next Lily— and then Miss Emma Lake, who, having received an introduction, was, like all alert and adventurous school-misses, on the *qui vive* for chums and accomplices. The Misses Rochester, two well-behaved and pretty school-girls from rural New York, — twins, by-the-way,—next joined the coterie. Lastly, Miss Lightner, the school-mistress,—a cultivated young lady, aged about twenty, completed the circle which gathered about Cora. Each one had some word or token of welcome to offer, as though the colony was consanguineal, and Cora a returning or rallying member of it.

An uncommonly agreeable evening sent Cora to bed with a cheerful feeling at her heart.

On the next morning, about eleven o'clock, a card was handed in to Cora. She took it and found the name— Cassel P. Rapid—engraved thereon.

" He wishes to see me ?" she asked.

" Yes, Miss Huron," answered the servant. " He is waiting for you in the large parlors."

Cora went down immediately. She did not touch a hair or smooth a fold. She was no longer afraid of Mr. Cassel Rapid, whom sight had transformed from a discreet, grave gentleman, into a rollicking sailor-boy.

Cora entered the parlors and looked around. Cassel was the sole occupant. He arose, bowed to her with perfect manner, gave her a chair, and seated himself in front of her.

Cora was almost overwhelmed with surprise and modesty. Before her was a young gentleman, seemingly taller than the sailor-boy of the day before, dressed in a suit of black the appointments of which were faultless, and, from top to toe, looking as elegant and distinguished as a young noble. The sparkle of his eyes had receded into their calm violet depths, and the boyish brilliancy and holiday glow of his countenance had given way to a magisterial, intellectual tranquillity, beneath which, to Cora's eye, slept the power and magic of a young god. She almost trembled with a sense of inferiority, as she looked upon this prince of manliness and beauty,—so rare, complete, and self-sustained. She waited, half demurely, for Cassel to lead the conversation, or broach whatever subject that might have prompted him to solicit her company. He commenced to talk. Before he had proceeded far, Cora forgot herself, attending to his speech, and watching the exquisite light and play of his comely and surpassing features. Cassel was making an effort for ascendency, and every little gesture that escaped him gave weight or point to its accompanying words. He continued to talk for almost half an hour, without giving her an opportunity of saying half a dozen words ; but she felt no disposition to say—only to listen. As the perfect flower unfolds itself to the genial sun, leaf after leaf, until the last one is open to be read of its beauty and snuffed of its fragrance, so did Cassel Rapid, as softly and consecutively as the opening of a flower, unfold to Cora the pages of her probable future in the giant city. Cora was given thoroughly to understand her status, which, from the evidence present and within call, promised to be an exceedingly gracious and agreeable one.

"Mr. Hope," concluded Cassel, breaking away from the magisterial air which he had assumed, and resuming his more characteristic one,—that of a brother to all young innocents who crossed his path,—"has favored me with this pleasant duty. Look upon me, therefore, as your elected knight and counselor,—not your tyrant,—to whom you may always come for advice, escort, protection, or vindication. You must make your requisitions on me as freely as you would dip water from a fountain, for the pleasure you will give me by doing so will be of the kind which never tires or cloys."

"Mr. Rapid," said Cora, with a thrilling sweetness which told upon Cassel's heart, "I was totally unprepared to meet so much tenderness and generous encouragement from your friends and yourself. I am conscious that to you in chief I am indebted, and hope you will believe me when I tell you that my gratitude will never sleep. I

confide in you, and therefore accept you as guide and
guardian, and hope to give you as little trouble as possible."

"You will cause me no trouble," said Cassel, and then
added, as if to himself, "such as, perhaps, you anticipate. But here," he continued, handing her a sheet of
paper, "is a Bill of Rights. I have drawn it up for you,
that you may know your privileges, and not be imposed
upon by the servants. You will be under no restrictions
except those of your own conscience. The house is free
to you, and Linda—that is, Mrs. Boyd—will be your sister,
if you will."

"I did not imagine," said Cora, "that there was to be
found such a home for me as this."

"You have found it nevertheless," replied Cassel, cheerfully, "and I do not doubt that you are worthy of it. This
afternoon—say at five o'clock—I wish to see you, here, to
arrange your studies and consult about your teachers.
You will please bring me a list of studies in which you
are thorough, another list in which you are advanced,
and still another upon which you have not entered but
wish to enter. And now, I will release you, until the
afternoon appointment."

As Cora withdrew, she cast a glance back at the young
gentleman who was so kind and gentle with her; his eye
caught hers, she blushed, they both smiled, Cora escaped,
and Cassel said to himself,—

"There goes my wife—if it is possible."

This was, by no means, love at first sight, for Cassel was
among the very last to be so flashed upon; and he was not
—when he said, "there goes my wife"—in love with Cora.
He did not know but that her heart was already pledged,
young as she was; and should it be, he would hardly attempt to distract her, or to undo the happiness of the one
to whom it might be given, by filching it from him. But
with Cora's unmistakable loveliness he was perfectly satisfied,—as much so as if he had known her for seasons; for
her beauty was of that delicate, pure, and sprightly order
—delicious with mingled vigor and softness—about which
there could be no question or after-opinion, and about
which seemed to be an atmosphere of enchantment. She

possessed it, beyond artifice or dispute, and the beholder, whether for the first or hundredth time, was sure to see it, and feel its influence. Her face was inclined to the oval or Italian cast, and was almost as white as milk, except where it was tinted by health and suffused with modesty. Her carmine mouth was tender and tempting, and her firm dark eyes were soft and true, and exquisitely conscious. Her character, as represented to Cassel by Mr. Hope, was as complete and lovely as her person. Her intelligence and natural chaste style he had already recognized. What more, therefore, could he wish to know? Although he did not love her yet, he was conscious that he would do so, unless some accident or change of programme should put her beyond his reach and sight. He felt that she would be his equal, and fully worthy of him, if not past-worthy. His first prudent action, therefore, would be to preserve the integrity of his heart if possible, until he should ascertain, probably from Mr. Hope, otherwise by finessing, whether or not she herself was intact. If he should be convinced that Cora was free from all entanglement, then would he endeavor to entangle her in the web of love.

Cassel Rapid's associates out in the city often called him Belvedere, referring to the unequaled Apollo in the Belvedere gallery of the Vatican. They also imagined that, on account of his youth, wealth, and singular personal beauty, added to which were many accomplishments both manly and rare, he had every reason in the world to be vain and haughty, and were upon occasions surprised at and impatient with him, when, for instance, he would stop a whole party of aristrocratic pleasure seekers of whom he was one, to shake hands and pass compliments with a tanned laborer, or lift a ragged little girl over a mud-hole.

But Cassel, notwithstanding the opinions of his associates, had no reason whatever to be either vain or haughty. It is not those upon whom Nature, in conjunction with Fortune, has bountifully showered her surpassing gifts, who are so inclined. It is only those to whom has been vouchsafed enough—just a little—to make fools of them. Some there be, who, having only a proper nose,

23

will nose their way through the world : or if it be an eye,
they will ogle you here and ogle you there: if the teeth,
they will grin out their mundane existence: and if the
form, they will strut their way to the grave. Cassel had
no special feature which he considered the best, or desired
to thrust forward. He did not make his diamond-mounted
finger any more prominent than his unadorned knuckles.
He did not attempt to repoise his head. His natural
walk being the easiest, he did not substitute a unique
style of locomotion. His voluntary smile being more
ready than a cultivated smirk, he did not excruciate his
facial nerves; a number seven boot fitting his foot comfortably, he did not wear an uncomfortable number six;
putting himself upon his individual merits, he borrowed
no brilliancy from distinguished relations, dead or alive :
and, altogether, he suited himself so well, that he essayed
no inordinate improvement upon the original work; he
would but keep it to the standard of its originality and
true capacity; the only trimming of Nature which suggested itself of any great importance, was the occasional
paring of his nails, and the shortening of his hair ; in the
multiplicity of his good looks, he could well afford to dispense with the greater portion of his capillary attractions;
for he did not aspire to the dirty-naped sect of the long-
haired *distingué*—and consequently his hair was never
suffered to soil his coat collar or draggle in his soup.

Cassel and Cora met at five o'clock in the afternoon.
She handed him a small memorandum-book, and then
stood modestly by his chair, pointing him to the entries
in the little book.

" Here," said she, " is Mr. Hope's enumeration of my
studies, including finished, unfinished, and not-commenced."

" Is this list complete ?" asked Cassel, looking up pleasantly into Cora's face.

" It is very flattering, and possibly in excess of being
complete," answered Cora.

" Mr. Hope is too old, and too sensible, to waste time in
flattering young ladies," observed Cassel, with negligent
truth.

" You consider flattery a waste of time, do you ?" ventured Cora, a little sportively.

"When a man has anything else in the world to do, as few have not, I can answer, yes."

"And when he has not?"

"Then he had better commit the Rash Act."

"What—marry?" asked Cora, with bright humor, and greatly at fault, for she remembered to have heard that marriage was considered the most uncertain, adventurous, and probably the rashest act of a person's life.

"No! not so bad as *that*," laughingly protested Cassel. "I meant suicide."

"Self-slaughter!" was Cora's surprised and grave response.

"In so extreme a case I would consider it justifiable homicide," observed Cassel, somewhat drolly.

"Don't you think 'justifiable' is a misnomer?" asked Cora, who felt prompted to sound the moral ethics of the young gentleman who was to be her guide.

Cassel, who was perfectly willing to dally with the young girl, asked, in pretended earnest,—

"What—in such a case as the one in question?"

"In any case, where life is involved."

Cassel gave a quick glance into Cora's face. Something in her voice arrested his attention. He asked,—

"Are you serious?"

"I am."

"Well, now, if it is a matter on which you wish to get my opinion, 'justifiable homicide' is, like almost every other phrase, both properly and improperly applied, as the case may happen."

"But *can* it be popularly and properly applied, in any case of slaughter by one person of another, except in the event of pure self-defense from imminent murder?"

"Are there no crimes which merit death? no exigencies which render the dealer thereof justifiable?" asked Cassel just a little sternly.

"But the laws should visit it."

"The law, in some of its functions, is like a broken and contemptible vessel, holding neither wrath nor retribution over the outlaw—holding nothing. It is the law itself which, in peculiar, instead of repressing or punishing crime, forces true men to become ferocious and bloody

gladiators, avenging their own unrighted wrongs. But
you are too innocent of the world to understand me."

"To kill is a wretched and extreme resort,—an act, in
my opinion, which kills the soul of him who slays the
body, be it his own body, or that of another."

"*Pallida mors*," said Cassel, reflectively: "it *is* an
extreme resort; but there are times when nothing but
death itself is due. When you have lived longer, you,
also, may think so."

Here again was that long-time prophetic asseveration
of "when you have lived longer,"—"when you grow
older,"—"when you see more of the world, to know it."
The woodland maiden asked herself "What is this mystic
knowledge which age and experience is to bring me?
Am I so unlike to others that I do not see creation and its
laws and duties as the intelligent, vast world sees them?
What is my lack, or my fault? I feel that my mind is
clear, but in all my contact with those who have gained
knowledge from experience I am set at naught as too young
to know."

Cora's reflections were interrupted by Cassel, who said,
in continuation,—

"However, we are off the subject entirely. Let us get
back to our books."

Cora had seen one man killed, almost at her feet. From
her earliest recollection she had lived in the same house
with a strange being, who, she had recently learned from
Carroll May's family history as written by Captain Gale,
was a man-slayer. Ordinarily, she avoided the subject of
human blood. But she was prone, by circumstances, to
think of it. As far as she had discussed it with Mr. Hope,
she had found him and herself well agreed. She was now
called upon to place herself under the guidance of Cassel
Rapid, a youth of whom she knew nothing except from
good report. Any subject, therefore, the discussion of
which might indicate to her his inner character, was likely
to be seized upon, especially the one just now so briefly
treated between them, however abrupt or slight the occasion might be. As she stood close up to Cassel, her
hand, which was pure of every stain, touching his, in fact,
as they were exchanging the memorandum-book, with

what freezing horror would she have sprung away from him, and shrunk from the touches of that hand, which, with all its mustered might, had driven the dagger to its hilt in a human heart, and would do it again and again, and a thousand times again under like incentive, had she but known or guessed the simple fact that there was human blood upon it! In Cora's code were copied the words, "Thou shalt not kill." They were underscored by well-remembered, painful experience, more of which she devoutly wished that neither age nor mystic revelation would ever bring her; for she felt that nothing which the future might reveal would ever temper her mind to forget or ignore the ancient saying, "Thou shalt not kill."

"Do you prefer male or female teachers?" asked Cassel.

"In most branches of learning I prefer the male," answered Cora.

"Why the male?" asked Cassel, who was already disposed to be a little jealous of the hours which Cora might spend with her masculine instructors.

"Because," answered she, "I think that possibly I might derive more benefit by coming in contact with the masculine mind."

"You regard the brain of our sex, then, as stronger than that of your own?"

"I regard it as different,—not so minute, but perhaps more comprehensive,—certainly ruder and stronger."

"Hence," said Cassel, jocularly, "the expression, 'strong-minded women,' as applied to those of your sex who affect masculine heads and masculine capacity."

"That may be," answered Cora "I know nothing about it; there are none such in my old neighborhood."

"How do you think that *I* would suit you as your instructor in General Philosophy?" asked Cassel.

"*You!*" exclaimed Cora, startled into an exhibition of too much surprise.

"Yes," replied Cassel.

"You are too young," said Cora, as if announcing an unquestionable fact.

Cassel felt himself blush beneath Cora's honest eyes and words; for she had told him exactly the truth. However well he may have been advanced in the different branches of Philosophy, he could not have combined experience with reading, and was not, in the broad sense, competent to distill those golden drops which Cora was in search of. She wanted the results and deductions of the gray head, and not those of untried and half-initiated youth.

"Please do not feel hurt, Mr. Rapid," said Cora very sweetly, as she saw Cassel's color rise.

"Hurt," replied Cassel while his eyes rested somewhat investigatingly upon her,—"I will answer you as Linda— Mrs. Boyd, I mean—once answered me: 'I am not hurt *at all*,—I am *ashamed*.' You have put your answer pertinently and upon the very point,—I *am* too young. But a less truthful person than yourself would have objected in some other and less acceptable way. Always treat me thus," said Cassel in a deep, impressive tone, "and we shall be the best of friends."

Cora's value had instantly doubled in Cassel's estimation, and he meantime had gained greatly upon her; for as she looked at him in his modest susceptibility and intelligent beauty, she felt that about him was a charm which would give him mastery wherever he might seek it. He continued:

"You have truly said that I am too young to teach you Philosophy,—for I am in the very springtime of my life and acquisition. What, therefore, could I tell you of Life's Summer—its Autumn—or its Winter? Under Mr. Hope you have progressed well, as I see from your notebook; especially in all ethical studies. You should have finished your philosophical education under him, so far as it can be finished at the school-desk. His venerable years, intelligent mind, and pure principles well fitted him for pouring out the limpid Truth; whereas, should I engage you an instructor here, I fear that he would mingle with the Truth the subtlety and venom of Metaphysics. I divide Philosophy into only two parts—tangible and intangible—material and immaterial. The first is demonstrable to the senses of the eye, ear, touch, etc.; the second must be grasped and turned over in the mind. In material Philosophy you are registered high by Mr. Hope, who has marked 'sufficient' opposite each branch upon which you have been engaged. To immaterial Philosophy numberless fountains contribute, but none of them are pure but one, which is not only pure but exhaustless. I have it for you, here—if you will come and look," and Cassel led the way to a center-table, on which was a handsome Bible. Turning to a fly-leaf, Cassel pointed Cora to an inscription which presented the book to Miss Cora Glencoe Huron, and beneath which was signed the names of all the members of the Boyd colony, including that of Uncle Jesse and of Lily Lake.

"Let this," said Cassel, "be your teacher, as I am satisfied it has been. No eye hath seen, or heart felt, or tongue told, what you will not find within its compass. If the lion is bold, this is bolder; if the sea is deep, this is deeper; if the world is wide, this is wider; if there is beauty in the universe, it is in the matchless pensiveness of the parables of Christ. 'Consider the lilies of the field, how they grow; they toil not, neither do they spin: and yet I say unto you, That even Solomon in all his glory was not arrayed like one of these.' Be you therefore, my young friend, a 'Lily' whose modest pure loveliness puts to shame the pomp and magnificence of princes, and is by Christ himself exalted above the glory and grandeur of imperial thrones."

Cassel was by no means pedantic in what he had to say, but earnest and tender. Cora was thrilled to the heart, and her speaking eyes told truly what she felt. She suitably acknowledged the sacred gift of the Boyd colony, and almost repented that she had not accepted Cassel as her preceptor in Philosophy, he seemed so gentle, and faultless, and firm.

Cassel and Cora, between them, arranged the programme of her studies, and Cora, whose means were ample, would soon be well provided with teachers, whose duty it would be to instruct her in various accomplishments, solid and light, at the Boyd mansion.

"Now for a matter of business," said Cassel. "Here is a blank check-book, with the name and style of the banking-house where your funds are deposited. When you need money, check on Sarazzin & Sarazzin, pass the check to me, and I will draw the money and deliver it to you. And although your cash account will be accurately kept by the banking-house, you must, as a sort of business lesson, keep it also, in this little book, a pass-book by-the-way."

"Is this not a Jew house?" asked Cora.

"Yes."

"Do you do business with Jews?"

"Why not?"

"I thought they were all dishonest."

"Who taught you that?"

"No one. I absorbed the opinion, seemingly from a rife atmosphere."

"And from the same atmosphere you might have absorbed rheumatism or earache. But did you ever see a Jew?"

"Do you mean a Hebrew?"

"Yes."

"I do not know that I ever did."

"Do you know what a Hebrew is?"

"A human being!" answered Cora, half amazed at the question. "A descendant of Abraham."

"Very true—and of whom are *we* the descendants? Of some other man, who, by all odds, is not near so illustrious or hoary with record as Abraham. A Jew or a Gentile, under the same circumstances, is pretty much the same manner of man, with the balance, if any, probably in favor of the Jew. Listen to me but a moment on this subject—for although I am not of their faith, there is a charm and invincible fortitude about the Jews, which excite silent wonder and admiration, if not open applause. Among all the races on the face of the globe, I do not think that there has been, or is *one*, which would have emerged from more than eighteen centuries of persecution, slaughter, pillage, and doglike treatment, with as many marks of its grand old ancestry upon it as have the Jews. There is probably not a race which would have left even an *idiot* to tell the tale of its former existence. The Chaldeans, who of old, crossed cimeters with them, are extinct. Babylon, which held them captive, is dust. Rome, which drew tributary coin from Christ himself, is in ruins, cowering beneath the mailed hand of an alien. Greece, which supplied an almost universal language for the Hebrew Scriptures, sits impotently upon the Mediterranean, the ghost of glory. On the contrary, the Jews now influence the councils of the greatest nations of the earth. But I will not preach you a sermon about the Jews. I will only say this—trust neither Jew nor Gentile until you know the man, and even then trust yourself the most. But back again to business. Linda tells me that you have need of a dress-maker. If it will be agreeable to you, we will all go out to-morrow, and arrange for your wants."

"Thank you," said Cora. "Nothing would please me better, or be more timely."

"It is very pleasant shopping when one has plenty of money," pleasantly observed Cassel. "Linda enjoys it so much that it is a delight to go with her. I believe, however, that such enjoyment is common and peculiar to the sex. In contrast, there are few things which gentlemen so dislike and postpone as the preliminaries necessary to the securing of a seasonable wardrobe."

"But when it is secured they are fond enough of displaying it," said Cora, with playful raillery.

"Not so fond but that the ladies are yet fonder."

"We are all weak," said Cora, "and abide in glass houses."

"And should therefore throw kisses instead of stones," somewhat encroachingly rejoined Cassel, at whose remark Cora, in trying not to blush, blushed the deeper and more charmingly.

On the following day Linda, Cora, and Cassel went to the establishment where Linda, under Cassel's auspices, had obtained her first nice-fitting dresses, and where the female portion of the Boyd colony were accustomed to deal.

Madame, very well pleased with the idea of securing a new and promising customer, and equally satisfied with Cora's looks and symmetry, exerted herself both professionally and socially to please to the uttermost.

She went with the trio to numberless shops where were kept all the fineries and niceries requisite to make a young girl look as Beautiful as a Butterfly. She selected, rejected, explained, suggested, and badgered the salesmen with effective ability.

"You," said she to Cora, "can wear any color you like. It is true, your face is very white, but your complexion is so pure and healthy and your blushes so accurate and enhancing, that you may dictate to the colors instead of being restricted by them. I propose to get you up a regular rainbow wardrobe—a different color for each day in the week, with intermediate tints for morning and midday lounging."

"I never lounge," replied Cora, laughing.

"But you must *learn* to lounge," humorously and sincerely insisted the madame, as if it were the most ravishing thing of all others to be done. "Mrs. Boyd has learned it," continued she, tapping Linda's cheek playfully and chucking her under the chin,—"and I know that Mr. Rapid indulges himself."

Cora was in a sea of novelty and enjoyment. Like every other sensible, spirited young girl, she was delighted with her outfitting expedition, and examined goods, laces, trimmings, and all sorts of female trumpery, with sparkling eyes and palpitating heart.

Back again at the dress-maker's establishment, after Cora's dimensions had been taken and recorded, the madame, apart with Cassel, said,—

"Mr. Rapid, your friends are so easy to fit. I have no angles to turn, bones to overlay, or hollows to fill. There is Mrs. Lake, and her children, and Miss Lightner, all good forms. Mrs. Boyd is still better. But Miss Huron is a young Venus, and as shy as a chamois. It is a rare delight just to take her measure." And madame smiled knowingly at the young man.

Cassel only smiled in return at this rather indelicate language—for madame was French, and he didn't care; he could stand anything which she might venture to say, particularly if it complimented Cora or developed her to him. He had not doubted the young girl's symmetry, and yet it was pleasure to him, faintly voluptuous, to have it confirmed and whispered into his ear by this female latitudinarian who was just from manipulating Cora's virgin form.

CHAPTER XXVII.

CASSEL'S day with Cora among the shops, dress-makers, and milliners, and the darling sweetness with which she conducted herself through all the turmoil and vexing indecisions consequent upon such a day, set him seriously to thinking. He was beginning to thirst for her society. He was sensible that he must get nearer to her, or get away from her altogether.

He wrote to Mr Hope. We will make a few extracts from the old minister's reply.

"I am satisfied," wrote Mr. Hope, "that Cora's heart is essentially free. She has had but little opportunity to form any but school-room attachments. She doubtless has had, and may yet have, her preferences ; but the only preference which might have fallen into a loving attachment, of which I have the least knowledge, was restrained from that course by the influence of events in the family history of either party. I refer in this connection to Carroll May. You have not seen him since you were both little curly-headed pets of Creswood,—you the elder, I believe, by a couple of years. He is a very promising youth, though perhaps somewhat hasty, or touchy, in his temper. He goes to New York this winter to seek his fortune,—and probably too confident that it is there."

Mr. Hope, at no little sacrifice of ease and expenditure of ink, then explained to Cassel the non-intercourse which had so long existed between Cora and Carroll, mentioned their many years' occupation of the same school-room, gave it as his opinion that they, though silent, had been somewhat affected toward each other, and would probably have become permanently attached, but for that life-long inhibition ordered by Oswald Huron, and of which the reader is well aware. What changes the recent developments in regard to Cora's parentage would superinduce, he was not able to foresee. He then gave Cassel, in this connection and anew, the history of the Huron war.

" The result," wrote he, "appears mainly to rest upon the finding of Maria Guthrie, the Huron nurse, and producing her or her depositions.

" Oswald Huron surprised every one by the consecutive calmness with which he conducted himself, and the ability with which he managed his cause.

"Neville Huron did not, in all probability, sufficiently heed the advice of Hector O'Dare, Captain Gale, and others, but placed too much reliance upon the lawyers, old friends of his, whom he sent here from Philadelphia. It has long been considered a tough stocking that—which 'Philadelphia lawyers' cannot unravel; but in this instance, they failed,—or fell behind their reputation. They probably did not anticipate meeting the first legal talent of Maryland, and when they learned that it was to be Sparta against Sparta, with all the advantages of arms and preparation on the other side, it was too late to correct their position. Hence the compromise, which they were glad enough to effect, and which they could not have effected had it materially changed the immediate destiny or disposition of Cora, as contemplated by Oswald Huron.

" But now to the matter which you no doubt consider as greater in importance than all the foregoing. 'Do I object to your striving to win Cora while she is under my guardianship?' I will answer you as though she were my own daughter, or you were my son. You may *win* her, if you can,—but you must not *woo* her: that is, you may simply secure her heart, but do not bewilder her, or fritter away her time. You will understand me I am convinced. I have an interest in Cora—I have almost raised her. She is overly dear to me, and will be to all who may know her. She will soon be sought after, whether I will it or not. You are just a little wild, my dear boy,—or have I forgotten my youth when I say so?"

Cassel thought that the old minister had certainly forgotten when he was a green sprig. The letter continued:

" However, I have an old man's affection for you; also, I trust you. Comply, then, with my wishes, and you have my consent to win, if you can, a precious little gem of 'purest ray serene.' But remember that *my* consent is a very limited one. It is that, merely, of Mr. Hope, whose propriety and right in the matter might well be questioned *in toto.* You, however, have had the sense and delicacy to perceive my moral responsibility and to regard my wishes,—which is an argument in your favor and against those anticipated ones of whom I know not, but who, I am aware, will be blind to the one and disregard the other. In conclusion, Cora is very young, but you cannot catch her with chaff."

Mr. Hope desired to do right,—not simply to make an appearance of doing right; for, as well as not, he might have referred Cassel to Cora's kindred. But what Cassel Rapid or any other young Rapid would have paid any heed to the reference? To have approached Cora's kindred on such a subject, at this time, would probably have opened anew the controversy of which the absolute possession of herself was the instance and aim. It was not likely that, at this period, either of the warring brothers would give up the contested child to a stranger, or look with much favor upon any who might seek, by carrying off the subject of dispute, to dissolve the feud. Before Cassel could court Cora's father, the law must recognize some one as being her father. And it was not, nor is it now, the fashion to speak to the "old gentleman" until all the arrangements have been perfected to do as well without as with his consent. Nowadays, when a political incumbent happens to oversleep himself in the morning, the departments are instantly flooded with applications to fill an anticipated vacancy Cassel did not wish to appear quite so precipitate as that with Cora's family. He thought it only due to Mr. Hope, in consideration of the reciprocity between them, and in view of the old minister's conscientious responsibility, that he should acquaint him, and solicit his consent Mr. Hope was aware of several things. Among them were, that early attachments are generally the most tender and lasting, if not the best; that Cassel would rarely ever find another Cora, and Cora hardly ever find another Cassel; that his refusal or objection would only restrain the young man during Cora's wardship,—if so long,—and that if Cassel had made up his mind to have Cora, he would *have* her if he had to seek her at the recently-discovered sources of the Nile, granting that she would have him. In giving his consent, Mr. Hope did his best; and few, if any, could have done better than the old minister's best.

Cassel was almost satisfied. His sky was pretty clear, but there was still a little cloud in sight.

What was the nature of Cora's preference for Carroll May? and was it very tender and very permanent?

What was bringing Carroll so opportunely to the city of New York?

Was it Cora?

Or was it the every-day necessity under which the young man rested, of providing for that unromantic exigency—a support?

Exigency may be defined as a short, quick want.

Life is short.

Its wants are quick.

Much quicker than its supplies.

Quicker than lightning—and more permanent.

The whole of Life is an exigency—an emergency—to which few of us are equal.

There never has been and will never be, probably, a temper better toned for happiness, enjoyment, and content than the temper of Cassel Rapid. Normally, his spirit was airy, free, and upward. To submerge it was almost impossible. Like the cork upon the billow, it would outride the wildest storms, and dance upon the foaming rage of the churned seas. But he had passed through a deathly experience, and, at times, felt its legacy most heavily. Although he had slain Jonas Aiken,—and would, without ruth, slay every such demon within reach of his arm,—he suffered from no pang of remorse; for under the incentive which had actuated him, he would, if need be, stand out against the whole *world*, and every voted law therein. But often—not too often—he went down into the very depths of sadness after the memory of his lost sister. His father's fate had been swallowed up by the fate of Diana—his matchless, thrilling young sister,—having been regarded by him as the heritage—a common one—of an adventurous life upon the verge of civilization.

But Cassel was constituted to encounter a great deal, and still be happy in the main. Unlike many who find it impossible not to be wretched, he found it equally impossible not to be habitually buoyant and joyful. Joy was the native element of his breast. Sorrow was an alien there, an invader, a tyrant; and his nature revolted against it, and cast it out, as the stomach rises up and expels the nauseating emetic.

. Cassel, though not vain, was nothing daunted when he came to think of Carroll May. He judged that Cora might have, in times past, preferred Carroll simply from looking at him across the room of a country school and contrasting him with his fellows. But he was satisfied that their souls were not entwined in that Gordian knot which no skill can untie, and which it would be a sin to cut. Nevertheless, when Carroll should come to New York, he would seek him out; and if he found him worthy of his lance, and so disposed, they would buckle on their armor, each, and tilt it out. The prize herself should be the umpress. Cora should drop the hat, and decide the contest.

But notwithstanding Cassel's superiority over Carroll in everything that lays its spell upon a maiden's heart, if Carroll should decide to enter the lists, victory might hover long before it perched. For although Cassel Rapid might pillage Cora's heart of all its store of tenderness, and wind her arms about his neck in an agony of love and passion, Carroll May was already templed in her secret compassion, and she might turn away from the finely-carved Parian which stood securely on its plinth, to support the coarser but tottering Granite from falling at her feet,—for compassion in the bosom of a noble-natured girl is only less potent than love, and, if properly cared for, may be turned to love. Between Cora and Cassel there were no time-hallowed associations. She now knew him for the first time. The only things in common with them were the few acquaintances whom he remembered near her old home, and the outlines of Creswood. But Cora and Carroll held much common property between them. They could go back and talk of their childhood, and of their early youth when at school they secretly strove to outstrip each other in their progress up the Hill of Science, and of the innumerable things which hedged their pathway up that immemorial Hill. They could talk of the neighborhood, the forest, the sea, the strand, the Tarpeian Rock, and of everything which Creswood held that to either of them was beautiful, strange, quaint, or cosy,— or had been. Carroll could throw out a skirmisher by telling Cora how he and Johnny Gale used to love her, and talk of her, and dream about her, when they were young cubs and she was a fay. In addition and conclusion, Car- rol was a sensible, handsome, engaging, resolute youth, who could create a sensation in the breast of almost any country girl whom he might endeavor to surround and capture.

Hector O'Dare's head-quarters were in the city of New York, where he kept a regular office. The day following the receipt of Mr. Hope's letter, Cassel Rapid went to O'Dare's office. The detective liked Cassel, regarding him, as he said, "clear stuff and diamond grit."

"Good-morning, Mr. Two-forty," said O'Dare, alluding to Cassel's name of Rapid.

"Good-morning, Mr. Nose," retorted Cassel, alluding to O'Dare's profession of nosing out things which were hid den or astray.

"I capitulate," rejoined the detective, laughing. "Take a seat and con over your sins."

"How's business?" asked Cassel.

"Oh, pretty brisk. I have on hand now,—let's see," and O'Dare turned to a ledger,—"one lost child, one runaway couple, two heavy swindlers, some big money, a four-carat diamond, the bones of a dead man, and the tongue of a live woman, or her skeleton, if dead. Also some old cases, and some cases *sub rosa*."

"I have a case for you myself," said Cassel.

"What is it?" asked O'Dare, with some interest; for he remembered Cassel's past peculiar application, and the stern result of it.

"It is certainly a case *sub rosa*, for I do not wish to be known in it,—and it may be a case *subsoil*, for all that I know about it," answered Cassel.

"I shall have to get me a platoon of grave-diggers, and keep· me a hungry hyena in leash," said O'Dare, drolly. Then, opening his ledger, he requested, "Let's have the particulars, Mr. Rapid."

"It is possible that I have been anticipated," said Cassel, "for there are others more directly concerned than myself."

"Give me an outline, or an odor, and I'll tell you in a moment if I have been put upon the scent."

Cassel explained to O'Dare the nature of his application.

"You are the third man in search of that woman's tongue, or, if she be dead, her skeleton," answered the detective. "First,—Neville Huron of Philadelphia; contest for a daughter. Second,—Carroll May of Creswood, Maryland; for family reasons. Third,—Cassel Rapid; reasons best known to himself."

"In whose service are you then engaged?"

"In Neville Huron's. He is wealthy and able to pay. Young May might be able, but it would take all he has. Furthermore, Mr. Huron's interest is prime, to my own knowledge. What young May's interest is I am unable to say. And what Cassel Rapid's interest is I do not care," said the detective, suggestively, "unless he chooses to tell me."

O'Dare's manner, in his last six words, conveyed the most delicately-pointed hint imaginable. When he was engaged upon any piece of business he endeavored to get into his own hands all radial or convergent lines to or from it. He would like to know Cassel Rapid's interest, therefore.

"I don't take your hint at all," responded Cassel, amusedly. "It is of no consequence whatever to either you or the case, O'Dare, or I would not hesitate to state my interest in full. To do so, however, would not assist you or obstruct you a flea's leap."

"But a flea leaps pretty far sometimes, and always jumps to the point," urged the detective.

"Never mind the flea," answered Cassel, who took up his hat and bid O'Dare "good-morning."

Cassel went home, wondering if Carroll May was interesting himself in the Huron war as a young lawyer, or in Cora Glencoe as a young lover. If the latter, might

it not mean more than Cassel would like to hear ?   He
was getting to be somewhat anxious about Cora, and was
becoming conscious that this anxiety was the outgrowth
of something else which had taken root and was sprout-
ing within.

Hector O'Dare, active man that he was, was again at
Creswood.   He had so timed his visit as to meet Captain
Gale at Gale Island.   He interviewed the captain, asked
him a round of questions about Maria Guthrie, and made
notes.

"What is her religion ?" continued O'Dare.

"Now, what in thunder do you want to know *that*
for ?" asked Captain Gale, who had already answered a
number of questions which he considered irrelevant.

"For a good and lawful reason," urged O'Dare.

"What is it ? I would like to know for curiosity's sake,"
said Captain Gale.

"Very well.   I'm to find Maria Guthrie, dead or alive."

"Yes."

"Suppose she is dead, and in heaven."

"*You* will never find her," laughed Captain Gale.

"Suppose, then, that she is dead, and not in heaven."

"You may, perhaps, reach her," again laughed the captain.

"I will at least rattle at the gate and inquire for her,"
said O'Dare, with a dare-devil look, which indicated that
he would almost as soon take a tussle with Pluto as not.
"But tell me, was she a Catholic, a Protestant, or a non-
professor ?"

"She was a Roman Catholic," answered Captain Gale.

"Now, you see," said the detective, "my whip has a
handle.   That single answer is equal to a month's search."

"When do you commence your search ?"

"I'm commencing it now.   But I have to go back fifteen
years and work it up to date.   It may take a year to find
her—two years even.   I can't do it at once any more than
you can raise a stalk of tobacco at once.   You have to
burn your bed, sow your seed, draw your plants, set them
out, wait for them to grow, keep the worms out, cut before
frost, and there you are."

Captain Gale now had an opportunity of making use of

a simile, which was one of a family of favorites with him, and which he was delighted to know he had never used in O'Dare's hearing.

"And," replied the captain, somewhat eagerly, and making sure of the opportunity, " as tobacco often ends in smoke, this search may end in smoke likewise."

" Just so, or ashes—the ashes of the dead," answered O'Dare. " But if she is alive, I'll smoke her out,—if she is buried, I'll find her head-stone in some Catholic cemetery."

" Are you a Roman Catholic ?"

" I am half Catholic, half Protestant, and half world-ling."

" You are one half too many," said the mariner.

· " No—I consider myself at least a man and a half. Here is the way I count. There is a class of men which I write down as 0,—another class which I write up and down as a stick, thus, |,—from which I go into an ascending scale of vulgar fractions, $\frac{1}{8}$, $\frac{1}{7}$, $\frac{1}{6}$, $\frac{1}{5}$, $\frac{1}{4}$, $\frac{1}{3}$, $\frac{1}{2}$, until I arrive at the standard, which is the unit, 1, and makes a very good man. I claim to be $1\frac{1}{2}$,—you are at least $1\frac{1}{2}$,—young Rapid is $1\frac{1}{4}$, and will make two, in time,—Johnny, your son, will make $1\frac{1}{2}$, but not before he is twenty-eight or thirty years old ; and so on, not to mention such men as Webster, Calhoun, Clay, Jackson, and others, who were, in their day, at least three figures—anywhere from 100 to 999. Of all the men in the earth, Washington is the only one who ever attained to the round 1000."

" You rank Washington, then, above the Roman Pontiff,—you do not subscribe to the dogma of the Pope's infallibility."

" I consider all men fallible—*very* fallible ; popes, prelates, preachers, potentates, presidents, politicians, peasants, peoples, Man, Adam."

" O'Dare, do you ever read the Bible ?"

" I rarely read any other book. It is the philosopher's stone which men have so long been searching for, but which few have found. They turn away from its hoary, moss-covered edges, to peck among agates, flint-blossoms, and drift, expecting to find it there, or its effects,—gold, dross,—and, like maggots working in corruption, spend fruitless lives burrowing in the vomit of volcanoes."

"Very good," said Captain Gale. "I am glad to learn that you are a philosophizer. Although some one has said that we all philosophize, and that philosophize we well or ill we *must philosophize*, yet you are a man, I take it, who is accustomed nicely to balance one thing against another, and to make all sides of a case fit."

"Just so," responded the detective.

"What think you, then, of the incident in Scripture where Christ casts out devils from a man, and permits them to enter into a valuable herd of swine, thereby causing the herd to pitch into the sea and be choked."

"I think it was fun for the devils, but pretty rough on the swine," answered O'Dare.

"Pshaw!" said Captain Gale,—"I do not want any 'negro minstrel' reply. How do you reconcile such apparently wanton destruction of animals and property to the character of Christ?"

"In several ways. In the first place, it might have been a very bad breed of hogs," said the practical O'Dare, at whom Captain Gale could not forbear a laugh. "Secondly, it was better for the devils to go into the swine than to remain in the man who was a terror to the neighborhood,—so that the situation was at least improved if not perfected. Thirdly, swine's flesh was by no means a favorite dish in Jewry, nor is it yet. Moses, by-the-by, must have known of, or anticipated, Trichina. But seriously, and lastly, and wholly, it was as competent and reconcilable for Christ, visible, to permit those malicious devils to destroy a few swine—probably as an illustration —as it is for God, invisible, to have permitted and still to permit the Prince of Devils to roam abroad in the Earth, wrenching, and distorting, and tormenting it with Wars, Famines, Fires, Floods, Earthquakes, Pestilences, Pangs, and Politics,—and yet it is so, and God wills it, else his will is not omnipotent. But do not clog and mystify your mind in a vain effort to comprehend and classify the universe—to reconcile or adapt human ideas to the facts which meet us at every step, or to fathom those facts. Why, for instance, is one person born to a palace and another to a plow? Why is one normally healthy another abnormally unhealthy?—one deformed, even hideous, and unfitted for any enjoyment, another beautiful and full of life and joy?—one naturally well-tempered and predisposed to good, another ill-gotten and predisposed to evil? You may say that Eternity will compensate for all this, if we only cast ourselves at the feet of Christ. But how is it with that part of animate creation, which, when it dies, will, according to the general belief, know no resurrection— the beasts, the birds, the fishes, the insects? One trout is hooked for dinner, while the next one escapes to live and sport in its liquid home. Go out into the forest—at your feet is a dead bird, while above you, in the tree near by, is another, of the same brood, merrily singing. Go among the farmers—one horse is bred a stallion, to be pampered, and another is unsexed, to sweat at the plow. One young chicken cock is garnished for dinner, and its mate is destined to be the Brigham Young of a dozen or more good fat wives. In the far untrodden jungle, one royal lion is captured and caged for the museum, and another continues to roam, the king of his haunts. I have seen beasts as wretched, and beasts as happy, as I have seen men and women. Their accountability is *nil*, and yet, like us, they have their vicissitudes as though under some elfin dominion. If, therefore, there is no future for them, what is going to compensate the unfortunate among them for the inequalities of this, their only life? Back again to immortality. At what time does the spirit enter into human flesh? It may be when the babe first kicks in its mother's womb.. Granted that it be so, a still-born child is necessarily sinless, and its soul has a swift, untried passage to heaven. Whereas, had the child lived, it might have chosen the road to hell. If I could have my choice, I would choose to have been born alive, but to have expired upon my first breath, and while my little body was being decked for the tomb, my soul to have been received into the arms of angels, and borne, without stain, back to God who gave it. But all these things are not only beyond our comprehension, but beyond our control as well. We are the abject creatures of an incomprehensible *Power*, whose manifestations, gauged by the square and compass of our philosophy, are by no means calculated to inspire the faith that He is all Love, all Compassion, all Mercy,

and all Justice. For such attributes, combined with omnipotent power, would, in our groveling opinions, have
avoided the necessity—if such there be—of sin, and sorrow, and mournings, and lamentations. But," said O'Dare,
breaking off, "we see where such investigations will lead
us—or rather, we do *not* see. The Bible, in one sense, is
like the road from Creswood to Snow Hill; it is the only
known route. Do not reject that Route for the reason
that it may, like the Snow Hill road, have numberless by-
paths leading we know not where. However," concluded
O'Dare, laughing, "I am not an ordained minister, and
can do no better with you than to leave you in the hands
of Mr. Hope, or his son Garland, both of whom I take to
be very excellent men."

As O'Dare shook hands with Captain Gale and left him,
the latter marveled to himself thus:

"Who would have thought that this wiry, sharp-nosed,
busy detective, had ever put his mind to such things. But
it is so,—each person imagines that he himself does the
most occult thinking of any, when the very next person—
the most improbable person perhaps—may suggest what
had never before occurred to the self-sufficient inquirer."

O'Dare left Creswood and went back to New York. He
felt more interest in the search for Maria Guthrie than in
all the other cases on his docket, for he had suffered his
feelings to become involved in the Huron war, attributable,
however, to his admiration of Cora Glencoe, and his love
of an intricate piece of business. Neville Huron had instructed him to prosecute the search without regard to the
cost, and he was preparing to weave a web over the entire continent, which, when he should draw it in, would
have Maria Guthrie or her remnants wound up it it.

"O'Dare," asked Cassel Rapid, stepping into the detective's office, "what is the news from Creswood?"

"Nothing."

"No news of Mrs. Guthrie?"

"None of your business,—I'm not in your employ,"
impudently responded the detective.

"See here, O'Dare, do you want me to loosen your
front teeth for you?"

"You could not do that, with all your athletic training."

" I might if I should try ; and you might have been in my employ had you been disposed to act the rogue. But to the point : I am Miss Huron's guardian, here in the city, and would like to know if there is any probability of supplying the absent link in the chain which is to loose her from one father and bind her to another."

" The link is as uncertain, and as unlocated, as the next gold nugget is to the miner. At this moment I am in a fog, and without chart or compass. I can tell you absolutely nothing, except," continued O'Dare, provokingly and maliciously, " that Captain Gale still lives on oysters."

With a gesture combining impatience, good-fellowship, and banter, Cassel passed out of O'Dare's office and strolled at random through the city.

At leisure, he wandered away from the turmoil of business, far among the thronged, pleasant, and stately mansions of the fortunate and wealthy, and gazed about him with an eye, not of envy, but rather of indolence. While thus recreating, he met a couple of fine, frolicsome-looking young fellows, whom, at a glance, he recognized as being from the country The two strangers were Carroll May and Johnny Gale, but Cassel neither knew them, nor they him. Carroll and Johnny seemed captivated with the singular comeliness, genial countenance, and faultless outfit of Cassel Rapid, and they regarded him so openly and with such undisguised appreciation, that he, as he passed them, bowed to them, and very pleasantly said,—

" How are you, gentlemen ?"

They spoke freely in response, and, as he passed on, stopped and looked at him, imagining, and with good reason, that he was the very tip-top of the young "bloods" of the city. After a few steps, Cassel, who was always attracted by anything fresh, rustic, and unsophisticated, turned about and discovered the two young fellows gazing at him and smiling. With considerable humor in his face and tone, he asked,—

" Are you lost ?"

The boys both laughed.

" Yes—we *are* lost," acknowledged Johnny.

" I knew it," said Cassel, with a friendly smile. " What part of the country are you from ?"

"Maryland."

"Maryland? What portion of the State?"

"From Creswood—on the eastern shore."

"Lightning!" cried Cassel, all the fun of his nature springing to his face. "Here's sport—right here. Hold up, now,—I want to name you This is Johnny, and this is Carroll."

The eyes of the boys widened with infinite wonder and anticipation. Presently Johnny Gale shouted,—

"It's Pony! it's Pony! God, but it's Pony Rapid!" And he and Carroll pitched on to Cassel and almost devoured him up.

A policeman approached and said,—

"Gentlemen, you must preserve order,—you are making entirely too much fuss here."

"Polly," said Cassel, turning to the mercenary, "you are so fresh, fertile, and green, that your club-stick is budding. Go back to your Station and get instructions. By to-morrow morning the trees on your beat will all have leaves on them, winter as it is."

The policeman walked away somewhat abashed, and in a state of mental perplexity regarding the true and practical construction of his orders; for that was his first day of service, and he was under a strict, though false impression, as to what constituted public peace.

Johnny and Carroll were almost wild with delight. Cassel was equally glad to meet them, but being, in a measure, *blasé* on travel and surprises, he was not so boisterous in his manifestations.

"Boys," asked he, "where are you bound?"

"We were hunting for our hotel."

"You are altogether out of the line of hotels here," said Cassel. "There is not a regular hotel within a mile of this spot. But come, we'll take a car, and you'll dine with me at a saloon."

Away they went, to a fashionable eating-house, and Cassel took the liberty of ordering for three.

"What brought you up to the city?" asked Cassel.

"I am going into somebody's law office," said Carroll.

"Johnny, what is your scheme?"

"Going into the exchequer of the Whitecap," answered

Johnny, with a laugh so ticklish that Cassel and Carroll were bound to keep him company.

"Johnny has a wild colt in him, I see," observed Cassel to Carroll, "and it will take a year or two to trot it out. As he will need no assistance in his particular, pleasant, and sonlike enterprise, I shall not offer him my good services; but you, Carroll, have you made an engagement?"

"Not a positive one. I have had some encouragement by correspondence, but I've no idea whether I shall succeed or fail in getting a position,—such a one as will support me. Johnny is studying civil engineering, and is here in that interest. Uncle Gale advised me to come here also, and to make or break at the law,—and furthermore," said Carroll, laughing, " to keep Johnny from breaking his neck."

"Carroll," said Cassel, "do not make any permanent arrangement for several days. I know of a good position which you can probably get, if it has not been filled. It is with a first-class law firm. They are particular, and have been trying for two weeks to get suited in an office man. They want some one for several years, and are not so nice as to what he may know in the beginning, but base their preference on the ultimate *promise* of the applicant. I think your face, fist, and tongue, with my recommendation, will suit them."

"I am much obliged to you, Cassel, and will be glad to advise with you. When can I see them?"

"I will take you round to-morrow. Meantime I will see them myself, this afternoon, after I have shown you and Johnny to your hotel. Have you any idea where you are?"

"Not the most remote. I only know that we are in New York."

"Come here—to the front door. Now look across the street. Do you recognize the building?"

"Jupiter! That is our hotel!" cried Johnny and Carroll with one voice.

"Yes," said Cassel, "but you get a better dinner here than you do there. Here the dishes are cooked separately; there they are all cooked together, where an oyster tastes

25

of pudding, and pudding tastes of hot salad, and salad tastes of mince-meat, and it all tastes of steam,—wilted as it were."

After a hearty, jolly, and re-enforcing dinner, Cassel went alone to the law office of Hallum & Gore.

" Good-afternoon, Mr. Rapid," said Mr. Gore, the only partner present. " Have a seat, sir."

" You are busy," suggested Cassel.

' " I can spare a few moments."

" Have you secured an assistant?"

" No."

" Do not close with any one, then, until I bring a friend of mine around to see you to-morrow. I think he will suit you. He is a fine young man, well educated, and gentlemanly. He has been a student of Maryland law, but can soon fall into your ways. His father was a better lawyer than either you or Mr. Hallum," said Cassel, with good-humored but incisive honesty, "and from what I have heard, and conjecture, the son will sustain his ancestry."

" You are very candid," replied Mr. Gore, with a smile half sardonic, half amused.

" On business, with business men, I'm as blunt as the back of a wedge. I am not depreciating you or your firm, but simply telling you the truth."

" The truth is quite refreshing," said Mr. Gore. " It is not very often that we get a breath of it in these precincts."

" I hope it won't make you sick," replied Cassel, gayly. " If it does, just swallow a professional prevarication by way of antidote or emetic." And Cassel went upon the street.

CHAPTER XXVIII.

CASSEL RAPID, who knew the family history of Carroll May, was generously disposed to assist the young man, and secure to him a good fair start in the race of life. Cassel's sympathy, wherever bestowed, was strong, active, and practical, and did not end in words if deeds were appropriate. Carroll was now an object of special interest with him, chiefly on account of his life-long orphanage and dependence,—subordinately on account of his life-long connection and disconnection with Cora Glencoe.

In Cassel's mind were several propositions. The first was one of benevolence ; for in his youthful, limited sphere, he was actuated by the same impulses of nobility and compassion which hallow the name of George Peabody, whose grand and solemn requiem has just been chanted by boundless, oceanic, and celestial voices, and the appreciation of whose gifted life bows down the famed heads of Europe and America now weeping out his world-wide obsequies. Cassel's benevolent purpose will explain itself when he acts upon it, which will be done almost immediately. Again, with regard to Cora it was Cassel's purpose to deal frankly and liberally with Carroll. If Cora loved Carroll—which he could scarcely bring himself to imagine except when he thought of the "family reasons" which Hector O'Dare had stated as the basis of Carroll's interest in the search for Marie Guthrie—then the die was already cast, and he would not attempt to upset it. For Cassel wanted *first love*, and not that which had been, or by any possibility might have been, kissed and whinnied over. But if Cora was free, then Cassel would endeavor to win her without wooing her, in compliance with the injunctions of Mr. Hope. Again: he would first establish Carroll May in business and in the line of promotion, after which he would seek an understanding with Carroll. His own position as *quasi* guardian giving him a certain and great advantage, should he see proper to use it, he felt that to be wholly generous, and to put himself solely upon his individual merits, it would be right to encourage, if not to urge, Carroll, if the young lawyer was in the least so disposed, to try his fortunes with Cora. He was sensible that Carroll, who himself possessed some advantages, might eventually succeed; but he reflected that he, Cassel Rapid, would never, if he knew or suspected it; become the husband of any girl unless she preferred him above all others,—and unless she had enjoyed the opportunity of bestowing herself in perfect harmony with the secret tender desires of her own heart.

If all persons were as fastidious as Cassel Rapid was, there would be few weddings in this world, for it is a very rare thing, particularly rare with a woman, to get the coveted one. Frail, weak, patient, lovely, and loving woman is generally the chosen—not the chooser. But God wills it so—else it would not be so. In this sinful and sacrificial world, the weak must succumb to the strong,—virtue must *lurk*, while vice stalks through the glorious and goodly places of the earth. Oh, for some keen, invincible, and universal sword of *Justice*, to flash throughout the broad round earth, and set all odds even! But we might as well invoke Christian charity from the Devil. It is Death, and only Death, who may solve the mystery of Life, and set all odds even.

In the morning Cassel took his two young friends to the office of Hallum & Gore. Mr. Gore was the leader of the firm,—the oyer and terminer. Leaving Carroll and Johnny with Mr. Hallum, Cassel and Mr. Gore retired to a consultation-room.

"Mr. Gore," said Cassel, "I have confidence in my young friend, and I have confidence in your firm, and I am satisfied you will suit him, and he will suit you. If he does suit you, what are you willing to pay him per year, and what advantages do you promise him?"

"I can answer you precisely. If he suits us, we will engage him for three years. For the first year he will receive as salary, five hundred dollars; for the second year, seven hundred dollars; and for the third year, one thousand dollars. At the end of that time, if he has the talent you credit him with, he will be a competent practitioner, able to take good care of himself. It may then be to our common interest to give him a junior partnership. If not, we will dismiss him with a moderate run of business of his own, upon which he can build his fortunes."

" The salary," said Cassel, " I consider rather low, for he will be an active and efficient aid to you. The advantages you offer are liberal enough. I have no doubt but that he will accept the position, and in view of it I have a request to make of you. In addition to the salary ·which he will get from you, I wish to give him, on my own account, for the first year, say four hundred dollars, and if nothing prevents, to continue this addition through the three years. But he must not know that I pay it until I choose to tell him, and you must not exact anything from him on account of this extra salary."

" I understand you," replied Mr. Gore. " It will be very easy to grant your request, for which I now give you our promise. His salary will then be, for the three years, nine, eleven, and fourteen hundred dollars."

" Yes."

" Just give me a brief article of writing, stating the case, so that, should you hereafter find it not convenient to continue this extra, he will not be in a position to demand it of Hallum & Gore."

Cassel gave the cautious lawyer the written safeguard required, and Carroll May was then called in. Cassel withdrew, leaving Mr. Gore free to examine the young applicant. Fifteen minutes passed, when Carroll came out smiling and successful.

" It is all right," said he softly to Cassel. " You are so very kind, and I am grateful. They give me more than I had any hope for."

" See, then, that you do your duty, both to them and yourself," said Cassel, with smiling but impressive earnestness, " for I am pledged for you, and I rarely ever pledge for anybody."

" I promise to redeem your pledge to the uttermost," said Carroll, in the full swing of that enthusiasm begotten of opening success.

This matter arranged, Cassel was impatient to adjust

25*

something of more immediate importance to himself.
Wishing to see Carroll privately, and not knowing exactly how he might well get rid of Johnny, he, at a venture, took the two young men to a museum.

Among the multiplicity of sights, Johnny and Carroll
became temporarily separated, and Cassel observing it,
took occasion to join Carroll May. He might have waited
until some other time, but what was the use of waiting?
Without prevarication or meandering he would go straight
to the point, as was his habit.

"Carroll," asked he, "do you know that Cora Glencoe
is in the city?"

"Yes. Have you seen her?"

"Seen her! I'm living in the same house with her."

"Indeed! Then you are a fortunate young man."

"Would you like to be in my place?"

"Yes,—with your name, and face, and fortune."

"Carroll, pardon me for abruptness, for I will be as
frank with you as I would have you be with me,—but do
you love Cora?"

"Yes—no—I don't know," answered Carroll, with a
sad mystification. He continued: "I might have loved
her, but, by a continual stamping out, I have kept down
what would have been simply wicked folly. You know
the reason why."

"But since her new history?"

"Since that I have not seen her."

"Does she love you?" asked the inquisitive Cassel.

"Me! I do not know that she ever wasted a thought
upon me. But why this catechism?"

"For several reasons. One of them is, I am, in a
measure, her guardian here in the city. Another, I do
not doubt that you were the most girl-winning young
fellow in Creswood while you and she were there. Don't
flash your eyes that way, for I am not making fun of you,
but am speaking in all sincerity. Another reason is,
Cora is the finest young girl within all my acquaintance,
and I thought that possibly you and she had formed an
attachment, if nothing more than a mute one, while being
reared as children in the same school and neighborhood."

"What might have been, may differ greatly from what

is. But do not talk to me about Cora Glencoe, because I am strenuously trying to forget-her."

" Carroll, the subject is too enchanting to be dismissed so summarily. I will be as frank with you as I have asked you to be with me. As I said before, I am Cora's city guardian. You are at liberty to win her if you can, provided you do not interfere with her studies. I reserve to myself the same privilege."

"You!" exclaimed Carroll, while he surveyed young Rapid's almost matchless *personnel.* "In that case I could hardly hope for success. You have every advantage of me,—authority, wealth, leisure, and an elegant comeliness to which I do not even pretend."

" I know of no one whom I would fear so much as Carroll May," answered Cassel. " But I glory in competition where I know that it is honorable."

" I will not strive with you," protested Carroll, "for should I by possibility succeed, there is a gloom which would rest upon the joint lives of Cora and myself which only the magic of an everlasting and never-waning honeymoon could effectually dispel,—and the spoken and written experience of the world teaches me that these matrimonial moons are wholly given over to waning. When I first learned of Cora's new prospective parentage, I thought of her in connection with my humble self as released from a bloody bondage,—that I was free to seek her. I was partly the cause of her coming to this city ; and therein I had a motive or purpose, which, however, upon mature reflection, ceases to exist, or sleeps ; and I have no present disposition to wake it up. I yield the ground entirely to you, and wish you joy of its possession. Under other circumstances I might wrestle with you."

Cassel was both pleased and disappointed,—pleased that the way was open and unobstructed, and disappointed that he should have no competitor ; not that he especially thirsted for competition, or wished to triumph over any adversary, but he experienced a feeling of dissatisfaction that any appreciative one, who had enjoyed good opportunities of judging of Cora's loveliness and sweet ways, and had once been under her influence, could so calmly, and conclusively, and in such a reasonable manner, make up his mind to forego her altogether. Could he, Cassel Rapid, make up *his* mind to such self-abnegation? Could he rest contented to forego the girl of his love under any circumstances short of impossibility? He thought not. Was it, then, a lack of ardor in Carroll May? or was it a deficiency in Cora, which caused the young man so tamely to submit to the tenor of the times? Was it an absence, to all but himself, of that thrilling combination of trait and person which makes men willing to go to the very devil if their way only leads them through the coveted portal? A man who is not disposed to be jealous, is well pleased to see a world of lovers worshiping at the feet of the girl whom he loves and whom he expects to make his own. It is not at all pleasant for him to think that, except himself, nobody is alive to her charms. Such undisputed monopoly would rob the luster, if not the intrinsic value, from the gem which he calculates to set in his breast and wear as a badge of wealth, and joy, and enviable success.

"Carroll," asked Cassel, "if you are not interested in Cora, why did you propose emptying your pockets by encountering the expenses of a search for Maria Guthrie?"

"How do you know of that?"

"Through O'Dare, the detective. I applied to him for a like object, and he informed me that both you and Mr. Neville Huron were in advance of me. Now I do not hesitate to admit that I was prompted solely by my interest in Cora. O'Dare told me that you were moved to it by family reasons. Can I, without impropriety, inquire what those family reasons are?"

"I am simply making an effort to vindicate my father and defend his memory." And Carroll went into an explanation of the cause which had induced him to engage in the search for Maria Guthrie.

"Your explanation is adequate and creditable," said Cassel. "But to return to our primary subject,—I cannot understand how any one with the ghost of a chance could or would yield Cora to another without an effort."

"My chance," replied Carroll, with an expression of countenance half pensive and half bitter, "is accompanied by the ghost of my father, which might frown upon me should I venture on the chance. However, my mind, in that particular regard, may be warped; and others may contemplate my position from a different stand-point from that which to me it has heretofore most vividly appeared. You yourself seem to do so. Cora, for all that I know, may do the same. You half banter me, Cassel,—kindling both my hope and my pride. If, therefore, you will permit me to retract, I will do so, and the future, under different urgings, shall determine the fates of Cora Glencoe, Cassel Rapid, and Carroll May. I shall hold myself free to outstrip you if fortune should favor me. Heretofore, I had put my love into a coffin and screwed down the lid, but the clods have not yet fallen on it. You have provoked it back to life and resistance. You have challenged me, old fellow," continued Carroll, with a strange gleam leaping from his eyes which Cassel did not altogether comprehend or like, "and I will endeavor to make your fight an exciting one, and your conquest valuable on account of its cost. But I warn you, that, when I launch, I will, if possible, sail over Cassel Rapid, or any other rapid, to get out into that sparkling champagne sea of joy which will be coexistent with the possession of this matchless little girl."

Cassel was again both pleasured and displeasured; he was gratified to know that Cora was properly estimated, but there was an expression in the eyes of the youth whom he had roused to antagonism which was not welcome to him. However, he reached out his hand and said,—

"Carroll, I give you my hand in pledge for a fair fight, without the accompaniments of jealousy and bitterness. Although your sudden resolution alarms me a little, it will give zest to the game, and whichever wins will have the satisfaction of knowing that the prize has been tested. Also, it is very possible that neither of us may succeed; in the latter event we can at least sympathize with each other while we suck our thumbs in defeat and despair."

"She is so well worth a battle," answered Carroll, "that it would be a pity should no lance be shivered or blade unhilted over her head. In one respect I have the advantage of you, Cassel. You are hopeful,—almost domineeringly confident; I am neither. If you are defeated, you will feel the galling edge of failure cut you through and through. I enter with but little hope; if I fail, I will be just where I began—almost. I am in a position to be cooler than you, for I have nothing to lose and everything to win. What my emotional status will be after the first encounter I cannot anticipate; but since you have spurred me to strive for Cora, I will assure you that rather than not come in contact with her at all, and hear her voice, and look into her eyes, and feast upon her blushes, I am in a mood to choose the exquisite misery of defeat, knowing as I do know that Cora will temper my defeat with a world of compassion and solicitude, in which all the loveliness of her nature will arm itself to soothe me, and make my failure there sweeter than success in any other quarter. It will be like dying upon some unequaled and ambrosial draught."

"Carroll," said Cassel, with something of impatience, "you know that you will not court any such distinction, or extinction, as that; or, if you should, that you are one among the last to bear it contentedly or derive pleasure from it."

"Some men choose to die for their country, others to die for mistaken honor, and yet others for such myths as Fame and Glory; but I would sooner sacrifice *myself* for the girl that I *love*, than, by a different immolation, to write my name upon the very keystone of Vanity's proudest spanning arches."

"I fear that I have roused a Cid, who will do battle in the very shroud and harness of the tomb ere he will relent in his warfare," said Cassel, with a look of incredulity and the faintest imaginable feeling and show of disdain. He was of the opinion that Carroll was talking foolishly and extravagantly, whether sincerely or not. In conclusion, he remarked, "Carroll, I intended this interview to be frank and simple. You have brought into it an element which I do not like; and we had as well rejoin Johnny, who appears to be immersed in the mystical but obsolete lore of those Egyptian mummies over there."

The interview had got to be distasteful to Cassel, who, from beginning to end, had intended and endeavored that it should be an open, knightly, and even boyishly frank, free conference; but before he had put an end to it, he saw

in Carroll's countenance and manner an expression and air
which he did not anticipate or like. For Carroll, though not
habitually on the *qui vive* for affronts, was very touchy,
and in many things morbidly sensitive ; and, out of pure
human perversity, altogether misconceived Cassel Rapid's
motives, writing them down in fashion as follows : " Now,
at this day, before me, Carroll May, a child of Poverty, a
vassel of Misfortune, and. the target of Circumstance,
comes Cassel Rapid, glorious in his youth and beauty,
and free by reason of his wealth, and deposes thus:
'Look at me, Carroll May. I am your benefactor ; I will
continue to befriend you if you will consent to amuse me
and enable me to pass my time agreeably, and mark the
dull days with a triumph here and there, which, though it
trenches upon your sensibilities, will gratify my vanity
and yield me an occasional crown of ascendency. I have
already, for my own uses, made you respectable by securing
for you a respectable place. I have under my charge a
lovely country-girl, whom I can monopolize at will by
virtue of my position ; but to do so, securely and entirely,
will be far too tame and insipid. Therefore, come you,
my convenient friend Carroll, and give spice to my pie
and pungency to my champagne. It is foregone that you
shall not share with me the pie or tip the champagne;
but you may have the wonderful, and for you the sufficient, pleasure of seeing me eat and drink when the ban-
quet is served.' "

Carroll had no conception what bitter injustice he was
doing Cassel Rapid by harboring such graceless thoughts
as these. Cassel's motives had been as pure as the limpid
spring-water, and as generous and free as the sun's goodly
ray. Carroll May was probably the only youth upon the
face of the earth to whom Cassel would have felt disposed
to proffer the unreserved, delicate, and confidential good-
fellowship manifested in his open-hearted and opportune
dealing. Instead of endeavoring to entrap Carroll for the
purpose of twitting and deriding him, or crowing over him
afterward, he was just away from doing him a first-rate
favor and secretly enhancing it out of his own pocket.
Had he been conscious of what was rioting through Carroll's mind, he would utterly have scorned him as an un-

gracious hound, unworthy even of a kick. But Carroll
was not absolutely, and without rebate, to blame : for instances of motive, pure, perfect, and unleavened, are so
very, very rare, that they pass us unrecognized, or unper-
ceived, like invisible angels silently gliding by. It was
well for the old amity existing between these two young
men, that Carroll May's bitter imaginings were as unde-
tected by Cassel as his generosity and fairness were unap-
preciated by Carroll. It is almost needless to state that
Carroll May would have writhed under insufferable shame
and remorse, had he been advised how well and truly
Cassel had acted toward him, and how egregiously and
ignobly he had suffered himself to misconstrue. From
this time forward, a breath of chillness seemed to hover
between them, bearing the least bit of frost.

CHAPTER XXIX.

WHEN Carroll May came to New York, he was by no
means determined to seek out Cora Glencoe, even for the
purpose of renewing old acquaintance. On the contrary,
he had almost made up his mind never again to look upon
her face if he could avoid it. He had generally considered
her as much beyond his endeavors as if she had been the
bride of another. But now that by others it did not
appear to be taken for granted that his father's blood would
cry out against him from the ground should he essay to
win her, he found no difficulty in convincing himself that
Cora's hand was not lineally stained by that father's gore,
and thereby forbidden to him. In view of her mooted parentage he could strive, then, for her hand, without vexing the
ghost of his slaughtered father. Carroll was a spirited
and combative youth, and with his ideas of Cassel Rapid's
motives, together with the influence of a life-long penchant
for Cora, it is not surprising that he resolved to compete
with Cassel, with all the vim which awakens at the touch
of love, pride, ambition, rivalry, and active sensibility.

It had not been Cassel's intention to provoke a sharp contest, but merely honorable and knightly emulation—but now that he dimly recognized a spirit of bitterness in the contemplated rivalry of Carroll May, he girded himself for firm, alert, and decisive battle.

Pretty soon a third champion appeared in the lists, and the contest bid fair to be a triangular one, with the probability of its angles increasing in number as the strife progressed.

This third champion was no less a personage than Harry Gray,—the Claude Melnotte, as he was called, of New York city. It happened in this wise that he became an admirer of Cora. Harry Gray had been pleased with the outward appearance of Linda Boyd, on a former occasion, when she was taking her first Park drive with Cassel Rapid, and had determined to make some investigations regarding her. But he had postponed doing so from time to time until now that Cora was established in the Boyd mansion. Cassel had promised to introduce the young gentleman to Linda whenever he should find it convenient to call at the mansion. When, at length, he came, Cassel and Cora were in the first parlor, into which Harry Gray was ushered by the bell-servant. Cassel presented him to Cora, and in a few moments slipped out to notify Linda and tease her a little—but Linda was absent. She and Mrs. Lake were making some calls in the city. Cassel left young Gray with Cora for the space of ten or fifteen minutes. When he returned, Cora withdrew. She would have withdrawn at first, but Cassel had left her so situated that she could not well have escaped without an appearance of panic or rudeness.

Young Gray was greatly attracted by Cora, and when she went out he turned to Cassel and asked,—

"See here, Rapid; what tempting little Greek is this whom you were kind enough to give me a glimpse of?"

"A young friend of mine, from Maryland; Miss Huron."

"What! Is she the one about whom the Huron brothers are waging such a war?"

"Yes."

"What is she doing here?"

"Educating herself."

26

" In whose care is she ?"

" Mine."

" Yours !" exclaimed young Gray, with surprise. " You are certainly offering me a joke."

" Not a bit."

" Who ever heard of such a thing ! Ha ! ha ! h-a !"

" Why not?"

" Are her friends all crazy ?"

" No more than are you."

" The idea ! Wh-e-w ! Cassel Rapid to have charge of two dainty little women, in a large city, and a thousand miles from their mammas !"

" What's the difficulty ?"

" Why, Rapid,—don't you know your reputation among the petticoats?"

" No,—please enlighten me."

" It is that you are a regular bohemian,—a rake,—a *blasé* sort of fellow with no appetite for anything except the fresh and untried."

" The character-makers are disposed to flatter me," observed Cassel, with an indolent, careless smile. " I might favor you with some current opinions in regard to yourself, if I thought it would have the smallest influence in reforming you. You are alternately wheedling at least a half dozen of young ladies to my certain knowledge, and——"

" Halt, Rapid. Do not take this occasion to sum up my sins against me; but tell me, is Miss Huron fancy free ?"

" I presume so. Why ?"

" Because I have already determined to seek an interest."

" You had better not."

" How so?"

" You'll find it hard."

" The way I like it."

" Very well,—I warn you."

" Oho ! *You* warn me, do you ?"

" Yes,—Cassel Rapid warns you off."

" I understand."

" No,—you don't understand."

" Is it not that you are a selfish fellow ?"

" No."

" Prove it," demanded Gray, laughing.

" Nothing easier," replied Cassel. "One word from me would close these doors hermetically against you, and you might try from now till doomsday and yet never succeed in seeing either Mrs. Boyd or Miss Huron."

" What a Sultan he is !"

" To complete the proof, you have my permission," continued Cassel, with provoking condescension, " to come whenever you like."

" What a merciful prince !"

" But bear in mind that Miss Huron is but a school-girl, and that you are not to interfere with the prosecution of her studies. She cannot probably see you every time it may suit your wayward fancy to drop in."

" How often may I call, you despot ?"

" Once a week, if it is agreeable to her."

" Who is to judge of the agreeability of my visits,—you or she ?" asked Gray, with a droll and significant look of inquiry.

" I leave it between you. You will not be apt to mistake any manifestation on her part."

" And Mrs. Boyd,—are you her Cerberus also?"

" She is her own mistress, and you will excuse me from striking a bargain which might not meet her approval. See her yourself."

" What is Miss Huron's name ?"

" Cora Glencoe."

" God ! but I love her already. Rapid, are you going in there ?"

" It's none of your business, Mr. Inquisitive. But you need not fear a dull time,—you will have plenty of opposition."

" If I had you out of the way, I would like the prospect better; for the battle is almost entirely within your discretion. If you should enviously observe me getting along nicely, you'll take it into your head to lock me out. Nevertheless, I'll try and get acquainted with her, and take the chance of your being struck by lightning."

Meantime, Linda returned, and Gray had the pleasure of seeing her. Linda rarely ever spent a more agreeable little while in her life than the half hour which Harry Gray devoted to her. When the young gentleman left the house with permission to come again and at will, he said to himself,—

"Cassel Rapid is in clover up to his chin.. I would give a fine pair of trotters to beat him. There's Mrs. Boyd, a sugar plum,—a ripe, blushing peach,—a regular little honey-bee. How I would like to kiss her, and have it accompanied by the faintest possible response from her own lips. But Miss Huron is a sweet, young dovey,—a gazelle,—with an eagle, or a young lion, to watch over her, and devour her up, perhaps. Oh, you rascal of a Rapid! Why are you such an unmitigated, fortunate fellow, as to come ever and anon between me and my fancy?"

A few evenings later, Carroll May and Johnny Gale called to see Cora. She received them as old friends, and entertained them balmily and with pleasure. They inquired for Mrs. Boyd, the young mistress of the mansion, in order to pay their respects to her. Linda soon came in, "beautiful as a butterfly," and ready to welcome the young gentlemen as Cora's friends. Carroll May paired off with Cora, and Johnny with Linda, and, apparently, a very pleasant evening ensued.

When the young gentlemen bowed themselves out, Linda said to Cora,—

"Your friend Mr. Gale is such a fine, handsome, hearty fellow,— so good humored and full of fun."

"I hardly knew him," replied Cora. "He has improved so very much since I last saw him down at Creswood. But what do you think of Mr. May?"

"He did not give me an opportunity of forming an opinion, being so entirely devoted to you."

Cora blushed, and Linda laughed at her, bantered her, and kissed her an affectionate good-night.

But we must follow the two young men.

"Carroll," said Johnny, as soon as they had cleared the front steps of the mansion, "Mrs. Boyd fills my eye exactly."

"She will fill your pocket if you can persuade her to become Mrs. Gale," said Carroll, with a sort of lack-interest reply.

" What do you think of her, Carroll ?" asked Johnny, who evidently felt more concern in the subject than did his companion.

" Well," answered Carroll, rather abstractedly, " I saw at a glance that she is very pretty, and upon that I presume she is very fascinating,—is she not ?"

" Yes,—she's as sweet as a cherry-pie, and as new as the first rose or the first strawberry in the Spring. She stirred up lots of mixed poetry in me, but it's been so long since I have anchored that close to a hoop-skirt that I hardly knew what to say or how to feel. I succeeded, however, in feeling first-rate myself, and she seemed to be mathematically pleased with my dialectics, notwithstanding she would laugh at me and call me droll. I am going to see her again, by Juggernaut. Carroll, it's regular hilltop. But how did you and Cora make it ?"

" Oh,—very well. She was particularly kind, and coy, and tender, as an old friend."

" Carroll," asked Johnny, while a street lamp lighted up the mischief in his cheerful, almost heedless, face, "you are rather staggering that way, are you not, old fellow ?"

" Can't tell yet," answered Carroll.

" Mrs. Boyd is so dainty, isn't she ?"

"As dainty as a young princess, I suppose."

"And she is friendly, and comes so near to a fellow."

" Yes."

" Then she is a virgin, although a widow. Did you know that ?"

" I reckon," replied Carroll, far away with his own thoughts.

" What's the matter, Carroll ?" demanded Johnny. "Are you asleep ? Wake up, and let's have a little hot supper at the Dolphin,—I'll stand treat ?"

" I'm not hungry, Johnny."

" Then go home, you squeamish fellow, and I'll go eat by myself. You must have met with a cross to-night."

Carroll and Johnny occupied, jointly, a furnished room, and took their meals at a restaurant. Carroll went alone, to his lodging, leaving Johnny to satisfy his appetite.

26*

Thoughts of women or girls had never yet dried up
Johnny's gastric juice, or interfered with his enjoyment of
a good meal.

Carroll May was now painfully in love with Cora, and
his interview, just ended, left him apprehensive that he had
suffered himself to take, and insist upon, a very imprudent
and damaging course. He had exerted himself to probe
into her heart, without alarming her, but after an assiduous hour spent in that behalf, he found himself rather
worse than better off. He had hot conceived that she was
so far his superior in emotional and single-handed finesse.
She baffled him at every point. Not that she strove with
him, but because she would *not* strive with him. In the
conduct of a successful quarrel, two persons must lend a
hand, or a tongue ; for if one declines to engage, the other
will find it a tedious and very unsatisfactory job to keep
the quarrel alive. Cora would not take part in a lover's
tourney between herself and Carroll. A soft answer
turneth away wrath ; it is a shield from which wrath
glances off; an oil which negatives poison ; a water which
stays and quenches fire; a smiling antagonist; a peace-
making alien, which comes in between wrath and wrath
and disarms aggression. It was thus that Cora disarmed
Carroll ; for when he slyly trenched upon her maiden
skirts, and delicately challenged an interchange of confidence and of feeling, she responded in words and manner
as foreign to the discussion which he was endeavoring to
initiate, as a kind and gentle word would be foreign to a
quarrel. She balked him with such easy and apparently
aimless tact, that he was at a loss to discover whether she
was altogether blind to his advances, or a most cunning
young diplomatist. Just so had Cora's brother Graham
been handled and beaten by her, when, as her cousin, he
was making or trying to make love to her down at Creswood. And as Graham had been bewitched by her, so
now was Carroll May bewitched and bewildered. When
he conversed upon familiar and general topics, Cora not
only went with him freely but often took the lead. But
when he would shift into the untrodden way in which *he*
would fain go, Cora would at once become an impracticable dunce or a deft little refugee, and he could advance

neither her nor himself the space of an inch. The two particular subjects on which Carroll tried to commit and convict her, were—the state of her heart toward the male world *en masse* and toward Cassel Rapid individually,—and whether her changed status and prospective condition in the world, did, in her estimation, set Cora Glencoe and Carroll May free to love one another, should they feel so disposed. But Cora would not exchange with him those little heart-coins which pass so currently between incipient lovers, for he had started radically wrong with her,—alarming her at the very outset, and causing her to lock up the treasures of her bosom, and hold fast to the key. He was not unaware of his failure, or of the consequences it might entail, and he already felt that the coolness and nonchalance of which he had boasted to Cassel Rapid, had entirely deserted him.

" I have made a fool of myself," said he, mentally condemning his management, " and, to make it yet worse, she knows it. Why was I so inordinately covetous and impatient? Why couldn't I let 'Cassel Rapid' and 'Carroll May' escape from the conversation, and permit her to talk upon subjects which did not drag so heavily? No! like a dolt I must go and make war upon her instantly, and now I have got myself hobbled and hindered and beaten. But when I see her again I shall rectify all this, and then take a different course."

Thereupon Carroll made very many sensible resolutions. But the question is, Will he, or will he not, act upon them? Will he have the patience? As a young lawyer, Carroll was patient enough, and professionally shrewd withal—but Blackstone on legal essence, and Cupid on a rampage, are two very different masters.

One evening when the Boyd colony was collected in the parlors of the mansion, and a general and spirited intermingling was in progress, Harry Gray, in his habitual fine humor, made his appearance, and, after running the sprightly gantlet of the colony, and devoting a few particular moments to Linda, captured Cora, and led her away to the piano.

" Now, Miss Cora, the favor which you have promised me is no longer unavoidably delayed."

Cora sang for him. In memory of Creswood and of
Larboard Strand, and her own feelings being in harmony
with the thrilling sentiment of the song, she chose
"Shells of Ocean."

> "And thus it is—in every stage,
>   By toys our fancy is beguiled ;
> We gather shells from youth to age,
>   And then we leave them—like a child."

"I always liked that simple, pensive song," said Gray,
"and I have never heard it rendered more sweetly or
touchingly." Cora blushed with pleasure, and Harry continued, "But it makes me feel too sad, and I do not wish
to feel sad to-night, for I came here to be joyful. Please,
then, play me a sweet confusion of operatic music, to drive
out the melancholy effect of this song of the Sea Shell."
And Harry Gray, venturing, stooped over and whispered
something into Cora's ear. She answered him nothing,
but, arranging her music, wheeled about on the piano-
stool and called,—

"Mr. Rapid ?"

Cassel came over and awaited whatever request Cora
should make of him.

"I wish," said she, "you would please turn the pages
for me. Mr. Gray has asked for opera music, and as he is
known to be a competent critic, I desire to secure every
advantage for my first effort within range of his ear."

"Why didn't you permit *me* to turn the pages for you?"
asked Harry Gray, who was discreet enough to recognize
the effect of his late fond whispering.

"Because I prefer to leave you free to close your auricu-
lars when you hear a grating discord."

"Very well," responded Harry, humorously putting up
his hands to be ready for stopping his ears,—"I'm in position."

The piece was slow and rich, but difficult of thorough
development, and Gray, with a good deal of interest,
watched Cora's fingers, as, with tremulous firmness, they
pressed the keys, and wooed from the willing instrument
its sweetest and most thrilling chords.

"That is perfectly delightful," said Gray, "and has recalled my more sprightly humor, so that I can enjoy another sentimental song if you will consent to alternate the pleasure which you are dispensing."

"Before I proceed further," answered Cora, "I wish to get something off my mind."

"Cast your burdens upon me," gayly volunteered Harry Gray.

"With all my heart," said Cora, who, with a business-like air, reached for a book which lay upon one end of the piano. "I brought this book here for the purpose of asking an explanation from Mr. Rapid, but you, probably, will give me the explanation just as well." Cora turned to a particular page, and handed Gray the book. "You will find on page 71, near the top, a Greek quotation. It is the key to the entire of pages 71 and 72. I am not able to translate the quotation, and cannot understand what immediately follows, until I am possessed of the significance of those Greek words. I beg pardon for introducing the subject at such a time as this, but it often worries me no little to have a difficulty hanging over."

Gray, who had by this time discovered that he had overcropped himself, very reluctantly took hold of the book, and then glancing suspiciously at Cassel Rapid, inquired,—

"Rapid, do you read Greek?"

"No," answered Cassel, without the slightest hesitation, but scarcely able to suppress a smile. As Gray's countenance cleared up of its shadow of perplexity, Cora turned with some surprise to Cassel, and was about to spring his trap-trigger. Gray was looking Cassel straight in the face, and the latter had no opportunity of making Cora a signal. Anxious not to have his trap sprung, Cassel dared to put out his foot and press the toe of Cora's slipper. She retreated in haste and panic, and expectantly waited for Gray to "unmuzzle his wisdom." Cocking his eye and looking into the book like a "magpie into a marrow-bone," Harry Gray translated the Greek, and Cassel Rapid, who had got a glimpse of it, immediately roared with laughter. Gray looked at Cassel as though it would be the acme of pleasure to seize him and choke him to death, and Cassel continued to laugh in that hearty, joyous, honest fashion which made his merriment either so very pleasant or so very provoking.

"What amuses you so, Mr. Rapid?" playfully asked Cora, who felt very much disposed to laugh herself.

"Let me see the book," said Cassel, still boiling over with appreciation of Gray's Greek lore.

Harry resigned the book much more reluctantly than he had at first accepted it, and when Cora was turned away and he could catch Cassel's eye, he went through with a most intense and vivid pantomime, to the exceeding amusement and inward delight of young Rapid.

"Mr. Gray," said Cora, finally turning to him, "I do not perceive what connection the quotation can possibly have with the text. Did you observe what immediately follows it?"

"I merely glanced at the quotation," answered Gray, feeling very miserable, and mentally cursing himself. "Why the devil didn't I read the connection?" asked he of himself. "I might have gathered an inkling of the significance of that confounded quotation. She will not only write me down an Ass, but a deceitful Ass." He then looked imploringly over to Cassel Rapid, who still continued, at intervals, to laugh with aggravating gusto. Cassel, with a warning shake of his head at Cora, laid the book aside. Harry Gray, beginning to feel a little safer, picked it up and said,—

"I observe, Miss Cora, that this is a work on Antiquities. Under whose gray-haired supervision are you prosecuting this particular study?"

"Mr. Rapid has lent me his collection of works on Antiquity, and volunteers to enlighten me when I am mystified, as I was—and am yet, by this Greek quotation."

"Mr. *Rapid!*" exclaimed Gray with assumed sarcastic, and genuine retaliatory amazement. "Mr. Rapid an antiquarian,—a Methuselah,—ha! ha! h-a! a compeer of Pickwick,—an admirer of hieroglyphics, Egyptian obelisks, and American mile-stones. Be cautioned by me, Miss Cora, and confine him to the Ancients. Don't let him descend to the Moderns with you, especially to the current generation."

" Why ?" asked Cora, preparing to act the impracticable dunce, as she had done with Carroll May.

" Because he is a gay bohemian."

" I thought he was a Marylander," answered Cora, with the most innocent look in the world. " However, I think the study of the current year as interesting as that of any preceding one, be it ever so remote. Look at the state of Europe, for instance,—hanging, as is supposed, on a verge. Even Bohemia may be turned topsy-turvy. Then, in America, the weather-vane points to the stormy quarter."

" She eludes me," said Gray to himself. Then aloud, " If you really wish an interesting modern story or subject, just investigate my young friend Rapid there. I think you will find in him a medley of misdemeanors."

" So trite a medley can readily be found elsewhere without the trouble of investigation," answered Cora.

" But try and ascertain, and tell me," said Gray, who did not regard Cora's last remark as particularly flattering to himself, for he might well answer for the " elsewhere," —" why it is that he is so winning with the girls."

" Probably because he behaves himself."

" By no means. For he exactly does *not* behave himself."

" His misdemeanors must then be very fascinating ones."

" They must be indeed," answered Gray, " for at this moment he has a dozen or more unhappy girls in love with him."

" Indeed! How many can *you* boast ?"

" Not one."

" Oh, how you would like to change places with him !" cried Cora, with sprightly, even teasing contravention, while Gray muttered to himself, " Caught again, by Jove !"

" But don't you think it very wrong," asked Gray, " for a young gentleman to have so many sweethearts ?"

" Very wrong indeed,—in the sweethearts," answered Cora.

" And in him also; for he can only love but one."

" Only one at a time, you mean."

" And he can marry but one."

" And thereby generously suffer the others to escape the misery of that one," suggested Cora, with a bright, sly glance at Cassel, who answered her with a smile. Cassel

was wondering what Gray was going to make out of this
somewhat episodic conversation. He was already half
convinced that it would end in nothing, and Gray was
himself apprehensive that he would, in the end, reach *nihil*.

"But what do you think of a youth," asked he, "who
always has a dozen or more strings to his bow?"

"I think that he is quite safe," answered Cora, merrily,
—"pretty well supplied with bow-thongs."

"Yes, but to go and get a dozen girls in love with him
when he knows that he can't parcel himself out to them!"

"He must be a very captivating person to do that, or
the girls must be very silly."

"But please be serious now," urged Gray, "and tell me
what you *think*—of—such—a—naughty—fellow?"

"To be serious, then," replied Cora, with the slightest
perceptible elevation of her brow, "I think absolutely
nothing about it."

Cassel broke out with a triumphant carol, which irritated
Gray, and caused him to color with vexation, while Cora
sat demurely looking on. Gray had essayed to tease Cassel, and possibly ascertain how Cora was affected toward
her gallant young guardian. But he failed to excite any
show of jealousy or concern on her part, and ended in
teasing himself. He got himself over on legitimate ground
as soon as possible, and by a run of sensible, pleasing talk,
endeavored to make Cora forget the poverty and weakness
of his ill-contrived foray upon herself and Cassel.

Cora had been very well pleased with Harry Gray. He
was excellent company, his manners were spontaneously
good, he had a look of native, unfailing amity and generosity about him, and very rarely, if ever, appeared self-
absorbed. He was frequently careless, and laid himself
open to raillery and attack, but by his very looseness he
frequently delighted his acquaintances by giving them
gratifying opportunities of pouncing upon him. His position was often like that of a fun-loving school-boy, set
upon by a bevy of snowballing maidens, each of whom
being half in love with the victim, takes good care not to
pelt him too hard. The most vicious of Harry Gray's
favorite female acquaintances would not have punished
him more severely than to slip a little snow down his back,

or to start a spear of tickle-grass up his breeches leg. There were at least a half dozen girls whom he kissed as regularly as he found a chance, and each girl knew that the others permitted it. There was nothing in life, so unsubstantial, which Harry liked better than to kiss a pretty, half-unwilling, girl. As a kind of feeler, he one day observed to Cassel Rapid "that he would give a bushel of shelled oats to kiss Linda Boyd,"—he did not dare to say "Cora Glencoe." Cassel very significantly replied, "Uncle Jesse stands no nonsense." Harry was shrewd enough to interpret "Uncle Jesse" as meaning "brother Cassel." So he did not get to kiss Linda,—poor Harry!

CHAPTER XXX.

JOHNNY GALE had taken a Juggernaut oath that he would repeat his visit to the Boyd mansion, and as he found the obligation more binding than burdensome, he did not outrage the sanctity of the Hindoo deity by forfeiting his oath. He went frequently to see Linda, and at length found himself just six feet—all that he measured —in love with her.

One day, after Johnny had done himself the pleasure of seeing Linda, he called upon Cassel Rapid, greeting him with hearty honesty, while his almost boyish face was covered with good humor mixed with apprehension.

"Come in, Hercules," responded Cassel, "and take a seat."

"Cassel," asked Johnny, half bashfully, "when a man wishes to reach a certain point, had he not better go straight to it, instead of moving upon it by detours?"

"That depends upon the topography of the ground or country which lies between you and your objective point," replied Cassel, thinking that Johnny's question was related to his pursuit of civil engineering.

"Say that a fellow is on a dead level," said Johnny, reducing his question to the simplest form.

27

" Then I would recommend him to take a bee-line and run for it," answered Cassel, who began to doubt that Johnny's inquiry was in pursuance of civil science; for Johnny's face and nerves were beginning to tell on him.

" Well, Cassel, on your recommendation I am going straight to the center at a single clip. I'm in love with Linda Boyd."

Cassel turned his eyes upon Johnny, who was looking comically lugubrious. Cassel regarded him for a moment, and then gave out a long whistle. Johnny wilted, and, in his confusion, retired almost into his boots. Cassel laughed at him, and Johnny, as if it was the funniest thing in the world,—this thing of loving Linda Boyd,—accompanied Cassel with his most ticklish giggle, while he blushed all over, and vented about a pint of perspiration.

" Have you cut your wisdom teeth ?" asked Cassel.

Johnny only looked at him.

" When did you commence this loving business ?"

" I hardly know," replied Johnny; " but I know that it's under full headway now."

" How do you know it ?" asked Cassel, with considerable inward amusement.

" How !" cried Johnny. " Why, by Juggernaut, I *feel* it—feel it *all over !*"

" It must be so then," observed Cassel, while he regarded Johnny with a half-serious, half-mischievous eye. " But does she love *you?*"

" Not that I know of. I can't complain of her way. She seems to like my company. I do my best, you know, old fellow, when I'm with her,—and, God bless her, if you will only sanction it, I believe I can get her to come aboard with me. What do you say, Cassel ?" And Johnny moved toward his arbiter as if about to devour him with anxiety.

" Did she refer you to me ?"

" No ; I wish she had. I haven't asked her."

" Then why do you come to me ?"

" Because you are the Sweet William of this mansion, and you can tell me to mosey in, or mosey out, just as it may suit your fancy."

" Do you talk that kind of slang to Linda ?"   .

" No."

" What book is that in your breast pocket ?"

" It is a work I am studying."

" But what is it ?"

" A Miscellany," replied Johnny, growing uneasy.

" Let me see it."

" You are changing the subject on me," objected the adroit Johnny.

" No ; I imagine that the book is in some way connected with the subject. You can let me see it at all events."

" Oh, you can see the *book*, if *that's* what you want," said Johnny, who, while passing it over to Cassel, endeavored to assume an innocent and careless air which was very poorly sustained by his feelings. Cassel glanced at the title of Johnny's "Miscellany," and then deliberately leveling his clear, mild, but incisive eyes upon the now sheepish-looking youth, said, with something of a smile,—

" I thought so."

He then turned to the book and read aloud, "Dictionary of Poetical Quotations."

".Johnny," continued Cassel, with an amused but admonitory expression on his handsome face, "don't get to running about after the girls with your shirt-tail full of violets and morning-glories."

Johnny felt very silly, and looked just as he felt. Cassel discovered here and there in the book, numbers of lines which Johnny had pencil-marked. He read them off to an imaginary fair auditor, in a tone which would have aggravated a saint. He then tossed the book into the glowing grate.

" See here !" asserted Johnny with an awakened, resolute protest in his face and voice ; "you are carrying your authority a little far."

" You are altogether mistaken," said Cassel, smilingly.

" No, sir,—I am *not* mistaken," replied Johnny, firmly.

" Hercules, don't get angry now, and split the earth wide open. I am doing you a service. I have heard Linda say, more than once, that she did not relish this lackadaisy, rhythmic hash,—that she almost despised it. She will like you the better, Johnny, with the ' Miscellany' in the grate."

"Cassel!" cried Johnny, his anger instantly flashing away, "you are a trump to tell me of it. *Damn* the book! —let it go to where the fires are made of brimstone, for all I care. And now if you will only say, 'Spread your sails,—I'll give you a puff,' you will prove yourself the glorious good fellow I have always esteemed you."

"Quite an inducement," replied Cassel; "but I'm getting more of this sort of business on my hands than I care to manage."

"Then grant my petition in short order, and you will not have so much to manage: you will then have more time to devote to your own little affairs with Cora," urged Johnny, with the slyest glance of insinuation.

"You are talking wildly," observed Cassel.

"My *eyes* are wild," retorted Johnny, laughing, "and I am apt to talk as they *see*,—only between you and myself, however," he added.

"Johnny," said Cassel, shunning the subject of Cora, "I want no foolery in this matter. Young men scarcely know their minds at twenty. I am but little your elder, it is true, but circumstances have disciplined me beyond my years. I will tell you what, in my opinion, you had better do. Continue to study your adopted profession, and endeavor to acquire more of that physical and mental polish which makes a man current·in good and chosen society. Visit Linda when you will, but do not propose to her inside of six months. That is a very short time in fact, though it may be very long in fancy. Meantime you can consult me if you feel inclined. I will advise you of this much to begin with—for I am better posted than you might have supposed—that Linda is pleased with you, you great, lubberly fellow," and Cassel laughed at Johnny, who was in no way disconcerted by the good news. "I, also, like you, Johnny, or I should·make an effort to halt you right here. Whether you can succeed or not, I am unable to say; but this I promise you, that, as time flies, if I discover any increase of worth in you, I'll take occasion to call Linda's attention to it, and—*vice versa*, remember."

"Cassel," said Johnny, with gushing enthusiasm, "give me your hand on it! I understand you. You want me to make myself worthy of her. I'll do it, by Juggernaut, or run the boat aground. I know I'm awkward, but then I am hardly grown."

"For Heaven's sake, and Linda's also, don't start to growing again! You are as big as a buffalo now. But you are not awkward, Johnny; at least, you will not be when the green sap that is in you turns to solid wood. A little more knitting of your joints together, the accumulated ballast of the next two years, the maturing of your black moustache and promising whiskers, together with a suit of fashionable clothes, two-story hat, and patent-leather boots, will make as fine a specimen of you as a woman, or a man either, would wish to see."

"Cassel," said Johnny, smiling all over, "you encourage me."

"All right now,—be a good boy and I may help you. But how is Carroll?"

"Oh, he's well enough, with the exception that he seems to be getting very irritable,—losing his temper entirely."

"What's the cause of his irritation?"

"I don't know, unless it's about Cora Glencoe. He is very often moody and impracticable, and I sometimes think that one of us will have to turn the other out of our room, which we jointly occupy. He used to be so bright, and as full of fun as Linda is of sweetness; but now he is either reading, sitting up all night dreaming, or scribbling away at something which he won't let me see."

"Has he not fallen out with me from some cause?"

"I don't know that he has, Cassel, any more than that he seems to have fallen out with me without any cause. I can't exactly understand him, and I don't like it as well as I do broiled quails, by a long flit. I have told him so a dozen times or more, but he doesn't appear to be in the least concerned whether I like it or not."

Carroll May was acutely conscious that he was endangering his whole scheme of life by continuing to venture within the enchanted air which floated about Cora Glencoe. And yet he *would* venture, notwithstanding that on each repetition of his hazard he came away feeling bitterly. Her impenetrability and adroitness exasperated him; and after leaving her, he would go to his lodgings, sit up at

night, and think and wretchedly wrestle over his almost
hopeless passion, and in the mean time mistreat Johnny
or ignore him altogether.   He felt that he had somehow
started wrong with Cora, and that it was now next to
impossible to get himself right.   When with her he
couldn't let her heart alone, although he saw that, like the
sensitive plant, it closed against him whenever he ventured
to disturb it.   In the face of this, he was becoming more
frequent and importunate in his visits to Cora.   Harry
Gray, also, was beginning to haunt the Boyd mansion, in
defiance of Cassel Rapid's injunction to come only once a
week.

Cassel's position of guardian was getting to be a delicate
and disagreeable one.   It had become necessary—his duty
—to interrupt this incessant courting, for Cora hardly
could claim a single evening as her own.   But for Cassel
to interfere would undoubtedly put his motives upon the
dissecting-block; if not with Cora, certainly with Carroll
May, and probably with Harry Gray, *et al.*   He had been
unable to discover or analyze her thoughts and wishes in
this special connection, except that he had now and anon
detected indications of impatience and protest on her part.
Before he should act, he determined to wait a given time,
much preferring that the proposition for reform should
come from her, and half anticipating that it would.

Day after day passed, and Cassel was beginning to apprehend that he should be compelled to exercise his authority, when, one afternoon while he was quietly smoking
his cigar, a servant handed a card into his room.   The card
was from Cora, and Cassel immediately went down to her.

"Do not throw away your cigar, Mr. Rapid," said
Cora, as Cassel was about to toss away his Havana.
"I dislike to take it into the parlor."

"Then I will see you in the anteroom, and while we
discuss some very grave matters, I will enjoy, what I confess to like, the fragrance of a good cigar."

In the anteroom, snugly seated by a coal fire, Cassel
said,—

"Now, Miss Cora, what can I do to enhance your comfort or pleasure?"

"Mr. Rapid," answered Cora, "I am perplexed."

"Who is not?" asked Cassel, smiling.

"Few are not, I suppose; but I am perplexed in the extreme."

"Not jealous, are you?"

"I am not quoting Othello," said Cora, with the slightest little pout; "and, by-the-way," continued the young girl, genially, "did you know that our red-haired dining-room maid contends that O'Thello was an Irishman?"

"Didn't know it. But back to your perplexity; what is the matter?"

"I see too much company," answered Cora, while a deep blush suffused her fair cheeks.

"Do you see too much company, or see the same company too often?"

"Too *often* would probably be the better term."

"Well,—what are you going to do about it?"

"I want you to help me."

"In what way?"

"Exercise your authority as guardian."

"And get myself into a difficulty?"

"Then don't do it. I will act for myself."

"And probably get into a still worse difficulty."

"Show me the way, then, you wise one."

"Tell me distinctly what you wish."

"My visitors come too often. Can I say more?"

"Your male or your female visitors?"

"Mr. Rapid, you are only trying to provoke me. You know well enough what I mean."

"Do you wish them to come at all?"

"They are welcome, if they choose to come more like angels."

"Making their calls few and far between?"

"Farther between than just heretofore."

"Very well,—I'll frighten them away," said Cassel, smiling. "You shall have no reason to complain in future. Whoever calls again, whom, at the time, you do not wish to entertain, just send his card to me, with your initials on the back of it. I will entertain him myself and be responsible for the issue."

"I daresay there will be but little 'responsibility' about

it, for they will not care. But I shall be none the less obliged to you for your kindness and trouble."

Cora arose to withdraw, but Cassel detained her, saying,—

"Please do not go yet, unless you are particularly engaged; for, now that we are here, I wish to talk to you."

"I have no urgent duty waiting upon me elsewhere," answered Cora, who resumed her seat, not wholly free from the apprehension that Cassel might have something *very* special to say to her. She could not well refuse him an interview, however, be his object general or particular.

"Do you not think that 'Cora Glencoe' is a beautiful name?" asked Cassel.

"I do—notwithstanding it is my own," answered Cora, wondering what Cassel was leading up to.

"Did you know that another once bore it—your little cousin?"

"Yes, sir."

"But for a lamentable accident, there would have been *two* Coras, and you would have escaped all the strife and uncertainty which has been crowded into your short career. The other Cora, whom you do not remember, and who was so very much like you, had she lived, would have negatived almost every element of discord in your history and experience."

"You know my history?" asked Cora.

"From Alpha to Omega."

"I do not know yours."

"Do not ask to know it. I could not tell it to you now. Some time I may tell you."

"Where are your relatives and kin?"

"Like Logan, I can say that there runs not a drop of my blood in the veins of any human being."

Cassel's violet glance rested upon Cora with infinite sadness. The young girl's heart thrilled with an agony of sympathy.

"And yet you are happy, Mr. Rapid."

"Because it is my nature to be happy,—I cannot help it. It is irrepressible, except, rarely, when the inseparable gloom of all temporal and perishable things darkly overcomes me, and makes me ready to welcome a premature summons from hither to Eternity. But my present object is to talk, not of myself, but somewhat of you."

"Please do not, Mr. Rapid—spare me—I do not like the subject—it will not bear discussion."

"You probably do not understand me, Cora."

"This was the first time that Cassel had not addressed her as *Miss* Cora. She glanced at him shyly, like some half-tamed bird anxious to escape, but confused or charmed into remaining.

"You may remember," began Cassel, "that when you first came to New York I claimed to care for you, and gave you what might have been denominated a preliminary lecture, surveying with friendly exactitude the ground upon which stood 'Cora Glencoe, the Pupil and Ward.' It has always been my wish and effort to be perfectly frank with you, and my desire that between us, as guardian and ward, there should be harmony of opinion and predilection. I am now going to make a review, with additions, of the situation, putting you in the light, not of Pupil and Ward, but of Young Lady and Ward, and in this review I am going as far back as your rocking-cradle. My own ideas and opinions I shall give to you without reserve, asking yours as freely in return, that in future we may thoroughly understand each other, that there may be no jar. In the first place, it is proper for me to inform you that Maria Guthrie, upon whose evidence your friends had hoped to terminate the controversy between your father and uncle, is dead. Your future is yet as complicated as your past has been, and it is in view both of your past and future that I now speak."

As Cassel proceeded, Cora, regarding him attentively, thought that there was no eye so clear and true, no voice so firm and gentle, no judgment so cloudless and correct, no countenance so comely, no soul so limpid, no heart so affectionate, and no manhood so knightly and glorious as Cassel Rapid's. As in her first interview with him, months away, she almost trembled with a sense of inferiority. When he had finished this, his second lecture, which ended in an interesting colloquy, Cora said,—

"Mr. Rapid, I know better now who and what Cora Glencoe is than I ever knew before. How is it that you

can so accurately divine my current thoughts, and wake
up others which perhaps were sleeping, and tell me so
truly what I feel, and even dream about ?"

"It is because I think *for* you, and feel for you, and
dream when you are dreaming," he answered.

This was the gentlest thing that Cassel had ever said
outright to Cora. She did not know exactly what he intended to convey by it,—the solicitude of a guardian or
the fondness of a lover,—but she repaid him by a glance
from her deep dark eyes which told him that she also felt
for him,—exquisitely.

The chief transient matter which had perplexed Cora
was the fact that she had been drawn into entertaining so
many young men, or a number of young men so often.
Considering her state of suspension, it looked to her like
fashionable, heedless, and even heartless dissipation. She
had come to New York to finish her studies, and to be
educated in the superficial ways of the world ; in pursuance of which it was very proper, even essential, that she
should enjoy some of the advantages of society, both male
and female. But any inordinate indulgence was condemned by her good sense, and the opposite of her incli-
nations. Before this interview Cassel was feeling a little
disappointed in Cora ; but when the interview ended, he
was better satisfied with her than ever before. She was
now become the Star of his helm, and by her stellar light
would he fain pilot his career. He now unfettered his
heart, and it throbbed for only Cora, in all the world, day
and night.

"Would you be displeased," he asked her, "if I should
take the liberty of being less conventional, and call you
Cora ?"

"If it would be because you like me better, I would not ;
if because I am losing your respect, I should not only be
displeased, but grieved also."

"The cause is, that when we are thus, alone, I would
strike out the Miss from between us, and get just that
much nearer to you."

Cora looked at her watch, a present from Oswald Huron,
and observed that it was time for her to recite French.
She arose, and Cassel, rising with her, held out his hand.

He did not see her so very often in private, notwithstanding they dwelt under the same roof. She took his hand and raised her glance as if to say adieu. As he gazed upon her face, chaste as bolted snow, a heavenly blush spread over it; but her eyes, as firm and dauntless as his own, never quailed before his steady, searching, and mesmeric gaze. Cassel ventured to put his hand upon her faultless head. Cora did not flinch. A crisis was upon her. She fully anticipated from Cassel the avowals of a lover, and she had fully made up her mind to reject him; for no one, however glorious and thrilling, who knew her history as he knew it, should ever successfully solicit her hand until the mystery of her birth and lineage was solved. She waited almost in agony for him to speak. "Cora," said Cassel, while all the gentleness and fervor of his nature was rife within his voice, "may the good God forever and forever *bless* you," and he took his hand away. An instant storm of revulsion swept through Cora's breast, and her eyes flashed fire into Cassel's soul, as, infinitely relieved and rejoiced, she turned away and left him, saying to herself,—

"I mistook him altogether, and wronged him; for he is too sensible and noble to insult and mock my unfortunate condition, as I feared he was about to do."

Although to the world in which he moved, Cassel's life appeared to glide away in an uninterrupted stream of pleasure, contentment, and happy tranquillity, the fact has been aforetime reverted to, that there were times when memory bore him down into the bleak lair of all grievous and agonizing things, wrenching his bold heart with anguish, and changing it from a ruby fountain of joy to one of vitriolic and bitter waters. But as, heretofore, we have respected the privacy of these absolute and deathly moments, we shall continue to do so, as, to intrude upon him while he wrestles with the poison of the past, is not essential to the full volume of this narrative, and would only bring pain to the sensitive reader as well as to the writer.

Neither was Cora free from care, as might have been imagined by those who only superficially and casually knew her; for she had her oft-recurring hours of mournful meditation and heartache. But she had lived all her life in a Gloom, compared with which her present existence

was bathed in sunshine and the tranquillizing sheen of
Peace. It is not then to be wondered at, that the anxiety
and uncertainty attendant upon her peculiar plight, should,
for the time, be subordinate to the tripping pleasures and
half-tried advantages which daily waited upon her and
greeted her at every step, in such captivating contrast with
her former experience. Like Cassel Rapid, Cora was constituted to enjoy exquisitely,—or to endure firmly; and,
as with him, the Angel of Joy would almost always whip
out the Demon of Grief from that chosen battle-ground,—
her tender bosom.

CHAPTER XXXI.

THE ensuing evening Harry Gray called to see Cora.
She sent his delicately-engraved card to Cassel Rapid,
with her initials indorsed upon it. Cassel smiled to think
how very soon it had become his province and duty to interfere between the young girl and her admirers. He also
laughed to himself in anticipation of the manner in which
young Gray would stomach such interference, and suspect it. He doubted not that Gray would regard it as a
very selfish interposition. He went down to the parlor,
ready for a rumpus.

"Now, Rapid," cried Gray, as Cassel walked in, "have
you brought yourself in here to be willfully *de trop*, and
to vex me with the unsolicited agony of your presence?"

To the surprise of Harry, who expected to hear a dis-
claimer and a round of excuses, Cassel answered,—

"Yes."

"Then, by Jove, you are ungenerous, Cassel, and inhos-
pitable. I won't stand it," said Gray, with some indignation.

"If you prefer to sit alone," said Cassel, "have your
way; I will retire."

"But I sent my card to Miss Huron!"

"Miss Huron is not at home."

"Not in the house?"

"Yes,—she is in the house. But Miss Huron is 'not at home.' Don't you understand the conventionality?"

"Is she ill?"

"No."

"Have I offended her?" asked Gray, with some anxiety.

"No,—but you have offended *me*," replied Cassel, smiling.

"Who the devil cares for *you?*" cried Gray, impatiently.

"I do. But Gray, to cut the matter short, don't you remember that I told you, in the beginning, that Miss Huron would see you, probably, once a week?"

"Well,—yes,—I believe I do."

"I also gave you good reasons why you should not come more frequently."

"You gave me reasons."

"*Good* reasons, my absent-minded friend Now, why don't you restrict yourself to weekly visits?"

"Because it's such a bore to be away from her."

"Well, who is to be bored, I wonder, you or she!"

"I'm thinking that *you* are the one who is being bored," answered Gray, saucily and insinuatingly.

"Very well, sir," retorted Cassel, "I don't choose that you shall bore *me*."

"All right, Mr. Tycoon," rejoined Gray, abandoning the controversy. "By-the-way, Rapid, did you ever tell her what a fool I made of myself over that confounded Greek quotation?"

"No need to have told her."

"She appreciated it, did she?"

"Of course she did. The next morning she laughed very gayly with me about it."

"And you, doubtless, were excessively gay over it. But why did you tell me that downright falsehood when I asked you if you were a Greek-reading *savant?*"

"I wished to gratify you by affording you an opportunity of making a display."

"And of showing my—— Well, never mind; I have yet to hear of the man who ever caught a girl by reading Greek."

"You'll never catch one that way, I am sure."

"Rapid, at times I can barely keep my hands from your throat; your laugh, at me especially, is so damnably provoking."

"Then why provoke it? Ha! ha! ha! ha! h-a!"

Harry got up and started out with a great load of disgust; but, halting, he turned about and said,—

"Rapid, come around and see me to-morrow. I am going to broach some wine and cigars,—just out of the custom-house,—honest transaction, too,—articles supposed to be genuine—come and judge—good-evening."

When Gray was gone, Cassel said to himself, "There goes as free-hearted a fellow as lives. He never bears malice or sees a bugaboo."

Cassel returned to his own room. In less than fifteen minutes, and while he was reading the history of the Tulipomania which made lunatics of all Holland more than two hundred years ago, another card was handed in to him. He took it and read "Carroll May" upon its face; turning it over, he saw Cora's delicate initials.

"I don't like this," said Cassel to himself, laying aside the Tulipomania. "I'm afraid that Carroll is not going to prove as tractable and reasonable as Gray. I am certain that he will vindictively feel that I am the mover in this business for my own aims or gratification."

Cassel went down-stairs and entered the parlor where Carroll was seated. Young May was by this time as quick as lightning to pervert the conduct of Cassel Rapid in everything which appertained to Cora Glencoe. He, without due warrant, had reduced Cassel's motives and recorded them against him; and he was now in that bitter and self-asserting state of mind which would go far toward rendering him impervious to reason or the religion of patent facts and circumstances.

"Good-evening," said Cassel, pleasantly, as he entered the room and offered his hand to Carroll.

Young May's greeting lacked its bygone cordiality, notwithstanding he did not divine the wherefore of Cassel's inopportune presence. A conversation upon indifferent subjects ensued, during which Carroll was rather abstract than concrete. Cassel hesitated whether he should tell Carroll of Cora's newly-chosen exclusiveness or wait for him to introduce the purpose of his visit himself. Carroll, becoming impatient, asked,—

"Is Cora at home?"

"Yes."

"I sent my card to her," suggested Carroll.

"She is engaged to-night, and will not see any one."

"Not see any one—why not?"

"As I tell you, she is otherwise employed."

"She might have sent me word."

"I bring you the word myself."

"By authority from her?"

"At her request."

"It is not your doing, then?"

Cassel had never warned Carroll to come only once in awhile to see Cora, as he had warned Harry Gray; for he thought that Carroll's intimate knowledge of the young girl's history, coupled with his own native good sense, would suggest to him a corresponding respect for her peculiar situation, and restrain him from encroaching upon her, and putting her at fault before the world. Cassel had for some time been sensible that Carroll May, entirely without just cause, was becoming more and more embittered against him. He could detect it in Carroll's eye, in the twitch of his lip, the impatience of a gesture, and the sarcasm of a word. He, out of compassion, and placid, native nobility, had borne with Carroll's whisks and whims until he was weary of them. To Carroll's last insinuating remark he answered, calmly but somewhat coldly,—

"Your words lack courtesy, Carroll."

"I discover no courtesy here which merits a response."

"Seek more agreeable environs, then."

"Not until I have searched this thing to the bottom."

"You are at the bottom of it now."

"If *you* are the bottom, I will go beneath and beyond you."

"Carroll, you are strangely unjointed of late."

"If I am, it is my affair—not yours."

"We were once friends."

"When we were children."

"And might well be, now that we are men."

"Tell me why I cannot see Cora Glencoe, and why she sends *you* here to deny me?"

Cassel very explicitly told him. Carroll answered,—

"If you were not my *rival*, I could see her."

"Whether I am or not, you *can* see her, but only at her pleasure."

"You require me to make my visits seldom, while you are always with her," said Carroll, bitterly and fiercely.

"I am with her less than you are."

"But you are in the same house with her, and see her every day. Is this what you call a fair fight?"

"You can come and live with us if you wish, and see her just as I, or the others do, who are in the house."

"It does not suit me to live here."

"You must suit yourself, as a matter of course."

"Neither does it suit me to be put off in this manner, and have this denial come through you."

"Possibly you do not accept it as authorized and genuine?"

"I would prefer to have it from her own mouth."

"You can obtain what you prefer, if you will await her convenience instead of endeavoring to substitute your own. You can afflict her, if you rudely choose to do so, by compelling her to repeat what I have already told you, and what I am well-nigh tired of insisting upon."

"I will not be put off at your dictation. I'll see her *to-night*, by thunder! and settle this matter."

Cassel's color deliberately rose. Fixing his firm, unyielding eyes upon Carroll, he slowly and with relentless decision, said,—

"You will not see her to-night, Carroll May."

"Then, by heavens!" cried Carroll, springing up and dashing his fist down upon a marble stand, "I'll *see you* in the morning!" saying which, he wheeled about and strode out of the mansion.

Cassel, who had entertained for Carroll none but sentiments of kindness which expanded even to indulgence, was shocked, grieved, and incensed by such headlong and unjustifiable behavior. He had anticipated something of a scene, but nothing so outrageous as this. Carroll did not seem to realize or care for the stern danger which he was daring, for Cassel was by far his overmatch, and had never accustomed himself to deal gently with men who insulted him. But out of charity, and knowing Carroll to be greatly distempered on account of Cora, he was willing yet to forgive the aggressive faults of the mad-hearted young lover, and continue to be his friend, if he would let him.

Still half reflecting and half wondering how *L'Amour* could so unhinge an otherwise clear-headed young man, Cassel, lapsing from his wonted discretion, sent his card to Cora. It soon came back, with her initials—now fatal to an interview—indorsed thereon.

"There!" said Cassel, rating and laughing at himself; "I am caught under my own deadfall. She treats us all alike. I was incautious and too precipitate. She is right not to desire an immediate discussion of the beaus whom I have turned away for her. Cora is most certainly 'not at home' this evening."

Cassel went to his room, turned up the gas, lighted a cigar, and once more essayed Tulipomania. From reading, he fell to dreaming, when, at the expiration of an hour or more, there came a tap at his door.

"Come in."

A servant opened the door and said,—

"A gentleman below wishes to see Mr. Rapid."

"Have you his card?"

"No, sir."

"His name?"

"No, sir."

"Request him to send one or the other."

The servant disappeared, and returning in a few moments, said,—

"The gentleman declines to send his card, but says that his business is important."

"Tell him that I decline to see him."

Cassel had already divined the errand upon which the gentleman had come, and he determined to exact of him to the outside limit. The servant reappeared with a card, on the face of which Cassel read "Charles Vermilion."

"Carroll May has chosen a red-named second, at least, to aid him in the spilling of red blood," said Cassel to himself. "I will go down and have a look at this Cochineal."

Cassel entered the anteroom where the gentleman was waiting, the parlors being occupied by some of the Boyd colony.

"Mr. Rapid, I presume."

"My name is Rapid."

"Allow me to introduce myself as Mr. Charles Vermilion."

"From where?"

"From the city of New York, sir."

"On important business if I mistake not."

"Yes, sir."

"State it."

Mr. Charles Vermilion handed Cassel a note in reply. Cassel took it and recognized the handwriting of Carroll May.

"Is your name mentioned in the body of this note?" asked Cassel, without breaking the seal.

"No, sir."

"Neither is it on the envelope, and I can't receive it."

"It was an oversight."

"I cannot receive it."

"Why, pray?"

"I never transact business of importance with an unaccredited stranger."

"Do you doubt my identity—or my respectability?"

"Your identity is no guarantee to me of your respectability; for this is the first time I ever saw or heard of either you or Mr. Charles Vermilion."

"What do you require, sir?"

"Since you have undertaken this business, I require that you shall conduct it in strict conformity with the Code. If you are a novice, go to some professional, and he will rejoice in giving you instructions."

"You are rather tart, sir,—but I suppose you have a right to demand this of me. Good-evening."

Aside from Cassel's scorn for these too often pompous and heartless go-betweens, he wished to give Carroll May an opportunity to repent of his precipitancy and suppress the hostile note. But he did not know Carroll as well as he was destined to find him out. Mr. Vermilion returned in half an hour, with his missive decidedly *à la mode*.

Cassel, who did not care to be troubled by meeting him below,—the anteroom being now without fire,—received the
warlike messenger in his own room. Vermilion had acted
in a gentlemanly though unsophisticated manner, and
Cassel had no further disposition to treat him harshly.
Cassel read Carroll May's challenge, and laid it on a table.
Vermilion withdrew, and, as it was getting late, Cassel
went to bed and fell regularly to sleep.

In the morning he met Cora in the lower hall, and taking advantage of a volunteer opportunity, he asked her
into the nearest parlor. Being seated, he said,—

"Cora, I turned off Mr. Gray last night."

She looked at him and blushed, then asked,—

"How did you do it?"

"Oh, I turned him off just as I would a gas-light. But
would you like to know how he acted?"

"Yes," replied Cora, laughing, "I would."

"Well, he conducted himself like a clever, sound-hearted
young gentleman, as he is; he was very anxious to see
you, but accepted the situation handsomely."

"I hope he did not feel hurt," said Cora, gently.

"I also turned off Carroll May."

"Like a gas-light, also?" asked Cora, cutely.

"No. He went off like a rocket. Here is the difference
between Carroll and Harry Gray," and Cassel handed Cora
the hostile note which he had received overnight, and requested her to read it. She took the note and glanced
through it, then hastly dropped it as if it had been a sting-
ing scorpion. Springing up, she set her heel upon it,
while her face turned as pale as pallid wax. Back to her
face again rushed the blood, and into her eyes leaped up
that invincible, desperate look of old with which she had
outstood the stormy master of Cliff Hall. Cassel had
never seen in all his life such intense and vivid loveliness,
standing out like some heroic fiery statue, and blazing
with an intrinsic and electric tempest. In a voice which
rang like steel, she said,—

"May woe be unto the hand that sheds blood over the
luckless head of Cora Glencoe!" and bursting into an agony
of tears, she threw herself upon a sofa, and sobbed out
the storm from her bosom. Presently she looked up and

said, "I, alone, have brought this hateful thing upon you."

The sight of Cora's wet face and the tear-drops hanging on her lashes, deluged Cassel's heart with tenderness for her.

"Do you not think that my honor is at stake?" asked he.

"No!" cried Cora, vehemently. "Let him go rave to the wind, or seek council from his father's grave. I *forbid* you to meet him on any plea of mine. I shall never speak to him again—never; or to you, Mr. Rapid, if you accept this challenge."

"Cora, do not be rash in your resolutions."

"Rash? I am not rash. There are other codes besides the technical, desperate code of *Honor*. I tell you that I utterly·*condemn* this systematic, diplomatic, cold-blooded slaughter, which is so frequently the sequel to a petty difference as trivial as the distinction between *honor* and *honor*. Carroll May's own father was killed by it, and my uncle, whom I thought my father, did the deed. *I once saw a murder*,—down on the beach at Creswood, in the shallow water. I can hear the words of the murderer ringing in my ears now,—'Go *home*, you sparrow!—the falcons of *Hell* are abroad!' But it is too terrible to think of or discuss; it curdled up my blood, and I fainted. I never wish to see or hear of such another crime."

Cassel, for the first time, learned that it was Cora who was sitting upon the Tarpeian Rock, looking at him, when he drove the dagger three times through the heart of Jonas Aiken. Should he ever tell her of that event in his history, —or rather, that the event, which she so vividly remembered, was a central part of *his* history? He would let time and circumstances decide.

"Mr. Rapid," said Cora, with that frankness which Cassel had insisted should operate between them, "if there is one on earth whose hand I would shield from the spatter and stain of blood, it is my kind, and patient, and knightly guardian. I know that it is the nature of men to rush hotly into fatal and fearful actions. But I know you to be cool and dauntless, and there is no need or exigency that you should *sacrifice* your honor by a mistaken effort to maintain it. Promise me that you will not meet Carroll May."

"Cora, you are the sweetest advocate that lives on earth. You tempt me sorely to break over a different barrier from that which you are erecting. But here is my answer to all you have said. This is a copy of the original which has already been sent." And Cassel handed her a sheet of paper, having first unfolded it.

Cora took the paper and read it rapidly. Over her anxious face flashed the light of joy and relief.

"Whatever the cause," said Cassel, "I would not bring your name out before the public, either on bullet or bulletin,—no, not for a thousand such points of honor as this."

With an approving, grateful, happy glance, Cora said, while she put one foot out as if ready to spring away,—

"Please let me go now;" and, as Cassel signified his consent, she ran out and up to her room, entered it and locked the door, where we will leave her to those wild and wakeful vicissitudes which thrilling love fails not to shower down.

Cassel's reply to Carroll·May was briefly as follows:

"CARROLL MAY, ESQ.

"SIR,—Knowing perfectly well the mistaken animus of your billet, I refrain from acting upon its suggestions, trusting, that when you have reflected, you will withdraw it. There might be provocations which would justify your note, but none such exist. In this matter, or lack of matter, I claim the privilege of judging for myself.

"As you will:

"CASSEL P. RAPID."

Carroll May, when he received the above communication, wrote a sarcastic, biting, and extremely personal article, which he appended to the correspondence already transpired between himself and Cassel Rapid, and in which he—as was customary, and is yet—denounced Cassel as a poltroon, coward, etc. etc. He went to the office of a city newspaper, to have published the correspondence and his additions to it. The newspaper-man through whose hands this fulmination passed for acceptance or rejection, happened to be acquainted with Cassel Rapid, and happened to be unacquainted with Carroll May. He was very well aware that if there was a person in New York city who was *not* a poltroon, coward, etc. etc., that it was Cassel Rapid. He therefore went to Cassel, out of motives half friendly, half cautious, and made an exhibit of Carroll's proffered newspaper assault, at the same time seeking of Cassel information in regard to the foundation of it. The flint in Cassel's soul at last was struck, and the fire flashed and scintillated from it.

"Wait a moment," said Cassel to the newspaper-man.

He then went up to his room, belted on a pair of pistols, came down again, and said,—

"Come with me into the city."

He took the editor to O'Dare's office, and carried him back into a shooting-gallery, the property of the detective. Lighting a couple of candles, he placed them on the target-stand. Retiring to the far-end of the gallery, he drew his pistols, one in either hand, and leveling them, almost simultaneously snuffed the candles with a double discharge. Turning to the newsman, he said,—

"So far as Cassel Rapid is concerned, he can afford to disdain that written article. But there is another besides himself involved, and I give you now distinctly to understand me. I'm obliged to you for coming to me first before deciding to publish what you know to be a lie. If that article is published by your newspaper, I will not only hold the author of it to account, but I will snuff out every responsible scribbler or proprietor of your establishment. I am not threatening you or daring you, but simply notifying you of a cold, congealed fact, which you will have to encounter."

The editor lighted a match and burned the manuscript before Cassel's face. When it was consumed, he observed, with dry humor in his countenance,—

"That ends the business. I am not yet prepared for your snuffing process."

The newsman went back to his items. Cassel stood in the front door of O'Dare's office, and amused himself talking to a raw Irishman, just over from the bogs of Killarney.

" What in the divil is that ?" asked Paddy.

" That is an American brunette."

" Be Jasus, an' I thought it was a she nager."

" What are you doing here, Paddy ?"

" Hunting room for meself, yer honor."

" Plenty of it, isn't there ?"

" Not in this city, jist."

" Why don't you go out West ?"

" Where is that, if ye plaze ?"

" Where the sun sets."

" Begorrah, what the divil is out there ?"

" Have you never read Hiawatha ?"

" Yis, yer honor,—high wather, and low wather, and bilge wather, and salt wather ; but it has been a bog of a stretch since I read any *whisky* wather. Would yer honor be so benivolent as to give Paddy a dime to wet the channel of Ould Ireland ? I'm off the immigrant ship jist, and have been drinking sea wather all the way over. My troat is as dry as the ashes of yer honor's cigar."

Just as Cassel was tossing a silver quarter to the Irishman, Carroll May, with inflamed eyes, approached, and, without warning, aimed a pistol at Cassel and fired. The bullet missed its mark, and Cassel, springing upon his antagonist, wrenched the pistol from his grasp. Seizing Carroll by the throat, he crushed him irresistibly down upon the pavement. Hector O'Dare came out to see what was the matter. Carroll meantime had swooned, and Cassel Rapid turned him over to O'Dare, requesting that he be taken to one of the city hospitals. O'Dare put Carroll into hospital, where he·lingered with delirious fever. When Carroll recovered, he was somewhat cooled of his hot distemper, though he was far from being cured of his hostility toward Cassel Rapid. But he was destined to be very suddenly and very painfully cured. Returning from sick leave to the office of Hallum & Gore (his employers), after sitting and talking awhile, he was handed a note, which read in words as below :

" MESSRS. HALLUM & GORE.

" GENTLEMEN,—On receipt of this, you will discontinue my contribution to the salary of Carroll May, your assistant ; as circumstances not anticipated have rendered the gratuity inexpedient.   " Respectfully,

"CASSEL P. RAPID."

Carroll turned to Mr. Gore for an explanation, which was very explicitly furnished him. It began to dawn upon his mind that he had branded himself with ignominy and black ingratitude by his headlong, vindictive, and dastard conduct. He picked up his hat, went out, sought his room, threw himself across the bed, and groaned in spirit. Carroll began to realize that Cassel Rapid, whom he was teaching himself to hate and abuse, had been his thorough friend, to the rare extent of secret *charity*, delicately chosen and bestowed. He revolted against the bitter bondage into which he had so madly thrust himself. What was now to be done ? How could he undo the pernicious, galling web which he had woven about himself, and purge himself so that no flavor of the past should be left to sicken the future ? With reactionary humility, he wrote to Cassel a long letter, which teemed with apology and repentance. In answer to it he received the letter below :

"CARROLL MAY, ESQ.   .

SIR,—Yours is received, and I allow its sincerity. But when, without cause, a once professed friend persistently seeks my life, there is no logic to convince me that there was not something radically wrong in his original friendship, or yet something strangely perverse in the man himself. I am willing to bury the past—the whole past, early recollections and all—and to meet you as I would meet a stranger, and be governed as I would be with a new acquaintance ; to wit : by the developments of the future. I have no extra sentiment or sensibility to squander upon shallow reconciliations.

"As you like it :
"CASSEL P. RAPID."

Cassel, who had been slow to anger, having been fully roused, was no vacillating child to offer blows at one moment and kisses the next, nor a heedless wight, to shift his friendships and affections with every breeze.

Does the reader remember what it was that convinced Carroll May of Cassel Rapid's genuine nobility? It was the knowledge that Cassel had secretly added a few hundred dollars to his salary as assistant in the law office of Hallum & Gore. How strange it is that a few ounces of gold should be accepted, as brighter and more weighty evidence of friendship than all the protestations and good fellowship in the world! Cassel had uniformly treated Carroll with especial kindness, amounting to brotherly tenderness and forbearance; and yet it required a paltry hundred dollars or so to prove him sincere!

Carroll, whose impulses were generous when not traversed by passion, felt abused to the very dust. He wrote another letter which Cassel, out of his wakeful compassion, could not forbear responding to kindly. "Come and see me," pleaded Carroll, "for I am utterly ashamed ever to intrude my face upon you, even to ask forgiveness." Cassel went.

"Oh, Cassel,—can you ever, ever forgive me?"

"Carroll, I have already done so. My coming is a pledge that the air between us is clear. If it becomes clouded again, I hope it will be no fault of mine."

"Cassel, you cannot conceive how wretched and humiliated I am. If ever I wrong you with bad thoughts again, may all the powers of heaven launch out destruction at me!"

"Let it be so; and let this thing be buried as the dead are buried. But where is Johnny?"

"I do not know. In my madness I drove him from me. I have not seen him for a week. When he left, after having tried to dissuade me, he sternly said, 'Carroll, what I heartily have to repeat, is, that I hope Cassel Rapid will put you out of your misery, which he *can* do, if he chooses, in the twinkling of an eye.' Since then I have not heard of him."

"Won't he come back?"

"Not until I send for him,—and I don't know where to send. He is the best fellow in the world, but when once he sets his head he is as stubborn as Gibraltar."

"You write him a little love-letter," said Cassel. "I am satisfied that he will be in to see me before long. I

29

will deliver the letter, explain to him, and let him decide for himself if he will come back to you or not."

In a few days, Johnny was back with Carroll.

Carroll May determined never to re-try his fortunes with Cora. He would not look upon her face again, as it would only aggravate an already hopeless case.

* ───────

CHAPTER XXXII.

WE have, up to this time, omitted to state that Linda occasionally paid a visit to her old home in Pennsylvania, where her family and the neighborhood petted her nearly to death. Also, that Neville Huron and his family periodically visited Cora. Having no room for new and unessential characters, however, we refrain from encumbering our history with the kith and kin of Linda and Cora.

Cassel frequently called upon O'Dare, between whom and himself a stanch friendship had early taken root and now throve thriftily. Each recognized in the other the genuine mettle of a proper man. One morning, not long after the little affray between Cassel and Carroll, in which the latter had attempted to shoot the former, Cassel stepped into the office of the detective, and was greeted with,—

" Good-morning, Mr. Lightning."

" Good-morning, Hector, thou spawn of Priam," retorted Cassel, who generally came prepared for O'Dare's drollery and impudence.

" I find you always ready,—too ready, in fact, for one of your age,—you'll come to grief yet before you marry."

" If not before that event, then most certainly *after it*, if the murmurings and mutterings which come like distant thunder to us from the wedded world are any indication of the incessant storm which might well be supposed to rage there."

" Rapid, what ever became of that young assassin, Carroll May ? I had no idea that he was such a viper."

" He is down in the Valley of Humiliation, clothed in sackcloth and ashes, repenting of his rashness."

"When I left him at the hospital, I expressed to him my kindest wishes that he might enjoy euthanasia at an early age."

" Do not judge too harshly of him," said Cassel. " He was laboring under the hydrophobia of an unsuccessful love-passion. But have you any Huron news,—any late developments ?"

" Rapid," replied O'Dare, impudently, "you don't pay me a cent, and yet you come around about once a week, suck me dry of 'news,' and then toss yourself off without even saying thanky. Remember that *my* information is the equivalent of gold, or trouble."

" I offered you gold, you blood-hound, and you would not receive it. I now offer you the other equivalent, trouble," said Cassel, stepping out into the middle of the floor and pulling off his coat.

" What does that mean ?" asked O'Dare.

" Come out here," cried Cassel. " You've always been bragging and bantering about your wrestling. I wish to give you a little 'trouble,'—I'll tussle with you for your cash secrets."

O'Dare, who was an expert wrestler, threw off his coat and willingly accepted the challenge.

" What 'holt' ?" asked the detective.

" Indian Hug," replied Cassel, and the champions instantly clinched.

The two men were about the same weight and inches, but Cassel was a model from top to toe, and was full of the activity and lithe strength of youth and symmetry. He was also an expert, trained in a Border School where such back-breaking sports are common. Before O'Dare knew what was the matter, Cassel spun him around and dusted his back for him. O'Dare got up somewhat crest-fallen, and saying,—

" Rapid, you've won it fairly ; but I don't acknowledge that there is another man in New York of your weight who can do the like."

" Pshaw! O'Dare. I can throw you any 'holt' you may choose,—side holt, Yankee holt, breeches holt, or grab holt."

"Try me Yankee holt," said O'Dare, hoping to redeem himself, for 'Yankee holt' was his forte.

They went at it again. The struggle this time was more equal, and Cassel came near to losing his feet, but by a dexterous recover he shifted O'Dare off his pins, and landed him square upon his hams.

Cassel's hearty laugh rang through the office, and was joined by that of an amused and admiring clerk who stood looking on, while O'Dare, still sitting upon the floor, gazed rather foolishly about him, as if to discover where he possibly could be. The sudden change in his polarity had disconcerted him. Cassel, mimicking valiant Jack Falstaff, mocked O'Dare, saying,—

"'And now, my lord, I'll caper with you for a thousand pounds,—if you'll lend me the money.'"

"Rapid," said O'Dare, getting up a little stiffly, "you are a hell of a bother. But, come; I'll see what's on the books," and turning to his immense volume of Secrets, he glanced over an open page, and continued: "I believe I told you that Maria Guthrie is dead?"

"Yes."

"Since then I have learned that her death was sudden, that she gave no verbal statement, and left no posthumous papers, in regard to Miss Cora Glencoe Huron. If she ever divulged the secret which she held, it rests under the seal of the Catholic confessional. I have here a transcript of her epitaph," and O'Dare read it off. "This is all that you have earned by the 'trouble' which you have just given me, but at your next regular intrusion I may have something fresh and forcible for you."

"And I'll pay you for it, if you will, in your own chosen coin."

"Now that you have got what you came for, clear out! I've no more time to spend unprofitably,—I'm busy."

"Good-morning," said Cassel, who left the detective to his webs, and traps, and snares.

Linda Boyd gave a large Dinner Party, and a gossiping, lively company was gathered in the Boyd mansion, in the midst of which were Johnny Gale and Harry Gray, conspicuously. Carroll May excused himself, being under a great "press of business." Johnny, as he afterward told

Cassel, " was doing his differential best to get Linda into integral calculus, and demonstrate to her that he was the most charming problem, and the most desirable upright cone, extant." As long as Cassel would joke Johnny, and Linda smile on him, he felt as luscious as a fig, and as gay as a spring lark. Neither was Johnny any ordinary "catch." He possessed good sound sense, was becoming polished, was already fine-looking, was industrious, was sober, was full of generous humor, could calculate and collect the interest on Linda's investments to the accuracy of an invisible fraction, and bid fair to become a bright utensil " about the house," as well as an ornament.

Harry Gray had fenced with Cora until they had got to be very good friends, and she was periodically glad to see him. Cora knew that Harry loved her, in his free-hearted kind of way, for he did not, in the same kind of way, hesitate to tell her so; but as he had discretion enough not to trench upon her maiden prerogative of yea or nay, she passed many a pleasing and pungent moment with him. Harry never missed finding the Boyd mansion on Thursday night of each week, and he managed to get an occasional extra glimpse of Cora by calling at odd hours on Linda.

The dining was *done* with all the delightful brilliancy of vivacious, sweet success, during which the tippling of delicate and enthused wine supplied the saddest and most tedious guest with intermittent wit

Rising from the table and resorting to the parlors, it happened that Cassel Rapid and Cora became seated in close proximity. While discussing the propriety of going to church oftener, Cassel was handed a sealed telegraphic dispatch. Taking it, he bowed slightly to Cora, and said,—

" I believe it is etiquette to read telegrams when and where they are received."

" It should be, if it is not; for the very sight of them implies haste," replied Cora.

Cassel tore the envelope, and at a single glance read the four words which had come over the wires. Looking up at Cora, he observed,—

" Here is a collection of words which would make some men shiver."

"How does it affect you?"

"It is a relief; putting, as it does, an end to a bad bargain," answered Cassel, with a smile.

"It is, then, on business?"

"Yes; prosy business."

As Cassel replied to her, the letter-sheet floated, as a gate swings, about in his hand, and the telegram, written in plain, bold characters, exposed itself to Cora's eye. She had no desire to read the telegram, but as it was so brief and distinct, her unprying eye mechanically and instantly caught and mastered the words, without an effort. The dispatch was directed to "Cassel P. Rapid," and read,— *"Your wife is dead."*

There is a very exceptionable, novelistic resort, where excuses can be found for singularly situated persons who *see* when they don't *want* to see, and who *hear* when they don't *want* to hear; compulsory sight-seers and compulsory eavesdroppers, they might be termed, who find it utterly beyond their power to escape seeing or hearing. Now,—unless the sight comes quick and vivid, as lightning, or the sound is loud and deep, like thunder,—there is no excuse for seeing, or hearing, against one's will. We can suggest an infallible and invincible escape from all this conscientious trouble. Here it is. When anything presents itself to the Eye, which the Eye does not wish to see, *close* the Eye, and the Eye won't see: a very simple and ready remedy, unquestionably. When, by fortuity, a confidential conversation is in progress, and catches an unseen Ear in an awkward proximity from which there is no escape, if the Ear sincerely desires not to hear the confidential conversation, stick a finger in the Ear, or fill it up with mud, and the Ear won't hear,—another very simple and ready remedy. So much for these *unwilling* spies and eavesdroppers, and their abettors, the unfertile novelists.

We are not endeavoring to excuse or condemn Cora for reading Cassel's telegram. It swung before her eyes, and she gathered its contents as the eye catches a flash of lightning, without premeditation. Cora was chilled with horror as she read those mortal words, *"Your wife is dead,"* and it was with the utmost difficulty that she could restrain herself from springing up and placing herself *en alto* before the assembled and watchful company. She kept her seat, however, and soon sat like a stone statue in front of Cassel Rapid. He was quick to discover her radically altered and extraordinary appearance, and, being alarmed by it, anxiously questioned her. She barely replied to him, and after sitting awhile she got deliberately up and went to her room. Cora felt outraged, indignant, and stricken to the heart. She remembered that Cassel had avoided telling her his history, escaping from it with the plea that it was then impossible or inexpedient, but that some day he might tell her. Who was this Cassel Rapid? and who knew anything about him, or his life? How did Mr. Hope know him, who had only seen him for a few days, except when he was a little boy? Who could tell of him, and of his hidden ways? Horror predominated over every other feeling which took possession of Cora's breast. "Who would ever have so wronged him," said Cora to herself, "as to have imagined from either his public or private tenor that he was a married man! But how coolly he received the tidings of the death of his wife, making a satanic joke of it, and hailing it as the finale of a losing and disagreeable contract! What sort of a creature she may have been, I find it difficult to imagine; an angel or a Gorgon. Who would dream, that knows him as I do, that so foul and horrible a spirit lighted up those pure and dauntless-looking eyes of his? Who would divine that a heart so callous beat within the breast from whence come words and winning numbers, so true, and tender, and soft? Who could look upon his blonde face, radiant with fatal beauty, and say that it was the reflex of a black night behind it? Who could look upon his manly, matchless form, and account it but the seductive garb of a treacherous devil? How art thou fallen from heaven, O Lucifer, Son of the Morning! Ah, but it is a bitter, bitter, *bitter* thing to me, to be driven to think of him as thus revealed."

Although Cassel, some months previously, had stated to Linda that he was a single man,—a young bachelor,—he had never made a similar statement to Cora, whose acquaintance with him was of more recent date than Linda's. Notwithstanding this, Cora could regard him in no conceivable attitude but that of a deliberate impostor. But could she openly fall out with him, and show resentment, because he had been married to a woman, and because that woman was dead, and because he appeared to consider it a good riddance,—the gratifying close of an originally bad bargain? Was it any of her concern whether he had or had not been married? Then, how many were there in the world who might regard the decease of a husband or wife as a welcome deliverance? How was she to make up her accusation against him? He had never declared himself her lover. It was true that he had evinced a tender and guardian interest in her; but was not every one about her very tender toward her? "Ah," said she, springing to a possible solution, "perhaps it is my tenderness for *him* that gives a bad color to this matter, and exacts of him what I have no right to demand. Can I go to him and say,—Mr. Rapid, you have deceived me; you have been a married man; your wife is just now dead, and you are glad of it? And yet, how can I meet him, or sit by him, as of old, or even pretend to do so, when I shall have to breathe, the while, an atmosphere loaded with horror and the rank poison of dissimulation—of my own dissimulation, in fact, if not of his?"

Cora at last determined to write to Mr. Hope, and positively request him to remove her. She wrote an explicit letter, which, out of the fullness of her confidence and reliance, acquainted the old minister with the true reasons upon which her special request was based.

She prudently determined to treat Cassel, if she could so compel herself, with customary civility and consideration; else, she might openly convict herself of being incensed against him upon grounds too painfully personal, and too near to her heart, ever to be admitted or hinted of.

How very bleak and lonely Cora now felt; as she stood in the vast world, an unconfirmed, unfathered child, rudely roused up from a sweet and thrilling dream in which she was just beginning to taste of the crystal, sparkling waters for which she had so long and wearily thirsted. She likened herself to the parched, desert-worn, sun-smitten traveler, who, being led by deceptive fortune to a bubbling fountain, is warned away from its delicious coolness by the roar of the lion, or the hissing of the deadly serpent.

But Cora, whose dicipline had been hard and stern, locked within the stanch vaults of her breast the griefs which clamored for free utterance, and suppressed with steady fortitude her ever-rising, full-forced sobs.

Cassel, when Cora left him in a manner so inexplicable, feared that she might have been seized with a sudden and acute illness. He went to Linda and requested her to follow the young girl and investigate the cause of her strange departure. Linda went to Cora's room. Finding the door locked, she tapped.

" Who is it?"

" Are you sick?" asked Linda.

" No. Please do not come in, now."

" What is the matter, Cora?"

" Nothing that need alarm you,—I am busy."

Cora was writing to Mr. Hope. Linda returned to the parlors and gave Cassel an account, *sotto voce*, of her non-reception. Cassel was far from being satisfied. He knew that Cora was acting under some extraordinary, painful influence, and he watched for her return to the parlors with much anxiety. But she did not come again that evening.

Cassel did not sleep as well as usual the ensuing night, and the next morning he was awake at daylight, thinking and wildering about Cora.

When she came to breakfast, she answered to his morning salutation, but he saw in her eyes a sterile response which he had never seen there before. She took occasion to withdraw from the breakfast-table while Cassel was listening to Uncle Jesse's account of the wonderful extent of the Russian Empire, and its wonderful progress in enlargement.

" What do you intend to do with your maps, Uncle Jesse?"

" Donate the copyright to American institutions of learning."

" Upon what plan are you now working?"

" My original plan. I have gathered all the different maps which have ever been published, so far as I have been able to get them. I have also the standard histories of the nations. Take the face of Europe, as an illustration. I have gone back to the mystic ages, and have mapped out what appears to have been the first authenticated features and divisions. Whenever, by war, treaty, or otherwise, a change has been made in the European countenance, my maps will show it and give the corresponding date. And so on with other quarters of the globe. You apprehend me Cassel, eh?"

"I do. Down to what period have you finished your atlantic and historical panorama?"

"To the time when Washington erected a free flag over the soil of America," replied Uncle Jesse, with pompous patriotism.

"An accurate, thorough work, such as you are engaged upon, would be inestimable in value. It would take rank with our most popular dictionary. No historian, scholar, or institution of learning could afford to do without it."

Uncle Jesse was excessively gratified. Cassel had long since won Uncle Jesse over. He spiced the old fellow's life in numberless ways. He would take him on a drive, to the minstrels, to the theater, to church, to the hotels, to the shops, sail him on the bay or up the river, amuse him with droll anecdotes, and put him at home in many new positions Uncle Jesse was always ready to "run" with Cassel, confiding everything to his consummate management, believing, as he did, that Cassel was invincible under any and all emergencies.

But Cassel was restless this morning, and, not relishing his breakfast, he escaped from Uncle Jesse and went to his room.

Cora, sitting alone in her room, received a card from Cassel, on which he requested the privilege of seeing her. She wrote a note in reply.

"Mr. Rapid will please excuse Miss Huron, who notifies him that she will no longer tax him in the capacity of guardian and mentor."

She folded the note, and sat awhile, holding it in her hand, and tapping it with indecision. Finally she tore it to pieces, saying to herself,—

"What need to send this note? I must remain in the

mansion for awhile, and an open rupture would make it
very unpleasant to Linda, who is so dear and good. But
Linda should know of this thing, and I will tell her of it,
but not until I bid her good-by. I will see Mr. Rapid.
Whatever he may secretly be or have been, his counsel
has been pure, and his kindness faultless."

Cora went down and met Cassel. With genuine interest
he inquired,—

"Have you been sick, Cora ?"

"No," said she, almost shrinking from his gaze.

"What is it that has chilled you,—have you heard bad
news ?"

She could not keep her eyes from meeting his. Anxiety
lent additional tenderness and magic to his gaze, and Cora
irresistibly acknowledged to herself that his countenance
was indelibly stamped with honor. Cora quivered at
heart. Could this indeed be Lucifer, Son of the Morning,
glorious and magical with beauty, come to snare her soul
to ruin ? She felt her heart giving way, but her mind,
trained to strength and resistance, she maintained inflexible. To his last question she answered as briefly as before,—

"No."

After an hour, Cora left Cassel, feeling as though she
had been tried by fire. She had never been put and kept
so painfully upon the alert, lest she should betray herself.
Her very soul was ravished by his artless, artful, deep,
but baffled solicitude, and trembled upon the tremor of his
words. His first offerings and requisitions were ingenuous
and playful. Cora shied from them. He then charged
upon her with numberless persuasions, which trooped in
on her in squadron after squadron, but without apparent
effect. Next, from ambush, he sprang suddenly upon her
with quick questions, as soft and unforeseen as velvet
leopards leaping from the jungle covert. But Cora, in advance, was armed to the lips against him. Whichever
way he turned he was met by an inflexible diamond edge.
Cassel elicited absolutely nothing; but deduction taught
him that, for some unimaginable cause, his status with
Miss Huron was what it might reasonably be with a
spirited and exacting girl, to whom, under very unfavor-

able circumstances, he had just been introduced   He was
conscious that the scepter had departed from him.   That
his kingdom was successfully revolted against him.   That
his gratifying and dulcet dominion over the waxing and
waning of a pure and priceless virgin, was at an end. But
why it was so, he in vain fathomed his heart and mind,
and questioned all his acts.

Two weeks passed away, and Cora was anxiously looking for an answer to the letter which she had dispatched
to Mr. Hope. Between herself and Cassel Rapid she
forced a tacit agreement that he should see to his own
affairs and she would see to hers.

Cassel, who intended and hoped that his abatement
would be but temporary, had also written to the old
minister, informing him that Cora had unaccountably
frozen herself up, and would not be melted ; and unless,
through Mr. Hope's influence, she could be induced to
explain or abandon the strange position she now insisted
upon maintaining, that he felt it to be his duty to notify
Mr. Hope to resume direct control of her, until he might
select some other suitable person to act in his stead, granting that Cora continued to abide in the city.   "She does
not particularly need a guardian here," wrote Cassel, "as
her conduct, except in the matter which necessitates this
advisement, is, as a rule, thoroughly well considered, and
well-nigh faultless.   But it is better that there should be
some person, some approved gentleman, to whom she
could appeal in any case which to her might prove an
emergency."

Mr. Hope was abruptly and woefully confounded when
he received Cora's letter one day and Cassel's a day or
two after.

"What, in the name of David, does all this mean?" he
questioned of himself.   "I wonder now if it is within the
outside limits of possibility that Cora is not the worst
mistaken little maid on earth ? Cassel a married man!
an impostor! his wife just deceased! and he perfectly
contented withal! Cora must be crazy. It is out of all
character. With all her advantages she does not yet
know Cassel as well as I do. As the sun shineth, so is it
clear to me that Cassel has never been in wedlock ; or,

granted that he has, the tomb of his wife would be the temple of his affections. And now," continued the old minister, with a touch of peevishness, "I shall have to write up a quire of foolscap to set this matter to rights. I'll do no such thing," asserted he, laughing complacently, with the relief of a timely and welcome idea; "but I'll send Cora's letter to Cassel, and his to her, and let them clear up the difficulty between them, without more ado. Cora may not relish the process, but I know that it is a thing of air which has alarmed her."

Mr. Hope was becoming very infirm, and it would have been quite a task for him to have conducted a correspondence which promised to be both voluminous and intricate; so he very wisely determined to make a double-barreled cross-fire, and kill the difficulty at a simultaneous discharge. If he was not intending to do conventionally right, he cannot be accused of intending to do wrong in thus exposing Cora's letter to Cassel's perusal,—not to mention Cassel's letter, which he would consign to Cora. He regarded them as mere children, and most old people are apt to forget or ignore the incipient punctilio of youthful modesty and unblunted sensibility. Mr. Hope, therefore, conscientiously cross-fired the letters, without a word of explanation, except the scoring on the margin of each, " If this does not settle it, write me again."

The same mail-bag brought back the redestined letters. Cassel was not in his room when Cora's written and explicit arraignment, under cover of Mr. Hope's envelope, was left conspicuously upon his writing-desk.

Cassel's letter, *via* Mr. Hope, was received by Cora, who read it with avidity. Her first thought was, that here was something about Cassel which had fallen into the hands of the old minister, and with which the latter desired to acquaint her,—something that would convict Cassel. It did not occur to her to consider that the letter was written by Cassel intentionally for Mr. Hope's eye, and that whatever confessions or exposures it might contain were, *in actu, et in rerum naturâ,* voluntary. At the first glance she conceived it to be a stray letter picked up by Mr. Hope, containing a damaging evolution of heretofore undeveloped facts in Cassel's history, which her old guardian deemed proper to lay before her. Having read the letter, however, she became mystified, and wondered why the minister had adopted so strange a method for satisfying her petition. And yet she was pleased with the contents of Cassel's communication. It evinced for her a correct and anxious care, and an unembittered spirit of self-abnegation, tinged with sadness; but was greatly at fault, as Cora judged, with regard to herself and "his inability to conjecture, or hatch out from a prolific and busy imagination, any cause or motive under the sun for her singular behavior."

When she met Cassel at the dinner-table, she vouchsafed to him the least bit more of kindness than of late; but still held herself distinctly aloof from anything like intimacy.

After dinner, when Cassel went to his room mentally discussing the propriety of, in some way, constraining Cora to state her grievances, that he might meet and annihilate them, he saw a new letter on his writing-desk. He recognized the ministerial characters of Mr. Hope, and, having torn the envelope and unfolded the inclosure, as readily recognized the delicate tracery of Cora Glencoe. He saw that the letter, or whatever it might be, was addressed to Mr. Hope. Turning to the signature, he read, "Cora."

"Here is some mistake," said he; and, getting up, he went and tapped at Cora's door. She opened it, and started with surprise as she saw Cassel Rapid. He bowed, and, handing her the document which he still held unfolded, said,—

"Cora, here is an errant something which I wish to return to its original starting-point."

She took it, glanced at it, and almost sank upon her knees.

"Cora," said Cassel, firmly but tenderly, "what is it that ails or afflicts you? You certainly are possessed of some terrible or annoying mistake, and yet you resolutely withhold all confidence from your friends. You are doing both yourself and your friends great injustice. Have you not the nerve to confront me, or Linda, with your troubles, or, if such, your hardships?"

Cora did not answer him, but putting her hand into her dress pocket, drew out a letter, and handing it to him, said,—

"I, too, have something of yours, Mr. Rapid."

"How did you get it?" asked Cassel, in surprise.

"By mail—from Mr. Hope."   .

Cora reflected a moment and then asked,—

"What have you to say to the contents of my letter?"

"I know nothing about its contents. I have not read a word of it."

"Mr. Rapid, is that true?"

Cassel would rather that a thunderbolt had fallen upon him than for Cora to have asked a question which plunged like a bitter shaft down into his heart. The wide estrangement which was implied in her cruel question reaped his tender-springing hopes down to the very stubble, and a frown gathered to his brow as black as the loaded cloud. Cora remembered no countenance as expressive or intense, except that corrugated, blazing face which, once upon a time, gleamed over the shallow sea down by the Larboard Strand. Cora repented. She hastily and earnestly cried,—

"Nay, *forgive* me, Mr. Rapid,—I will not insult you with such a question. I am the guilty one, for, I am ashamed to confess, I have read your letter a dozen times;" and Cora hung her head while her pure cheeks blushed scarlet. Finally, Cora looked up into his face and said,—

"Mr. Rapid?"

"Well?" asked he, with an expression half curious, half smiling.

"Has it occurred to you that Mr. Hope intended that each of us should read the other's letter?"

"It has, since I have just learned that he has returned them both—and crosswise."

"See here," said Cora; "on the margin of my letter are the words, in his handwriting, 'If this does not settle it, write me again.' I find the same words on the margin of yours."

"What then do you propose?"

"In consideration of the fact that I have read your letter, I offer mine for you to read. Having done so, return it to me. I will then, with Linda, meet you below, in the rear parlor."

Cora felt that now was the auspicious time for dispos-

ing of Cassel Rapid. He took the letter and went to his
room. When he had finished it and re-read it, he was in
one sense more mystified than before. How could Cora
ever have conceived or imagined that he had been married
and was an impostor! Notwithstanding his mystification,
he felt a world of weight lifted from his breast. Here,
then, was the germ of his trouble, and the occasion for
Cora's chillness. He would go down into the very substrata, and drag the thing up by the roots—whatever it
might be. He proceeded to the rear parlor and notified
Cora that he was ready to receive her and Linda. The
two girls soon entered, and sat down. Linda had noticed
that there was something wrong between Cora and her
brother Cassel, but she little knew the beginning or the
extent of the alienation. Cassel met them with a smile,
as open, and pleasant, and triumphant as ever came upon
the face of man. As the interview between Cassel and
Cora progressed, Linda looked on and listened with
wonder.

"So," said Cassel to Cora, "you regard me as an impostor, do you?"

"If you are not, I trust that you will be able clearly
to prove it," replied Cora, firmly.

"Tell me," said Cassel, "from what unknown world of
ideas you have gathered this most singular idea of all."

"I come here," said Cora, "from no motive born of curiosity to pry into your life-history; but as Mr. Hope has
referred this matter back to its sources, it becomes my duty
and exigency to cut our communication, and in future to
take care of myself. For Linda's sake, I will tell you
plainly why it is that henceforth I choose to be freed from
any authority which heretofore I have, for good reasons,
acknowledged and willingly submitted to. Accident put
me in possession of a fact, in the concealment of which
you have been unmanly, and so far criminally distinct
from honorable custom as to justify the impeachment of
your moral integrity. I will state to Linda, that very recently I saw you, with a smile on your countenance, and
with after-comments as heartless and ruthless as stone,
read a telegram announcing unmistakably the *death of
your wife*. I speak now in that frankness which you have

so often coveted. Linda," said Cora, turning to the girl-widow with an eye of superlative interrogation, " did you ever dream of such a thing?"

Linda came near to fainting, and looked to Cassel with a wild, thrilling appeal that he should purge himself of this strange and damaging accusation. Cassel, who had been standing up, put his hands to his face and shuddered down into a chair, overwhelmed with this terrible and unexpected revelation. His breast heaved, and he shook with the active shame and ignominy of detection, was it? No; but with a full jolly-boat load of suppressed laughter, until finally he broke out with a contagious carol, as ringing as the notes of a silver trumpet. Cora started to leave the room.

" Please wait a moment, Cora," cried Cassel, with a joyous, mischievous face; " I understand it all, now, and can demolish this monster in a twinkling."

Cora resumed her seat. Cassel drew out a ring of keys, selected one, gave it to Linda, and said,—

" Little sister, will you do brother Cassel the favor to go up to his room, that there may be no suspicion about the matter,—open the red leather trunk at the foot of the bed, look in the left hand far corner of the tray, and bring down a package marked in red ink, ' Chicago Dispatches?' I am interested in some beef and grain contracts out there. Those contracts are my wives. One of them is just deceased,—that is, a contract has proved bad, as wives often do, and has been suffered to die."

"Mr Rapid, I would prefer to go now, and you can explain to Linda."

" No, Cora. You have confronted me with an accusation; you must needs confront my exculpation. And furthermore, I'm going to wind this thing up in a frolic,— I never felt so saucy in all my life."

It began to steal in upon Cora that she had put her foot into it up to the ankle. She was very anxious to beat a retreat, but Cassel wouldn't let her. Her joy, however, equiponderated her confusion, for it would be as joyful as it would be shameful to her—far more joyful—if Cassel should prove innocent, as he now seemed able to do.

Linda soon came back with the package of dispatches. Cassel took it and said,—

"Cora, you may act as judge, jury, and prosecuting attorney; but I think that before I am done, you will dismiss the suit, or at least enter a *nolle prosequi*."

Cassel handed one dispatch after another to Linda, in the order of their dates, and Linda read them to Cora. It appeared from these dispatches that Cassel had been married almost as often as the Sultan; that some of his wives had died, some were yet thriving, and, strange to say, some who had died seemed to have been relumed by the Promethean heat of a little, extra, smelted, precious metal.

"What in the name of goodness does it all mean?" asked Linda, her large, soft eyes looking wonderingly at Cassel.

"It means that I am a Brigham Bluebeard, looking out for another victim to follow in the train of those several wives whom you have just read about."

Cora, in utter confusion, but still with boundless secret gladness, ran out of the room. She was not yet at the bottom of the matter, but she was certain that Cassel was a live young bachelor, and that she, to use her own words, was "most essentially a live young fool." Up in her room she stormed at herself, before her mirror,—

"You illimitable and unmentionable little *fool* you!" she cried at herself, while she stamped the floor with vigorous foot. "*Pshaw!* I almost wish I was wicked enough to swear. I have heard men say, that, at times, nothing but a round of hearty swearing would empty them of their feelings. I feel just that way *now;* and if I wasn't afraid, I'd *ring* it at you, you *goose! Don't you look at me!*" she almost shouted at her reflection in the mirror; "I've no *patience* with you."

Cora was as fidgety, and as serio-comic, as ever was Lotta upon the public stage. We will return to Cassel and Linda.

"But what *does* it mean?" asked the bewildered Linda.

"It is one side of a commercial, telegraphic correspondence. I will explain it to you."

Is it necessary to explain to the reader also? If so, it can be done by substituting "wheat" for "wife," or, for the dear creature, you can substitute "beef cattle." But an explanation can *best* be given by referring to numerous dispatches of like facial import which passed from the City of Washington to the city of New York during the late war, when gold gamblers kept foxy agents in the capital city, as newspapers kept correspondents there, to nose around and smell out the very freshest item, and then run frantically to a telegraph office and send it off by a flash of lightning, substituting "wife" and wife's afflictions, for the Federal army and its vicissitudes. No official watch-hawk, placed to guard the wires and embargo their tell-tale capacity, could decently refuse the transit of a dispatch notifying an anxious husband of an event so melancholy and tax-free as the death of a darling wife, but would certainly and absolutely light his pipe with all such dispatch slips as might, for instance, prematurely convey news of the defeat of McClellan, or Hooker, or Pope, or Meade, or Burnside, the latter of whom a certain bold song sings out to be a "clever fellow." A man who was so fortunate as to be located in New York, and to possess an espoused myth in Washington City or its environs, whose patriotism and sympathy caused her pulses to wax and wane with the successes and reverses of the Federal arms, and whose symptoms, like the finger of a barometer, warned the desolate husband in advance of a storm (of good or bad news), before the stormlike reverberations had reached Wall Street, such a man, we say, was well-nigh sure of an oft-recurring gold crop. It was a good thing in those days for a manipulator of Gold to have a tremendously vicissi-tudinous wife in Washington City.

Cassel was engaged in no gambling operations, but he and Mr. Lake were, with a large capital, successfully competing with a presumptive monopoly, and, to guard against their prying rivals, and against telegraphic treachery, the commercial lightning which came to Cassel from the West, sometimes told remarkable tales on his "wife," or his "uncle," or his "grandmother." The dispatch which Cora had seen, and which had announced to Cassel the *death* of his wife, was a mere notification, from an agent, of the unfruitfulness of one of his commercial and least-favored spouses.

Cora felt as if she never could face Cassel Rapid again, and yet she determined to face him at the first opportunity. All her confidence in him was back again, and augmented. Notwithstanding she was conscious of having acted from proper motives and upon apparently sufficient grounds, she could not forbear storming at herself as an "illimitable little fool." She met Cassel before nightfall, and found him as joyful as Spring, and as lively as a volume of wit.

"But why did you not tell me, or accuse me, sooner?" he asked of Cora.

"Because I thought you were a *monster*," she laughed.

"Cora, would you like for me to tell Harry Gray about this exquisite complication?"

"Tell *nobody*," she cried, with pleading, mischievous eyes. "Linda has already promised me."

"Do you think it possible for two girls and one man to keep a secret?"

"*I'll* never tell it," answered Cora; "Linda will never tell it: so, sir, if it escapes, you will be the responsible party."

"Personally responsible?"

"Yes; 'personally responsible,' as the braggarts say."

"I have yet to see the brace of girls whom I fear; but I already know a brace of them to be loved," said Cassel, adroitly.

"And I," said Cora, "know of a similar brace of quails, in the forest at Creswood. They would make such a nice morning lunch," and Cora ran away to her own room.

Cora was again at ease and happy. When we say "happy," we do not mean that she never reflected upon her condition, for she very often did so. But she was much more charmingly surrounded than, of yore, she had ever been. As a tender flower which has struggled up through storm and gloom will, if transplanted into sunny soil, lift up its head and repay the floral nurse with vigorous and fragrant evolution, so Cora, coming out of the dismal den of Cliff Hall, and into the genial atmosphere of the Boyd mansion, felt as reinforced as the newly-nourished flower which opens and courts the nostril or the bee, and as blithe as the sunny bee which ravishes the opened flower. What girl, naturally teeming with all the elements of joy, and possessing a mind, healthy, firm, and elastic as a Toledo blade, could have been otherwise than chiefly happy, we do not say contented, situated as Cora was? In addition to all other bright things immediately around her, she was in that blissful, ravishing, and unreturning state which comes but once upon the fresh heart and whispers " Eureka,"—the finding of the very thing to *love*. During her late interview with Cassel, that in which he had vainly endeavored to capture or expose her motives, and out of which she had come as from a fiery furnace, she had more than one time imagined, that if he was actually a monster, then were all men monsters, and that he was the most brilliant and fascinating monster of them all. Fronting him with an outward stoicism which baffled his eye, she nevertheless had felt him pillaging through all the sacred places of her heart, like an active chieftain of Free Lances sweeping through a city, and laying a dominant hand upon its citadel, its shrines, and all its hallowed spots. If Cassel was so strong with Cora in the character of Lucifer, how glorious and conquering would he be, as the radiant Apollo, prince of the blonde Day?

Johnny Gale was getting along with Linda so well that it began to be pleasant with her for Cora and brother Cassel to tease her about him.

The last letter which Johnny had written to his father, after having hinted at his " ambition " in very ambiguous terms, closed with the following characteristic words: " Now, father, I think I've struck oil, and I want a couple of hundred to test the well. That is, I must be fashionable in the cut of my coat, and keep up with the tailors. You will reflect, father, that a spider without a web would stand a frosty poor chance of catching flies."

Captain Gale and his wife held a consultation over the letter of their " wild boy," which eventuated in Captain Gale sending Johnny the wherewithal to weave his web. But he took the fatherly precaution to write to Carroll May, and inquire what it was that Johnny was driving at.

" He'll go and tangle his hawser with some loon of a girl,

like as not, and think that she is a born and bred princess,"
observed Captain Gale to his wife.

Carroll May replied to Captain Gale's letter, but referred
to Cassel Rapid that particular portion of it inquiring about
Johnny's " ambition."

Cassel wrote a spicy communication to Captain Gale,
giving a good, though amusing account of Johnny's court-
ship, and satisfying the parents that, in the matter of his
" ambition," Johnny was no fool by a fathom. " Mrs. Boyd,
who, with equal propriety, might be called Miss Linda
Medley, is," wrote Cassel, "just such a girl as I imagine
Mrs. Gale was, at Linda's age, and promises to make just
such another excellent lady-woman."

" I don't ask any better, Sallie," emphatically spoke out
Captain Gale, as he read the letter aloud to his wife. Mrs.
Gale's motherly and still handsome face rippled with smiles
at this double compliment to herself, and at this cheering
and undoubted testimony confirming Johnny's good discretion and probable good luck.

" Wife," said the gratified captain, having finished reading the letter, " I think I'll send Johnny a couple of hundred more. It's well enough to help him along a little
when he is disposed to do a good thing,—and both Cassel
and Carroll say that he spends his money judiciously
though freely."

"Just as he *should* spend it," responded the mother.
" And nobody has a better right to furnish it than you
have, for you made it yourself. But let me read Cassel's
letter over again."

When Mrs. Gale had gone over it herself, she observed,
complacently,—

"I never read a more pleasant letter in all my life."

" Cassel knows how and where to launch his compliments," said Captain Gale humorously. " Now, he knew
it wouldn't be worth his time to try and honey-fuggle *me*,
the young rascal." But the captain was honey-fuggled,
nevertheless; for in Cassel's comparison was a retroactive
compliment which flattered the rugged mariner's youthful
good taste and discretion.

By way of dismissing, for the time, the subject of Matrimony, and winding up this chapter, we will peep in upon

Uncle Jesse and Cassel Rapid, who are engaged in a confidential conversation. In fact, all of Uncle Jesse's conversations were confidential.

"Uncle Jesse, why didn't you marry?" asked Cassel.

"Why *didn't* I!—You mean why *don't* I, eh, Cassel?" suggested the old man, straightening up his collar.

"Well—yes—didn't I say *don't*?" asked Cassel, adroitly.

"Yes, you didu't," maladroitly replied Uncle Jesse.

"Well, why *don't* you, then?"

"Because, Cassel," said the old man, with an invincible, harsh, testy look, "I stand no nonsense."

"But would it be nonsense, Uncle Jesse, to persuade some charming woman to become Mrs. Jesse Medley, who would tap you lovingly on the check, and beat up the bed for you?"

"A-hem—Cassel—don't mention it. Before I could turn around three times I'd have a trundle-bed full of brats, and an everlasting caterwaul and nursery *pot-pourri* ringing and raging and dinging and damnably donging in my ears. No, sir,—one Medley in my establishment is the complement exact. My grandfather Moore had just thirty-three and $\frac{1}{3}$ children. The $\frac{1}{3}$ child was a deaf and dumb idiot, his last, and, by-the-by, his favorite, for it slept three-fourths of its time, and when it was awake it made no more noise than an expeditionary mouse. The old gentleman advised me, if ever I should be fool enough to marry, to search me out a free-martin—ha! ha! h-a! eh, Cassel?"

"Marry the Moon, Uncle Jesse. You will then be Platonically safe," laughed Cassel, who abandoned the incorrigible old bachelor.

CHAPTER XXXIII.

TIME passed smoothly away, Spring came and went,
leaving in its train the delightful month of June, through
which our narrative must now plow. The mornings were
bland, and the days were quiet; everything in the Boyd
mansion was quiet, except two or three busy, throbbing
young hearts; everything at Creswood was quiet, except
Oswald Huron; and all along the Potomac of our little
history, quiet chiefly reigned.

Cassel Rapid went around to O'Dare's office. O'Dare
was away—in Philadelphia. "Could the clerk give him
any Huron news?" The clerk "could not."

"Are you not a new hand here?" asked Cassel of the
clerk.

"No."

"Do you remember me, then?"

"I do not,—we see so many people."

"Were you in the office one day when O'Dare and I
had a wrestling match?"

The clerk smiled, and answered,—

"I recollect you now; Mr. Rapid, is it not?"

"Yes."

"You were interested in the case of—let's see—whom?"

"Huron,—I told you when I first came in."

"Are you prime in the case?"

"How?"

"Number one—first—principal?"

"Yes,—that is, I am acting for myself."

"About what is the date of your application?"

"You are so very special," said Cassel, "that I imagine
I had better wait until O'Dare returns. When will that
be?"

"Don't know."

"What *do* you know? Anything?"

"Nothing."

"This is a regular know-nothing office—when O'Dare is out of it," said Cassel.

"Just so," answered the smiling clerk.

"Maybe *you'd* like to tussle a round or two?" said Cassel. "Possibly I could bang something out of you."

"No objection to it in the world," promptly replied the clerk. "Just walk this way, into a back room, and I'll try you one fall, if it kills me."

Cassel had only intended to rally the clerk a little, but now that his banter was accepted he could not well back out. He followed the clerk into a rear apartment where the floor was carpeted.

"You pick a soft place I observe," said Cassel. "You probably anticipate a fall?"

"I don't wish to break your bones," answered the clerk. "But what 'holt' do you prefer?"

"I'm not particular."

"Nor I," retorted the clerk; "but wait until I take off my coat and watch."

"Take your shirt off, for all I care," said Cassel, who had already determined to turn the clerk a double-and-twisted summerset.

The office-man quickly stripped himself of more than his coat and watch, and to Cassel's unbounded astonishment O'Dare stood before him *in propria persona!*

"The *Devil!*" cried Cassel, surprised into an absurdity.

"Whist," softly replied the detective.

"What!" cried Cassel, still in amazement.

"Just so," admitted O'Dare, "but not so loud."

"What are you up to?"

"It's not up, it's down."

"Down where?"

"Into 'hell'."

"What do you want down there?—to take lodgings in advance? That's not fair, old fellow," said Cassel, drolly.

"I've got to go down there to-night after a trinket, and I've been trying my disguise all day to see if it is proof."

"Well?"

"Not a soul has recognized me."

"Put it on again, and let me look at you."

31

O'Dare resumed his disguise, and demanded,—
"Now."

"O'Dare, I would never know you, unless possibly by your eyes. I was as much surprised just now as though you had risen from the grave-yard."

O'Dare turned about, took a vial from a pigeon-hole, sprinkled from it a yellow powder into his palm, and then rubbed some of the powder in his eyes. Soon his eyes became bloodshot, and the last twinkling vestige of his original appearance was destroyed.

"Don't that hurt?" asked Cassel.

"It smarts a little; but I am occasionally under the necessity of using it."

"How long does the effect last?"

"Well, half an hour or so; but I carry it like snuff in my vest pocket, and can renew it at will and without detection."

"Now, O'Dare, about Huron *vs.* Huron?"

"I'm on another trail in that interest."

"What are the prospects?"

"They fluctuate just as I succeed or fail."

"What sort of a trail is it?"

"I am tracing a positive daguerreotype with which to confront a negative one."

"A shadow," said Cassel.

"A shadow which, if I can catch it, I engage to transform into a luminary, under whose light Miss Huron's lineage will stand out in bold and undeniable characters, so that she, or her anxious lover, can read her title clear."

"I hope you will succeed," said Cassel. "Meantime I will not be overinquisitive."

"A very discreet conclusion," replied O'Dare, who, after a moment's reflection, asked, "Rapid, are you cool?"

"No.—I'm rather warm," answered Cassel, who thought that O'Dare was facetiously alluding to his somewhat heavy woolen coat.

"I don't mean caloric," said O'Dare. "Have you a good, sound nerve?"

"I'm healthy,—if that answer suits you."

"If a dangerous and desperate desperado (to be superlative by way of tautology)," said O'Dare, "after an ex-

citing interlocutory controversy, should come at you with
a drawn knife to cut your heart out, but by some good fortune was prevented from entering upon his well-intended
enterprise, could you, immediately after your peril was
passed, sit down and write, without a shaky hand, a note
to your sweetheart, inviting her to the juicy joys of a
strawberry festival ?"

" That would depend somewhat upon the season."

" Say that strawberries were ripe."

" Well, — I imagine I could, almost; but not having
tried it I can't positively say."

" Again," said O'Dare ; " are you grateful ?"

" Yes ; but not beyond a double return for an original
favor.   If a man should assist me to pull my boots off, for
instance, I wouldn't be willing to set him up in the boot
and shoe business, and bolster him every time he might
be likely to fail.   Gratitude has a limit, as well as patience."

" But don't you, when you come to reflect, after you go
to bed, without having said your prayers,—don't you consider yourself resting under some unrequited obligations
to Hector O'Dare ?"

" Well, yes,—I can answer that question without the
reflection implied in it."

" Would you not, then, like to lighten those obligations
by doing him a service ?"

" I don't know but I would ; but quit your hyperbolical
and diabolical rhetoric, and bring yourself down to the
preciseness of a financial budget; I then may be able to
divine your meaning."

" Very good.   I am going down into 'hell' to-night,
and I want you to go with me."

" That is demanding too much even of the most active
or morbid gratitude.   But tell me of your expedition and
its object."

" I wish to steal a ring from the finger of the Devil.
Some of my understrappers are away, and among all that
I can command, I do not know of one who has the nerve
to go with me, and the quick discretion to do the exigeant
thing."

" I'm not contracting for the performance of any exigeant

feats just at present. But can't you dash a chunk of ice at the Devil and freeze him out ?"

" To be plain, Rapid, if you are so disposed, you can do me a favor by coming with me to-night. You have heard of cutting vessels out from under a battery. I wish to cut a man out from the dangerous precincts of a den, without making too much noise about it. At all events I wish to form his acquaintance in my present disguise."

' Why don't you call on the regular police ?"

" Regular deuce,—they are boobies."

" Can't the New York police arrest a single man ?"

"Yes, and spoil my game, perhaps. In this nest I have eggs which hatch me out a stingeree every now and then. I don't wish to break up the nest,—only to rob it of a fledgeling."

" What do you want with the man after you get him ?"

" I don't particularly want the carcass, but something which I suspect to be in the clothes-pockets of the carcass."

" Is there no way of getting it without going down into Pluto's dominions ?"

" Money will get it, but I won't have it that way, not even if I could buy it for a cent. My professional pride and standing are involved, and I must all-wise fail before I resort to money."

" O'Dare, I thought you were a prudent man."

" Prudent ! By Jupiter, I am exercising the very acme of prudence. Don't you know that if I suffer myself to be blackmailed once, I lose prestige with my friends,—the rogues and evil-doers,—and that every devil of them would try it on me ? When I am after a wretch I *never* compromise with *him*, though I am often constrained to suborn some of his pals."

" You use one rogue to catch another."

" I set A to catch B to-day, and to-morrow I reverse the eccentric and set B to catching A."

" It is a poor rule that won't reciprocate in its workings," said Cassel. "But which am I to consider myself, your A or your B ?"

" You are my Bee, if you will be, whom I intend to put into the nose of the Bruin who is stealing your honey."

"*My* honey! What interest have I in your Bruin?"

"I shall not tell you until the job is over; but you are interested, I assure you."

"O'Dare," said Cassel, "you have taken the pains to bottle me up; now you can uncork me or not, as you will. But, be it remembered, I never do anything or go anywhere unless I know the reason why. I intended to go with you, on the score of your past services, and on a piece of business strictly your own. But now that you have brought me in as an interested party, I will not budge an inch until you tell me explicitly wherein I am interested. I have a right to know, so that, when in action, my own judgment may be the ready fountain and mainspring of my acts."

"Rapid, did I make such terms with you when, in your interests, I went down upon the Larboard Strand?"

Cassel's eyes flamed, and his face grew hot with rushing blood. Getting up and fronting O'Dare, he stretched out his right arm, and in a voice which cut its way to the hedged heart of the detective, said,—

"May the arm *wither* when it ceases to serve you! Come,—I will go down into the bottomless *pit* with you, and never ask a question as to my errand. If you have war to make, let it be war,—red-hot and up to the very hilt. If I flinch, may all the heavens on high come down and dash me to pieces!"

O'Dare, with some regret, saw that he had sent a bolt of fire into Cassel's inmost soul. It had not been his thought so thoroughly to electrify him. Rather gently, he said,—

"Sit down, Rapid. You are entitled to more confidence in this matter than I have admitted or bestowed. It is true, as you first contended, that if you go with me you should precisely know what you are to act upon. I will now precisely inform you, and leave you to judge whether or not you are an interested or sympathizing party. So. When I discovered that Maria Guthrie was dead, I went to see Neville Huron; he was disheartened, and so was I. Nosing about for a new trail, I learned that he had preserved the clothes which were upon the infant when it

31*

fell over the bluff; also a locket that was about the little thing's neck.

"'But,' said he, 'they were dressed exactly alike, and wore lockets which could not have been distinguished the one from the other.'

"'Did the lockets contain anything?' I asked.

"'Each contained a miniature of myself,' said he.

"'What style of miniature?'

"'They were daguerreotypes.'

"'Taken at the same time?'

"'No. The miniature in my child's locket was taken first. I sat for it. About a week afterward, when I was on the eve of visiting my brother Oswald, I had a copy taken from the original, and incased it in a locket similar to my own child's locket.'

"'And the copy you gave to your brother's child?'

"'Yes.'

"'One of these daguerreotypes,' said I, 'was a negative and the other a positive. Now, can you prove in any way which one it was that you gave to your brother's child?'

"'I can, by some old family servants, who were really more interested in the trinkets at the time than I was. I can also prove by them the battered locket which came back to me hanging to the neck of the little corpse. They have seen it often. The plate of the miniature is bent, the result of the little one's terrible fall over the cliff's side.'

"'How have you been accustomed to part your hair?'

"'On the left side.'

"'All your life?'

"'Yes, since I was grown.'

"'Now, Mr. Huron,' said I, 'the proof is at hand. If the head in the battered locket which you have here, parts the hair on the left side, it is the copy which you gave to your brother's child, and that child, to a demonstrated certainty, lies buried in your vaults; and the living one, Cora, now in New York, is, to a demonstrated certainty, your daughter.'

"'Have you ever entertained any doubt of it?' asked he.

"'No,' said I, 'but a certain Maryland court has. If

you prove up this locket by unimpeachable testimony, the court is bound to be with you, and your daughter becomes your own. Go get the locket and let me see it.'

"He brought me the locket. The hair was parted on the left side, and the whole trinket peculiarly battered so as to be very distinguishable. I then gave him my opinions as to his best mode of procedure, and came away to New York. Now, Cassel, the sequel to this conference between myself and Neville Huron is almost enough to discourage even Hector O'Dare. Every time I roll the wheel of Cora's fortunes up the hill of difficulty, Neville Huron manages to roll it down again. What damnable fool's work do you suppose he made of it after I left him? Still confiding, it seems, in his brother's sense of justice, he took the locket, went down to Creswood, stated the case to Oswald Huron, showed him the locket, and begged him to abandon his claim. Oswald Huron requested a couple of days for deliberation. Meantime he secretly went off and consulted with a villainous lawyer who is popularly known as the rider of a nag called 'Famine;' and the upshot was that the locket was stolen from Neville Huron before the two days expired. Oswald Huron then bid his brother bitter defiance, and cunningly wrote to little Cora, here in New York, to send him, as a *souvenir*, the *other* locket, which she had fondly preserved. Innocently she sent it to him. The rider of 'Famine,' specifically designated as Mr. Attorney, having learned the value and bearing of the locket which had been stolen from Neville Huron, managed to get possession of it. He is a professional *black-mailer*, and considered the stolen locket as an egg which would hatch out wealth. But he could do nothing with the locket by remaining within ken at Creswood. He lived a starving life there at best. So he turned out 'Famine' to thrive or succumb, and ratted his way to New York, for the express purpose of black-mailing both the Huron brothers. By this means he doubtless hopes and expects to see-saw his way to a heavy purse. Neville Huron referred the whole matter to me, acknowledging his gross and lamentable indiscretion. I went to see him. I then went down to Creswood, got upon the scent, traced Mr. Attorney to his den in this city, and now have an eye on him. He is in fellowship with some desperate characters. Now for your idea of getting out a search-warrant, and calling in the police to arrest him, etc. etc. That would never do. He would go to law about it, and if he saw no other escape he would compound with Oswald Huron from whom he extracted the locket, and the important trinket would find its way back to Oswald Huron, and in all probability be destroyed. Where it now is, it is safe from destruction, for the thief holds it as a kind of collateral assurance for anticipated cash. He has already made written overtures to Neville Huron, who, having more financial than genealogical sense, declined to respond. I wish to get this locket quietly, if possible, for more reasons than one, or two. If the locket is restored to Neville Huron without any fuss or blazon, the impregnable position which he once held, by reason of its possession, will again be his. But if we get into a lawsuit over the locket, it will become as difficult, probably, to prove up the trinket as it has been to prove up Cora Glencoe. Don't you see?"

"I do," said Cassel. "But now for your plan of operations."

"It is impossible to prearrange a plan, and that is why I want you to come with me instead of some damned numskull. Everything will have to be done upon the suggestion of the moment. We may accomplish nothing whatever to-night, except, in my disguised character, and your unknown one, to make the personal acquaintance of our man. But you will have to look more like a 'rough' than you do now. However, I'll fix that when the time comes. I shall have to wear this disguise, for among the wretches whom we are likely to meet are many who know me of old, and who would disembowel me on sight"

"What time shall I be in readiness?" asked Cassel.

"About nine o'clock this evening. Can you shoot?"

"Yes."

"But can you shoot well?"

"I can beat you," replied Cassel.

"No,—you can't do that. I am certain."

"Come into the gallery, and we'll soon see."

In the gallery, O'Dare said,—

"Take your choice of pistols," pointing to a rack which held at least a dozen.

"All I want is a true one," said Cassel. "Choose for me."

A lively contest ensued, in which there was so little difference that it was agreed to be a draw. But O'Dare frankly said,—

"Cassel, with your own pistols, you would beat me, if I left any room for you."

"Do you expect to use pistols to-night?"

"Only in self-defense. I took the precaution, however, to get legal warrants, which, if I am compelled to plug a man, will bear me out."

"Me too?" asked Cassel.

"Or any other man," answered O'Dare, with a humor in his tone and face which, with the slightest recalled brogue, made him, at will, so droll and racy a companion.

At nine o'clock Cassel called at O'Dare's office and said to the detective;—

"I am now ready to make a dash for the Devil's finger-ring, or privy signet, which is it?"

"It may turn out to be your wedding-gift ring," said the detective, insinuatingly. "But strip yourself to shirt and drawers, and put on this suit. Take those diamonds out of your bosom and sleeves, and put in these pastes to make you look flashy. Rapid, I would give a dollar to see you perfectly nude,—I imagine that every inch of you is athletic symmetry itself, and I always admired symmetry, mental or physical."

"If you are fond of looking upon nudity, visit the Cancan, or advertise for a skinned cat," replied Cassel. "I strip for no man alive."

Cassel arrayed himself in the clothes which O'Dare had provided for the occasion, and stood out for inspection.

"Damn it," said O'Dare, a little impatiently, "your face is too bright and handsome. Let me put some yellow powder in your eye."

"No, I'll be switched if I do."

"It will never do to go with that face. It looks like the silver shining moon peeping out of an old clothes-bag. Something must be done. Here, take this, and rub it over your phiz."

"What is it?"

" Nothing but a mixture of grease and gunpowder."
Cassel rubbed his hands and face with the mixture.

" Now " said O'Dare, "wash in cold water, without
soap." Cassel did so, and asked,—

" How do I look now ?"

" Like a handsome coal-heaver with his Sunday duds on,
—just right."

" Are you ready ?" asked Cassel.

" Yes. Are you armed ?"

" I have my pistols. They are lightning to the center
at every fire."

" Take about eight inches of this kind of stuff," said
O'Dare, handing Cassel a double-edged dagger. " Its glitter makes the flesh creep. Here, also, are some brass
knuckles. I have something better still, but I doubt if
you would use it."

" What is it ?"

" Pulverized Cayenne pepper "   •

" Now, that's *too* bad," said Cassel, laughing; "you
must be anticipating a fight with a 'hell of ugly devils'."

" I always go *prepared*," replied O'Dare, picking up a
small black-walnut case and concealing it under his loose
coat.

" What is *that* for ?" asked Cassel.

" I am going to open a faro-bank. But listen, and tell
me if this contrivance which I now put in my mouth
changes my voice beyond recognition."

" It does, most assuredly."

" You've heard faro-dealers articulate. I must not only
change my voice, but modulate it, à la Faro, to the low,
soft, tender, briefly sweet and unctuous grunt of a grazing
sow. But come on, and I'll explain as we go along."

In about three-quarters of an hour Hector O'Dare and
Cassel Rapid stepped into a saloon located in one of the
most dismal parts of the city. O'Dare handed money to
the bar-keeper, and said,—

" Give me a ticket for a vacant table,—a table against
the wall, mind you, and not out in the center of the floor."

The keeper passed over a numbered ticket and then
glanced at Cassel. O'Dare pitched him an additional coin.

" Here, Ned, show these gentlemen below."

" Does he know you ?" whispered Cassel to O'Dare.

" No; but he knows what the money is for; it is our entrance fee to ' hell,' the gambling-room."

" I thought a fellow could get to hell for nothing,— by simply letting himself loose and naturally dropping into it."

" No," replied the humorous O'Dare; " he must commit some overt act; he must do a turn or two for the devil."

CHAPTER XXXIV.

THE apartment into which our two adventurers were ushered was capacious, underground, and so situated in respect to the street and the upper stories of the building as effectually to hush up the sounds of revelry and brawling so common to this subterranean precinct. The apartment was lighted by a single central chandelier, which was fed by a single gas-pipe. The uses of the room were similar to what were those of the basement of the " Bull's Head," in San Antonio, Texas, where, some years ago, any man conforming to the regulations, and who could muster the means, might possess himself of a table and spread his gambling snares.

Entering the room and mixing with a couple of dozen men or more, O'Dare and Cassel found themselves in the midst of a piratical, pugilistic, cut-throat, brazen, desperate-looking crew. O'Dare saw many old acquaintances, whose recognition of him would in no way have conduced to his pleasure or safety; and among the men who were betting at an active faro-table he discovered Mr. Attorney, the gentleman whose personal acquaintance he desired to cultivate. He took quiet occasion to point him out to Cassel; he then stepped to a vacant table, corresponding in number with his ticket, went in between the table and the wall, spread out the customary gambling devices of the place, and struck a bell which was attached to the table, the silver sound of which notified all lovers of " hazard" that their love was waiting and willing. O'Dare's object in thus ignoring the Statute vs. Gambling was to give himself character, influence, and respectability in "hell;" for no one than he was better aware of the fact that among this habitually impecunious and spasmodically pecunious substrata crew a gold-banked dealer was envied and respected, and admitted to be the very top-gallant of aristocracy and the sky-sail of grandeur.

O'Dare not only succeeded in his immediate design, but unexpectedly and fortunately arrived at a decisive point in the ultimate business upon which he was venturing. A number of fortune-fighters gathered at his table; Cassel bet freely, and O'Dare at one time was solicitous for the stability and solvency of his bank. Several, who were having bad luck at the other table, now came over to O'Dare. Among these recruits was Mr. Attorney. He bought a number of "chips" and lost them; he bought more, and lost again. Turning to Cassel, who was in luck, he asked a loan of five dollars. Cassel let him have it. He soon lost it. He then asked O'Dare if he might bet jewelry. O'Dare consented that he should. He pulled out the very locket which the detective so earnestly desired to get hold of, and asked,—

"How much do you value this at?"

"Let me see it," said O'Dare.

The battered locket was passed over. O'Dare balanced it in his hand as if to ascertain its weight, and then with some difficulty sprung it open. There was the daguerreotype of Neville Huron, and the detective was not slow to perceive that the hair was parted on the left side,—proof positive to him that this was the kernel of the obstinate nut which he had so long been endeavoring to crack.

"What is it worth?" asked Mr. Attorney.

"Fifteen dollars, locket and chain."

"Say twenty, and I'll bet it all at once."

"Very well," said O'Dare, willing to do a favor. "Make your game."

Mr. Attorney coppered the locket upon the King, but slyly retained the end of the chain in his fingers. The King lost, and O'Dare was deliberately reaching out to take in the coveted trinket, when Mr. Attorney dragged it off the cloth, and put it back into his pocket. Every eye now turned upon O'Dare. Even among the lowest gamblers, the act of which Mr. Attorney was guilty is regarded as an unpardonable breach of fellowship and honor, and such an act is always disallowed when referred to the "gentlemen present." But the "gentlemen present," however ready they generally are to *decide* all important questions of this kind, never or rarely take it upon themselves to *enforce* their decisions; and, in the end, it amounts simply to a contest of words or weapons between the aggressor and the aggrieved, with the sympathy on the side of the aggrieved, but with the battle to the strongest, nevertheless. Although O'Dare had suffered the locket to slip through his fingers, he was conscious that he had gained an advantage and an opportunity, each so great and unexpected that he was determined neither to release the one nor neglect the other.

"You lost," said O'Dare, pleasantly.

The man said nothing.

"Pay your loss," insisted O'Dare, coolly.

"It is worth more money than twenty."

"You accepted my valuation, and I raised it at your request and to your satisfaction. If I had valued it at a thousand dollars, the result would have been the same, for you undoubtedly lost it,—on the King."

"But I am not willing to take twenty dollars for it," said Mr. Attorney. "I'd sooner go and get you the money;" and on that plea he was about to escape, when Cassel, drawing a knife and taking him by the throat, sternly said,—

"*Deliver, or die!*"

There was a steel-like ring in Cassel's voice which hushed the by-standers. Mr. Attorney, looking into Cassel's face and discovering the imperial and relentless courage which looked upon him and held him by the throat, cowered and yielded up the locket. O'Dare, with well-concealed triumph, politely thanked Cassel, who quietly observed that "game was game, and that he stood no nonsense from either side of the table."

Mr. Attorney continued to grumble about the locket, that it was a *souvenir*, etc. etc., and was endeavoring to borrow the money wherewith to redeem it. O'Dare became alarmed lest the man should succeed in getting the money, when, under the customary "practice," the locket would have to undergo redemption. To hedge this new danger, he looked over to Cassel and asked, blandly,—

"Will you favor me with your name, sir ?"

"My name is Rapid," replied Cassel.

O'Dare found it impossible to repress a smile at this exquisite candor.

"Thank you," said he, with all the gravity and polish of the most dignified faro-table. "This is a small matter, but business is business, and as I expect to do business here, I want every one to understand that I work strictly on the square. Will you, therefore, be kind enough to take this locket to the nearest jeweler's, ascertain its carat and value, and bring me the jeweler's certificate to the same ? Whatever it is worth, I will pay this gentleman the amount, or he will pay me and retain the locket. I leave it to the 'gentlemen present' if anything can be more fair."

The "gentlemen present" decided that nothing could be more fair and lovely, and Cassel, putting the subject of dispute down into the bottom seams of an inside vest pocket, was about to go upon his errand, when Mr. Attorney said to him,—

"I will go with you."

"No," said O'Dare. "I object to that."

"Do *you* object?" asked the man, of Cassel.

"Go or not, as you please," answered Cassel, with an optic gesture to O'Dare, which caused the latter to withdraw his objection.

Cassel understood O'Dare's game, or, if not, he would make a game of his own. He would go out, elude Mr. Attorney or knock him down, put the locket in some place of security, return, report, and he and O'Dare would take the most favorable opportunity of escaping from Pluto's dominions. But Cassel, accompanied by Mr. Attorney, had hardly taken three steps away from the table, before he was arrested by a sudden crash and uproar, which was increased by the fierce yell of,—

"*Foul,—by God*, boys, it's *O'Dare !*"

Cassel turned instantly about. There, at quick and

desperate defense, stood O'Dare, partly stripped of his disguise, backed by the wall behind his table, with drawn pistols, and with the audacity of the very devil in his half-grinning countenance, while his brilliant, fluttering eyes seemed by rapid glances to be holding a dozen men at bay. Cassel saw that a dangerous crisis, however it had come, was at hand. Without a moment's hesitation he drew off and knocked Mr. Attorney as cold as a wedge. Quickly throwing aside his coat, to be unencumbered, he sprang over the faro-table and took his position shoulder to shoulder with O'Dare, at the same time presenting in either hand a cocked revolver, and saying to the crowd,—

" Come on, if you like the look of it !"

One half of the crowd prudently or timidly left the room ; but a dozen or more ferocious-looking fellows, inverted friends of O'Dare, loudly swore that he should never leave the room alive—neither his accomplice. They formed a frowning and threatening semicircle, but, for the moment, stood with drawn weapons at a respectful distance, seemingly spell-bound by the unflinching aspect of the two dauntless-looking men who were braced to defend themselves and each other to the last gasp.

While O'Dare and Cassel stood together, with their eyes and pistols leveled at the fierce and hungry looking desperadoes about them, they carried on the following whispered conversation :

" What do you propose, O'Dare ?"

" To surrender myself on condition that you shall go free."

" I am no deserter, O'Dare."

" But you have the locket. When you are free, I'll beat them, somehow."

" No. We'll beat them together."

" How ?"

" I'm going to shoot out the light. We can then strike for the street."

" Rapid, if you miss we are gone."

"But I won't miss ; and I see no other escape."

" This is no place for *us* to disagree," said O'Dare, drolly. " Is there but one pipe ?"

" Only one."

"Then we'll both shoot together, to make certain of it, and at one, two, three."

"You understand, O'Dare, that when we shoot we will drop to the floor and secure our pistols. The table will protect us a moment. You will give me your left hand, and with our brass knuckles we'll fight through the confusion until we reach the street"

During this rapid whispering, the black-browed semi-circle was beginning to move for attack.

"Count," said Cassel.

"One,—two,—*three*," said O'Dare, and in a twinkling the chandelier fell with a crash, and the room was in total darkness. A dozen pistol-shots succeeded, the ruffians roared and raved, and the gas poured in, filling the room with stench.

"Strike a light!" cried some one.

"*Never!*" shouted O'Dare, in an assumed voice, "you'll fire the gas and scorch our breath."

"Open the doors!"

"Hang on to O'Dare—whoever has him," was heard, in deep, fierce tones.

"Close in on them!" shouted another.

Meantime Cassel and O'Dare, with locked hands, burst through the deadly cordon, and succeeded in finding a door, leading they knew not where. It was locked. They kicked it open, and came upon rising steps. Ascending, they came to another door. It yielded to the turning of the knob. They found themselves in the dining-room of the establishment. The whole house was now in an uproar, and roughs were collecting from adjacent fastnesses. Opening another door, Cassel and O'Dare discovered that they were upon the rear threshold of the saloon. They were instantly recognized, and a general, tough mêlée ensued.

"Use your knuckles, Rapid, and let's keep together," hastily said O'Dare, "If it gets too fierce, blow them to hell with your pistols!"

"O'Dare, you're excited," said Cassel, knocking a fellow heels over head with a vigorous, scientific stroke.

"I'm alive," answered O'Dare, as he kicked one fellow in the groin, and sent another one buttocks over stomach into a far corner of the saloon.

The two gallant and athletic men fought their way out, receiving, *en passant*, some stunning blows themselves. Escaping into the street, they soon gained a place of safety. O'Dare was without a hat, and Cassel, having thrown off his coat at the beginning, was both coatless and hatless.

"You call that doing things quietly, do you, O'Dare?" asked Cassel, with provokingly gay criticism.

"But for a damned accident it would all have been smooth and quiet enough," said O'Dare.

"What changed the scene so suddenly just as I was about to leave?"

"A drunken fellow stumbled against me. Clutching at me for a support or a break-fall, he pulled off my head-gear and exposed me, and but for you, you bold, stanch fellow, I would have been in an almost inextricable fix. Rapid, you are the most complete man that I ever saw, let him come from Dan, or Beersheba, or from betwixt the two; and I do not judge you simply by the operations of to-night, either. I've studied you before, while you were asleep—or should have been, you young tiger-cat."

Catching up a cab, they were soon at O'Dare's office, and in the best of humors. O'Dare brought out some wine and cigars. Lifting a glass, the detective offered a toast,—

"Success—the measure of genius."

Cassel responded, significantly pointing to O'Dare's face,—

"A skinned cheek—the unmistakable trade-mark of desperate enterprises."

"You came cleaner off than I did, Cassel," said O'Dare, rubbing his bruised cheek. "But here; although I lost my faro outfit, I beat those fellows out of several hundred dollars. Shall I divide with you?"

"Give me fifty of it, O'Dare. I know a woman who needs it badly—the invalid mother of a little newsboy who brings me my papers."

"Here, Cassel, let it be a hundred; I will credit my account of *Mundus* vs. *Cœlum* with fifty dollars' worth of disinterested charity. Bring me a receipt from the
32*

woman," said O'Dare, with facetious absurdity, "for I preserve all such vouchers for the Last Settlement when the celestial book-keeper shall strike a balance throughout the Universe. I have some pretty good figures to show on that day."

Cassel resumed his own clothes, gave O'Dare the locket, and went home. He did not sleep well that night, for an active and annoying idea intruded upon his mind, and would neither be banished nor browbeaten. Early the next morning he repaired to the office of the detective.

"O'Dare," asked he, "has it occurred to you during the night just passed, that, if a sudden requisition was made upon the city of New York for its two most egregious fools, the committee of selection might, without useless hesitation, spot Hector O'Dare and Cassel Rapid?"

"Don't put me first, if you please," answered O'Dare. "But what's the trouble?"

"How is this locket, now that we have it, going to do us or anybody else any good?"

"Why not? It will prove up Miss Huron."

"But how?"

"This is the *copy*, mind you, and the copy was given to Oswald Huron's child, and was about the neck of it when the little corpse was brought to Philadelphia."

"But how are you to determine, legally, that this is the copy, to say nothing of to whom it was given?"

"I omitted to tell you," said O'Dare, "for the sake of brevity, that the daguerrean, who took the original, and from it the copy, is still operating. On his old books are charged to Neville Huron an original and a copy, a few days intervening between the entries. The dauguerrean is willing to swear that subsequent to those dates he never has taken similar pictures for Neville Huron."

"He must have a deuced good memory to swear by," said Cassel.

"No; his memory has a backer; for, a day or so after he had taken these pictures, his books show that he quit operating on daguerrotypes, and confined himself to the more recent styles of photography."

"He might have *copied* one, nevertheless."

"He is willing to swear that he did not. But admit

that he might have done so, this battered locket and bent plate will prove themselves."

" That will do, so far as the daguerrean, the locket, and the miniature are concerned ; but it won't yet prove to a court that this is the copy."

"We can prove that the copy was given to Oswald Huron's child, and that the child habitually wore it. Do you grant that ?"

" Yes."

" We can prove that this identical locket and miniature was about the neck of the dead infant. Do you grant that ?"

" Yes."

" We can prove by Mr. Neville Huron's invariable custom of parting his hair on the left side, that this is a copy. Do you grant *that* ?"

"No."

" The devil you don't !"

" No, I don't. If it was a blind eye, I would admit the proof. Or if his hair was friable, like glass, and he had been born with it parted on the left side, I would admit the proof. But as it was, and is, flexible, how can you establish the fact that it lay this way or that, on any particular occasion ? Nobody but himself, an excluded witness in this case, could swear to it. His own wife could not swear to it. Cora Glencoe's hopes are indeed vanished into invisible, thin air, if they are to hang for existence upon the scalp-locks of Neville Huron."

" Ph-e-w !" whistled O'Dare, like a man who had been suddenly halted—nonplused—countermarched.

" I knew a man once," said Cassel, " who sat down, and, as he supposed, made a careful estimate. Upon that estimate he embarked in business, and conducted it flourishingly for twelve months. He was to sell so many goods at such a profit, and his aggregate expenses were to be so much, and his yearly gain was to be the respectable balance between debit and credit. He oversold his calculation, and underwent his estimated expenses, but at the end of the year he found himself bankrupt. He went and looked over his old estimate. He had omitted to carry the figure 1, and it made a difference of ten thousand dollars against him. O'Dare, I think that in this matter you have omitted to carry the figure 1."

" Cassel," said O'Dare, with the assured gravity of Methuselah, " a cunning fox always has two entrances or exits to his burrow. To all that you have said, or may say, I emphatically answer—*buttons !*"

" O'Dare," replied Cassel, with some impatience, "don't be a downright fool."

O'Dare got up, unlocked a case, took out the locket, also a microscope, and with apparently inimitable nonsense, said,—

" Cassel, I repeat, and insist that it is—*buttons* "

" Well unbutton the thing and spread it out, that I may have a look at it."

O'Dare shook out the plate on which was copied in miniature the bust of Neville Huron, and placed it under the microscope.

" Here, said he, " are coat buttons on one side, only, of a single-breasted coat. Here are vest buttons, on one side, only, of a single-brested high-pressure vest. An open plait in the shirt-bosom shows a peeping button similarly situated. Any tailor will tell you, and swear to it, that in the make-up of single-breasted clothes the single row of buttons is always put on the right-hand side of a garment. So you see that '*buttons*' gives me the decayed timber, the rotten log, the gopher-wood, upon this question of copy identity. Look at your own clothes, and look at mine, and then take a microscopic view of the miniature, and retract your insinuation that I am a downright fool."

Cassel looked, and saw that it was so.

" How did you ever think of such proof, O'Dare ?"

" To tell the truth, I only thought of the buttons after I had gone to bed last night. My difficulty was the same as yours. I couldn't sleep. I beat about for a counter-irritant, and found it. It was buttons, only buttons. They are better proof than any head of hair, though it be as fine a head as Cassel Rapid tosses."

" You are quite certain now, are you," asked Cassel, "that you have a faultless case of it, and that the legal mind, after a thorough scrutiny, will feel absolutely convinced that Neville Huron is the father of Cora ?"

" No," positively replied O'Dare.

"What! I thought the locket was to be the keystone to your arch?"

"It is a difficult thing," said O'Dare, "to prove, to an absolute certainty, who is the *father* of *anybody's* children; but you can risk your happiness on the chance that *Mrs.* Neville Huron is Cora's *mother.*"

"O'Dare, you are merely a two-legged absurdity,—a fork-ed humbug."

"I beg your pardon," said O'Dare, with great impudence; "I had forgotten that in this Play of the 'Huron War' you are acting in the character of the Lover."

"If you were not such a useful leash-hound, I'd scalp you, O'Dare."

"See how he blushes! As red almost as a scalping Indian. You need not be ashamed of loving Cora, for I tell you, Cassel, she outshines the most of girls as the moon outshimmers the stars at night; and I am glad to know of you that your cheek is accessible to the pink spray of a modest youth's sweet shame."

"O'Dare," said Cassel, "you are so very awkward."

"No, I am as nimble and as softly-moving as a cream-seeking tabby-cat. Go you home now, put yourself on your mettle, and make your propositions. Get ahead of Harry Gray and all other sickish swains; close in as rapidly as Rapid may be, and clinch your happiness. I would myself bear Cora the news of her approaching emancipation, but I will not rob you of the prestige which good tidings always carry with the bearer. Tell Coy all about it, Cassel, and then drop like a shot hog down upon your knee-pans and blubber away at her. I have already telegraphed to Neville Huron."

"O'Dare, you are one of the seven Plagues; you are also the most audacious fellow in all the catalogue of brazen men. I was struck with the latter fact last night, when I turned about and saw you standing like a veritable and grinning Satan, surrounded by howling and revolted devils. But don't you feel a little sore from some of those heavy blows we received?"

"I do feel somewhat battered. I saw stars several times last night. But Mr. Attorney must have had just time enough to imagine that he had been struck by light-

ning when you hit him. That was the most sudden, cap-
sizing, and nicky thing of the night. But go, Cassel;
Coy is waiting for you."

"Why do you call her Coy?"

"That was the pet name for her when she was a child."

CHAPTER XXXV.

WHEN Cassel went home he found that Cora *was* actually waiting for him. He encountered her in the front
parlor. She was dressed in pure white—in gala costume
—in swiss, and hat, and flowers, and feathers, with peeping bosom and bare round arms. She looked like a blushing, sweet young Grace, hugged about by the soft and
feathery snow. Cassel had never seen her so surpassingly
lovely and ravishing, and he felt the wildfire kindling in
his blood. As he looked upon her the thought entered his
head that if Cora should ever turn against him, then would
the whole world drop out of existence.

"Mr. Rapid, I have been searching for you. Where
have you been so early?"

"Out into the city. What is your pleasure?"

"I have a favor to ask of you," said Cora, modestly.

"Not the half, but the whole, of my kingdom is subject
to your requisitions. I give you *carte blanche.*"

"I do not intend that you shall be so extravagant,"
replied Cora. "The favor which I am encouraged to ask
is very simple, though, if granted, will be highly valued."

On that day there was to be a procession of school-girls,
pupils of Miss Lightner, the young mistress heretofore
mentioned. Miss Lightner had the intellectual charge and,
to-day, the processional conduct of these school-children.
They were to march through certain pleasant streets, take
an excursion train, and go out to a rural picnic, where the
air was free and the trees were full of birds, whose June
throats sent twittering melody upon the soft summer wind.
Miss Lightner had requested Cora to accompany and

assist her. Cora had agreed to do so, and also to ask Cassel Rapid to act as Marshal of the Day. Cassel promptly consented. Nothing was more delightful to him than to grant a request from Cora; and to be out an entire day with a lot of little virgins, and with Cora for the dearest of them all, promised to be very pleasant to him.

"You are to go on horseback,—that is, through the streets," said Cora, persuasively,—"and you are to wear a sash."

"That doesn't disconcert me in the least. I think I'll go all the way on horseback."

"But how will you keep up with the cars?"

"Easily enough. There is a fine road running along by the track for some miles, and a good racker or trotter can beat the common time of a locomotive, in a short heat. At all events it will be a diversion to the school-children to see me try it."

"We shall laugh at you if you come up lagging"

"Laugh and grow fat," said Cassel. Not that he thought Cora in need of a single ounce of flesh; she was just right,—just upon the verge of voluptuousness, five feet four inches tall, a one-hundred-and-twenty-four-pounder, and every pound symmetrically bestowed, if the word of madame, her dress-maker, was entitled to belief.

Cora retired and completed her gala array. Cassel rigged himself, and appeared in front of the Boyd mansion mounted upon the proud stallion with the black mane and black feet. Linda and Cora were out on the balcony. Cassel saucily threw a kiss at them. Linda responded with a blushing rose which she dropped down to him.

"Little sister," said Cassel, "please go into my room and bring me my lasso. It is hanging in the rack, on the left."

Linda disappeared, with the backward glance of an affectionate, fond sister. How radically different she now felt herself to be, compared to the green and outrageous little bumpkin which she was when Cassel first took charge of her steps and education!

While Linda was absent, Cassel said to Cora,—

"I'll show you something of my cow-boy training

to-day, if we should happen upon a loose animal in the vicinity of the picnic. Did you ever see the lasso fly ?"

"I have seen it wielded, once, but have never seen it cast," answered Cora, with a sensation of horror at her heart, for she never could forget the pursurer and pursued, down on the Larboard Strand.

Linda came back with the lasso.

"Heave it down," said Cassel.

She threw it, and catching it, he fastened one end to the pommel of his saddle, and hung the coil in a ring hook at the side. He then rode away to the rendezvous, and soon, to the stirring clap-trap of a kettle-drum and brass band, he led the gay and flowery procession past the Boyd mansion, where Cora came down and joined with Miss Lightner. The school-girls were delighted with the knightly pomp of their handsome young marshal, and Cassel exerted himself to give *éclat* and spirit to the enterprise.

Taking the cars, the excursionists passed slowly out of the city into the country, where the engineer spurred up his iron steed and the pale horse had to buckle down to work. Away they went, the horse of iron and the horse of flesh contending for the decisive neck. A cut would ever and anon flash between them, but again they would emerge, neck and neck together. The engineer looked with admiration upon the emulous and splendid animal, whose proud crest was forward, and whose busy feet came down as regular and rapid as the ticking of a Swiss watch. The school-girls waved their handkerchiefs, and cheered with enthusiasm. Cassel threw kisses at them, to which they gayly responded. He ventured to throw a kiss at Cora. With instant propriety she sent him back a flying air-kiss—for was she not a pupil, and should she distinguish herself from the others ? He was even bold enough to assault Miss Lightner, but she was not competent to notice it otherwise than by a graceful wave of the hand, and a thought of "what a fine young noble he is !"

The excursion proved to be delightful beyond the ambitious pitch of even Miss Lightner. The uncaged school-girls capered with lithe limbs over the green pasture, and blushed with exercise and pleasure.

Cora and Cassel were sitting to themselves, in the wavy shade of a low spreading tree whose branches yielded to the soft force of a gentle though fickle wind. Cassel felt that compensating Time had shivered the tenacious seal which circumstances had set upon his heart, and that he could now enter upon whilom forbidden things. He indulged in beautiful pastorals, which he was very capable of doing, and swept with nimble thought and imagination through all the known fields of real and unreal enchantment.

"Mr. Rapid," said Cora, "what teaches you to talk so well?"

"To talk *well*," answered Cassel, "is simply to tell the truth. If a person can talk at all, it must be here, where everything is so pure, and fair, and suggestive."

"And so free," rejoined Cora. "It has been a long time to me since I have been out in the forest and among the birds. I feel now like a hind let loose. I imagine that the deepest secret could not live here, but would needs peep out to enjoy a little freedom, and thereby die of discovery."

"What you say is so aptly true," replied Cassel; "for under the influence and pervasions of this spot, which to me is to be the sweetest or bitterest spot on earth, I can no longer fetter the clamoring secret that I love you."

Sudden though it was, Cora did not start, seem overcome, or exhibit the least surprise. The announcement had been made so gently and so naturally, and was so entirely divested of the customary ill-conceived accompaniments, that it fell upon her and melted in, like a snowflake falling upon a warm rock. Cora blushed and pouted, and looked at Cassel with an infinitely sweet and relenting reproach. He was confident that there was never such a *ravissante* little maid in the wide world, as she dared his feasting, inquiring eyes, with her blush, and pout, and sweet reproach.

"Are you surprised?" asked Cassel.

"No—yes."

"A definite answer—but are you angry?"

"No."

33

"Then what means that little beacon-light of reproach which warns me to beware?"

"To be candid, Mr. Rapid, I am disappointed in you."

"Why, Cora? Is it a fault to love you?"

"Yes or no, as you like. But to dismiss the subject as lightly as you have introduced it, I can refer you to no 'parent,' should I feel ever so slight a disposition to make such a reference."

"There, Cora, is your mistake. I have transgressed neither the law of etiquette nor delicacy. The hour has come, in which I may speak and you may respond. Do not be excited now, and I will read you the latest pages of your history."

But Cora *was* excited, and she listened with exquisite sensibility and interest to Cassel while he detailed the history of O'Dare's last night's operations, and then made her understand the sure results which would follow. He then pressed Cora for an answer to his special plea.

"But why are you in such hot haste about it?"

"Haste! My most exemplary patience has snapped its cords. And then," said Cassel, telling a fruitful fib, "I am afraid of Harry Gray."

"Pshaw!" protested Cora, who, in her eagerness on the one hand, betrayed herself on the other.

"You *do* love me, don't you, Cora?" said Cassel, with sweet and gentle urging.

"Yes—I—*do*, if nothing else will satisfy you."

"Nothing else in this world will. How long have you loved me, you little dove?"

"Only since your avowal—a few moments."

"Now, Cora," saucily and joyously objected Cassel.

"Not longer, then, than you have loved me, I can tell you."

"Are you sure?"

"Yes,—unless you are the most deceitful fellow in the world."

"I confess that I have been very deceitful with you, you rose-lipped darling; for never by word or look have I intimated to you the thousandth part of my affection. Not until I have the opportunity fondly to show it will you be able to conceive how deathly dear you are and ever shall be to me."

"Why so very dear?" asked Cora, thrilled by the deep tenderness of his voice.

"Because you are pure as mountain snow, warm-hearted as love, and stanch as steel. I could load the air with reasons. And, as I once told you, I am the Logan of my house, having no living thing, but Cora, to love. You are dearer to me than vengeance to the vengeful."

"Vengeance! Why do you mar the moment with that painful, crimson word?"

"Because it suits my comparison, being *priceless* in the estimation of men."

"I did not know it."

"I will not teach you of it. Whether it comes from Above or Below I know not; but it has been, and is, in the heart of immemorial Man, and the blood of Christ has failed to wash it out. But come away from it," said Cassel, humorously, "and let us be foolish as all fresh lovers are."

"I'll play the fool with no one, by request," said Cora, with mock sobriety and unwillingness, while her eyes rested with infinite tenderness on her lover.

Cora, who was as fiery as she was firm, had thought that she loved Cassel before; but now that her heart was unlocked, she felt in her roused bosom the headlong gush of all her soul, spangling through her veins, and thickening in her throat. At this moment she could have wound her arms about her lover's neck and died upon a kiss. Out of the gloom of Cliff Hall had she been plucked, and transported into a sphere of active life, and light, and happiness, and love, like a sweet star, hitherto without form and void, sent singing into the field azure of a summer evening sky. And now her lover was impatient to garland her way with flowers, and make the air about her hazy with the gossamers of love. How bright the future seemed to her, intrinsically bright, but more brilliant still, when compared with the past! She felt now that wickedness, and sorrow, and anguish, and ills, had fled the world, and that only rainbows spanned the heavens, and only music swept the air; that life was not indeed a gloomy vale, nor its charms but lurid meteors, nor man but evil, nor gold but dross. The primrose chaplet about the giddy head was now all appropriate ; the flowery circle of dancing school-girls was all appropriate; the trained melody of chords and pipes was all appropriate ; the music gushing from the free bird's throat, as it swung in the green bough, was all appropriate ; strike the cymbal ! let God be praised, and. man rejoice, for O this is a happy, happy world ! So felt Cora Glencoe with her lover beside her. In less than an hour she would feel as one dead and yet conscious to suffer. ·

Cassel found no occasion or opportunity for displaying his skill as an expert *lazador*, except that he had already cast the invisible loop of love over the white neck of the coyest little antelope of a girl, and drawn her to him with a charmed cord and so gently, that she was soon subdued, and happy, and confident at his side,—ready to skip with him over the lawns, or bask with him by the waterfalls, and in the pleasant places. Cora and Cassel, giving sigh for sigh and pledge for pledge, plighted themselves for-ever.

> "I am thine, and thou art mine,
> Body and soul forever."

Miss Lightner came and requested the lovers to lend their voices to the singing of an anthem which was to close the rustic pleasures of the day.

> "Praise Him,—praise Him,
> Ye shouting nations praise Him."

The school-girls, with their conductors, then repaired to the railroad, to be in readiness. Cassel put his ear to a rail and notified the company that the cars were coming. Here was an opportunity for Miss Lightner to give her pupils a practical lesson in the philosophy of sound, and in a few moments every pupil had her ear upon a rail. Cassel, a rascal, stood off and compared their ankles.

"Are you going to race with us again?" asked Miss Lightner, pleasantly.

"No," replied Cassel. " I must be kind to my horse, for he has been very kind to me.. He is now eight years old, and since I first got upon his back and subdued him, he has never failed me a single step. The only thing about him which I dislike, and at the same time like, is, that he is too fierce ; he will let nobody groom him but me. Our stableman has to lower his food to him from the loft, and unless I curry him myself he gets no currying at all. He will admit of no hair-dresser or valet but me. But I love to fondle him, he is so affectionate and grateful. Would you like to see him and me in a play?"

" I would indeed."

Cassel threw the reins over the pommel of the saddle, and ran out upon the lawn. The horse rushed after him, neighing, and rearing, and snorting, and wheeling about him. Lightly as a young panther, Cassel, disdaining the stirrup, sprang into the saddle and stretched away. Back again he came with furious speed, and, when just abreast of Miss Lightner, he swooped from his saddle, plucked a white wild-flower from the ground, recovered himself, and instantly brought the proud horse upon his haunches with his forelegs buried to the knees almost in the spongy soil. As Cassel sat upon his quivering wild-eyed steed, his cheeks rosy with the violence of his feat, and holding up the little bloom which he had snatched from the sward, Miss Lightner, whose mind was classic and artistic, thrilled with the consciousness that she had not dreamed of a life-picture so vivid and heroic. The school-girls were actually frightened, until they saw that Cassel was safe and un-hurt. Into Cora's heart came a pang. Whence it came she could not divine, unless from the memory of the deed down on the Larboard Strand, which Cassel's swift action had recalled.

" Mr. Rapid," said Miss Lightner, " you have electrified me. I have read of such deft and brilliant feats, but put them down as merely fanciful. I see plainly that I have many things to learn. But permit me now to thank you thoroughly for the favor you have done us all, and me espe-cially, by coming with us and making our little excursion so delightful a success."

" Miss Lightner," replied Cassel, with a covert glance at Cora, " I can very well afford to assure you that I am amply repaid by the distinction with which you have honored me, and the pleasure I have enjoyed in company with so much loveliness and intelligence."

The young school-mistress was unaffectedly grateful to Cassel, and gratified at the prosperous issue of the day.

"The cars are in sight," said Cassel, who rode away to meet the excursionists in the city, form the procession, and conduct it to the point of disintegration.

The pleasure-party were soon again in the city, and, this time without music, were moving gayly along a wide and handsomely-built street, when from far up the street came cries, and shouts, and yells, and reports of pistol-shots, while, from his saddle, Cassel could see a commotion of people dashing here and there into doors, and actively seeking places of security. The commotion and alarm drew nearer and nearer, until Cassel discovered the rapidly-approaching cause. A brace of infuriated, half-wild Western steers were rushing down the street, maddened by their strange surroundings, and by the missiles and wounding pistol-balls which were launched at them, lunging and goring at every salient object in their way. Cassel saw that his little school of children were in direct and imminent danger of being scattered and gored and trampled upon the pave. Luckily he had taken his pistols with him to the picnic, as a law against roughs and strolling vagabonds. Knowing that he had not a moment to lose, he spurred his trained horse forward to meet the mad brutes. The leader made directly for this new antagonist, savagely shaking its head, and leveling its pointed horns for ripping, bloody work. Cassel sent a pistol-bullet into the brain of the foremost animal and dropped it dead in its tracks. Its companion, rendered yet more furious, came bolting forward and lunged desperately at the pale horse. Cassel had barely time to spring his horse aside and escape the formidable horns. The mad steer plunged by him, and started for the school-children who were now in frightful peril. They had kept together, along the sidewalk, backed by a blank wall. They had not appreciated their danger, which was multiplied tenfold by their red sashes, and Cassel had no time to tell them of it. As the mad brute escaped him, with a glance of fire Cassel wheeled his fierce stallion, and as no pistol-shot from the rear could halt the danger, with the quick, sharp cry of the *lazador* he waked up the bold breast of the stallion, wielded the lasso above his head, and came like a rushing thundershaft down the street. It was now that the champion of the prairies was in full career, and now it was that something, more dreadful than any wild brute's hoof or horn, *gored* through the heart of Cora Glencoe, and overthrew her, and trampled out her life. Here again was pursuer and pursued; and here again, coming like an angel of death, was the matchless and terrible horseman, who, in fierce pursuit, had spurned the sands of the Larboard Strand, who had driven Jonas Aiken into the sea, and three times plunged the dagger to his heart. Here indeed was the unknown murderer! Recognition, like a flash of lightning, pierced her soul, and all her recent full-hearted happiness and wildering joys were scorched and withered up and consumed, as grass before the wind-driven fire. Cora drooped senseless to the pavement, just as Cassel, with an unerring cast, lassoed the forelegs of the wild brute, and tripped it almost at the feet of Miss Lightner, who stood her ground, but with pale terror in her face. In another moment, Cassel put an end to the danger with his pistol. His action had been brave and magnificent, and waked up the enthusiasm of every one who saw it. He was greeted with cheer after cheer from the street, and the waving of handkerchiefs from the overlooking windows. But soon he saw Miss Lightner kneeling and supporting Cora. He sprang from his horse.

"She has fainted!" said Miss Lightner, quickly. "Get some water!"

Cora was soon restored to consciousness, but when Cassel offered his tender assiduities she turned from him with a look of mingled horror and unutterable reproach. He thought it but the effects of still lingering fright. He arranged for Miss Lightner to accompany Cora to the Boyd mansion in a carriage, and he would take charge of the children, and dismiss them home.

When Cassel returned to the mansion, he felt a bleak fear enter his breast with what he was told. Linda informed him that Cora looked like marble, and was almost as quiet. That she was perfectly rational, and was not,

in any ordinary sense, ill.   That she had already written
a letter, which Linda herself had read, *demanding* of Mr.
Hope that he should take her home; that if he did not
send for her, she would go herself to Cliff Hall at the expiration of a stated day.

"She will give me no explanation, though she is still
affectionate to me, or tries to be," said Linda.   "She
sheds no tears, complains of nothing, but looks at me as
if her heart was dead within her; as if her whole body
was dead, and her soul was yet inhabiting the corpse.
Oh, it is *terrible!*" and Linda broke away with tearful
lamentations.   Coming back, Linda said, "I asked her to
see you, but she went into ice, and coldly spurned the request.   Brother, there is something out of common that
is pressing upon and afflicting Cora.   Oh, if you could
only see her desperate, hopeless-looking eyes, you would
think that murder had been committed upon everything
in this world which she had loved and cherished!   I know
not what to do, and her immovable opposition bars me of
your assistance.   Why it is, God only knows."

Cassel was most agonizingly confounded.   Cora, whose
mental constitution he knew to be cast in the healthiest
mould, and whose rosy lips but an hour ago had formed
the sweetest words in the universe for him, now to turn
about and spurn the very sight of him!   It was beyond
all earthly alchemy to analyze the motives of such extreme
and dreary conduct.   But Cassel had a hope, that when
Cora recovered fully from her fright, as he conceived it,
she would again be as she had been.   He was urged by
all the tenderness which he felt for her, to go to her,
break up what evidently was an illusion, and soothe her
back again to lively joy, but he prudently decided first to
get Linda to give her some composing draught, which
would steady her shaken nerves, or put her to sleep.

"Cora, take this," said Linda.

"What is it?"

"Something to restore you."

"I do not want it."

"Brother Cassel sent it."

"*Take it away!*"

Linda came back and told Cassel that Cora would not
have it.

The blighted young girl held but one imperial, overpowering, disastrous feeling to her heart. He, whom she had
given herself to love as a god, was a *devil.* Lucifer had
come upon her and exalted her, only to break her cruelly
against a stone. Her tender heart was now as bleak as
the snow-clad wastes of winter. Cut away from all the
world, she felt alone like a dying cygnet drifting upon a
boundless tide. Bootless was it that at Creswood was a
venerable man who loved her: bootless was. it that in
Philadelphia were arms ready to receive her, for with
them she had not grown up and intertwined. Fate had
cast her out, and there was nothing under the vault of
heaven to which she might fondly cling, or upon which
she could rest in peace.

Never again did Cora sit at the family board of Linda
Boyd. She took her meals in her room, and would neither
see Cassel Rapid nor communicate with him. Cassel's
heart was completely harrowed up by anxiety, suspense,
mystery, and painful vigil. Cora's conduct was so strangely
and stubbornly inexplicable. Except upon the hypothesis
of partial insanity, he could find no shadow of reason or
excuse for her, and even upon that ground, the calamity
which confronted him would be superlatively painful, and
disastrous to his hopes for both Cora and himself. He
often contended against a strong and active impulse to
force himself into her presence, imagining that he could
bring back the color to her cheeks and the live light to her
eyes; but he hardly could thrust himself upon her in the
face of her repeated and positive denials, lest it should aggravate her condition, granting that hallucination was the
ruler of her otherwise unaccountable ways. Days passed,
and Cassel, remembering her mad uncle, could not otherwise conclude but that Cora was suffering from partial
insanity superinduced by fright. The suddenness and
singularity of the peril which had so rudely threatened
her and her companions, and possibly the additional aspect
of her lover being in the very jaws of the danger, had
caused her, as Cassel thought, to faint. When she recovered her consciousness, it was accompanied by the
glamour that her lover was himself the peril, and that, by
reason of his swift and vivid action, a fear of him had

lodged within her breast and was ever present to her mind, making her think of him with an insane dread, which time alone would cure. Cassel was satisfied that there was no other foundation in the broad world upon which to build an explanation.

Cora had occasion and incentive, greater than ordinary, to cut the words, deep and sharp, into the tablet of her code, that she would "countenance no man-slayer;" for the subject had been brought home to her, crimsoned with the red wash of human blood. Her uncle had again and again insulted and spit upon a man, and had then killed him for resenting the injuries. But he was her father, as she had thought, and the lock of lineage had held her to him. But with her own eyes she had seen Cassel Rapid rush like a tiger upon his fellow and *kill* him. She felt that, knowingly, she could never touch a bloody hand. She was outraged that Cassel, knowing her principles so well, should have come upon her with his sealed history and fatal beauty, pillaging her of all she had, only to repay her with the hated offering of a red hand. But, like alms to an impostor, her heart was given, and could never be recalled. Not that she regarded Cassel as still worthy of her love, but there were now *two* Cassel Rapids in her little world: the one was her matchless lover and the child of the Sun; the other was a man-slayer and the slayer of her peace. From the remembrance of her *lover* she could no more escape than the stars can escape the Infinite Glance which lights them. She must still love what Cassel Rapid *appeared* to be—but what he actually was, *never!* She must worship the myth, but never again the man.

Oswald Huron was unmistakably and violently deranged. To all who were compelled to remain with him, he made Cliff Hall a foretaste of what they might expect, should the devil wait upon them at their death-beds, and carry them below. Vindictively his mind ran upon the subject of Cora, and he had already determined to spurn the agreement which he had made, and summon her home. If need should be, he would go for her himself.

He went out one day where the accident occurred which leads to a great portion of this narrative, and leaned over

the bluff to look down upon the spot where, more than sixteen years previously, an infant was broken and mangled.
The sight of it seemed to madden him and charm him.
He lingered there all day, steeped in acrimonious gloom,
under the influence of the Apollyon, which, to his own
knowledge, haunted him. Late in the evening, the evil
spirit that was in him seemed to rend him, and with a
frantic cry he rushed forward and sprang wildly over the
precipice and was dashed to pieces. One of the negroes,
who had been detailed regularly to watch him in his
wanderings, but who feared to approach him, saw his sui-
cidal leap, and sped home with the news of it.

Before Mr. Hope could send for Cora, Neville Huron
came up from Philadelphia. He brought her the first
tidings of Oswald Huron's death, and qualified the news
by suggesting to Cora that however much the fatality was
to be lamented, it struck from her pathway the only obstacle
to her peace and permanent happiness. But Mr. Huron
found his daughter in a condition, of which he could get
no satisfactory understanding, from her or any one else.
She would only tell him that her life was bankrupt; that
it had almost ever been so; and that he must take her
home as a flower that was dead. The father was inex-
pressibly grieved. He urged upon Cora that her trials
were over, that she now had a father, and mother, and
brother, and sisters, who would hedge her about with love,
and coax or steal away the poisonous residuum of the past.
He regarded Cora as having been wearied out by the constant strain which life had put upon her. He was now
prepared to cut the straining cords, give her a cheerful
range, and bring out the sun to shine upon her, and restore
her. But Cora's hopes had been wrecked, just as the
clouds had broken away and let in the light of the dearest
day of all her life. Her happiness in the very hour of
its birth had been beheaded, as by the sweeping cimeter
of Saladin. Although she was now possessed of a home
where wealth and affection would greet and gird her, she
felt that she would carry into that home a shadow which
would darken its walls, and a burden which would oppress
its joy. She felt that "Cora Glencoe," as she had not
been in the past, would not be in the future, essential to

the happiness or integrity of the house of the Hurons; that the family circle was complete without her; that no accustomed niche was there for her to occupy; and that instead of inhabiting she would *haunt* the house that gave her birth. Could her sisters love her as they would have done, had the associations of childhood locked and linked them together? Could her parents love her as though she had learned to coo upon their lap and knee, and vex and delight them with the importunities and enchantments of early childhood? Could any of them love her at all, and would they not weary of her, coming among them, as she would, with a cheek that was wan, and a heart that was faint from the sappings of that vampire—Care? The element of steel in Cora's composition, which had sustained her in her miserable life with Oswald Huron, was melted by the heat of the fiery furnace through which she had just passed, so that she drooped beneath the weight of her crosses, and swayed with the behests of the pitiless blast.

CHAPTER XXXVI.

CASSEL RAPID and Cora Glencoe were each in that condition which induces many faulty-headed people to commit the Rash Act—Suicide. But neither of them thought of such a desperate way out of their desperate troubles.

Of the two, Cassel was the more hopeful, and consequently the more restless. Although he was as one lost in the night, without star or beacon to guide him, he trusted that the morning would come again perhaps, and smiling Aurora light up his pathway, that he might pursue it. But he was compelled to admit to himself that his trust was a wretched one at best.

Cassel had suffered before, when anguish, deep beyond the reach of soothing plummet, had overwhelmed him. But *then* he knew the wherefore. Now, he could not conceive or conjecture, far or near, why it was that Cora, so immediately after having given her heart to him, should utterly turn against him as though he had done her an aggravated and unpardonable wrong, disdaining even to accuse him, but, by her actions, telling him plainly that he himself well knew the great sin which he had committed against her.

The idea that Cora's condition arose from glamour or insanity, no longer stood him in stead, for both Linda and Miss Lightner insisted that Cora was as sane as he was himself, and that she was undoubtedly acting from an unclouded and intelligent will.

Cora had gone home. It seemed useless for Cassel to follow her; but not to do so, and never to find out what this unimaginable thing could be which had come between them, would harass him through his whole life, let that life be what or where it might.

Cassel was not a man to give up. Neither was he a man to waste himself in bootless enterprises which promised nothing. If, therefore, Cora *would not* see him, hear him, or communicate with him directly or indirectly, what could he do? But for his unlimited confidence in Cora's truth and justice, he neither could nor would have undertaken anything whatever. He would have acknowledged the stroke as once before he had acknowledged a deeper and more disastrous one. But, convinced as he was that Cora, in her opinion and action, was conscientiously true to herself, he determined to do the only thing left for him to do. He would endeavor, by watching and waiting, himself to solve the mystery, despite her absolute taciturnity. But how should he go about it, and where should he commence? His first step was to write to Mr. Hope (by Garland, who had come up to New York for Cora, not knowing that Neville Huron had taken her home), and inform the old minister of everything that had ever transpired between himself and Cora, then solicit the minister's advice and intervention. Giving Mr. Hope time to write to the young girl, hear from her, and then write back to him, he waited impatiently for the result of his first step. Finally a letter came, and Cassel, expectantly, opened it. But it broke like an apple of the Dead Sea, containing little else but ashes.

"Do not ask me to *write* it to you," Cora had only written, so far as the cause of her attitude toward Cassel was involved in the correspondence.

From this reply Mr. Hope inferred, and so intimated to Cassel, that, should he ever have the opportunity, he might induce Cora to *tell* it to him.

"I am confident," wrote Mr. Hope, "that she would tell me, if I could only see her; which, at present, I cannot."

Cassel reflected that Cora was in Philadelphia and the old minister in Creswood, and that they might never meet again. She would certainly not go down to Creswood to confer with Mr. Hope, and it was not to be expected that the old minister would go up to Philadelphia to interfere with Cora. Cassel could not ask it of him. But notwithstanding that it was a long and tedious journey for age and infirmity to undertake, and that the errand was a presumptuous one, this venerable and goodly man *did* go to the far city, in behalf of the son of his benefactor,—but not until other events in this, our history, had transpired.

Cassel, upon receipt of Mr. Hope's letter, appreciated the difficulties which contravened a natural or probable meeting between the minister and Cora; also, could he even bring them together, the slim, rare chance that the obstinate girl would be more communicative with Mr. Hope than with others who had been as sisters to her,—namely, Linda and Miss Lightner; or than with himself, who had been her tender guardian and still more tender, outspoken lover. Cassel had played his first and strongest card, and the trick was against him. A long night of anxiety and oppressive thrall was before him.

But, as drowning men will catch at straws and bubbles, or the wounded leopard seek familiar haunts, Cassel, from somewhat similar impulses, looked in upon Hector O'Dare; not that he anticipated consulting him, but O'Dare, professionally, was intimately connected with the Hurons, could talk about them, and probably tell him next to nothing about Cora. But that would be better than absolutely nothing at all.

Cassel liked O'Dare; first, because O'Dare liked Cassel, and had done him unforgotten favors; second, the detective was a capital fellow; third, he was the best of company, and never below par.   When O'Dare had the leisure to gossip and joke with him, Cassel, who was something of a loafer, could not find in all New York a more pleasant lounging-place than the office of the detective.

O'Dare was a cautious man, as well as a cautious detective, and trusted no one implicitly; but he probably did trust Cassel to greater lengths than he trusted any other man alive, not excepting his confidential clerk.   And he frequently amused the young man, by the hour, or the half hour, according as time was precious, with details of inimitable incidents and casualties which had interlaced and befallen his professional career.

When Cassel entered the detective's office on the occasion in question, O'Dare met him with his usual droll bravado, slapped him on the shoulder, and bantered him for another wrestling match.

"No," said Cassel.   "I am not in the humor to-day."

O'Dare's quick eye detected that Cassel was inclined to be serious, if not dejected.   He rejoined,—

"It's not far from here to Philadelphia, Rapid.   What are you down in the mouth about?   If you have no money to pay your passage, I'll dead-head you."

"Sit down, O'Dare, and act like a sensible human."

"That is to say, act in character—act myself—act Hector O'Dare, for instance," replied the detective, laughing. "But, by the other way,—(most people preface by saying 'by the *way*,' but Hector generally admonishes with 'by the *other* way,' for you can always anticipate a change of direction when you hear that significant 'by the *way*'),— therefore, by the other way, you have been indulging in a little adventure lately, and all by yourself."

"What?" asked Cassel.

"What! Why, the papers were full of it.   '*Tremendous*' is no adjective at all.   '*Magnificentissimus*' is a dwarf compared with the string of type which printed you a hero.   A frantic drove of wild-cattle were about to run, hoof and horns, over the city.   You halted, shot, and lassoed the last one of them.   Why didn't you whistle for me, and let me share the glory?"

"O'Dare, your enthusiasm outstrips your discretion.

You would earn a good salary as 'local' to a sensational column."

" These roustabout locals *do* get a little droll sometimes, don't they ?   But, by the other way, what is the drollest thing in life that you ever read ?"

" It would be an endless job to consider your question."

" Well, I can tell you the drollest thing that Hector O'Dare ever read, and make a short job of it at that."

" Suppose you tell it, then," said Cassel.

" It is the last clause—second verse—sixteenth chapter —Genesis, — and reads so: ' And Abram hearkened to the voice of Sarai,'—ha! ha! ha! h-a!" and O'Dare laughed as heartily as if the Bible, which in the main he venerated, had been a collection of facetiæ.

" I don't discover anything very droll in that," said Cassel, who was not very much inclined to laugh.

" I know you don't.   But you will, when you go and look at the context."

" Which I shall probably not do," carelessly observed Cassel.

" I don't care whether you do or not."

Chatting awhile, O'Dare finally asked,—

" What the devil is the matter, Rapid? I never saw you look so sober, or heard you laugh with less unction in all my life.   In fact you don't laugh at all, but put me off with a grin so dry that it actually makes me athirst.   Is there anything swagging, or rotten, in the build of ye ?"

" We all have our serious moments."

" To be sure; but you are not only serious, but despondent.   By the other way,—that is, to change the subject entirely, don't you think, Cassel, that I am entitled to your confidence in a matter in which I did you prime service, but about the sequel of which you have never vouchsafed me a word ?   I have respected your silence," said O'Dare, with true feeling, which made him both dignified and graceful, " and will continue to do so upon the slightest intimation. You know what I mean."

" I do.   You wish me to tell you in what manner I met Jonas Aiken and killed him."

" You have stated it with a perspicuity absolutely frightful," exclaimed O'Dare, who did not appear very much frightened however.

Cassel described, more minutely than we have done, the tragedy of the Larboard Strand where Jonas Aiken was so swiftly sent to his well-deserved doom.

" Just as I or any other man with a heart in him would have done it," said O'Dare. "And now, while you are in a confiding humor, tell me why you are so dashed to-day. Maybe I can help you."

" I fear it is beyond the reach of all your skill."

" There are few things which cannot be manipulated or managed by deft hands."

"And this," replied Cassel, "proves thus far to be one of the few."

" Is it money ?"

" No."

" Then I know what it is."

" What ?"

" Disappointment here," and O'Dare touched the region of his heart.

" Why do you fly so quickly from the pocket to the breast?"

" Because, when a man is brave, honest, wealthy, in good health, young, unmarried, handsome as a Greek ideal, and is without kindred to lose, or bring him into trouble, there is but one thing which can rule him so dreadfully below par as I find you to-day. Why, Rapid, your countenance is not worth two bits on the original dollar. Tell me of the complication, my young sweetheart of a boy, and I may be able to untangle the tangle for you. I may possibly help you *some* at the very least. Is it little Coy who is troubling you? I know it is, and you need no longer try to hide your elephant behind a handkerchief."

" O'Dare, you have shrewdly guessed, and your shrewdness shall be the purchase-money for my confidence. I *am* in trouble, and it *is* Coy, as you call her, who is the cause of it. But it is not the ordinary trouble of a lass-lorn school-boy which is affecting me ; there is something strange about it,—so strange that I can in no way account for it. I will tell you."

Cassel detailed to O'Dare the particulars of his tribulation, and then asked,—

" Now, what do you think of it ?"

"As you said, it is a very strange thing indeed," answered the detective, who, after reflecting a moment, observed, "You remember that her Uncle Oswald was insane; and, by the other way, did you know that he is dead?"

"I remember his insanity, and also know of his death; but I am well assured that insanity has nothing to do with Cora's actions."

"Fright cannot have superinduced such conduct, for she is a girl of as fine nerve as any that I know. I have seen her often, and I especially tried her once myself, down on the beach at Creswood;" and O'Dare told Cassel of the time when he gave Cora the gem pistol while she was sitting alone upon the Tarpeian Rock.

"She was sitting exactly there when I sent that hellhound to his doom," said Cassel, with a lightning glance which indicated that his soul would never sleep over that deed and the cause of it; "and she saw me do it, for it was done right before her eyes."

"Has she ever recognized you as the party?" asked the detective.

"Not that I know of,—in fact I know that she has not."

"You were riding that fierce stallion?"

"Yes."

"And came up the strand in hot speed?"

"Yes."

"Wielding your lasso?"

"Yes."

"Rapid, I have it," said O'Dare, quietly, but with a gleam of triumph from his cool clear eyes.

"Have what?"

"I hold the mystery in solution."

Cassel sprang up, and in a voice half stern, said,—

"O'Dare, do not mock me, I warn you!"

"I am *not* mocking you, quick thunderbolt that you are. You are the last man on earth whom I would either dare or desire to mock. Sit down, and I will hold up to your view the *solution* as in a crystal goblet, that you may look it through and through."

Cassel sat down, with his eyes fixed upon O'Dare, who continued, distinctly and succinctly,—

"When, the other day, you came rushing down the street, after the mad steer, riding the identical pale stallion, wielding the identical lasso, and with war and exigency in your countenance, in the vivid picture she recognized you as the identical man who sent that devil Aiken to judgment. Cassel, she regards you as a *murderer!* There is the solution."

"O'Dare!" cried Cassel, again springing up, "you are a wizzard! You are the very Ithuriel at the touch of whose spear this monster of a thing stands revealed. But, thank Heaven, it is less terrible when revealed than when in disguise. Give me your hand, you cunning captor of secret and mercurial things; you have struck a light in the black firmament which overhung me and imprisoned me with its close horizon."

The two men locked hands and wrung each other vigorously. They were each elated with the discovery, for in it the detective triumphed and the lover hoped to triumph.

"Now, sir," said O'Dare, "do not doubt my willingness to serve you; and, above *all* things, never doubt my *capacity.*"

Cassel was exalted from his vale of despondency. That O'Dare had found the key to the troublous secret was beyond question. Neither did he question that Cora, when she should learn *why* it was that he had slain Jonas Aiken, would give him back all that she had so relentlessly taken from him.

"Cassel, your face is appreciated to six bits on the dollar, at the very least."

"O'Dare, I shall never again doubt your capacity. I have come to believe that in your subtlety you can almost tell me why water runs down hill."

The new aspect of his affairs had already induced Cassel to reoccupy his old familiar position of joking antagonism with O'Dare. But the detective, somewhat at length, replied,—

"There, lovely youth, you are mistaken altogether. I would greatly prefer an undertaking to put this and that together and block out a *reason* why one man *does*, and one woman *doesn't*, than vainly to endeavor to explain the mysteries of creation. I might tell you that water runs down hill under the influence of the attraction of gravitation, and that the attraction of gravitation is a mutual attraction between matter and matter, which draws the lesser to the greater; but if for the term 'attraction of gravitation,' I should substitute the equally illustrative term 'tom-fist-i-cus of the ox-cox-i-jis,' you would know just as well, under the latter term as under the former, what that influence *actually is*. Wiseacres describe Electricity as a fluid, for the sake of identification or of recording their wisdom, but Hector O'Dare is bold enough to *deny* that it is a fluid. Electricity, to the brainless creation, bears the same relation that *thought* does to brain-ed creation. Brain is the galvanic battery of thought, and sends it even beyond the invisible suns in the twinkling of an eye. Electricity is the corresponding essence or scintillating flint of the Material, sleeping as the child sleeps, or musing as man muses, except when Deity directs it in the heavens, or man vents it with artificial contrivances. To call Electricity a *fluid*, you may as well say that the letter A or the figure 9 is an ink spot or a chalk mark; whereas, each is an Idea. You may object to the assertion that Electricity to Materiality is what Mind is to the Flesh, on the substrata, that is, on the ground, that thought will traverse space and penetrate everywhere at will, while Electricity will shy from a feather bed, or halt before a wall of glass. I will answer that objection by suggesting that as there are some substances which are bad conductors of Electricity, or with which it has no affinity whatever, so are there some conditions of the brain which restrict thought,—for example, ignorance; also some very bad conductors of thought,—for example, *nonsense*,—ha! ha! ha! h-a!"

"By which very bad conductor, *nonsense*, you have endeavored to convey your ideas or thoughts to me. I can acknowledge the receipt of no single one of them. O'Dare, you talk like a wise fool."

"*Like* a fool, or *to* a fool?" laughed O'Dare. "I sometimes pick up a fool and literally larrup him with learning, and I was congratulating myself upon having secured an audience."

" Who would ever have dreamed that a simple rogue catcher was so ambitious, or so positive a wit! But give me a cigar and I will suck wisdom from you as a sponge sucks water."

" Shall I tell you all I know ?   Can you stand it ?"

" I do not wish to hear what you absolutely *know;* that would be too uninteresting and matter-of-fact.   Tell me what you suspect,—what you *darkly suspicion,*" said Cassel, with all his old humor creeping to his countenance.

O'Dare set out some wine.   Lifting a full glass, he said,—

"Cassel, I stick to my old toast,—' Success, the measure of genius.'   When you came in here you were only worth two bits on the dollar.   I have dragged you out of the Slough of Despond, and, by mixing a little sense with a good deal of nonsense, have bulled your market value to about ninety cents on the dollar.   I leave to Coy the pleasure of tossing you way up beyond par or price, if she chooses to do so.   But take your carcass out of my office, for I have not a single other minute to spare ;" and O'Dare rang for his clerk, whom he had dismissed when his interview with Cassel first promised to be a confidential one.

"I am going down to Creswood—have you any messages ?" asked Cassel.

" Yes.   Remember me to Captain Gale, of the White-cap ; and present the respects of the ' Geologist' to young Hope, the Creswood minister, a very clever, upright gentleman no doubt, but, on a well-remembered occasion, a most aggravating bore,—a regular curculio, spiking all my green fruit ;" and O'Dare rapidly explained to Cassel how the young minister had innocently annoyed him and almost upset his character of ' Geologist' once upon a time.

Cassel repaired to the Boyd mansion and notified Linda that he should be absent for an indefinite period.   Though anxious, she did not turn pale with dismay or break into a shower of grief, as she had done on a former occasion, for she now felt self-sustaining : her good-by was a smiling one, though a few tears which forced themselves out and rolled, like dewdrops from a blushing rose, off from her healthy cheeks, fully attested the presence and wakefulness of her affection and tenderness.

Cassel went down to Creswood, and with him went the pale horse. As the young man approached the house in which he was born—"Gift Home," but more generally spoken of in the neighborhood as the "Parsonage"—he saw Mr. Hope sitting bareheaded and alone upon the portico, watching the bold beauty of bulging, towering thunderheads, as they rose up from the sea and caught the golden flash of a summer evening's sun. With his snowy hair and patriarchal beard, and his benevolent countenance pensive with undefiled Religion and lighted with the halo of Faith, he seemed as an aged warrior resting from his battles, and confidently looking Above, from whence would come his everlasting victory. As Cassel came forward, this old man, hoary with good deeds, and ripe with duties well performed, and dreaming as it were in the holy reflection of that heaven to which he was so manifestly near, the youth experienced in his heart that the rare picture before him was far more noble and beautiful and touching and instructive than all the glittering panoramas of the vain and folly-seeking world. Cassel took off his hat and reverentially approached, as a stripling should approach a venerable grandfather whose works had made him worthy, and whose years had crowned him with majesty. Mr. Hope arose and met Cassel. Putting his broad right hand upon the uncovered head of the youth, and in a voice tremulous with fervor, he said,—

"May the blessings and mercies of God rest upon thee, my son,—now, henceforth, and forever."

Cassel leaned his head against the old minister's breast, and choked down his rising emotion. In a few moments the family was about him and he was receiving from every side a genuine and sprightly welcome.

During the evening, after tea, Mr. Hope, with reference to the things which he knew lay heavily against Cassel's heart, said, in answer to the youth's inquiring and pleading eyes,—

"To-morrow, and we will see each other."

CHAPTER XXXVII.

CASSEL rested as well as he might until the morrow. Mr. Hope, after breakfast, took him into the pastoral study, closed the door, and locked it.

"Now, my dear boy, tell me all."

Cassel felt that his fortunes were about to be put into the balance and weighed out to him ; that before him sat the future architect, moulder, and arbiter of his fate. Notwithstanding this, and that the pure truth might shatter his hopes forever, he came prepared to tell only the truth.

"Mr. Hope," said he, "since my last letter to you, I have had suggested to my mind what I confidently believe to be the foundation upon which my trouble is built."

"And you came to see me, and to tell me about it, that I may, if possible, remove the foundation, so that your trouble shall tumble to its own destruction ?"

"I came for that express purpose. But before I can ask you to befriend me in the new phase which my difficulties have assumed, I must tell you of a fact in my history which involves, not only the cause of my present trouble, but a *feature of humanity*, which feature few men regard differently from myself, but which, to you, may present an insuperable objection to the extension of your sympathy."

"Tell me all," said Mr. Hope. "I can then be the better friend and counselor."

"Have you ever imagined," asked Cassel, with an almost rigid face, "who it was that slew Jonas Aiken ?"

Without an instant's hesitation, the old minister replied.—

"The brother of Diana Rapid slew him."

"That is the *truth*," said Cassel, firmly ; "and the fact that you divine it so readily, proves in your own correct heart that I ought to have slain him."

"Thou shalt not kill," was Mr. Hope's reply.

Cassel looked into Mr. Hope's face, long and earnestly.

Then, in a tone which fulmined through the old minister's breast, he said,—

"Man mocks the earth with his laws and licenses. Diana Rapid was purer than the drop of dew on Vesta's morning wreath. *Hell* came upon her; and where is my young sister now? Mouldering in the lonely soil of a Western wild, where hymns are never sung and prayers are never heard. Oh, what a life was in her bosom, to be quenched and polluted by this fiend of hell!" The brother's eyes gushed with tears, and his breast heaved. Presently he continued: "She had a lover,—a noble boy. Where is he? Rotting in the trenches of the Crimean dead. Have I sinned? I do not claim it as a godly act, for I am no god. I do not feel that I am guilty. I have *never* felt so. I hold fast to this deed of puny retribution and justice, as you yourself cling to the good deeds of your life. But tell me, my revered friend and father, if this act, which my whole life will sanction, and the recent knowledge of which causes Cora to regard me as a murderer, bars me from your sympathy and aid?"

"Christ would not have done it, my son."

"Ay, but would *you* have done it?"

"Christ would not have done it," repeated the old minister, mildly.

"Nor would the Angel of the bottomless pit have barely done what that *wretch* failed not to do. If reeking Evil must needs stalk the earth, whenever it crosses my path I'll assault it in the teeth of every law that pusillanimous demagogues may *dare* to fashion. I'm an *outlaw* in the eyes of dastard codes, and I thank God for the spirit which makes me such."

"Tempt me no more, my son. I am but an old man, and the fire of my blood is quenched."

"Moses slew an Egyptian for a lesser crime. Brutus killed Cæsar for a lesser crime. Cromwell killed Charles for a lesser crime. Washington, the rightful nonpareil of men, killed André, *hung* him, for a lesser crime. And millions have been slaughtered by wars and laws for crimes which pale before this wretch's triple work."

"Urge me no more, my dear boy. Speak no more of it now. I will seek God, and to-morrow I will bring you tidings."

"But you must understand," said Cassel, "that Cora winessed the act; that she considers it a cold-blooded murder; and has just learned that I did the deed, but does not know *why* I did it. All I desire is that she shall thoroughly understand; after which, if she frowns upon me, I would not snap my finger for her smile. I would disdain to touch the hand of any girl or woman who would not justify me."

"In the morning, Cassel," repeated the old minister, "I will bring you tidings."

Cassel waited patiently and hopefully until the next day. His conversation with Mr. Hope had relieved him, and he felt much more at ease, for he saw that the good man was with him, and trusted that Cora, in the purity of her youth, would be as chivalrous and independent as was the minister in the purity of his age.

On the morrow when the minister met Cassel, his greeting was, cheerfully,—

"My son, in a few days I go to Philadelphia."

Cassel's heart bounded. He knew what it meant, and half of his anxiety and care was expelled. Cassel had hoped much, but not quite so much as this. He replied,—

"But, my dear sir, is it necessary for you to take upon yourself this weary journey? Can you not write? If you desire it I will be your amanuensis."

"No, Cassel, I could neither write nor dictate all that I would say to her; and I am certain that the impropriety of my having an amanuensis at all in this matter, and especially for it to be Cassel Rapid, has escaped your perceptives. A little jostling will probably not hurt the old joints in me, and recreation may do me good."

When this brave old veteran of the Cross started upon his weary and peculiar mission, Cassel accompanied him during the days of toilsome cart-road travel which it was necessary to endure before they could reach a railroad station, making him as comfortable as possible, and caring for him with ceaseless assiduity. Cassel would remain at the station, take charge of the carriage and horses, and await Mr. Hope's return.

The old minister arrived safely in Philadelphia, and Cora's sad heart was surprised into temporary joy at the unexpected but welcome presence of her dear old guardian and friend. But her aching, active sorrow soon smote upon her joy, beating it down and utterly away. Mr. Hope's breast was scourged with anguish at sight of Cora, pale, hopeless, and almost silent, while her desperate dark eyes appeared to avoid the intelligence of his glance. Deliberating in his own mind, the minister changed his original plan. The next day, Cassel, at the lonely station, received the following note:

"MY DEAR BOY,—Go back to Creswood, but leave the carriage and horses at the station. I will start for home to-morrow, and Cora is coming with me. I have not spoken to her yet in your behalf, and will not do so until we arrive at Creswood. I think I am doing for the best. You, of course, cannot be my guest while Cora is with me, unless I can prevail upon *her* to give you the welcome. You had better go down to Gale Island and remain there. I will act speedily and notify you."

"Your friend,
"ST. JOHN HOPE."

Although Mr. Hope's note did not change the status of affairs, Cassel was encouraged. He went back to Creswood and to Gale Island. Captain Gale, who had been in port for some time, was making ready for a short cruise. He invited Cassel to take a sail with him. Cassel accepted the invitation with pleasure and purpose. He would get himself clean out of the way, and relieve the situation of whatever suspicion Cora might have entertained that premeditation was decoying her down to Creswood to throw her in the pathway of her lover. Cassel was a pretty good sailor, and no mean addition to the crew of the Whitecap, for the weather was warm and lazy, and the sympathetic sailors felt warm and lazy likewise.

Garland Hope had for some time considered himself a success, both as minister and educator,—so much so, that he had induced Rebecca Ruthven to abridge the time which should elapse before each should make the other perfectly happy. Consequently, they were to be married the coming autumn. Rebecca was seventeen years of age, and was fully developed into a woman. What, therefore, was the sense or utility of waiting? She was entirely free from that mercenary spirit so common to the safely-engaged girls of 1870, of " seeing Life " before taking the marriage-vows. Now what does this " seeing Life " mean ? It does not mean *seeing how to live !* But it means that a girl who feels secure of, or indifferent to, her lover, prefers first to expend her bloom and plumpness in all sorts of dissipation and the devil knows what, and, having broken herself down, become literally tired out, and *blasé*, then affectionately to surrender herself, a withered old skin full of bones, to the patient fool who is waiting with open arms and purse to receive her. She will spend the honey-moon in his arms perhaps, and the balance of the moons in his purse, perhaps not.

Rebecca Ruthven did not contemplate going to her lover looking like a dried herring or a starved heifer. Her love-liness was mild as the light of an astral lamp ; her blonde beauty and voluptuous figure gave her an appearance at once angelic and ravishing ; she was in the vigorous dawn of womanhood, and she was willing to give herself fresh to Garland, and let *him*, her lover, gather the bloom from her cheek, instead of brushing it off in giddy contact with a superficial non-repaying world.

Rebecca was not as intellectual as Cora Glencoe, nor was she as exquisite and statuesque, but she was very sweet, and fair, and affectionate, and would doubtless make as good a wife as Cora, and as good a mother, which, after all, constitute the chiefest sources of happi-ness and comfort in a family. Intelligence—mutual intel-ligence—is essential to the higher joys of existence ; but a person can be intelligent without, in the matter of intel-lectual culture, having ever acquired more than a sound, symmetrical, rudimental scholarship, reinforced by obser-vation and instructive reading. For what is more disgust-ing or malapropos than a thoroughly well-lettered fool? or what, on the contrary, is more agreeable than native in-telligence allied with a good heart? It is better for a woman to understand how to dress a fowl, or a man how to wield an axe, than for either of them to be able to dive out of sight into some bottomless question of science or art,—the science of government for instance, or the polite art of torturing an unfortunate piano.

Rebecca's education was, in greater part, practical. She anticipated becoming a minister's wife, and was neither too modest nor too lazy to fit herself well for the trying sphere. And she bid fair to be as amiable, useful, and well-ordered a helpmate as any minister or plain man need want, or is entitled to.

Garland was as perfectly satisfied, and as serenely happy, as it is in the nature of mankind to be. He did not see a single cloud in his sky of which he could not smilingly and confidently say, *Nebicula est: transibit.* His betrothed was all that he desired her to be, and his way in life, pleasant and fruitful now, opened yet fairer down the vista. His experience had not been absolutely painless, but it had been peaceful and full of purpose. He, like all of us, met with occasional brambles, and stumbled here and there against a stone; but he trusted in his Religion and his Love, and always rallied to his either trust, instead of railing at the bramble in his way or the stone at his foot.

If peace, and quiet content, and unostentatious happiness ever rested anywhere in this world, they abided with the excellent households of the Hopes and the Ruthvens. But a shaft from Hell was already aimed at them. Who, but God, can catch it on his shield?

A few days after the Whitecap sailed, Johnny Gale very unexpectedly arrived at Gale Island. Johnny had improved greatly, both in appearance and manner, and had a look of elegance about him which contrasted well with the home-clad denizens of Creswood. On his arrival, his mother and sister Caddy smothered him nearly to death two or three times before they could let him alone.

" Is the old man in port?" asked Johnny.

" What old man ?" asked his mother.

" The governor."

"Johnny, what do you mean ! For whom are you inquiring ?"

'Why, *father*, of course ! Whom do you reckon ?" and Johnny looked at his mother with impudent amazement.

"Did—you—*ever !*" exclaimed Mrs. Gale, turning to Caddy, who, like her mother, was astonished at the enormity of Johnny's assurance.

Johnny bolted out at the door, went around the house,

stood up in a chimney corner, and vented one of the most ticklish suppressed laughs imaginable. His shoulders shook up and down for a full minute. He then returned to his mother and Caddy, and began to busy himself unpacking his trunk of clothes. Coming to a pair of socks with holes in the heels, he turned and tossed them to his mother, saying,—

"There, old lady,—I wish you'd darn those darned socks for me"

With an amazed and threatening air, Mrs. Gale got up and walked over to her son.

"John Gale! Is *this* the sort of education you are getting in New York? You needn't laugh so ticklish, sir, or I'll get one of your father's rope's ends and tickle your tail for you, big as you are."

Johnny now broke out into an open roar, while Mrs. Gale looked at him, angry, bewildered, and amused in spite of herself.

"Ma, he's only teasing you,—he don't mean it," cried Caddy, while Johnny continued to roar.

Mrs. Gale, thus enlightened, jumped on her son, and beat him with motherly blows until Johnny put his arms about her and squeezed the tears out of her eyes.

"Mother," said Johnny, as soon as he could command his voice, "when the 'old man' comes home, don't you tell him; I want to try it on with *him*,—just for fun."

"You try that with your father, and he'll buckle you down and spank you," replied Mrs. Gale, with a laughing threat.

"He's not 'old man' enough for *that*," said Johnny, saucily.

"Yes he is, sir,—old and young enough too."

Mrs. Gale was as proud of her husband's stalwart strength as she was of her son's good looks and promise.

"Johnny," said Caddy, "what brought you down so suddenly, and without any notice?"

"Nothing sudden about it. I have not been here for months. And what's the use of a notice? You wouldn't make any preparation for me if I were to give you a fortnight's warning and come in a coach-and-six."

"Preparation indeed! We are always prepared for you,

you young buffalo," said Mrs. Gale. "But I can tell you, Caddy, what brought him down so like a thief in the night. He has come to ask his mother if he may marry that young widow up in New York."

"No, I'll be smashed if I have," protested Johnny, laughing and blushing, and asserting his independence. "That's one of the things which I intend to do—or not, without anybody's yea or nay but hers. Remember, mother, I'll soon be twenty-one."

"And much of a man you'll be, you great booby of a boy," laughed his mother. "Think of *him*, Caddy, with a wife. It will be like a young gander housing with a pullet."

"More like a giant nursing a doll," said Caddy.

"Or an elephant fumbling with a mouse," rejoined Johnny, helping them along. "But whatever it is like, I expect to like it."

"You'll have to, whether you do or not," said Mrs. Gale, while Caddy laughed at the Irish bull of which her mother was guilty.

Is it to be supposed that Johnny Gale, an open, headlong, and unguarded youth, was going to wait six months—notwithstanding Cassel Rapid's injunction to that effect, and Johnny's promised submission—before he leveled his gun and popped the question at Linda? Whoever has supposed such a thing is an egregious failure. Johnny did not *intend* to break his promise to Cassel; but it will be remembered that there is a certain well-ordered place, which, for economy and convenience, makes its *pavements* of intentions—good intentions at that. Johnny conscientiously meant what he had promised, and contemplated "holding his horses" until the six months should expire, and possibly for a day or two over, to make good count. But Linda was so *very* bewitching, and Johnny was such an awkward hand at holding back, and the girl-widow once gave him, as he conceived, such a winning chance to rush ahead, and he was so well in remembrance of the old adage "now or never," that he let all "holts" go, his team ran away with him, and he found himself landed and sprawling, with all the ticklish foolery of the love that was in him overgushing at Linda's feet.

"But I will *not* give you an answer, you great giant of

a good fellow," insisted the blushing, laughing, delighted, and coying Linda, "until I have seen my brother Cassel," and Johnny was compelled to gather himself up, and accept the situation until brother Cassel could be consulted.

Meantime, a little frightened, he determined to see brother Cassel himself, and to see him first; for that excessively important individual might take it into his head to come down upon him heavily for disregarding his strict injunction and outstripping the expiration of the agreed probation. He would go see brother Cassel then, who, to his growing fears, began to loom up more terrible than any castle he had ever read of in any child's book of legends.

That, and nothing else, was what brought Johnny Gale down to Creswood He had not come because he loved his father, or his mother, or his sister,—which he did,—but because he loved Linda Boyd, and Cassel was the arbiter of his fate, and Cassel was supposed to be at Creswood.

"By Juggernaut," was Johnny's constant apprehension, "it will never do to let him discover from anybody else but *me*, that I have stolen a march on him in his absence."

Pretty soon Johnny inquired if Cassel was in the neighborhood, and, almost afraid to meet him after coming so "frantic and far" for that express purpose, learned, somewhat to his momentary relief, that he had put to sea on the Whitecap.

"How I would like to be with him!" exclaimed Johnny, inadvertently.

"*Well*," said Caddy, pertinently and pertly, "that is saying a good deal for him and very little for us. You have been with him for months, and now that you are here, at home, with your mother and sister, you must still be pining after Mr. Rapid. I thank you, sir; very kindly, sir."

Mrs. Gale looked to Johnny for an explanation.

"But now that I've seen you all, here, I want to see father," was Johnny's very lame excuse; "and you know, Caddy, how I always loved to sail?"

"But, son," interposed the mother, humorously, "tell us about that Mrs. Boyd."

"Oh, she's the sty of my eye," replied the blushing young Hercules.

"But are you the sty of *her* eye?" asked Caddy.

"She says I'm a good fellow, and referred me," answered Johnny, putting a fun-face upon it.

"I hope," said Caddy, who was something of a plague, "that she did not refer you to 'Uncle Jesse,' for Mr. Rapid says that Uncle Jesse stands no nonsense."

"He will have to stand a devil of a sight of it if he expects to stay in *my* family," and at this conceit Johnny fairly roared with laughter.

"Johnny," said Mrs. Gale, severely, "never do you use such a word as 'devil' in the presence of your mother again."

"Nor anywhere else," added Caddy.

"No—nor anywhere else," agreed Mrs. Gale.

"Did I say 'devil'?"

"Yes, you did," spoke up Caddy.

"I declare I was not aware of it. I beg pardon all around."

"I would rather you *had* been aware of it," said Mrs. Gale. "Not being so, argues that you are so accustomed to the use of such words that you do not know when they escape you."

"No, mother; it is because I feel so free here."

"Never get so free *anywhere*, my son, as to lose respect for your mother."

"Never indeed, mother. When I lose respect for you I hope to go to the dev——"

"Hold, Johnny!" cried the wide-awake Caddy, springing up. "Ma, he was just going to say the *very same thing* over again!"

Johnny ran out of the house and rolled in the grass. He felt some inward reproach, but, at the idea of inadvertently suffering the identical offense to return and kick the heels of his apology he *couldn't* suppress that ticklish laugh which lived in him. He went back to fib out of his difficulty. He protested that he meant to wish himself "to the dogs," but that Caddy's reprehensible practice of interrupting him had not allowed him to finish what he had intended to say.

CHAPTER XXXVIII. .

CORA was again at Creswood, among the scenes of her earliest recollections. What a melancholy attachment possessed her for Creswood, with its hills, and abysses, its strands and familiar places! Cliff Hall was now her own. Oswald Huron had left it to her in his will, and although he was known to have been fitfully insane, and although the will would not have been admitted to probate, or, being admitted, might easily have been overthrown, Neville Huron, the legal heir and representative of his brother, confirmed the document, and gave to Cora the entire wealth of Cliff Hall, as her due for the lonely and painful life which she had spent there, and for which he, the father, was in a measure originally responsible. It was a valuable and desirable hold, but Cora had earned it, in fee-simple, with her dripping, bitter tears, her anguish, and heartache, and solitary, sad songs down upon the strand.

After resting the part of a day and the ensuing night, Mr. Hope lost no time in holding an interview with Cora. He could not bear to see the young girl so bereft, and would, if possible, become a restoring physician, giving her back all that she conceived herself to have lost. His venerable years endowed him with the privilege of speaking freely, and sanctioned the propriety of Cora's willingness to listen. He told Cora of Diana Rapid: of her cloudless purity and loveliness and youthful prospects. Cora had never known that there had been a Diana Rapid. With a solemn grief which awed the young girl, he then told her of Diana's fate. Tears coursed their way down his aged cheeks. He spoke slowly, and with tremulous—almost terrible, earnestness. Cora sat perfectly still, shedding no tear, and giving no sign. Her stanch, warm heart was frozen in its fountains. She crept to the old minister's breast, and nestled there as if shielding herself from some

icy wind, while shudder after shudder swept through her
body from head to foot.

"It was for *this—damnable* deed, that Cassel slew the
spoiler." The old minister continued to speak slowly and
impressively. He was playing no part, but felt and doubly
felt all that he said. "Such blood as he has spilled will
never stick to his hand. In the breast of that boy is as
noble and pure a heart as ever beat. His arm is valiant
against lurking Evil, and in his conscience virtue will
always triumph. For his cause he has faced a hundred
deaths. He is the chief among thousands, beautiful, and
brave, and worthy to be loved, as *I* love him, with the
whole heart. My little one——"

Cora could stand it no longer. She sprang wildly from
the old minister's arms, out into the middle of the room.
Her cheeks were flaming hot with the furious rush of the
pent blood. Her eyes blazed, and her every glance was
a glance of fire. Like some tempestuous, tameless thing,
she uttered a genuine war-cry, stamped vehemently upon
the floor, and fled away. The old minister was bewildered,
but he was too infirm to follow and overtake her. He
waited for her to return to him. Half an hour passed, and
Mr. Hope was beginning to get impatient. He heard a
light step coming along the hall, and Cora, calm and blushing, appeared at the door.

"Come here, Cora."

She approached, knelt down, and rested her head upon
the minister's knee. He waited for her to speak. Without lifting her head she said,—

"And you would have Mr. Rapid and myself to be
friends?"

"That is what I wish. I knew of all that I have told
you before I placed you in his care in the city of New
York. In fact, immediately after his home was broken up
in Texas, I corresponded with him regularly, and was the
first to notify him that his foe was here in Creswood. I
solicit no more from you than I grant myself. I am unreservedly his friend. He eats at my table, sits by my
daughters, and associates with my son."

Cora, not yet looking up, said,—

"You have been my father. At your knee I learned to

pray. I have always contemplated you as the safe link between me and God. I know that you are venerable with good deeds which would crowd a century of ordinary good men's lives. It cannot be that we are both mistaken." And Cora handed up to the old minister a note. "Here," said she, "is my decision."

"What is here, Cora?"

"Open it and read, and then transmit it to Mr. Rapid, for I know not where he is."

Mr. Hope glanced through the note, which was a model of brevity, and read,—

"Mr. Rapid,—Forgive me. I am wiser.—●ORA."

"My dear child," said Mr. Hope brightly, "there is no balm in Gilead like this for his earthly troubles."

Cora's heart again trembled with tenderness for her lover. A mountain had been heaved from her bosom. The blood seemed to spangle like spray of ecstasy throughout her body, and tingle at her very fingers' ends.

"And now," said Mr. Hope, "for the last few words which either of us need ever speak upon this subject."

The old minister, after talking some time, concluded with these words:

"Although men cannot be as gods, it is no excuse for them to be as devils. It is better that all the sons of Beelzebub on earth should die than that one Diana Rapid should be wrecked. The law was too lame even to *catch* this Jonas Aiken, and would only have chastised him had it caught him. Therefore the brother made a law unto himself and the spoiler, and, in its execution, wrote *Tekel* against the statutes of his country. What is a man's country? Patriotically, and poetically, it is a broad land, teeming with busy millions. Practically it is his Fireside. What, then, is all his country to the man who, suffering from boundless wrong, can only sit by his fireside mournfully, and watch the sparks fly upward? I venture the assertion that there is not a proper man or virtuous woman in America, or in the world, in whose secret heart Cassel would lack justification. My little girl herself would have scorned him, had he done other than what he did. But I am not now attempting to justify *him*, but *myself*, as a minister of the gospel, in the view which I have taken of

this thing. Neither would I urge this view from the pulpit, for it might eventually lead to an excess of violence
—of undue violence, under other heads of grievance. The
law is what should be changed, that its workings may har-
monize with the genuine sentiment of the American breast.
Have you followed my meaning?"

"I believe I have; and yet, you feel yourself to be in a
dilemma, and that I shall judge you as not quite true to
the gospel which you have preached so long. But from
that very gospel," said Cora, smiling, "I can explain your
position in much fewer words than you have used."

"Let me hear you," said the minister.

"Christ, in his teachings, eschewed and condemned ty-
ranny; but, out of the fish's mouth, himself paid tribute
to a tyrant."

"And out of the mouths of babes and sucklings pro-
ceedeth wisdom," rejoined the old minister, patting the
young girl's cheek. "You can teach me, Cora. I am
growing old and feeble, and have lost my logic and aptitude of thought."

"Mr. Hope," asked Cora, "can you conjecture why it is
that mankind is so afflicted?"

"The Lord loveth whom he chasteneth."

"But some are miserable and some are happy,—some
are born *filled* to be happy, others to be miserable, without any apparent cause for the distinction."

"That is an argument against Universalism," replied
the old minister, "which maintains that an all-merciful and
all-just God would destroy his own attributes by punishing his own creation. This world is an *existence*, as truly
as will be the future world. If, therefore, punishment is
visited upon us, *here*, in an apparently indiscriminate manner, for the same, or other inscrutable purposes, punishment may as surely be visited upon us beyond the grave,
in a *discriminate* manner. But do not tempt me to preach
you one of my old sermons."

Cora mused awhile, and then, with a long, deep sigh,
said, as if to herself,—

"How infinitely I am relieved. I was in a total and
hopeless eclipse."

Cora was thinking of her lover.

"But now, my child, I trust your eclipses have passed over and away, forever. And that reminds me, Cora, that to-morrow afternoon we are to have a partial eclipse of the sun. Did you know that?"

"Yes, sir. There is nothing so grand or suggestive to me as an eclipse. Not that the eye can see so much, but the mind grasps the huge and wonderful fact that it is the Supreme Hand which is placing these vast worlds in the vaster universe with greater ease and precision than a boy would place his marbles tit-tat-tow, all in a row."

The old minister smiled at Cora's apt illustration.

"Yes," said he. "To His infinite power, worlds are as marbles; and to His infinite glance, the planets wheeling about the sun are as fire-flies circling the lamp. But did you ever read Cooper's description of a Total Eclipse?"

"Not long ago I read it. Although I never saw a total eclipse, I am satisfied that Cooper has given a due and accurate picture of the grand phenomenon." Hesitating a little, with a faint blush and half-diffident eye, Cora asked, —"Mr. Hope, will you laugh at me if I tell you something?"

"Yes," laughed the old minister in advance, "I will, if it is very amusing."

"It is not amusing at all,—but it may be very laughable, nevertheless."

"Whatever it is, Cora, I will endeavor to treat it as it deserves," replied Mr. Hope, with an encouraging look.

"You remember, when I was quite a little girl, how you exercised us in the class which you called 'Praise'? We had to compose hymns and praises."

"I do,—and I also remember that you wrote many little verses of praise and petition, which God must have regarded as a tender mother regards the sweet prattle of her child."

"I can hardly realize now," said Cora, "how pure my heart was then, and how near I felt to God, when writing my little verses to him."

"Cora, did you know that I shed tears over some of them?"

"No *indeed*, Mr. Hope! For why?"

"Because they reflected a dreary, desolate childhood,

and, in their simple pathos, breathed an exquisite plaint, or elegy, which went to my heart like arrows tipped with fire."

Cora got up and put her hands half caressingly upon the old minister's shoulders, and with a gaze which was rife with affection and just a little saucy, shook him playfully, and demanded,—

" *Why* didn't you tell me *then* that you loved me ? I might have known it from your ceaseless kindness, but I was too young to make discoveries. I lived through all those desperate years thinking that there was no one in the wide world who cared for me. Ah, *dear!* how desolate I was in yonder Cliff Hall, with none but my fitful uncle."

" But you have strayed from your text, Cora. What was it that I am to laugh at which you are going to tell me ?"

" Nay, sir,—it is something which you are *not* to laugh at," protested Cora, merrily.

" Oh !—the laugh is to be on the other side of the mouth ! Very well,—I am ready to hear you."

" I have dared to write some verses," said Cora, blushing most charmingly. "They were suggested by 'Cooper's Eclipse,' and by the inquiry, 'How is it possible for man to look upon the wonders of Heaven and Earth and yet say,—there is no God?' Which, you are well aware, some persons do say, and many seem to think, judging from their acts. I would not show these verses to a living soul but you," added Cora, laughing; "but I wish you to read them and see if they are at all fit. I have them with my little souvenirs—in my trunk."

" Go get them."

Cora brought the manuscript, and sat demurely, while the old minister, having adjusted his spectacles, critically read the young girl's effusion. As they will detain the reader but a few moments, we introduce the verses here, not so much on account of their merit, as to give a glimpse of Cora's mental cast, additional to what may have been evolved or disclosed thus far in our narrative.

"IS THERE NO GOD?"

The Fool saith in his heart—" There is no God ;
   That Man no Maker has, but withers down
To tomb like grass—resolves into a clod ;
   Reaping on Earth what he on Earth has sown."

What though a Summer Evening's pomp bestow
   A prouder court than emperor ever trod,
And all the heavens with matchless splendors glow ?
   The Fool saith in his heart—" There is no God."

What though the whirlwinds wrench, and wreck, and rave,
   And cowering Seas are scourged as with a rod,
And cowering Hills cry out to the whipt wave ?
   The Fool saith in his heart—" There is no God."

What though the Sun vouchsafes the goodly Day,
   And countless worlds, obedient to His nod,
Gem the far Night with infinite array ?
   The Fool saith in his heart—" There is no God."

" Let there be Light," Jehovah simply said,
   And from His glance there gathered in the sky
A dazzling fiery Wonder which has sped
   Its ceaseless way, and baffled every eye.

A lesser Wonder rolled from out His palm,
   And put its silver belt about the Earth ;
Changefully changeless, 'tis as sure and calm
   As when the God that made it gave it birth.

No stranding argosies bestrew the sky,
   Or crash each other in that lawlike realm ;
Obedient to the First Command they fly
   With faultless sail and still unerring helm.

" Now comes the Eclipse," said Mr. Hope, smiling at
Cora, while she turned off, askance-like, that he might
finish.

Away, up in the heaven, an opaque shield
   Superbly wheels the Sun and Earth between,
Catching the sunlight from its wonted field,
   While strange untimely shadows supervene.

Lo ! like a hallowed sheen from Paradise,
   Corona crowns the errant Queen of Night,
And while from wildered Earth awe-whispers rise,
   Celestial luster-plays before the sight.

Man, Beast, and Bird, admit the viewless Power
  Which worketh wonders in the firmament,
And where the belt of undue shadows lower,
  A superstition and a Faith is blent.

But when the Sun is darkened in his course,
  The Fool looks up and mutters, "It is odd,—
How is it thus that Night comes on perforce?"
  And never once bethinks him of a God.

"Cora," said Mr. Hope, looking over his spectacles, "I am neither a poet, nor the son of a poet, but in my hasty judgment this is very good   At all events, it is much better than I am able to do myself, and I shall not attempt to criticise it."

Cora, with modest, diffident pleasure, was abashed. Mr. Hope continued,—

"It is very difficult to compose a good *short* piece of poetry. There is not sufficient space for the mind to gather impetus. The mind is something like the bird, the horse, or the locomotive : a certain distance must be traversed before it can get under full headway."

"Your comparison is apt, when speaking of *Talent;* but *Genius,* to which I do not aspire, is like the lightning ; its first leap—its very first *inch* of flight, is at high speed."

"You, then, are among those who divide talent from genius,—rating the one as a faculty and the other as a gift. Now, it is as difficult to tell where one ends and the other begins as it is to run a line between the blended yellow and orange of a rainbow. Genius is merely a name by which to distinguish the highest order of talent."

"The space between them might then be compared to the space between tweedle-dum and tweedle-dee ?" laughed Cora.

"Just so," replied the old minister, "granting that you are on an ascending scale."

"The highest notes," said Cora, "are not always the sweetest."

"Nor the safest : the strings are more apt to stretch into discord, or snap into confusion."

"I am so contented with your estimate of my little poem that I do not think I shall ever attempt another."

"I should have abused it and put you on your mettle,
as the Reviewers did Byron."

"All the abuse in the world would neither provoke nor
taunt me into a poetess."

"Wouldn't you enjoy turning rhymes?"

"Aha!—but can one extract gold from granite?"

"By no means. But many make the endeavor."

"And fail,—miserably fail."

"As people do in most things else."

"But then it is more bitter, is it not, to try and be a poet
and to utterly fail?"

"Because rarely do any ever make the trial but the sensitive, and *none* but the sensitive ever succeed."

"Those who are so quick to feel," said Cora. "And
failure bears a double sting,—that of the mere intellectual
bankruptcy, and the still more venomous one of rebuked
presumption."

"True,—and you, Cora, can very well forbear to try, for
you are witching enough without the laureate chaplet."

"Mr. Rapid told me once that you never flattered," observed Cora, saucily.

"That's more than he can aver of himself, I dare say,"
replied the old minister, humorously.

The dinner-bell now warned them to whet their appetites, and the interview was abruptly closed with the following question and answer:

"Cora, why did you leave me so wildly; in the very
midst of our conference?"

"Because I felt like *War*,—like a cannon, charged and
red-hot shotted to the mouth, impatient to burst and destroy—the *Spoilers!*"

CHAPTER XXXIX

CORA GLENCOE and Rebecca Ruthven had always been
the best of friends, probably from the circumstance that
they were different in character,—Cora being self-acting
and decisive, and Rebecca being mild and malleable.

Rebecca had called to see Cora, just after her interview
with Mr. Hope as per last chapter, and on the morrow,
the day of the sun's eclipse, Cora was to go over to old
Mr. Ruthven's, some half a mile through the forest from
the Parsonage, and she and Rebecca, with pieces of smoked
glass, would seek a pleasant spot of which they knew,
just half way between the Parsonage and Mr. Ruthven's,
where they would chat, view the eclipse, chat again, and
separate, each to return to her lodge.

This arrangement had been made at the instance of Rebecca, who longed to unbosom herself to Cora in respect
to her maiden anticipations and dreams of the precious delights which awaited her just behind the front veil of the
Future, and which the coming autumn, assisted by the
young minister, would shower upon her. Cora's own
little secrets were so crude, and fresh, that she felt no apprehension that they would become too mellow, or spoil
on her hands, should she keep them locked away for a
season.

After dinner, on the day of the eclipse, Cora, with her
dog companion, which Mr. Hope had cared for since the
death of Oswald Huron, and which remembered the young
mistress well enough, started through the forest for Rebecca's home, guided by a foot-path here and there almost
choked up by the summer growth of twigs and bordering
shrubs.

The spot where they were to take their celestial observations was a knoll, bare of trees, rocky, and patched with
grass and moss. It was called White Mound, and afforded
a view of the sky, spacious enough for their astronomical
purposes.

Cora, out in the wildwood, where her voice and footstep
might claim elfin freedom, was very happy. She had just
sent a *salvia* to her lover, and soon would he come to
her. She tripped along, agile as the chamois doe, singing
snatches of forest glees, mocking the birds, catching at
flowering woodbines, racing with her dog, and indulging in
every little jaunty air and motion which prudery frowns
upon. None but her dog, however, saw her garter, or eyed
the tricksy dash of her pretty foot, as she rioted in the
luxury of the new and joyous life which had come upon her.

When she reached the half-way spot, she found Rebecca
there in advance of her, seated and waiting. Rebecca had
become impatient, for she had "something sweet to tell."

"Why, Becky!" cried Cora, "am I tardy?"

"No,—it is I that am early. I thought I would meet
you, instead of waiting for you at home."

"But I wanted to see your mother and your grandpa."

"You can see them another time. To-day I wish to
have you all to myself."

Cora sat down on the grass. She soon perceived Rebecca's drift, and encouraged her in the way she wished
to go. Rebecca, by degrees, unlocked her full bosom, and
Cora saw, in the midst of it,—in the holy of holies,—
the image of Garland Hope. She met Rebecca's confidence
with intelligent sympathy; played upon her just as she
wished to be played upon; and teased her just as she
longed to be teased.

Rebecca was full of joy.

Cora, through her smoked glass, glanced momentarily
at the sun. Presently she cried,—

"Becky!—look!—the eclipse is at hand; the moon is
just upon the edge of the sun. *There* is the power and
precision of the Creator!"

A low, deep growl from the dog caused them to turn
about. Terror! Dismay! aha! *impotent* are all the tongues
on earth to supply that word of unlimited import and give
a name to the *fearful* thing which swept into the souls of
these young, helpless virgins, as out of the thicket two
jungle demons sprang and rushed upon them. In a moment
Rebecca Ruthven was dragged into the thicket, and Cora,
with the desperate strength of a captured gazelle, was

struggling and writhing and shrieking in the grasp of Pollution. The mastiff, with a savage bark, rose to the rescue of his mistress, and tore the enemy with fierce fangs. Cora was freed. Wild with terror she sped away, leaving the dog and demon struggling on the ground, while the shrieks of the lost Rebecca Ruthven lent wings to her feet. She burst into the Parsonage like a pallid messenger fresh from the throne of Panic. Mr. Hope and Garland hastened to her.

"*Go!*—to the *White Mound!*—*Rebecca!*—*Hell* is there! —great *God* for a thunderbolt!" and she stamped her feet in the fury of her excitement.

Mr. Hope sank down, an impotent old man. Like a wild stag Garland rushed away, only to look upon the ashes of all his hopes. Coming upon the spot, he saw the faithful dog, ripped open by a knife blade, and gasping in the throes of death. Searching swiftly, he found the sweetest flower of his holiest heart, pale, lifeless, and abased with the doom that was sealed upon her. Like an angelic ruin she lay along the ground, limp from the stroke of Satan. As Garland Hope stood over his ravished love and gazed down upon her, what was it that overwhelmed and congealed his breast? Was it sorrow? No. Was it pain? No. Was it agony? No! Poverty of my mother tongue, where is the *gigantic* word that will tell me what it was, that I may score it upon the hearts and stamp it upon the foreheads of the living, and strike it into the tombstones of the dead?

And ah, the broken virgin! Think of the extreme moment when her all of life and hope and joy was *shattered* to atoms while in the grasp of one whose lightest word was terror and whose kiss was death. Would that I could gather all the shrieks, and cries, and moans, and slogans of revolt which have startled and rent the air since the world began, put them into one vast crucible and reduce them to a single white-hot word! With it I would tell the tale of Diana Rapid and Rebecca Ruthven. I would write it upon the brows of my countrywomen, as a damning reproach upon our lawgivers and the chivalry of men. A few years, forsooth, of strict, safe, and wholesome labor, to balance all this misery and coal-black infamy!

When Cora, by ministering to the stricken old man beside her, had, in a measure, forced herself into necessary calmness, in view of the confidence which had recently passed between them, she ventured to ask, what punishment the law would visit upon the Spoiler for blasting the life of the guileless Rebecca, and turning the peaceful, joyful houses of Hope and Ruthven into habitations of woe.

"The farce which usually follows the tragedy," replied the old minister feebly, "a term in prison,—I know not its duration, so subject is it to abridgment."

"It should be *death!*" said Cora, sternly, and stamping her foot as if spurning the law; and as she thought of Rebecca, she cried out, with vehement intensity, *"Oh, it should be death—a thousand times* DEATH*!"* and her hands clinched and her eyes blazed with revolt.

Cora was never fitful, frivolous, or blindly passionate, but a girl of disciplined mental strength and fortitude, trained to hardship and self-command, and accustomed to speak from reason rather than emotion. When, therefore, she said it should be *death*, she not only felt it through every fiber, but thought it in mind and soul and every faculty of intelligence and judgment.

But who can go into the once peaceful cottage and placid life of the Ruthvens, and tell of the heart-breaking scene which followed, when Rebecca, piteously moaning, was borne in, and with constrained solemnity placed, like a defiled but still sacred image, upon a chaste white couch! Let everlasting woe be unto the soul which does not pity and double pity her! and let a blacker doom, if can be, come upon him who would withhold his voice and vote from justice, simple justice—which is death! Yes, *death!* we do not fear to say it, and repeat it, and ring it aloud. If *démons* elect themselves to die, let them *die*—and let good men and chaste women *live*.

The grandfather and the mother had not known of this terrible blast upon their house and name until they saw their broken child and jewel brought in before them. Mrs. Ruthven's lungs were constitutionally weak. This sudden stoop of agony, shame, and horror sent the panic-stricken blood surging through her bosom, breaking its boundaries, and gushing from her mouth. She fell across the couch on which, like a pallid wreck, her sweet, young, only daughter lay. The white-haired, tottering grandfather, whose honest pride and every hope was centered in his grandchild, in whom he blossomed anew, reeled like an aged oak uprooted by a descending thunder-shaft, his heart burst within him at the clash of his calamity, and he fell headlong to the floor, a spent, rifted, and lifeless thing of clay. He was dead. *Tragedy* was there, in that once peaceful, hopeful cottage, more deep, blood-red, and rending, than ever pressed down upon the couch of Desdemona.

Where was Garland Hope?

Out in the woods, the young minister was stretched along the ground, like some prone and rigid statue cast upon its face, and impotent to move.

Creswood was chilled as by an overshadowing winter-cloud shuddering and shaking down its frosty rime. Then came the reaction, and swift, bold feet traversed the hills and glens of the forest, and stern men stood guard to intercept the Spoiler. But more of this anon.

The days passed gloomily away. Cora, in grief herself, but surrounded by a family steeped in the gall of bitterness, spent the most of her time alone. She went out one morning into the orchard, then to the pasture, which was near the house, and climbed up on the fence. She sat there looking at the animals peacefully grazing, or quietly reposing in the shade of the scattered trees.

Not far from where she sat, she saw a pale horse stretched in the shade.. Cora shouted. The horse raised his head, and looked around. Seeing Cora, he got up, shook himself, and woke up the hills with his clarion neigh, clear and reverberating as the peal of a silver trumpet. With a proud and imperial step, he slowly approached the young girl. Cora, forgetting the fierce temper of the stallion, having recognized him as the rapid favorite of her Rapid lover, got down from the fence and went out to meet him, by which indiscreet action she put her life in jeopardy. The horse came up to her and rubbed his head against her shoulder, with low, soft whinnies. Cora caressed him, and laid her cheek against his velvet jaw. She felt in her pocket and drew out a little paper of salt. She had been in the orchard eating apples and salt, after the manner of girls. She emptied the salt into her palm, and the horse ravenously licked it away. He then begged for more, but she had no more to give him. In the great trouble which had rushed upon the Parsonage, the animals had been neglected. The pale stallion, unsatisfied and impatient, reared upon his hind legs and fought the air with his hoofs. Cora sprang back. The stallion rushed upon her, and around her, leaping, rearing, prancing, and breaking away, and spurning the ground in the glory of his strength. Cora was frightened and dismayed. Whenever she attempted to move away, the horse came about her like a whirlwind. One stroke of his hoof would break every bone in her body. He bit at her, as if he would seize her in his gleaming white teeth and shake her to pieces. She could see that at each return his eye was gathering fire and ferocity, and she quaked with terror as she found herself in the jaws of a strange and unanticipated peril. In the midst of it, she heard a voice of command so stern, metallic, and even fierce, that the very roots of her hair tingled. The stalli stopped with the suddenness of a pistol-shot. Turn about, Cora saw Cassel Rapid hastening to her. With a which meant almost everything, she sprang toward him and ran into his arms. She put her arms tightly about his neck, and hid her face in his hair. He forced her face in front of him, and kissed her passionately in the mouth. Cora did not revolt, but clung to him, almost frantically, as if he were the sheet-anchor of her safety. She felt the need of *protection*, not only immediate, but for always, and she buried herself in his dauntless breast, like a child fleeing from the terrors of darkness into its mother's bosom.

"You understand me, now, little one?" asked Cassel, while he held her in his arms.

"You are my war-eagle," said Cora.

"You are my dove," rejoined the lover.

"You are my *lion*," cried Cora, almost ready to shriek with happiness and accumulated excitement.

"You are my lamb," was the gentle reply, and Cassel again forced Cora's lips to his.

After numberless endearments, Cora looked into her lover's eyes with a long, thrilling, agonizing gaze. She was thinking of Rebecca, and the Hopes, and the Ruthvens.

"I know it *all*," said Cassel.

"What shall be done?"

A black frown gathered to Cassel's brow, and a lurid, *relentless* light leaped to his violet eyes. Cora felt that in her lover was an invincible spirit that would draw blades with Apollyon himself, in a question of right and wrong.

"Please do not look so terrible," pleaded Cora.

"I cannot help it. I am thinking, not only of what *is*, but of what *might* have been. *You* were there, my pure young love. Great *heavens!* if this thing had come upon *you*,—and, for the second time, upon *me*, I would have devoted my life and fortune to slaying every spoiler upon the face of the earth. If that is not the truth, may the great Jehovah annihilate me *now!*"

Creswood was in arms, and every honest heart was stern and fixed for justice,—if justice *can* be visited upon a crime, *unprovoked and inexcusable damnation*, which transᴵs the retributive power of the mortal arm. Rebecca ᴴᵛᵉn had given the name—nay, the *names* of her destroyers, for she knew them well. They were two men—demons—who had recently been employed as carpenter and plasterer in repairing the Ruthven cottage, in anticipation of the young girl's approaching bridehood. There they had seen Rebecca, in her blonde loveliness, and she had parleyed with them, daily, in respect to the repairs. Premeditation had long been in their guilty souls.

The sheriff with his aids, and all the arms-bearing males of Creswood,—among whom the Hopes were sacred and the Ruthvens honored,—were now afield. Every passway from the original "Crescent Wold," of which "*Creswood*" was a contraction both in name and fact, was guarded day and night, and the destroyers, like hyenas surrounded in the jungle, were being hunted to the center, without intermission or time for rest.

There were several bad characters in the neighborhood, chiefly men who, like Jonas Aiken, had boarded with Amy Turnbolt down among the huts on the Starboard Strand, and who yet sojourned there at convenient or inconvenient intervals. Consciously guilty of many misdeeds, they were alarmed at the rousing of the people, and were by no means satisfied that the sheriff did not carry in his pocket warrants for their arrest, or that the people, now that they were out in full force, would not make a clean sweep of the neighborhood. They therefore rallied to the destroyers of Rebecca Ruthven, banded themselves together, and, finding escape hopeless by land, the whole guilty party determined to seize the Whitecap and put to sea.

The outlaws, for we may well call them such, were known to be burrowed somewhere in Creswood, and plans were being perfected by which to capture them, without bloodshed if possible. But it was the tacit understanding among the more prominent citizens, and all who follow in the train of determined leaders, that the two destroyers should, when captured, be *hung*,—the sheriff and the laws to the contrary nevertheless. But a rumor, which gradually ripened into a well-authenticated report, was rapidly spread abroad, that Miss Ruthven was mistaken in the names visages of her destroyers. A respectable and well-kn country merchant,—our old friend Mr. Nutt,—who ke store in the next-to-nothing of a village back in the woods a few miles from Gale Island, with several other honest and disinterested citizens, affirmed that the accused were both at the country store, a quarter of an hour before the eclipse began,—the time at which the outrage was said to have been committed,—and continued there until sundown. This they would swear to in a court of justice. But Rebecca Ruthven did not vary from her original and positive accusation, and although the citizens were not so ready to organize a mob as they had at first been, they were equally determined to catch the men, whose actions, in secreting themselves, did not conduce to establish their innocence, but the contrary.

Captain Gale was sitting on his portico. Better from that point than any other, he could watch, with his spy-glass, up and down the beach for more than three miles each way, to see that no skiff put to sea to carry the outlaws beyond the strict lines of Creswood. At night, the skiffs along the strands were gathered at Gale Island, and guarded.

It was late in the afternoon. Several watermen, in obedience to improvised regulations, had brought their skiffs to anchor in Gale Island Bay, and were now on the cottage portico, conversing with Captain Gale about the excitement, and interchanging conjectures and rumors. Cassel Rapid, coming down from the forest, tied his horse on the verge of the canal, and hailed the island for some one to ferry him over. One of the watermen, at the request of Captain Gale, brought him over in a trice,—no, in a skiff, for we are now relating facts.

Johnny Gale, and Caddy, and Cora were sitting on the Tarpeian Rock, Cora's old favorite seat. The two girls were raking Johnny fore and aft about Linda Boyd, and Johnny was retaliating by accusing Caddy of having no sweetheart at all, good or bad,—and attempting to tease Cora by pronouncing Cassel Rapid a humbug; the meanest and most conceited fellow he had ever observed between two New Years.

"You shall not abuse him," said Cora, "unless you do his face, and you dare not do *that*."

"I've already done *that*, to my heart's content," fibbed Johnny, "and now I expect to abuse him the world over."

"He'll thrash you," said Caddy.

"By Juggernaut, he isn't man enough," replied Johnny, glancing complacently down at his proportions.

"But he's b'hoy enough," said Cora, laughing; "and I'll tell you, Mr. Johnny, if you whet your tongue against him, I will hint to him to cut you out with Mrs. Boyd."

"And he'll take the hint,—as a matter of course,—that is, he would, if he didn't have to paddle over Lake Huron, or *some* sort of a Huron, in order to be able;" and Johnny roared with laughter at his clumsy pun. "But I've already got *my* little fate bottled up, corked, and sealed. I 'laid' for Cassel, and caught him upon the hook of one of his most precious proverbs."

"How did you accomplish so great a feat of angling?" asked Caddy.

"You know, Caddy, if you ever read your Bible, how Nathan 'laid' for David, caught him fast, and the

nounced him with, 'Thou art the man!' Well, I am-
bushed Cassel pretty much the same way, and then came
down upon him with the announcement of, '*I am the
man.*' He saw that I had horn-swoggled him, and like
the best fellow in the world,—which he is,—he told me
to pass in my checks and mosey along to glory."

"Love has made a most cunning diplomatist of you
Mr. Johnny," laughed Cora.

The conversation was suddenly broken off by the report of a pistol-shot from the direction of Gale Island.
Another similar report quickly followed,—then three or
four more in rapid succession, among which could be distinguished the louder discharge of a shot-gun.

"What is it?" asked Cora.

"It's at the island,—I must go!" cried Johnny, who
started away.

"Are you going to leave us here alone?" screamed
Caddy.

Johnny halted, undecided whether to go or stay. Looking homeward, he saw a man rush up to the pale stallion,
which was tied close to the edge of the canal, and mount
him. The fierce animal reared, and plunged, and shook
off the man, then struck him to the earth with his forefeet, and trampled upon him. Cora turned as pale as
marble,—she feared that it was her lover, and she strained
her eyes to see if he would rise from the ground; but he
did not. She was just about to rush away to her lover's
assistance, when a man appeared over the bank of the
canal, and started up the beach, running with all his
speed. In a few moments an agile form sprang upon the
prancing stallion, wheeled him, and launched forward up
the strand in swift and magnificent pursuit. Nearer and
nearer came pursuer and pursued, and Cora, in the highest
pitch of excitement, stood upon the Tarpeian Rock; for
she had recognized her lover, with the lasso poised above
his head, and in chase of another Jonas Aiken. She fully
expected to see the man rush into the sea, and the pale
horse breasting the waves and carrying his rider within
dagger-stroke of the fugitive; she fully expected to see
the vigorous arm lifted, and the steel, upon its deadly
errand, flash downward with three decisive strokes; for

it was all but as the realization of a vivid dream, long past. But the pale horse came like the wind, and with an unerring cast, the coil of the lasso dropped like a serpent about the neck of the fleeting fugitive. Sudden as the stroke of a hammer, the stallion stopped, with his forefeet buried to the fetlocks in the solid sand. The fugitive was violently overthrown. Johnny Gale hastened forward, and recognizing one of Rebecca's destroyers, he seized him by the throat, dragged him up, and in a voice of passion said,—

" *You* are one of the *hell-hounds* who have brought woe into this community !"

Raising his arm, he was about to strike the man to the earth, when Cassel cried,—

" Hold, Johnny !—this is not your game."

Cassel dismounted, and the man was secured. Turning to the two girls, Cassel said,—

"Come,—we must hasten to Gale Island,—there are some wounded men there,—Cora, will you go with us ?"

" Good God !" cried Caddy. " Is father hurt ?"

. "Only a flesh wound, in the arm,—there is no danger, as far as he is concerned."

But Caddy thought there was.

" What has occurred at the island ?" asked Johnny.

" Come on, and I'll tell you as we go. But first, Cora, do you know this man ?"

" No," replied Cora, looking at the prisoner. "But what has happened ? Why, your clothes are ringing wet !"

" I swam the canal,—that is all."

As they proceeded to Gale Island, Cassel explained.

" Six men attempted to carry the Whitecap to sea. Captain Gale discovered that a strange crew was aboard of his vessel, and that the anchor cable was cut. He quickly mustered a force of three watermen and one landlubber, the latter being me, who chanced to be at the cottage. We were all well armed. The rogues were trying to work the vessel out of the canal into the open water. The cabin and hatchways were closed, and the enemy were obliged to remain on deck and stand their ground, or jump overboard into the bay. One of our men fired a shot, and a man dropped. We came to as close quarters as the situation would allow. I fired and another man dropped. The rogues returned the fire, and one of our men was wounded. Captain Gale opened on them with his shot-gun just as a ball from the enemy passed through his arm. Three of the enemy were down, one threw up his hands and surrendered, and two jumped overboard.

" ' There they go!' shouted Captain Gale.

" ' Who ?'

" ' The fates of Rebecca Ruthven.'

" Our two unwounded watermen ran for their skiffs. The fugitives escaped up the opposite bank of the canal. I swam the canal with one of my pistols in my teeth. When I got upon the beach my horse was pawing one of the men, while the other—this devil walking before us— was fleeing up the strand. I mounted and pursued. You saw the rest."

"Are you hurt?" asked Cora.

" No,—I lost a lock of hair, and my wrist is grazed, but no damage."

When they came to the canal, the man who had been thrown and hoof-beaten by the stallion, was dead. Cora, as soon as she saw his face, sprang back and whispered with horror,—

" ' *Tis he!*"

" Who ?" asked Cassel.

"The man who *killed my dog.*"

Cassel understood her. Turning to his horse, he patted him affectionately, and said,—

" This is the horse who ' knoweth his rider ' in more ways than one."

The party were ferried over to the island, and soon entered the cottage, where they found no little confusion. There were five prisoners, three of whom were wounded severely, and two unhurt, except that the fugitive whom Cassel had lassoed was jerked nearly out of joint in the region of the neck. A surgeon—or rather, a physician— had been sent for : also the sheriff.

" Captain Gale," said Cassel, " let me dress your wound."

"My wife has dressed it, but I'm afraid she's a raw hand at the business,—it feels too much bound up."

Cassel took off the binding, washed the wound, passed a skein of white silk through it, and skillfully bandaged it.

"That's a powerful limb of yours, captain; and all you need do to bring it around as good as new, is to keep it cool and beat off the fever."

"That's about all a man has to do to *live*," laughed Captain Gale, "keep Death out and breath in. But thank you, Cassel, I feel much easier under your manipulations."

"What do you propose to do with these prisoners?" asked Cassel.

"Turn them over to the sheriff."

"But the one whom I captured?"

"Him also, unless you claim him."

"What is his name?"

"Hines."

"I wish Garland Hope were here;—I'd know better whether to claim this wretch or not. He ought to be hung."

"Let the law hang him."

"But it *won't* hang him"

"Well,—I've nothing more to say, just now. You know there is a report that Miss Ruthven is mistaken."

"I am sure she is *not* mistaken," said Cassel.

"Why so sure?"

"Because Cora has recognized the dead man on the opposite bank of the canal as the one who was in company with this Hines when the deed was done. What is the name of this dead man?"

"Butler,—he was a plasterer."

"Exactly. Hines the carpenter, and Butler the plasterer; the very names which Miss Ruthven adheres to. She knows them well, and cannot be mistaken. Cora herself recognizes one of them."

"It's a hard thing," said Captain Gale, thinking of all the anguish which the Ruthvens and Hopes were suffering, of the bankrupt Rebecca, and the bankrupt young minister.

"Hard! It's *Hell!*" said Cassel Rapid, with corrugated

brow. "Captain Gale, you shot a man to-day. What did you do it for?"

"For turning pirate and attempting to rob me of my property."

"Would the loss of the Whitecap have been an irreparable loss to you?"

"By no means, though it would have been heavy."

"Did you try to kill the fellow?"

"Of course I did. I had a right to try, and to succeed, too, if I could do so. But I am glad that the affair ended with so little mortality."

"If you had killed a man during this attempted piracy upon you, the law would have said *Amen.*"

"Yes."

"And yet you are justified by an *attempt*, merely, to *steal your boat;* and this attempt was, in one sense, a measure of self-preservation with the pirates. Suppose, however, that they had not only *attempted*, but had *succeeded*, to pillage Gale Island of its *chastity*, and *honor*, and *joy*, and *peace*, and *very life!* What then?"

"I see your drift, Cassel; but proceed."

"A blind man could see it," replied Cassel, sternly. "An injury which can never be amended, an outrage which can never be canceled, a wound which can never be healed or even soothed, an *infamy* which can *never* be blotted out, has been put upon an innocent, pure-hearted, and blameless young virgin, and about her now sweeps a maelstrom of woe which engulfs not only herself but many of her heart-aching friends. The power and prayers and riches of the *whole earth* are impotent to restore her, or even patch up this most superlative wrong. The same with Garland Hope. What would have been the loss of the Whitecap to *you* in comparison with what *he* has lost! Can you even imagine what that gentle true heart within him suffers? Old Mr. Ruthven, an honored patriarch of your county, is killed by it. Mrs. Ruthven, as amiable and sweet a mother as ever caressed a child, is stricken to her bed, from which she will never rise until summoned by God himself. Rebecca will be a living and polluted statue until the grave redeems her. Gloom rests like a pall in the home of the Hopes. It is *done*, and Omnipo-

tent power itself cannot undo it. *Who did it?* The
wretch is here in your own house, a very poison to the
air. Rebecca is almost without a champion. Her lover
is as mild and gentle as a lamb. He is, moreover, a minister and priest of Heaven, and cultivated conscience may
make him shrink from the red task which clamors for
performance. But is it not enough to make him curse
God and die? Is it not enough to make him dash the
Book to earth, spurn the commandment 'Thou shalt not
kill,' and rush to vengeance, retribution, justice, *everything* which might be fierce and rectifying? Suppose he
does. The pusillanimous letter of the Statute will *hang*
him. If he does not, the spoiler goes to the penitentiary,—
in this State for life, in many other States for a few years.
What does 'for life' signify? It means simply until a
change of government, until a certificate of good behavior
is presented, well underwritten with the signatures of
scheming men, or until some candidate needs another vote
perhaps."

[NOTE.—Without desiring to make a distinction, we refer
the reader, as an illustration of Cassel's truth, to the fact,
that, among the convicts *pardoned* during the year 1869
by the Governor of Illinois, were *seven*, each of whom had
been convicted and imprisoned for Rape. Where are
their victims?]

Calmly looking into Captain Gale's honest face, Cassel
Rapid said, in continuation,—

"Captain Gale, you are a man whom I respect in every
sense of the word. You are an exemplar to your neighbors. You have lived a life of propriety, integrity, order,
and peace. Since you had a voice you have sustained the
laws of your country. Your hobby has been, 'let the
Law take its course.' You have even subjected the
Whitecap to this, your hobby. But coolly,—do you not
think that this wretch should die?"

"But I am not the person to kill him."

"Who is the person?"

"I cannot say."

"Suppose that it had been *Caddy*, instead of Rebecca;
who *then* would have been the person?"

Captain Gale, without reply, looked out of a near window. Cassel continued:

" It is written in the hearts of the people, and upon every leaf of chivalric history, that *death* should be the sequel to this *worse* than death.   The *Law* should visit the punishment, like an unquailing and champion executioner ; and that Law should be set in unnumbered frames, and enriched with flowers, and hung upon the walls of cities, and in the trees of the forest, as the jewel of our statute books, and a pledge to our countrywomen that we are *men*.   Great Jehovah! when I suffer myself to think of it, I *thirst* for the blood of the Spoiler !   *I—killed—Jonas—Aiken*, Captain Gale.   Tell that to the winds, and let them carry it to the four quarters of the globe.   Tell it to the sheriff, as it is your lawful duty to do, and let him arrest me.   I *dare* you to do it.   I tell you again, that I, Cassel Pontiac Rapid, *killed* Jonas Aiken.   What say you ?"

" Hush, Cassel," was Captain Gale's reply.

" We agree," said young Rapid.   " I would engage to revolutionize America upon this one question, if I could only reach the ears of my countrymen.   They don't *think* about it, unless it is brought home to them, and then it is too late to think, and they have to *act*."

Cassel's words may read as though he were unduly excited, but he was not.   He was in earnest, and his voice was as stable and regular and clear as the ring of silver.

CHAPTER XL.

To those of our readers who feel an interest in the *Cause* which this narrative advocates, we promise that the ensuing chapter shall be exceedingly interesting,—and the promise is not a piece of presumption on the part of the author, for we are, and have been, dealing in *facts*, paramount to the creative powers of our pen, and demanding simply a concise and truthful record.

The sheriff with his posse came down to Gale Island and took possession of the prisoners.

Hines, the jungle demon, was confined in jail under two indictments,—one in connection with the ruin of Rebecca Ruthven, the other for piracy upon the Whitecap. His bail was very heavy, and he could not raise it. We are disregarding legal and mystifying technicalities.

In the midst of the deplorable incidents affecting the *commune* of Creswood, there came a letter from New York to Captain Gale. The sturdy mariner was not upon his island, but was back at the little village gossiping, with his wounded arm in a sling. Mrs. Gale, recognizing the handwriting of Carroll May, did not hesitate to open the letter in her husband's absence. Carroll's communication was peculiarly apropos. It began by stating that Johnny had left New York without giving any definite idea as to where he was going. "It is likely," wrote Carroll, "that he has gone out with some surveying expedition; but wherever he may be, you need give yourself no care, for Johnny is big enough to take his own part, and that of two or three more, if necessary,—*one* more, at all events," and here Carroll hinted at Linda.

Carroll wrote of himself as "getting on finely," and as being in "very good spirits," which gives additional proof that it is possible for the human heart to continue its regular beats, even after it has been broken all to pieces by a love stroke. The letter continued :

"Uncle Gale, I have often thought of that engraved dagger with its *Tekel* on the point, and of Jonas Aiken and his undoubted crime. Recently I have figured as associate counsel for the plaintiff in a case of a similar and exceeding outrage. The plaintiff is a little girl not more than fifteen years of age, and the criminal, or defendant, a banker of wealth, resident in this city. The banker was sentenced to a few years' imprisonment, with the prospect of a speedy, *purchased*, pardon. He would have been mobbed but for the strenuous efforts of the police—efforts, by-the-way, worthy of a better aim. We are now preparing to strike high in the figures of his wealth, for damages. The little girl was poor, but lofty minded, respectable, and pure, and language could not tell you of the depths into which this infamy has plunged her and her kindred. Our law firm is engaged in the suit for damages, and we

intend to succeed, or put it through every court of justice
and equity in the land. But if the mountains were of gold,
and she had it all, it would never give back to that sensitive and sweet young girl the normal peace of her soul, or
the integrity of her contemplations. Her life is envenomed,
and she feels that a leprosy will always hang about her.
She feels that she is utterly blasted by this caress of Hell;
that she must hide her face in shame ; that she must forego
her lover ; forego all the delights and pure proximities of
life ; everything in fact that lights the eye or glads the
heart,—and spend her time in solitary tryst with the heartache. It is a *shame* upon American manhood that these
deathly grievances should not be met with *Death.* A term
in prison,—an abridged term in all probability, to offset
the ruin of our women ! Every honest man should *revolt*
against the law, defy the law-makers, or become law-makers
themselves and to some purpose. This little girl's father,
and brothers, and cousins, all swear, by their eternal souls,
that the ravisher shall die as soon as his foot is free from
the gates of his confinement. They are a resolute family,
springing from Revolutionary stock, and will wait a hundred years, if life were so long, that they may visit justice."

When Mrs. Gale, with tears in her eyes, had read thus
far, thinking not only of the little New York girl, but also
of Rebecca Ruthven, she earnestly said to herself,—

"And God grant that all of her kindred may live till the
hour of retribution comes. What woman could love or
respect *any* man who would not defend her purity, or
avenge her spoliation ? I know what *my* old lion would
do, notwithstanding his reverence for *Law,* and his preach-
ing about the 'law must take its course.' If demagogues
will *not* protect us with their laws, which are chiefly gotten
of corruption, then let our household lions themselves rend
the demons who crouch in the jungle, watching for their
opportunity. *That* is a Right, for the exercise of which I
shall *always* contend, whether it be called Man's Right,
Woman's Right, Humanity's Right, or *God's* Right."

The conclusion of Carroll's letter had no bearing upon
this little history, and it is therefore suppressed. Mrs.
Gale, having finished it, mused awhile.

" Laws," said she to herself, " are strange things any-how.   Suppose that one of these demons should come in here right now, and that I, knowing his purpose, should take that pistol there and shoot him dead.   What would the *law* do ? Nothing.   But suppose that I could not shoot him, and that he should make himself the master here, and my husband should come home, and I should tell him, and he should hunt up the demon,—as I know he would,—and shoot him dead.   What would the *law* do *then*?   It would *hang* my husband for murder, or imprison him for man-slaughter.   And mind you, *I* kill the demon *before* he is the master, and, in the other case, my husband kills him *after* he is the master.   What sense is there in such laws as that ?   Again,—suppose my husband is *here* when the demon comes in at *first*, guilty of *intention* merely, and my husband shoots him.   The law sleeps.   But if the demon should bind my husband, and then master me and make himself guilty of the *act*, and my husband should break loose and follow him out and kill him, to-day, to-morrow, or next week, *then* the cranky and abominable *law* wakes up *against my husband!*   What sense is there in such laws as *that?*   Will our legislators tell me ?"   And Mrs. Gale looked scornfully toward the Seat of Government. "There's too much gingerbread work and fine lace about *law* anyhow.   Why don't they make it simple, so that they can understand it themselves,—the simpletons ?"

It was some time before Hines was able to secure coun-sel, as almost everybody was incensed against him.   Dur-ing this self-dependent interim, fearful that a certain trick which he had played upon the country merchant Mr. Nutt, and upon several other good men and witnesses, might not stand him in stead, he marked out for himself the follow-ing line of procedure and defense.   He would, if possible, get himself tried first for his lesser crime, of piracy.   He would declare himself innocent of the ruin of Miss Ruth-ven, plead guilty to the charge of piracy, but extenuate his guilt by reminding the court of the great hue and cry against him, and which, for self-preservation, had compelled him to an extreme resort; to wit:—an attempt to escape by means of the Whitecap, but with no ultimate design of destroying the vessel or keeping it permanently from the owner. He would maintain an intention to have run the vessel into port, safe from the fury of Creswood, from whence he would have notified Captain Gale, that the property might have been recovered with as little loss or delay as possible. He would then appeal to the mercy of the court, secure for himself the shortest term of imprison-ment, at the expiration of which, when he came to be tried for his greater crime, he would have the advantages of the lapse of time, with its changes and forgetfulness, a calmer community, and whatever of sympathy his past imprison-ment might beget for him. The prisoner discovered some tact within himself.

But " circumstances alter cases," and the circumstance of his having at length secured the aid of counsel, and the knowledge that he would be tried in the order of his crimes, and the cheering information, through his counsel, that he would be able to establish an *alibi*, caused him adroitly to reverse his battle front, and willingly to accept the " ty-ranny of the docket," as he had at first been pleased to term the consecutiveness of the judicial calendar.

We have already alluded to the puzzling fact that mer-chant Nutt and several other good citizens had expressed themselves able conscientiously to swear that both Hines and Butler were at the store of the merchant *before*, *during*, and *after* the precisely-timed coming of Rebecca's calamity. Their oaths would be based upon the infalli-bility of Mr. Nutt's clock-dial, which prided itself in keep-ing tick and time with the sun.

The prisoner, who was not unprepared for this different phase, but who had all along had reason to calculate on it, in the event that the merchant and his co-witnesses did not, in the general indignation, turn their backs upon him and bridle their capable tongues, now determined to prove an *alibi*—an *elsewhere*,—and in his second trial, whenever that might be, to plead " not guilty," and sustain his plea upon the good ground that all Creswood had been in arms against him without cause, thereby coercing him into piracy upon the Whitecap, as a measure of pure self-defense,—a pressing and absolute life-measure.

The day of trial was near at hand. In addition to the

38

hackneyed officer of the law, the prosecution had engaged able counsel and whetted tongues.

Cassel Rapid had written the following letter to Carroll May :

"CARROLL,—Within ten days after the receipt of this, I earnestly desire to see you at Creswood. You have heard of the fate of Rebecca Ruthven. I wish to engage you as associate counsel for the prosecution of one Apollyon. My reasons are numerous and multiform.

"I know how the trial will terminate. The criminal will prove an *alibi* and be acquitted by the jury. But as he is most certainly guilty, I do not want the citizens to acquit him.

"You are just out of a case almost similar, and are therefore fresh from the arena, and fully primed with the strength and aptitude of the first talent of New York, with and against whom you have recently been engaged.

"It will afford you an opportunity of seeing your friends, earn you a good fee, for which I am responsible, increase your importance with your employers, and advance your reputation in the professional sphere.

"Auxiliary to your own peculiar logic and force, I wish to inoculate you with some of my own gathered fire, and have you pour it out, scintillating with volcanic heat, to nerve this people, not to mad fury, but to intelligent, decisive, and irresistible *action*,—I need hardly add, *righteous* action.

"Lastly,—I have sent up a wish to the Great God, that He shall strike me with His thunderbolts the moment I cease to stand for the purity of my countrywomen, or to make war to the hilt upon the spoilers of our virgins. Come.   •"Your friend,
                                              " CASSEL."

Carroll May responded in person, and, on the day of the trial, sat within the bar with numerous doctors of the law. While waiting for proceedings to begin, a packed throng devoured with hungry eyes and ears every indicative sight and sound.

Garland Hope was at home. He felt utterly incapacitated to meet the public details of his bitter woe. He had intrusted his interests wholly to Cassel Rapid, confident that the untiring energy, courage, and discretion of his young friend would accomplish all that was possible.

Early on the morning of the day of trial, Garland was in consultation with Cassel, to whom he poured out his heart freely.

"If he is convicted," said the young minister, "and, under our statute, imprisoned for life, I shall feel constrained to let it rest at that. But if, by virtue of this *alibi*, he escapes all legal punishment, *what shall I do?* I alone of all the earth am left to visit justice upon his head."

"I almost wish that I could take your place," said Cassel, with a glance which told well enough what *he* would do. "You know what I *have* done," continued he, "or if you do not, I will tell it to you as an example."

"I know," replied Garland, with a haggard look. Then, with earnest eyes and voice, he asked, "But have you never, in the silent night, or the contemplative day, *repented* of what you did,—or, to be milder, *regretted* it?"

"*Repented!*" cried Cassel, with a glance of fire. "Jehovah, in whom I trust, *knows* that I have not. But I have *groaned* that all I have done, or could do, was so like a feather's weight in the scales of justice. If Albro Ruthven were living, there would be no need of statute, judge, or jury in this case."

"It is not that I fear the laws of Man, but of God," said the young minister, with a look of agony.

"Bring me the Laws of God," said Cassel.

Garland handed him the Bible, and Cassel quickly read from Deuteronomy, chapter xxii., verses 25 and 27:

"But if a man find a betrothed damsel in the field, and the man force her, and lie with her; then the man only that lay with her shall die.

"For he found her in the field, and the betrothed damsel cried, and there was none to save her."

"There," said Cassel, "is authority for you, from the very foot of the Throne,—a precedent more than twenty centuries old. It is the Law of Moses and his God. And it was given in a barbaric age, when women were the pup-

pets and toys of men. I know that the Mosaic Dispensa-
tion has been modified by that of Christ, but it is chiefly
by way of simplification,—and the God-given laws of Justice and Nature are immutable,—the same yesterday, to-
day, and forever. Who shall change them? If there is
any truth in Moses the forerunner of Christ, and if Hebrew history is not all a fiction, then the spoiler must surely
die. A Russian serf slew the prince of his house when
his young daughter came from the castle to his hut dripping with the gore of her own undoing. He fled down
into Europe and up into the mountains of Switzerland,
where, in his Alpine freedom, he defied the far power of
the Russian Empire,—and the world applauded. An
humble but proud-hearted butcher of Rome, unable to cope
with the tyrant emperor, slew his own child, Virginia, in
the public market-place, to save her from imperial pollution.
The mightiest bards and most trenchant pens have praised
him, and his name *now*, after ages have passed, occupies
the niche set apart by sentiment and history to commemo-
rate Heroic Virtue. Garland, I am a Christian, though
not a member of any church. I offer up my little sacrifices, alone, in my closet, and appeal to Heaven for guidance and strength to do right and be a good man. But if
ever I could consent to abandon *one of my own* in the days
of her calamity, I should feel as though I had clasped
hands with Satan, and had submitted to his dominion.
My conscience would *rebuke* me, as utterly unworthy ever
again to seek blessings from above. I *could not* kneel to
God while neglecting and ignoring so great and clamoring
a duty. This spoiler with whom we have to deal will be
set free to-day. I have already given you an outline of
what will be his defense. How it is that honest men will
swear him innocent I do not even imagine; but that they
will do so I have no doubt, and am equally certain that
they have not been suborned. He is guilty. You know
it,—and I know it. Who, then, will assert Justice? Where
is the champion of Rebecca Ruthven?"

The young minister, who had listened attentively and
excitedly, seemed ready to shout the slogan of Justice
and Retribution, and wield the sword of execution. Reaching out his hand, which Cassel firmly grasped, with quivering lips he said,—

" Whatever the *end* is, you, my bold brother, are the chief of all my friends. May God bless you, and may He strengthen and direct *me.*"

" But I am not done with this matter yet," answered Cassel; and he took from his pocket-book and unfolded a sheet of closely-written manuscript. "I have referred you to the Olden Law, and now I wish to give you the law of the present day upon this prime subject. America is a broad country, and its multiform government might well be called a many-headed monster. Out of these many heads, however, there are a few which spit no venom except for the Evil Doer,—and when, in this connection, I speak of the Evil Doer, I refer to the present interest, the Ravisher of Chastity. Let me give you an introspection of diversified moral and legal ethics. There are some American communities of which I am proud,—there are others of which I am utterly ashamed." Cassel then read from his manuscript.

" In Louisiana, the Ravisher suffers *death*, by the *law.*

" In South Carolina, the Ravisher suffers *death*, by the *law.*

" In Delaware, the Ravisher suffers *death*, by the *law.*

" The above three States are the Golden-Heads.

" In Maine, the Ravisher is imprisoned for life.

" In Massachusetts, the Ravisher is imprisoned for life.

" In Connecticutt, the Ravisher is imprisoned for life.

" In Maryland, the Ravisher is imprisoned for life.

" In Alabama, the Ravisher is imprisoned for life.

" In Mississippi, the Ravisher is imprisoned for life.

" The above six States are the Silver-Heads.

" In Pennsylvania, the punishment is fifteen years in prison, and not exceeding one thousand dollars fine.

" In Rhode Island, it is ten years or upwards in prison.

" In New York, it is ten years or upwards in prison.

" In Missouri, it is five years or upwards in prison.

" In Iowa, it is any term or for life in prison.

" The above five States are the Copper-Heads.

" In New Hampshire, it is not less than seven nor more than thirty years in prison.

" In Virginia, it is not less than ten nor more than twenty years in prison.

"In Kentucky, it is not less than ten nor more than twenty years in prison.

"In *Texas*, it is not less than five nor more than fifteen years in prison.

"Under *that* law I killed Jonas Aiken.

"In Ohio, it is not less than *three* nor more than twenty years in prison.

"In Indiana, it is not less than *two* nor more than twenty-one years in prison.

"In Georgia, it is not less than *two* nor more than twenty years in prison.

"The above seven States are the Cobra-Heads. But the following *two* are the heads of the Old Serpent himself.

"In New Jersey, the punishment is not less than a fine of a thousand *dollars*, nor greater than fifteen years in prison.

"In Vermont, the punishment is not less than a fine of a thousand *dollars*, nor greater than twenty years in prison.

"Of the remaining States I am not advised.

"Now," continued Cassel, "what sort of a legal panorama is this for lawgivers to present—ranging from a purse of gold up to the scaffold? Is chastity only worth one thousand dollars in Vermont or New Jersey, when in Massachusetts it costs imprisonment for life, and in South Carolina it costs *death!* What is it that makes this shameful schedule of prices, but the fact that good men suffer themselves to be governed by the senseless regulations of pusillanimous idiots or scheming knaves? Let me put this question before you in a shape which cannot fail to convince you that statutory law in this connection means *absolutely nothing;* and that good men can well afford to trample it under foot on their way to justice. What is the difference between the price of cotton at New Orleans and at Liverpool? What is the difference between the price of wheat at Chicago and New York? What is the difference between the price of beef cattle on the Texas prairies and in Philadelphia? What is the difference between the price of· *any* commodity *here*, and the same commodity *there? The difference is merely in the cost of carriage, with a fractional margin for legitimate and well-earned profit.* This is *Commercial* law, mind you, and is a true, well-digested code, applicable to the whole world. On the other hand, what is the difference between the *legal* value of a woman's chastity in New Jersey and Delaware? On the New Jersey shore of the Delaware River it will cost, perhaps, a thousand dollars. On the Delaware shore—just across the stream—it will cost *death*. In Augusta, Georgia, it will cost, perhaps, two years in the penitentiary. Just across the Savannah River, in Hamburg, South Carolina, it will cost *death*. In Vermont, it will cost, perhaps, a thousand dollars. Within a distance of ten feet, *two* feet even, over an imaginary line and into Massachusetts, it will cost imprisonment for life. *Who* must rectify this thing, and purge the land of these abominations? Can modest wives and daughters come before the public and challenge the chivalry of men on such a question? They have the *right* to do it; but it should shame the veriest dastard in the broad earth should they be so compelled. But, Garland, I must leave you now and go to the court-house."

Cassel went out, mounted the pale stallion, and rapidly traversed the forest, mile after mile, until he reached the county seat.

As soon as Cassel had gone, the young minister fell upon his knees, and besieged Heaven with prayer.

"Thou who hast created us, and breathed into us the breath of life, and revealed to us Thy Kingdom, and charged us to build it up pure and undefiled, I come before Thee as a child cometh to its father, and beseech Thee for the moving of Thy Spirit upon my soul, that I may *know* and *feel* that which I should do. Tell me, O thou Great Jehovah, shall this demon die? Not that *I* may reap vengeance, which is Thine, but that he is a *Spoiler*, and goeth about as one sent from Hell, seeking of innocents that he may destroy them. Is it sinful, just God, for me to feel that every man who meeteth him should slay him? Teach me, in behalf of Thy Kingdom on earth, and if my soul has grasped the wrong, withhold me by divine and potent influence, and I will bow the head while this mighty evil passeth by. Seven times will I come before Thee, O Jehovah, in my extreme; and the seventh shall be the Sabbath of the soul,—in which I *implore* Thee, Lord of Hosts, to purge me pure, and give me to know if I shall go forth and smite this Philistine."

Never did man pray, and beseech, with purer motives, or more fervent, passionate sincerity. Rising from his knees, the young minister sat himself down and waited, as for a Voice, or the sensible motion of the Spirit over his soul. Seven times he prostrated himself, in all the agony and ire of earnestness, and waited each time for the interposition or direction of some invisible monitor. But neither Voice, nor Spirit, nor secret helmsman came to him, to influence or direct him. He was left utterly and singly to his mortal resources. Finally, to himself he said,—

"God, whose ways are past finding out, suffers me to determine this temporal issue by the light and weight of temporal wisdom. All that is in me of intelligence or emotion urges the decree that this demon must *die;* and by the love which I bear to Rebecca, and by her purity which has been polluted, and by her life which has been ruthlessly blasted, and, *by the living God*, he *shall* die !"

Garland quivered with emotion. No voice or print can tell of the agony of that day—a day of prayer, and wrestling, and storm. But his mind was now made up, and he became as calm as a statue of Retribution.

The hours passed, and the afternoon was waning. But already a stern and illustrative scene had been put upon the stage of human life, away at the county seat where throngs had gathered to witness the eccentric workings of the law.

The pale stallion stretched gallantly away through the forest, and the woods and the hills rang with the music of his hoofs. At length the sound of his busy feet was borne upon the wind through the open windows of Garland's study. The young minister recognized the rapid hoof strokes, and waited in a deathlike calm for his friend to appear. Cassel opened the door, and stood upon the threshold, like Hero in the very front of Victory. A stern but celestial beauty beamed from his matchless countenance, and his right hand was pointing aloft as if in triumph. Garland, as he looked upon him, knew that he had hardly dreamed of a more glorious incarnation than the youthful, rosy, and invincible form before him. Mustering his voice he asked,—

"Watchman, what of the night?"

Cassel, still keeping his position on the threshold, with a smile of stern triumph replied,—

"Moses yet liveth: and the Law of God and Human Nature is paramount to the statutory *fulmen* of imbeciles."

"What is the decree of the court?"

"Of the *court!* It is naught: but there was a Mosaic decree *outside* of the court, and the spoiler is *dead.*"

Garland uttered a cry of surprise, of relief, of satisfaction, of almost everything except of joy, for joy was forever banished from his breast. The two young men looked into each other's eyes long and earnestly. A fascination drew them together, and as they locked hands in a manly clasp, they were of kin. The fates of Diana Rapid and Rebecca Ruthven bound them each to each with a peculiar tie. And although Cassel had slain his foe, and Garland had deliberately elected himself to do in like manner, in all the broad land of the free there were not two nobler hearts at beat, or gentler, purer souls.

"Garland, sit down, and let me tell you of it as briefly as may be. We had *two* courts to-day—one *de jure*, the other *de facto*. Carroll May almost set the building afire with an irruption of burning and sententious eloquence which amazed every one, even myself who had primed him for this occasion. But no speech could amount to anything in the face of an invincible *alibi;* and Carroll's effort was not so much leveled at the accused as at the *Crime*, wherever it might be committed, and in the latter respect it carried conviction with it. The trial in the court-house ended as I predicted to you; but a trial in the grove hard by, where were gathered all of our best citizens, closed with the sentence of death and the execution of the wretch. The structure of this widely-discussed *alibi* was based upon a trick, which was thoroughly exposed by an honest and truthful old negro man belonging to the Widow Hopkins, but whose testimony in the legal court was inadmissible. He was on the ground to-day, having driven the carriage of his mistress, who was in attendance on the trial. It seems that the negro had told his mistress something about Hines and Butler, and that she came to court to-day to see what could be done in behalf of justice. She was soon in consultation with Captain Gale, and very promptly thereafter the captain was in consultation with a number of staid citizens. A jury of sixty men, the best men in the county, was organized, among whom was Captain Gale himself, and an immense throng of people followed this jury to the grove just in the rear of the court-house. I was appointed to question the old negro and elicit what he might know. I have his testimony here, written down. I wrote it myself, and then, for conscience sake, cross-examined him before the jury. He had told the simple truth in the beginning, and he did not vary from it in the end. The consciences of the jury were set at rest. I will read you the old slave's testimony in his own words.

"'On the day that the sun was eclipsed I was at Mr. Nutt's store, waiting for my mistress, who was visiting some of her friends in the village. I had a watch which master give me just before he died. I wanted to set my watch with the sun, but there are so many hills and trees where I live that I can't see the sun when it rises and sets. I asked Mr. Nutt to look in the almanac and tell me the minute when the eclipse would begin. He told me to put my watch with his clock, because he said his clock was right. But I was not satisfied, and young Mr. Ashton, who was always kind to me, looked in the almanac and told me to set my watch at twenty-two minutes past three, at the very first beginning of the eclipse. He then lit a candle and smoked a piece of glass and give it to me, because I was thinking I could see the eclipse without any blind over my eyes, but he told me I couldn't. I went out, and when the eclipse commenced I set my watch, and then I went to see if Mr. Nutt's clock was right. It was very near right, maybe a minute too slow, and I didn't think it worth while to tell him of such a little difference. There were several gentlemen in the store talking neighborly, and I went and stood just outside the door and was listening to them. One of them proposed to see if the eclipse was begun, but another said it would be such a small affair that it wasn't worth looking at. More than twenty minutes after I set my watch, I saw Mr. Hines and Mr. Butler come running over the hill road from the east. When they were in a hundred yards or so of the store, they stopped running and walked the balance of the way. When they come up they blowed like they were tired, and I thought they had been running a race. They began to talk to me, and the gentlemen in the store, hearing them, all came out and commenced talking and took seats on a bench at one side of the door. Mr. Nutt came out also. Then Mr. Hines and Mr. Butler went into the store to get a drink of water. The water was at the back end, just under the clock. They drank, and then they talked together, and then Mr. Hines turned the clock back. I saw him through the window I began to think that something was strange about Mr. Hines and Mr. Butler, and I couldn't keep from watching them and listening to them. Mr. Butler's breeches were torn, and pinned up with a thorn, and I thought I saw blood on his clothes, but the spots were covered with dust and I was not certain. They then came out of the store and asked Mr. Nutt if his clock was right, and he said that it was. Then they told the gentlemen to remember the time when they got to the store, because they said they had made a bet with some of the men that live down in the shore cabins on the Starboard Strand, that they would travel from the strand to Mr. Nutt's store in a given time, and that Mr. Nutt was to set down the time of their arrival and be referee. Mr. Nutt looked at his clock and wrote down the time on the outside of his store door, on the upper panel, and all the gentlemen looked at it and promised to remember it. Then I thought Mr. Hines and Mr. Butler were just playing a trick, and I said nothing. Late in the evening just before sundown, and just as my mistress was coming to start home, I saw Mr. Hines go and get some more water, and he then turned the clock forward again, while Mr. Nutt and the other gentlemen were talking to my mistress I didn't think much more about it until I heard that Mr. Hines was in jail, and was going to be cleared by proving that he got to Mr. Nutt's store before the time that the eclipse

commenced. I knowed he hadn't got there before the
eclipse, and I told my mistress about it. She told me to
keep my tongue until the day of trial, and she brought me
here to-day to see if I could do any good by giving my
evidence to the people.'

"That," said Cassel, "was what exploded the theory
which up to this time had withheld the arm of the people.
Mr. Nutt and several of the witnesses by whom the *alibi*
was established in the court-house, were brought before
the court in the grove, and confirmed the negro's testimony, except only that none of them had seen Hines tam-
pering with the clock. The evidence was conclusive to
every one, and when the question was put, 'Shall Matthew
Hines be hung?' sixty stern voices responded '*Ay*,' and
the multitude shouted an *Amen* which made the grove
tremble in all its leaves. When the criminal came out of
the court-house, his face beaming with wicked triumph,
the jury of sixty took him from the sheriff, and told him
to prepare for doom. Finding himself suddenly hedged
about by a frowning array of honorable citizens, he became
trepid, and cried for mercy. But his cry was as unavail-
ing as the cry of his victim, and no man gave ear to it.
He acknowledged his guilt,"—here Garland shivered,—
"and refused to say his last possible prayer. He was
hung, and his body delivered to the coroner. Now.let me
tell you who composed the jury of sixty. One-third were
members of your church. About a third were personal
friends of *hers*. The remainder were citizens, strangers
to both you and her, whose sense of justice alone actuated
them." After a pause, Cassel continued: "Garland, I
will not mock you with my sympathy, for I know how
like the stars this visitation is beyond the reach of anything on earth. But I have a word of counsel. Do not
you mock *her* with an offer of your hand. I have seen
her. My own history gives me the right to see all such.
And I tell you truly that the only wish that lives within
her heart is the wish to die. She grieves for you, Garland,
and bears her world of woe gently as a broken angel, as is
her nature. She hopes to meet you beyond the skies, with
all her vows intact, and wed you There. I have felt it my
duty to be able to tell you all, and to tell you of her. Forgive me if I have done it rudely."

The young minister bowed himself in unutterable anguish, and Cassel softly withdrew and left him in the boundless desert of a hopeless life. Ah, the sweeping agony that rushed like bitter, *bitter* seas over his soul, and continually overwhelmed it! There was no goodly spot this side the tomb which would ever again give rest to the weary feet of Garland Hope and Rebecca Ruthven.

[NOTE.—The statutes to which Cassel, in the foregoing chapter, has referred, were cotemporary with the scenes then enacting. What changes may have been wrought by the subsequent American confusion, we are, at this time, unable to inform the reader.]

CHAPTER XLI.

CORA returned to Philadelphia. She became the light of the house where she had erst been the shadow.

To account for this great change she had to tell her mother her sweet little secrets.

Cassel came to see Cora in her own home, and the Hurons, including Cora, were delighted with him.

Cassel still kept his head-quarters in New York. One day he appeared at O'Dare's office, and said,—

"O'Dare, the world is soon coming to an end."

"And I suppose you think that when it does, Cassel Rapid will be at the tip end of it," responded O'Dare, with his usual impudence.

"Yes,—and I hope you'll be at the *other* end," laughed Cassel.

"Just so. We can then see-saw the old craft out of existence."

"But, O'Dare,—I'm going to be married!"

"What of that? Any leatherhead can be married."

"But, my complimentary friend, it suggests a subject in connection with which I may have been unpardonably remiss."

39

"What kind of a subject? Is Legion the name of it?"

"Notwithstanding our long and intimate association—"

"I beg your pardon," interrupted O'Dare, "I never become intimate with anybody but my wife."

"The very subject in question," persisted Cassel; "for I cannot for the life of me say whether you have a wife or not. I have all along presumed that you have not— nor ever had."

"Nobody ever appears to think that it would be 'regular order' for me to have a wife."

"Precisely," answered Cassel. "You are so confoundedly self-sufficient, that an appendage strikes the inquiring mind as altogether superfluous."

"The devil it does! Why can't Hector O'Dare enjoy the tender and essential rib as well as you, you green goose?"

"Because it don't appear in character that you should ever have been a pensive and elegiac swain, blacking your mustache, and curling your hair, and writing sonnets to your 'mistress's eyebrow,'" laughed Cassel.

"Never answered to that description in my life. But in a world of pangs and penalties, where good to bad is like pigmy to giant, do you suppose that Hector O'Dare would ignore the main chance! That Hector O'Dare,— I like that name,"— drolly observed the detective, "that Hector O'Dare, who never misses his man, would stand by like a split stick and *miss* his *woman?* No, sir! He would never make a miss, but a mistress, of her. There's a pun for you, if you have the sense to comprehend it."

"A very silly one, requiring about as much brain to comprehend as to perpetrate."

"You know what I told you once," said O'Dare, "about my choosing a fool for an audience?"

"For that matter you need never lack an audience; just talk to yourself," laughed Cassel.

"What time do you dine?" asked O'Dare, abruptly.

"I keep banker's hours."

"It wants half an hour, then, to your dinner-time. I take my meals whenever I can get the chance. But come dine with me to-day, and I will show you what, when you are married and housekeeping, you will never be spry enough to show *me*—that is, a well-served dinner after ten minutes' notice."

O'Dare took Cassel to his residence, which, in appearance, was perfectly respectable in exterior, and even luxurious within, but in no sense ostentatious from either point of view. Entering the parlor, the detective sprung a bell. A tidy little girl appeared in a few moments, and stood for orders.

"Ask Mrs. O'Dare and the children to favor us with their company," and the little handmaid disappeared.

"Aha!" exclaimed Cassel, "you've been married some time, I begin to see."

Presently, Mrs. O'Dare, with a little boy and girl, respectively six and four years of age, entered the parlor. The gentlemen arose, and introductions followed.

"I am glad to see my father's guest," said young Hector.

"And I am glad to see your father's boy," replied Cassel, patting the sprightly boy on the cheek.

"Father told you my *Sunday* name," said little Kathleen.

"And what is your every-day name?" asked Cassel.

"Froggie."

"That's because she can go like a frog," said young Hector.

"Jump like a frog, or sing like a frog?" asked Cassel.

"*She* sings, and *I* jump," answered the little brother.

Mrs. O'Dare was a fresh-looking and fine-looking brunette, with flashing eyes, active countenance, much grace of person, good manners, and was, on rare occasions, when she got her dander up, *master* of the house.

Conversing readily, and with a genial face, she was pleasantly at ease with Cassel, whom she well knew by repute through her husband. Turning to O'Dare she inquired,—

"Are you very busy to-day?"

"No," incautiously replied the husband.

"We'll dine, then, at four."

"Half-past three," suggested O'Dare.

"That will be in ten minutes," protested the wife.

"Just so," admitted O'Dare, trying to give her a wink.

But she wouldn't take any wink. Turning with a half-saucy smile to Cassel, she said,—

"Mr. Rapid, did you ever see such a man? He will even come home from a week's absence, and at an odd hour, and he must have his meal in five, ten, or fifteen minutes. I can generally give him all he deserves within the required time. But when he brings distinguished guests, and expects me to act Lamp to Aladdin, I sometimes revolt," and she cast a mischievous, daring glance at her lord. "However, he shall have *his* meal in ten minutes, if business is pressing, but I invite *you* to stay and take *dinner* with *me*." Saying which she arose, went out, and soon returned with, "Mr. O'Dare, your meal is ready, and I am ready to serve it." With the least possible dash she turned away, casting a black-eyed, half-defiant glance over her well-set shoulder.

O'Dare was whipped,—and he was aware that Cassel, with keen enjoyment, appreciated it and would run him heavily. Cunningly he observed,—

"She knows exactly how to make me love her."

Cassel could stand it no longer, and his hearty, silver laugh rang through the house.

"Did you see those black eyes?" asked O'Dare, actually blushing.

"Yes,—and I see whom they vanquish," laughed Cassel.

"My odd hours *are* too bad," said O'Dare. "She stands it just a little longer than she ought to, and then she raises the standard of revolt. I glory in her spunk."

Mrs. O'Dare came to the door and inquired of her husband,—

"Will you have your hasty pudding, or dine with Mr. Rapid and myself?"

"I believe I'll not hurry the cook," replied O'Dare, and the trio laughed merrily.

Mrs. O'Dare, pleased and relenting, came in and sat down. A very agreeable half hour preceded a very well-served dinner, and O'Dare behaved himself for several consecutive weeks afterward.

Cassel Rapid, whose faultless symmetry was the delight of his tailor, and Cora, whose bridal loveliness we fain would, but cannot, describe, stood up before the venerable Mr. Hope, and a host of gathered friends, in the house of the Philadelphia Hurons, and were married.

Prominent among the guests were—the Hope family, except Garland—Captain Gale and his family, who came up in the Whitecap—Linda Boyd and Miss Lightner—Hector O'Dare and his black-eyed wife—and Harry Gray. The latter, when the ceremony and numberless congratulations were endured, came forward and said,—

"Cassel, you beat me,—but I always thought you would, for you had the near way on me. I've been preparing for this for some time, and although it is bitter-sweet, I bear no malice, and truly hope that you will be as happy as I *would* have been."

"Mr. Gray," said Cora, who always liked Harry, and felt willing to indemnify him, "I have a sister far lovelier than myself. See her there."

Harry looked about, and saw Gussie Huron, fresh, ingenuous, and sweet as Hebe. He got himself desperately in love with her, and eventually succeeded in making her his bride.

Johnny Gale stood six-feet-one in his wedding-boots, and was as fine a pyramid of flesh, good humor, and good sense as ever took the vows. His rich, abundant black hair, fine forehead, *rouge* cheeks, scarlet lips, shaded by a boyish mustache, together with his splendid physique, gave him an appearance brave, commanding, and superb.

"Did you ever see a person improve as Johnny has?" whispered Cora to Cassel. "He looks like a young nobleman."

"He *is* a young nobleman," answered Cassel. "Look at Linda,—fresh and delicious as the blush side of a ripe peach. She becomes 'Mrs. Gale' with ideas very different from those with which she became 'Mrs. Boyd.' She is in *love* now for the first time. She calls Johnny her handsome giant."

"She is greatly indebted to you, 'her brother Cassel,'" said Cora.

"Not more than I am indebted to her for her innocent, beautiful, and unfailing affection. There was a time when

none but Linda could refresh the waste places in my breast.
I have always been *rejoiced* that she returned Johnny's
love, for they will suit each other as the clapper suits the
bell."

Johnny, being married, abandoned his engineering
studies. He sold out the oil farm in Pennsylvania, gathered together the financial resources of his wife, invested
them in real estate, and contented himself with collecting
rents, and, eventually, making fireside trips to Banbury
Cross.

Carroll May devoted himself to business, with one eye,
however, fixed upon a certain stylish girl, the daughter of
Mr. Gore, of the firm of Hallum & Gore, his employers.
Carroll promised to succeed with some brilliancy in his
profession.

Cassel Rapid had recognized in Miss Lightner the most
of those excellent qualities which belong to our superior
women. Although she maintained herself bravely, she
was entirely self-dependent, in sickness or in health, in
success or failure. Cassel, whose heart was as tender as
it was imperial and dauntless, felt a sympathy for her
which would not let him rest. She was too modest, or
too something-or-other, ever to " catch " beaus. Cassel
determined to catch one for her. " Why shan't *she* have
a honey-moon as well as the rest of us ?" asked Cassel of
himself. He and Cora continued to conspire against Miss
Lightner's maidenhood, until they succeeded in making her
the mistress of a comfortable establishment, and of a
worthy husband whom she found no difficulty in loving
and esteeming.

Rebecca Ruthven is a living statue, dead to the world.
Her mother never recovered from the pulmonary illness
superinduced by the destruction of her family. Rebecca,
an orphan, lives in the family of old Mr. Hope. Garland,
who could not bear to be near her and not with her, left
Creswood, and accepted some distant Christian mission.
It was his wish that Rebecca should live with his father's
family, and be treated in all respects as a daughter.

Time passed, and brought its inevitable changes. The
sea had long been encroaching upon Gale Island, and its
banks had been gradually tumbling in, until the anchor-

age was destroyed. A furious storm, which maddened the ocean and shook the Atlantic shores, and wrapped the island in a shroud of foam, while it rocked and trembled with the shock of thundering, frantic waves, beat down the loamy bulwarks, cleft the soil with deep gulches, and rendered the island uninhabitable. Captain Gale, who had made his fortune, abandoned his island home, and settled in the suburbs of Philadelphia, where Caddy met with her fate, and was married.

O'Dare is still upon the *qui vive*, and malefactors had better continue to look lively.

Uncle Jessie, who lives with Johnny and Linda and the children, at the "Gale" mansion, was at length forced to fall back, for self-consistency and excuse, upon the old couplet, that,—

> " A little nonsense now and then
> Is relished by the wisest men."

Postscript, in lieu of Preface.—Reader, this is no tale of Fiction, or of Faction. Neither is it *factitious*, but a feeble presentation of Fact. We have not drawn upon Imagination for either incident or example, for every morning paper, almost, has vouchsafed us both. Our trouble has alone been in the finding of *words*, active and potent enough to tell the simple Truth. Neither have we any such wrongs to avenge or lament, near or remote. But if, by this indirect instrumentality, we shall be able to save a single pure woman or innocent virgin from the *Spoiler*, we shall ever feel well repaid for this our labor in that behalf. If we can but direct the attention of a single intelligent and honorable legislator to the disgraceful, senseless incongruity of American statutes which bear directly upon the core of every honest, virtuous heart, we shall indeed feel greatly gratified and encouraged. The price of *Gold* is the same throughout the Union. Is *Chastity—the purity of our women*—less precious, or less to be considered, than *Gold!* Who will dare assert it?

ADIEU.